I KNOW HOW THIS ENDS

ALSO BY HOLLY SMALE

Cassandra in Reverse

I KNOW HOW THIS ENDS

HOLLY SMALE

MIRA

MIRA™

ISBN-13: 978-0-7783-6863-2
ISBN-13: 978-0-7783-6034-6 (International Trade Paperback Edition)

Recycling programs for this product may not exist in your area.

I Know How This Ends

For questions and comments about the quality of this book, please contact us at CustomerService@Harlequin.com.

TM is a trademark of Harlequin Enterprises ULC.

Mira
22 Adelaide St. West, 41st Floor
Toronto, Ontario M5H 4E3, Canada
MIRABooks.com

Printed in U.S.A.

For my grandad—
who always saw me

"If you can look into the seeds of time, and say which grain will grow and which will not, speak then to me."

—WILLIAM SHAKESPEARE, *MACBETH*

1

IT'S NOT HARD to see the future.

We do it all the time without thinking: search the skies above us for what's coming. A red sky at night is a shepherd's delight, but in the morning it's a sailor's warning, so a sunny day is either behind or ahead of us. When dew is on the grass, rain will never come to pass (high pressure), but when clouds appear like rocks and towers, the Earth's refreshed with showers. For thousands of years, humans have looked upward to catch a glimpse of what the future holds and thus plan accordingly.

Then rhymed about it to ensure that it sticks.

But when it's literally your job to keep an eye on what lies ahead, it's not just the heavens that hold the clues: they're scattered everywhere, like raindrops. Data that's easy to miss if you're looking in the wrong direction.

The signs are always there, as long as you're paying attention.

"SO, BASICALLY YOU'RE a Weather Girl."

I lean back in my chair and study the face of Date Number Fifteen. According to his online profile, the key to John's heart is "Cuddles and Coffee," and he doesn't like "people who don't message back—we r hear to talk!" (But not to spell, apparently.) John enjoys "long walks on the beach," "honesty LOL" and randomly adding LOL to basic statements. He claims to be forty-two years old, a Gemini ("whatever that means haha") and a "six-foot-stop-asking" accountant who drinks "socially" but "never smokes" and is looking for his "next big adventure—is it you?"

At no point did John say he enjoys smugly demeaning his dates, yet here we are.

"Sure." I take another sip of red wine. "Why not."

"But not on telly." There's a manic, slightly feverish glint in his eyes, like a light bulb about to pop. "So not a *real* Weather Girl. Bet you would look very nice in one of those perky little suits, though. Just saying."

John winks and takes a huge swig of his pint: fingertips stained yellow.

"I wouldn't know," I say brightly. "As you say, I'm not *On Telly*."

"You *could* be, though." He leans forward and I catch a strong whiff of the cigarettes he never smokes. "You're hot enough, Margaret. Like, an eight. Maybe. Not quite. Seven and a half, but with the right lighting . . ."

I grin at the waiter as he arrives with two plates of pasta.

"Thank you so much." Picking up my fork, I attack my tagliatelle. "Could we also please get a side of garlic bread—make that two—a burrata with pesto and tiny tomatoes, a Caprese salad, stuffed artichokes, garlic mushrooms and . . . ooh, a bottle of your *most* expensive red wine? And a tiramisu, please."

John chokes slightly on his free bread roll and I smile sweetly at him.

"How rude of me," I add. "Was there anything extra you wanted? Coffee, obviously. It *is* the key to your heart, after all."

Date Number Fifteen glances at the menu, boggles slightly at the prices, then forces a smile at the patient waiter.

"No, I'm good."

John looks me up and down, presumably to work out what my body will look like after £65 worth of Italian side dishes and whether it'll be worth the financial investment. He says he's an accountant; I'd imagine he's calculating it to the penny.

"I like a girl who isn't afraid to eat," he says uncertainly as

I pile pasta into my mouth and wipe carbonara sauce off my chin. "It's very . . . sexy."

"What a relief, John." I finish my wine. "You're a true gentleman."

This pleases him: he *is* a gentleman. Here, finally, is a woman who *sees him*.

"You're a breath of fresh air, Margaret." He shakes his head, ruefully picking at his ravioli. "Online dating is the worst. You would not *believe* the amount of crazies I've met. Absolutely bonkers out there."

"Oh no." I tilt my head at him. "How awful for you."

"At least you look *mostly* like your profile photos," Date Fifteen grins at me with an errant piece of crab stuck between his teeth, "although obviously they're flattering—but we all tweak now and then, don't we?"

"We do." I feel my nostrils flare slightly. "Which beach do you favor for your long walks, in this non-coastal city of Bristol?"

"Oh." He blinks. "I went to Weston-super-Mare last year."

"True commitment! And what's an average weekend like in the life of Gemini John?"

He's starting to look irritated now, and I think I can guess why.

"You know, just . . . normal stuff." John rubs his finger yet again, and I make a mental note of it: number seven.

"Wonderful." I beam at him. "And last weekend, specifically?"

"What is this?" John tries to laugh, which is unfortunate because the crab is still protruding, as if making a final doomed bid for freedom—possibly encouraged by all the talk of beaches. "A first date or an interview?"

I glance at my watch. "Are they not the same thing?"

Just in time, the waiter arrives with my order. I grin at him and he grins back.

"Actually." I put my fork down and pat my stomach. "Can we get all this to go? I want to make sure we have enough *energy* for later, if you know what I mean."

I wink at John and his surliness evaporates like water droplets on a hot car bonnet.

"Ooooh, bad girl. Straight to the point. I like it."

"I'm thirty-six years old," I say calmly, wiping my mouth and watching as John rubs his finger for the eighth time. "I haven't been a *girl* for two decades. But thank you so much for repeatedly overlooking that chronological flaw. Much in the same way you have overlooked your own age, which I'm guessing is what—forty-seven?"

Date Number Fifteen winces. "Like I said—we all tweak. Right?"

"Absolutely!" I grin at him. "It makes sense to strategically alter the data to make sure you hit a younger female demographic. What an interesting way to reject the burden of time we all carry."

The waiter saves him from responding by arriving with the bill and, with a twitching mouth, placing it in the middle of the table. I keep my hands flat and dimple at John for a few seconds—playing a game of bill chicken—until he sighs slightly and reaches for it. The muscles under his eyes twitch, and I watch his internal struggle. Am I worth extra garlic mushrooms? He glances at my breasts and decides: just. With a gallant flourish, Date Fifteen pays the whole bill, leaving no tip.

"So." With my most seductive eyes, I push back my chair. "Shall we go?"

Poor John's face lights up with such ferocity, I almost feel guilty. Almost but not quite. "Absolutely. My place or yours?"

I grin. "Both."

"Um, how does that work?"

"Well, John." I put a twenty-pound note on the table, stand up and grab my raincoat, handbag and giant umbrella. "I am going to go to my house, and you are going to yours. So that's how it will work."

"But—"

"You've failed this date, John. Sorry."

"I don't—" He stands up too and stares at me for a few seconds with his mouth open (crab still present), then looks at my tip lying on the table. "*Why?*"

"I'm so glad you asked." I smile at the waiter, who is holding a paper bag. "Because you haven't asked me a single non-rhetorical question all evening. You have stared at my breasts for the entire, uncomfortable hour. And not a single thing on your profile is true, including your height."

All five foot ten of him bridles. "I am *six foot.* It's not my fault you're wearing bloody heels."

"Oh, and you're married."

At this, his face completely changes, which immediately erases the one percent uncertainty still remaining. "What the—"

"With children."

John pales. "You're—"

"Crazy?" I laugh properly for the first time this evening. "I doubt it, John. You've rubbed the indent on your ring finger eight times. You also have one piece of dried alphabet cereal stuck to the back of your jacket, along with baby spit-up on your collar. Having assessed this data, I surmise that you have two children. One is less than six months, the other learning to read, so I'm guessing three or four years old. It's an A, by the way. In case he or she is missing a vowel."

John—or whatever his actual name is, I'm assuming I'll never know now—starts to froth like an overloaded washing machine. "What the hell kind of business is it of yours if my wife and I are—"

"Except your phone has pinged six times this evening and you checked it as soon as I went to the bathroom. So I'm guessing you are currently 'stuck at work,' sad-face emoji. Don't feel too bad. Statistically, thirty percent of people using online dating apps are secretly married, so it's not just you. You're just shockingly bad at covering it up."

Suffice to say, John isn't LOL-ing anymore. It's a good thing this little Italian restaurant in Clifton is so quiet on a Monday, because I think *now* he's really "hear to talk."

"So, you knew you weren't interested and just let me pay for dinner anyway?"

"Yes." I pick up my takeout bag. "Thank you. Much appreciated." I hold up the bottle of wine to the waiter, along with the previous glass I'd already poured. "I'll bring this back next Monday, OK? Washed, obviously."

The waiter laughs. "Gotcha."

I glance out of the window—yup, just as expected—and sling my raincoat on. John told me when we met that my raincoat and umbrella were "overkill in August," but I've been watching the cumulonimbus clouds gather all afternoon. The sky doesn't lie, unlike the majority of my online dates. As I walk toward the front door, I can feel John crackling behind me, the way you feel electricity in the air just before a thunderstorm.

"By the way," I say, holding up the bottle of wine, before he can start yelling. "My name is *Margot*. And I'm not a 'Weather Girl.' I'm a bloody meteorologist."

Then I open my umbrella just as the first few drops begin to fall.

And walk straight into the rain.

I PROBABLY SHOULDN'T have enjoyed that as much as I did.

In fairness to him, Gemini John was unlikely to be a perfect match for me; I'm not sure I want any man with a heart that can be "unlocked" at the local Starbucks. But I didn't have time to line up another option, and Monday is Date Night. And no—I don't normally make them pay for the entire meal. I've decided to save that as a special treat for the men who merrily tick the "single" box on a dating app and then ask their wife why they're "being so neurotic" when they get home.

Irritated, I unlock my front door and attempt to get into my house.

Huge cardboard boxes have migrated slowly down the hallway over the last couple of months, and now one of them has fallen off the top of a teetering stack, barring my entry. With a few huffs, I ram the door open and stare at the broken plates lying in an accusatory heap on the floor. The box says "MARGOT WAYWARD'S KITCHEN SHIT" on it, which now seems slightly pouty.

"Fuck's sake," I sigh, pushing it to the side with my foot.

Then I step over the crockery pieces and carry my food to the small kitchen I'm still not used to. I put most of my free Italian fodder in the fridge, take my bra off with a sigh and grab a fork so I can peacefully make my way through the remaining tagliatelle without my date silently calculating how much each bite costs.

Still chewing, I pick up a pen and my little purple notepad. Then I quickly scan the contents.

DATE ONE: *fifty minutes late.*

DATE TWO: *said the woman on neighboring table was "too old to dress like that."*

DATE THREE: *sent me eleven unanswered texts in a row, followed by an unsolicited photo of his genitals.*

DATE FOUR: *ate with mouth open, then helped himself to my mushrooms.*

DATE FIVE: *asked for a "Body Count" ten minutes in.*

DATE SIX: *rude to waiter.*

DATE SEVEN: *told me, while wearing a shirt with three buttons missing, I could have "made more effort."*

DATE EIGHT: *casually claimed "all my exes are crazy."*

DATE NINE: *used phone to work out his share of olives.*

DATE TEN: *immediately told me "not to get too attached," then winked.*

DATE ELEVEN: *homophobic, racist, anti-women, anti-deodorant.*

DATE TWELVE: *doesn't normally date his own age but will "make an exception" for me.*

DATE THIRTEEN: *monologued for two hours about his exercise routine.*

DATE FOURTEEN: *gave me marks out of ten as if scoring an ice-skating competition.*

"Get back out there," they all said. "Plenty more fish in the sea."

Except nobody pointed out exactly what is swimming around in the depths of the online dating ocean in your thirties and forties: it's all jelly and teeth and transparent organs and protruding eyes jubilantly announcing that "they want to find that special connection" as long as she's a "nine or above."

At least now when they ask for my "Body Count," I tell them it's currently zero, but I'm looking to change that and have dug a large hole in my garden.

With flared nostrils, I write:

DATE FIFTEEN: *married with kids.*

Then I flip to the back of the notepad and scribble under my rapidly escalating List of Dating Criteria:

25. Doesn't already have a secret family.

Flopping onto my sofa, I switch my burner phone back on. Suffice to say, after a few months of waking up to unasked-for images of body parts, I bought a second phone I could throw at a wall as hard as I wanted.

With a sensation of faintly impending doom, I start scrolling through images of men as if I'm looking for a vacuum cleaner in an Argos catalog: occasionally handy but not exactly enjoyable. The more faces you look at, the more identical they start to seem, until they're reduced to a simple slide show of human features in a variety of positions: eyes, noses, teeth, beards that cover rapidly disintegrating jawlines, though they still "prefer women without make-up" and "will buy the first drink if you actually look like your photos."

Nope, nope, nope, nope. Rather switch my toaster on and stick a fork in it.

Then I abruptly sit forward: *Henry, 39.*

This fish has a kind, open face, blond hair, a wide, dimpled smile. Henry is a fireman, six foot two, and has made no passive-aggressive statements about saying "something more interesting than 'hi' if you want to impress me," as if he's the eighth of his name and holding court. Henry is on top of a mountain, laughing in a pub garden, wearing a suit at a wedding that hopefully (but not definitively) isn't his own. Henry is—quite possibly—a dolphin in an ocean of sludge-sliders and bottom-crawlers who try to stick their tongues down my throat without asking for permission first.

Surprised, I swipe right and hold my breath to see if we match.

Jackpot.

Then I send my normal message:

Hi Henry! Shall we save getting to know each other for a meeting in person?

Do you fancy dinner next week? Monday any good?

Margot

Straight to the point, as everyone should be.

The reply is almost immediate.

Hello Margot! Good idea. Sounds great! Henry

Frankly, I don't have time to pen-pal for the next week while we sporadically discuss our favorite holiday destinations. Romance can wait until we know if the other person clicks their fingers at waiters or not.

Date Sixteen set, I put my phone down and stare around my tiny new flat.

Two months here and it still doesn't feel like home yet.

Leaving aside the scattered boxes—which I very much have—it's still a home for a person I no longer am: half of a pair. The bathroom even has His and Hers basins, which feels slightly aggressive. This is a flat for *more than one person*, those basins say. A *couple's* flat. Don't you dare come in, with your one face to wash, and store make-up and skincare in the second one.

After a few seconds, I reach forward and stare at my burner phone again.

I shouldn't. I won't.

Except I already know I will, so let's save the internal struggle for when there's actually someone to pretend in front of. Holding my breath, I open the social media account of an imaginary person I made up called @Lucy_Jones7. Lucy has a jaunty squirrel as her profile photo, works vaguely in "The Arts" and has uploaded a few pictures of flowers and pancakes to her profile so she looks like a real human, not a completely unhinged stalker faking an entire identity and then getting angry at men for doing exactly the same thing.

The latest post is a firm punch to the gut, as always.

Lily is beautiful: lit with the healthy iridescence of someone who doesn't eat takeout six days a week. Her naturally red hair waves to her waist, her cheeks are rosy and she's holding a pint of beer up to the camera with a beatific smile of contentment and triumph. On the table in front of her are two chicken curries, two bowls of rice, two saag aloos, another beer. All even numbers. It's the dining equivalent of my His and Hers basins, and she wants us all to know that someone is using the second one.

Underneath, she's written: *Simple pleasures are the best. <3 <3 <3*

Quite the original statement, Lily: you should trademark that immediately.

Teeth gritted, I "like" the post ("Lucy" probably would, after all). Then I throw my phone across the room and listen to it hit the solid oak floor with a satisfying crack. It'll be fine; it's used to being lobbed regularly. Strapping on my boxing gloves, I carefully step around the green screen still stapled to my living-room wall and go toward the corner, where a heavy bag hangs from the ceiling like a stuck pig.

I'm just about to take my first gratifying punch when a cold wave runs through me. I feel dizzy, misplaced, and suddenly see two hands: one mine, the emerald ring my grandfather gave me glinting, and the other belonging to someone else.

This hand is large and tanned, and something is scribbled in large letters across the back of it. Two letters, dark blue and slightly blurred. *IR*? A flash of orange. I watch in surprise as my hand reaches forward, fingers touch briefly, the orange falls—and a wave of liquid heat shoots up my arm.

Blinking, I pull back and the hands abruptly disappear.

Blimey. Where did that come from?

Grimacing—I need to get more sleep—I recalibrate for a moment.

Then I take a deep breath and start punching. I punch and punch until the burn feels sugary and my arms hurt and the rage inside me begins to dissolve. Sweating, I kick the bag for good measure and stick out my tongue at it like a child. I take the gloves off, wipe my forehead and pick up my other phone: the phone I never throw, can't throw, need to stay close to at all times.

And I turn my real life back on.

2

I'M ALL ABOUT the data, so here's mine:

NAME: *Margot Wayward (or "Maggie"/"Meg" to my grandfather)*

AGE: *36*

NATIONALITY: *British/Australian*

LOCATION: *Bristol*

PROFESSION: *Meteorologist*

HEIGHT: *5'10" (or "six foot" if you're a man on a dating app)*

WEIGHT: *None of your damn business*

STAR SIGN: *I'm not even going to humor this question*

PETS: *No thanks*

LOOKING FOR: *Still very much figuring that out, with the help of a collection of data and multiple notepads lined up on my kitchen counter*

It tells you almost nothing about me, right?

I love information as much as anyone, but the truth is usually in the details we try to hide. What this data doesn't tell you is that I haven't washed my current bra in eight days but would rather die than admit that to anyone, I use hair grips to pick my ears when nobody is watching, and I have an errant hair on my cheek that grows to whisker length if I don't regularly cut it with scissors. It doesn't tell you that I frequently close kitchen cabinet doors by kicking them or that I will "leave a saucepan to soak" for a full three days and once got drunk and bought a new one instead of just washing up the old one.

It doesn't tell you that I have a PhD from Imperial College but don't know the alphabet without singing the song first, or that I clip my toenails over the toilet and don't always pick them up if they shoot across the bathroom. I am snappy and entitled with my Alexa, even though she's never anything but helpful, and I only wear navy, black and white because I like to convince myself I'm sophisticated and French, which I am very much not: I'm just lazy.

I am acerbic, judgmental, impatient, hypocritical, sometimes imperious.

I can be both arrogant and also deeply insecure.

I am a slob but irritatingly meticulous, childish and prickly; I instinctively don't like seventy percent of humans and make that painfully clear within seconds of meeting anyone new; I'm not a fan of most animals (with the exception of tortoises, armadillos, hermit crabs, turtles, basically anything with a hard, impenetrable shell—you see where I'm going with this metaphor).

I'm nowhere near as funny as I try to convince myself I am.

Or as self-aware.

And none of this is written on my dating profile, because if it was, there would be no Married John, no Mister Olive Calculator, no Sir Body Count. If I told the truth about who I actually am, it would be a wasteland of nothing and nobody, so instead I judge others for editing themselves favorably too. I search relentlessly for the data in others while keeping the data of myself locked safely away behind a password I refuse to share.

I hide the truth behind other, lesser truths: from men, if not from myself.

Frankly, it is exhausting and my love life is not unlike one of the cardboard boxes lying in my hallway: packed up with swear words written across the front, Sellotaped shut and easy to ignore until it falls over and smashes everywhere.

At which point, I simply step right over it.

EIGHT MONTHS AGO, I left my job as chief meteorologist at the Met Office in Exeter, moved back to my home town of Bristol and started @MargotTheMeteorologist, an Instagram account where I, Margot, talk about—shockingly, prepare yourselves—the weather. I used to spend my work days sitting in an office and examining enormous swathes of data coming in from approximately two hundred and sixty synoptic weather stations from around the UK, but I now spend them making short videos about special clouds and bending winds, flash floods and graupel.

Bored and lonely, I started responding to every comment and to everyone in my inbox, where people started turning up in ever-increasing droves to ask extremely specific questions about what the weather might be like at their granddaughter's christening next Saturday, in Hull, at 2 p.m. (Raining, always raining.)

A couple of celebrities shared my posts, and my followers rapidly grew.

Before I knew it, my page had grown to 250k+ followers and I was making enough money from advertisers and sponsors to stop looking for a meteorology job because I had found one, entirely by accident. Enough money to put toward a deposit on a Clifton flat with a tiny, unnecessary guest bedroom. Enough money to live off takeout and buy clothes online at 3 a.m. when I'm too tired to sleep, which I then fail to return because I'm too tired to go to the Post Office. Enough to enjoy literally none of it while I keep up with a work schedule that has escalated from time-consuming to time-obliterating. It's also steadily giving me the posture of an orangutan as I hunch over my phone or laptop, eating pot noodles and optimistically scanning the ingredients for a vitamin content that patently isn't there.

Not that I'm complaining—it's my digital baby—but it's making it hard to stop the rest of my life from unraveling as fast as I frantically knit my career together. Every day, in between making new content, looking up data and responding to messages and emails, my phone peeps like a hungry newborn penguin.

Today's missed notifications:

EVE: How was Date 15? Is it love?

JULES: It's obviously not love or
she'd have told us already

EVE: She could still be enjoying the love haha ;)

JULES: Then she'd definitely have told us.
Probably during. Stats and observations etc

EVE: laugh face

JULES: You can't just say "laugh face"
Eve what's wrong with you

EVE: It was supposed to convert
automatically sad face

Missed call: Mum and Dad

EVE: Maggie? Worried. CONFIRM ALIVE STATUS.

JULES: It's OK, I've just seen a new post
on Insta—she survived D15 hurray

Missed call: Mum and Dad
Missed call: Mum and Dad
Missed call: Mum and Dad

GRANDAD: Hello Meg thin

GRANDAD: king of you

GRANDAD: hop you gah

GRANDAD: well make

GRANDAD: sure

GRANDAD: you are wearing substreet

EVE: Maggie are you still coming?

JULES: That's what he said

GRANDAD: Substreet

Missed call: Mum and Dad

GRANDAD: SUBSTREET

EVE: Shall I resend address?

GRANDAD: I MEAN SUNSCREEN. Grandad

In the meantime, my burner phone has been chirping up like a younger sibling dancing in front of the television for extra attention. Not that I have any siblings, but I spent enough time at Jules's house when I was a child to know exactly how annoying it is.

Morning Margot! How's your day going? Henry xxx

It's hot today isn't it? X

I think I've burned my eyelids
LOL. Not a good look. Xx

What are you up to? Xxxxx

Sighing, I put my laptop down for the twentieth time.

Last night, Henry was looking so promising—delightfully succinct and Darcy-like, a man of few words and, hopefully, knee-high boots—but he's already irritating me. It feels like I've accidentally subscribed to a mailing list simply by adding an item to my cart. Why doesn't he have anyone else to text?

Why *so many* kisses? Why does he think the logical solution to three unanswered texts is to send yet another one?

Ping.

And a totally unrelated GIF of a dancing cat.

Teeth gritted, I reply:

Hello! Sorry, super busy with work.
Yes, super hot. Nice cat.

Can we leave it until our dinner to chat?

Margot x

There's a short silence while I wonder if Henry is single because his last girlfriend walked him up a mountain, took his profile photo and left him there because he wouldn't stop sending her unrelated GIFs of otters holding hands.

Ping.

Really sorry. I've only just started
online dating. I'll rein it in. H

I'll just go ahead and add *nasty cow* to my long list of character flaws.

No—I'm sorry. Just overwhelmed with work.
Really looking forward to meeting you. Hope the
eyelids are better soon. See you on Monday! Xx

Then I rub my eyes, yawn and blink at my watch.

It's nearly 6 p.m. already and yet another day has disappeared, evaporating like the ocean carried by strong trade winds. Everything hurts. Back, hands, neck, arms, the deepening frown line between my eyebrows. I'm steadily becoming one of those projections of what humans will look like in a hundred years: a semicircle with claws for hands and no discernible chin.

My phone peeps again.

EVE: Where are you? Should we wait?

What do they mean, where am—

It's Tuesday. Panicking, I glance down at myself—black shorts, navy tank top, something crusty stuck to the front (freeze-dried carrot?)—then give up and sling a long, bobbly navy cardigan over the top so I look a bit like a grandma getting ready to flash someone in a park. I thrust on some cheap flip-flops, hop over the smashed dinner plates, grab my keys and trip over yet another box on the way out.

"Fuck fuck fuck—"

Nearly there!

I lie as I start shuffling down the road.

Sorry sorry.

My Instagram account may be my baby—in a figurative, emotional, physically draining sense—but there's another, much more literal baby that needs my full attention now.

"BLOODY HELL," JULES says as I burst into the clinic room. "We could hear you clacking all the way down the corridor like a shire horse."

"Or someone having sex," Eve says from the bed. "Badly."

Then she starts giggling and quickly clapping her hands together to demonstrate. *Somebody* has already been given valium.

"Sorry," I say again, adjusting my face mask and hairnet. "I told Alexa to set an alarm, but I shouted at her yesterday and I think she's still sulking."

The nurse, physician, embryologist and sonographer have all paused so they can assess the obligatory turquoise gown I have accidentally put on backward, like a superhero cloak. This is Embryo Transfer Number Six, and it makes fifteen dates look like child's play, inappropriate pun intended. At the end of a bad date, I have a belly full of Italian food and a slightly grumpy sense of despair and more time wasted. Eve gets to go through cramps, bloating, hormonal fluctuations, nausea, fatigue and an enormous series of hefty cheques, and—so far—her poor little belly has remained empty.

The nurse frowns. "And this must be—"

"The third member of our exotic throuple," Jules says chirpily, from where she's holding Eve's hand. "We don't like her as much, but every couple needs a third, slightly taken-for-granted partner who can do the domestic chores and organize holidays."

I laugh and an extremely dozy Eve looks alarmed.

"That's not true, but if we *were* a throuple, we'd be *lucky* to have Maggie. We love you, Mags. You're the winds beneath our toes. I really need to pee. I think my bladder is going to pop like a pigeon."

Jules squeezes her hand. "Spaced-out numpty."

"We're all just friends," I explain as I take my place on the other side of Eve and grab her hand too. This particular procedure isn't supposed to hurt, but Eve is generally terrified of anything medical, which makes this an even more impressive journey to go on. "Since primary school. No sex going on here."

"You can say that again," Eve giggles. "That's why I'm using a donor."

We explained all this the first time, obviously—the escalating endometriosis, the ticking biological clock that is deafening Eve and so on—but after five failed procedures, Eve consulted her tarot cards or whatever and decided it was "bad luck" to return to the same clinic, so we switched it up to encourage her, even though that's not really how any of this works.

"Great," the embryologist says with a slightly strained air of practiced patience. "We don't normally allow this many people in the room, but we'll make an exception this once."

"Once is all we'll need," Jules states staunchly. "Just one more."

Eve nods emphatically, legs akimbo.

These two women are the reason I'm not still curled up in a ball on an Exeter floor, screaming incoherently into some tiles. They were the little girls who took me under their sparkly, elasticated wings when I emigrated from Australia to England as a child, then became the teenagers who drank Archers with me for the first time, puked in a garden bush with me for the first time and avoided peaches together for the first time (ongoing). We have grown together like three sunflowers in one pot, each going on our own separate journey—independently reaching for the sun—yet permanently joined together, roots entwined.

There is nothing I would not do for these women.

Other than get to the most important date in Eve's calendar on time, obviously.

I squeeze her small, pale hand as the sonographer scans her stomach and her pixelated gray internal organs shift on screen like outer space. She's watching it with wide, anxious green eyes, and I feel another burst of tenderness for her. It's almost painful, my love for Eve. Like pressing a nearly healed bruise. Of the three of us, she has always been the kindest, the most positive, the most instantly lovable. I just want to reach across and grab the speculum, somehow take control of the uncontrollable for her.

"Got to say," Jules says, watching the screen too, "I've seen better movies. Two stars, extremely low quality, would not recommend."

But her dark eyes are slightly wet and her gravelly voice is too tight, like a pair of double-knotted shoelaces. The tight black curls around her face are frizzing slightly, which means she didn't sleep well last night either. We smile faintly at each other: the two of us sharing humor as deflection, always.

"Right," the nurse says gently as she hands the embryologist what looks, frankly, like some kind of worm that lives deep under the desert. "This is the catheter which contains your fertilized egg suspended in liquid, Eve. We're going to slowly insert this into the thickest part of the lining of your uterus, then we'll inject it in. It shouldn't hurt."

Eve's eyes get bigger—she's a tarsier, hanging on to a branch—and she nods.

"Happy swimming, little one," she whispers, and Jules and I glance at each other. Nothing is going to be "swimming" anywhere, as far as we're aware, but we'll let her hold on to this sweet image if it helps. In Eve's valium-befuddled mind, I suspect it's also wearing armbands and a little inflatable vest.

In sensitive silence, they inject my best friend, and there's a flash on screen.

"Finally," Jules says. "A bit of action."

"That's an air bubble," the embryologist explains patiently. "So we know that the egg is where it needs to be."

"Somebody gave it a snorkel," I whisper, and Jules snorts lightly.

"All done." Instruments that always seem too large—like kitchen utensils—get removed and Eve is cleaned up. "You just have to rest for five minutes, and then you can be on your way. Remember to keep taking your drugs. That's super important."

The team exits the room, leaving us to find Eve's errant knickers.

"He meant me, right?" Jules says as she picks up an abandoned floral shirt, socks and a patterned scarf from a heap on the floor. "As if I'd forget."

Then she picks up a pair of giant, graying, frayed knickers.

"Fuck me," she adds, throwing them at Eve. "I think we've just answered the question of why you need a sperm donor."

Eve giggles again as she tries to get dressed in a horizontal position.

"Speaking of sperm donors, aka male humans," Jules adds as a doped-up Eve puts her leg through the wrong jeans hole. "How's the epic experiment in date-a collection going, Margot? What was Number Fifteen like?"

"Very handsome," I say, taking the jeans away from Eve,

turning them the right way round and handing them back. "And married. With kids."

"Ew." Jules screws up her nose. "If Sim ever divorces me, I shall get me to a nunnery."

Jules and Simran have been married for eight years now—a relationship that continues to amaze me simply by being so painless.

"Lots of single women there," Eve says hopefully. "Good idea."

"Maybe Maggie should spend less time on the internet," Jules points out for the sixteenth time this month. "Then she might actually meet a man in *real* life."

"I do meet men in real life," I say lightly. "It's not my fault that the postman and the food delivery guy aren't impressed by my food-stained tracksuit."

Eve stands up with a tentative deer wobble and we all laugh.

Then the three of us pause for a minute of awed silence, trying to process the enormity of what has just happened. Again. It's not pencil cases and sparkly wings and Archers anymore. A whole life may have just started.

Please, please let it finally start.

"Seriously." Eve holds out her hands, her pupils the size of doorknobs. "What would I do without you guys?"

"Wear your jeans backward and your knickers on your head." I bend down slightly and push her wavy blonde fringe aside so I can kiss her shiny forehead. "Not for the first time."

We all smile at each other—briefly nine years old again, with plaits and sticker-covered backpacks and hopes of love letters and magic—and for just a moment I see Jules glance to the left of her, where a fourth member of our group used to be.

And I wonder, briefly, what Lily does without us.

Because, of all the raindrops I have watched fall over the years—of all the clouds I could read from a mile away and protect myself from if necessary—that was one storm I never saw coming.

3

ATMOSPHERIC PRESSURE IS measured in hectoPascals. As I explained during one very early and not particularly well-liked video, it describes the force exerted by the weight of the air above us, and this pressure changes depending on the area around it. On a weather chart, thin lines called isobars join places with equal sea-level pressures, and they are helpful in identifying areas of high pressure (anticyclones) and low pressure (depressions).

It also makes the sky look as if it has fingerprints, which is lovely.

I just have no idea what pressure is called when it's coming from your parents.

"DARLING, YOU'RE NAKED."

Scowling, I wipe water out of my eyes. I've been submerged for forty minutes, sporadically surfacing just to take a deep breath and dive again, like a humpback whale. Apparently, nothing is sacred, not even my own nudity.

"I'm in the bath, Mum," I say, angling the phone so she can just see the top half of my head. "Nakedness is kind of a requisite."

"It's nearly midnight." My mother's nostril takes up half the screen. "Why aren't you in bed? You need to get more sleep, sweetheart. You're starting to look a little haggard."

"Thanks." I rub more water out of my eye. "Just hold on while I drown myself."

"Don't be so dramatic, darling." Mum turns slightly. "George! She's still up. Come and say hello. Quickly! Put the pot down!"

For a moment I wonder if my parents have taken up a brand-new, illegal Australian hobby, and then I realize Dad is gardening in the background.

"Can you let me get out of the bath first, before we have a family meeting? And if you want me to sleep, you could think about not calling me at this time."

"We're still getting used to the time difference," Mum explains, as if nine hours ahead was advanced algebra, not math a six-year-old could accomplish without a calculator. "We just wanted to see how you're doing."

Ten weeks ago, my parents retired and immigrated to Australia, to the sunny little northern town my mother is from and where I grew up. Now they're micro-managing me from the other side of the world, which is, frankly, more efficient for everyone concerned.

"She's doing fine," Dad says from out of shot. "Stop worrying."

"She doesn't look *fine* to me," my mother objects sharply. "She looks like she has the bath too hot. Darling, one day you're going to get up too fast and faint and knock your head on the toilet and die alone on the bathroom floor, with no clothes on and nobody to find you for days and days, maybe weeks, and then what will we do?"

This was worryingly specific.

"Get a hobby that isn't harassing me?" I sigh. "Hang on. I'll get out now."

Slightly dizzy, as predicted, and now scared of my own loo—thanks, Mum—I put my phone face down, climb out of the bath and grab my dressing gown. "Right." I hold my phone back up. "How can I help you this evening, at this completely antisocial time?"

"You haven't picked up your phone for weeks," Dad explains

gently. "We just wanted to check that you're doing OK because we can't truly relax if you're not. Well, we can. It's really very nice here. But it's not *as* relaxing as it could be."

I smile fondly at my father. As spicy and resentful as I pretend to be—because it's fun, mostly—it was actually me who told them it was time to leave England. I kept finding brochures scattered around their dark little Bristol house, with images of sunny beaches and golf courses circled in purple ink and "*Not Yet*" written next to them. When what they actually meant was *Not Until Maggie Is OK Again and When Exactly Will That Be?* And day by day, the little lines around me grew denser and denser until I could barely breathe.

"I'm doing brilliantly," I say as cheerfully as I can. "My Instagram page is growing every day."

My parents glance at each other patiently, as if starting your own successful business is the equivalent of knitting your first scarf, and it's cute but not what anyone particularly needs details about.

"That's not what we meant, darling." Mum puts her glasses on like a little owl and gets closer to the phone camera, as if that's how technology works. "Tell us you've at least unpacked."

I look around the living room. Nope. "Yup."

"Great. Show us."

"Ugh. Fine." Feeling like a teenager, I hold up the camera at the apartment, filled with cardboard boxes and broken floor plates. "No. Happy?"

"Margot Elizabeth Wayward." Now I know I'm in trouble, because I don't even have a middle name, she just makes one up whenever she's scolding me. "This won't do, will it? Do we need to come back and sort you out?"

Dad looks momentarily horrified. "Joanne, we've got dinner with the Gilberts tomorrow and I've been marinating the chicken." He gets a dark glare from Mum and reassesses. "Which is not as important as the welfare of our only daughter, obviously." A bolt of hope. "Or Maggie could come out here? We can send you the money for tickets."

"I'm *fine*. If anything, I am *thriving*."

(I say while staring at five empty pot noodles lying on the coffee table.)

"And are you Getting Back Out There? Not just spending all your time browsing the internet or with Julia and Evelyn?"

I am not *browsing the internet*, Mother, I am *developing content*. We've had this conversation multiple times, but clearly it's had zero impact.

"Yup," I say through gritted teeth, staring at a box that says "MARGOT WAYWARD—PHOTOS." That one can stay firmly Sellotaped shut, thank you. "Just yesterday I met a man who wanted to extend his family to include me."

Mum beams with palpable relief. "Well, that sounds promising!"

"Without the permission of his wife."

"Ah." There's a silence. "Keep trying. Darling, you're not getting any—"

"If you say *younger*," I hiss, towel-drying my hair with one hand, "I swear to God you will both be put in a very cheap retirement home without any extracurricular activities. I'm thirty-six, not eighty-six."

"Actually," Dad says calmly, still subtly repotting his plant just out of shot, "I recently read about a woman who met her first true love at ninety. A lovely meet-cute in neighboring hospital beds. Fell for each other immediately. Very romantic. Admittedly, they only lasted a few days together, I think some kind of infection, but it's never too late, that's what I'm saying."

"Fuck me," I say flatly. "Something to look forward to."

"*Language*, sweetheart," Mum sighs. "You have a PhD, Margot, so you clearly have a bigger vocabulary than you pretend. And I was *going* to say, *you're not getting any more healed*." This is palpably untrue because that's not a normal sentence. "Open yourself up, Maggie. Let someone in. Give someone a chance."

"Please stop buying *Live Laugh Love*–adjacent pillows, Mother."

"Does the coffee filter need changing, Joanne?" Dad sniffs his mug. "It tastes weird."

"If you want the coffee filter changed, change it."

"Well, I will, but I don't know when to."

"When it tastes weird, George."

"It's been a pleasure," I say sharply, glancing at the clock. "Thanks for this essential update. I'll be sure to pick up next time you call."

"Keep looking for a real job!" Mum leans urgently toward the phone. "There has to be *something* out there. And go see your grandfather! He's all on his own now, Maggie, like you."

"Bloody hell," I snap, and put the phone down.

BUT THOSE LITTLE pressure lines keep tightening, and I'm still wide awake at 2 a.m., perambulating the flat like an impatient ticket inspector and prodding boxes with my toes. I can still see Aaron: humming while he stirs a home-made soup in the kitchen, lying outstretched on the sofa with his huge feet on my lap. He is everywhere I look: scattered like clouds across a summer sky, casting shadows all around, blocking my light. Aaron would have found something fun to do with the spare bedroom, which he'd have unpacked immediately. He'd have loved the tiny garden and would have built a barbecue, or at least started and then talked about it for the next six months.

Except Aaron's not here, and never has been. It's a house haunted by his absence, and I can almost hear him say, *Blimey, Margot. It's been nearly eight months. You need to start moving on.*

I want to say, *I am trying, Aaron, I promise.*

But I can't, because he's not here.

I can't, because it's not true.

WITH A BOLT of supreme effort, I grab a pair of scissors, open one of the "KITCHEN SHIT" boxes, pull out a spatula and carefully place it in a kitchen drawer.

For a few seconds, I stand back and stare proudly at it.

That wasn't so hard, was it? Tomorrow, I might upgrade to

the pair of tongs I have literally never used because takeout just doesn't require any.

Yawning widely, I crawl into bed, pop in my mouth guard to stop me grinding my teeth to powder and try hard not to see Aaron, his heavy arm casually flung over my waist. The space around my middle feels weirdly empty. That side of the bed still has him lying in it, even though it's brand-new. New mattress, new sheets, new covers: I made absolutely sure of it.

Clamping down on plastic, I pick up my burner phone and methodically trawl through all five dating apps I've downloaded for variety, of which there is none. If online men were like weather, meteorologists would have a much easier job and there'd be fewer complaints about "inaccuracy." The messages are alarmingly predictable, and it's difficult to decide which is less attractive: a generous offer from a stranger to lick me or an inability to distinguish between a possessive adjective and a contraction. One has opened with a detailed explanation of what he'd like to do to me, as if I'm a woodwork project looking to be sanded.

Instead, I find myself searching Henry's profile again.

This time, I'm looking for the data he hasn't included: the signs of what's really going on, hidden in plain sight. But all I can work out is that Henry wears a yellow tartan scarf when it's cold, like a children's cartoon bear, and his ears go extremely pink when it's hot (*sunscreen*, Henry). He hasn't co-opted a child or dog that isn't his, and there aren't any group shots of friends simply to prove he has some, but which accidentally show every woman in a twenty-mile radius that he's not the most attractive one. He is a tantalizingly blank canvas—the dots of him are drawn in the things that aren't there—and for the first time since I started online dating, I feel . . . faintly excited.

Henry has sent me his phone number, even though I stopped giving out mine at Date Three: i.e. the unexpected introduction to a stranger's genitals.

But he seems lovely, so I impulsively text from my burner phone:

Hi Henry. This is Margot. It's 2:32 am so apologies if I look a bit mad—can't sleep. I don't suppose you fancy dinner this evening instead, do you? X

I study the message for a few seconds: uncharacteristically impulsive.

Send.

To my surprise, there's an almost immediate response:

Hi Margot. I'm on a night shift right now so also awake. Tonight works for me. You pick a location. Henry x

And there it is: hope.

I haven't felt it for so long, I barely recognize the airy lifting of my insides, like a blast of heat under a hot-air balloon. I feel myself expand very slightly and rise. I'd forgotten what it feels like. It's nice. Sweet. But the dark, cold, tugging undercurrent running beneath it—that, at least, is familiar.

I am absolutely terrified.

Great! Here's a link to the restaurant. Hope you like Italian! Margot. X

Outside, rain hammers against the windows: the sky bellows, shatters, breaks apart. It's comforting, knowing I'm not the only one. That the sky is out there, doing it too.

Then I roll over and stare at the empty space next to me.

One storm at a time.

4

HERE WE GO: Date Sixteen.

As I wait, I scan the Criteria List in my notepad.

One date every week for the last sixteen weeks, and I only have four left to go. Twenty first dates, total. A data-collecting experiment in which I prove that I've given it my Best Shot: to myself and to everyone else. But all I seem to have gathered is exactly what I *don't* want, in laborious detail.

Which is, it appears, *literally everyone.*

"Can I get you anything to start?"

The waiter hovers politely over me like a kestrel and I shake my head while I scan my list more carefully. My list of Red Flags is long enough now to overflow onto a second A4 page, sporadically highlighted and double underlined, with capital letters. In meteorological terms, a *red flag* is a warning of fire. It's a danger alert sent out when high temperatures, low humidity and strong winds mean an increased likelihood that things will literally burst into flames. But it works the same way with dating and love, so what are the signs you should run?

How do you tell if this whole thing will burn to the ground?

The answer: I collect, I analyze and I watch.

Do they order for me? Do they suggest a change to my physical appearance? Could they be controlling? Do they only talk about themselves? Are all their ex-partners "psycho"? Have they lied on their profile?

The problem is that the more you look for Red Flags, the

easier they are to find. Until you're no longer looking for fire: you're looking for just the faintest bit of smoke, a hint of heat, a puff of ash, and you're out of there, running for safety.

A fire is a terrifying prospect when you've already been burned.

CAREFULLY SLIDING MY notepad and pen back into my handbag, I focus on the door and try to breathe slowly. Henry is already nine minutes late, and this demonstrates such disrespect and carelessness, such hubris, it strongly indicates he's selfish in other areas of his life too, better nip it in the bud now before it gets any worse—and I'm doing it already. *Fuck.*

Then the door swings open and I take a deep breath.

Henry is gorgeous and as we lock eyes, my stomach wriggles. He smiles widely and a pulse of lightning shoots through my shoulders, down my arms and into my fingers. Heat flashes. Warmth glows. Fire or chemistry?

I smile back; his smile broadens, dimpled at the corners.

For a surprising moment, I find myself thinking: is this it? Is this the arm I want around my waist at night, the man I want filling the empty frames still sitting in a cardboard box in my hallway?

"Margot!" Henry's voice is deep and warm. He approaches me as I stand cautiously and all six foot two of him bends slightly to kiss my cheek, smelling faintly of cinnamon. "What a place! I've never been here before! Thank you for choosing somewhere so lovely for us to meet."

A flush of fierce pleasure, completely undeserved: I have literally brought every date here for the last four months.

"Thank you for coming at such short notice."

As if this is a Zoom meeting I've just decided to hold after lunch and nobody really wants to be here but me.

"My pleasure!" Henry holds the back of my chair so I can sit down again. "I was going to take an extra shift, but this is a much more fun way to spend an evening."

He takes his seat and grins at me while I study his handsome face.

What am I even looking for? A twitch of a muscle that shows he can't be trusted? A strain around the eyes that indicates disappointment in me? I look briefly at his large, tanned hands—no wedding ring or imprint—and the collar of his T-shirt: no lipstick, accidentally rubbed. Is he actually a fireman? That much remains to be seen, obviously, but he looks like he *could* be.

And now I'm staring at him as if he's a frog on a table, waiting to be dissected.

Which, in so many ways, he is.

"Sorry," I say quickly, looking away. "It's just rare to meet someone who actually looks like their profile."

"Why, thank you." Henry laughs warmly, teeth glowing white. "As do you, Margot. Thank goodness for photography. Imagine if we were dating in the 1500s and all we had were watercolor portraits to go by."

"Anne of Cleves springs to mind," I smile. "The worst possible outcome for a too-flattering dating profile picture."

"Divorce, ridicule and public shaming." Henry is studying my face too, and I try my hardest just to let him. What does he see? That my eyes are too large, that my nose is too sharp, that my mouth is a little too small for my head? Or is he just looking without pulling me apart? If so, *how*? "I remember that bit from school."

"Yes." I pick up the menu. "Luckily, now the consequences are just being loudly labeled a catfish in front of seven other diners."

"No!" Henry laughs. "They wouldn't dare."

Date Number Seven: he of the three missing buttons. He said that my hair was "more red" in my photos, which was "misleading," and wouldn't accept the existence of hair dye as an answer.

"Oh, they do dare," I grin, still pretending to scan the menu. "The internet is full of people who dare continuously, in my experience."

"This is actually my first online date ever. I think I mentioned that already. It's all very exciting. Although you're making it easy on me so far, which I appreciate."

I briefly think back a year to when online dating apps were a beguiling mystery to me too, full of exciting romantic opportunities just waiting to be unearthed. I'd sit next to Eve while she scanned reluctantly through them, glibly telling her how "fun" it looked and how I was "a little sad I didn't get to try it." Safe in the knowledge that I was exempt from this particular adventure.

Frankly, I still shrivel in shame. I was the woman who rolled smugly around in her own love life while pretending she envied others their freedom, and I got everything I deserved.

"I'll try not to traumatize you for the others," I flirt slightly.

"If it goes well," Henry says, glancing across the room at the waiter with a wide smile and then back at me, "maybe there won't be any."

It feels as if somebody just trickled icy water down my back, and I have to fight an urge to stand up, shout "NO, THANK YOU" and flee the scene, taking the olives with me.

"Whoa, boy," I say as lightly as I can, taking a large swig of wine as the waiter approaches. "Let's have starters before we become exclusive."

"OK." Henry smiles. "But I'd quite like marriage before we finish pudding."

He's joking and it's sweet but also terrifying, and I can feel my eyes pop like a hamster held a little too tightly.

"I'm teasing, Margot," he says gently. "Obviously."

"Yes!" I straighten my striped top with suddenly sweaty hands. "Ha ha! Brilliant. I . . . um . . ." I look wildly around as the waiter pauses. "Just have to pop to the bathroom. Be right back. Please tell the waiter I'll have the pasta carbonara."

Fuck.

Breathing too fast, I scamper through the maze of tables—knocking over a vase with a fake flower in it—and into the bathroom, where I promptly slam the stall door shut, sit on the lid of the toilet, drag my legs up to my chin and pull out my phone while I hyperventilate into my knees.

HELP

EVE: Oh no! Is D16 awful? Shall we call you and fake an emergency getaway?

JULES: Breathe, Mags. What's going on?

He's nice.

There's a pause for about thirty seconds, as well there might be.

JULES: Maggie I say this with love but GET FUCKING THERAPY

EVE: Maybe you're not ready to date yet?

Obviously I'm not ready to date yet.

That's been clear every time I sit down at the same restaurant table and scan the man in front of me for ways I can dismantle him, as if he's a life-size game of Operation and I just need to pull him apart carefully without his nose lighting up. It's not the satisfaction of a healthy, well-balanced and emotionally open woman, that's for sure. Every time I see a Red Flag, all I feel is triumph: *there* it is, you didn't trick me. No shocks here.

But I had to at least *try*, right? Twenty dates. That's all.

Because if I didn't try—if I didn't conduct this experiment—I'd probably just never date again. The hurt would solidify inside me, harden and brick me into myself, leaving me comfortable inside a tower I've built: isolated and alone. Month by month, I'd find a new excuse—a new focus, a new distraction, a new ick—and the cement between my bricks would become permanent.

It's been eight months: time to get back on the bike.

Even if the last one threw you directly into oncoming traffic when you weren't even wearing a basic helmet.

It's OK. I'm better now. Just needed a quick panic attack.

JULES: Gnocchi him dead ha ha

EVE: You've got this, Maggie! We love you!

Breathing out, I unlock the door and stare in the mirror: I have the wide-eyed expression of a wild horse some cowboy just tried to tie to a lamp post.

Stop being such an asshole, Margot.

Carefully, I smooth my expression back to neutral. Then I return to the table, where Henry has apparently already ordered food and is now drinking a beer, completely unfazed by my freak-out.

He smiles. "All good?"

"Absolutely." I'm feeling calmer already. "So tell me about yourself, Henry."

DATE SIXTEEN PASSES with flying colors.

He's the age he claims to be (he shows me ID); he's never been married, has no children; he asks me questions too, which is a disarming change. He doesn't refer to me at any point as a "girl," or immediately delve too hard into my past as if relentlessly foraging for historical truffles. It's his first online date because he "normally meets women organically," but he is "looking for a real connection now." Our political beliefs align and what we're looking for in a relationship matches. OK, he doesn't know what a *meteorologist* is—he thinks I study stars—but he accepts my correction with grace and aplomb.

Henry is intelligent, erudite, honest, incredibly warm and charming.

He's almost painfully beautiful.

By the time the bill arrives, he has ticked almost every single box on my List of Dating Criteria. More importantly, he hasn't gone anywhere near the Red Flags list, and yet somehow

I haven't freaked out again. Possibly because the air around us is charged with electricity. Every time we accidentally touch—reaching for garlic bread at the same time, filling a water glass—a white-hot line of heat runs across the back of my neck, sparking in showers like a Catherine wheel. For the first time in four months of dating, I actually *want* a Second Date. What happens now, I have no idea. From now on, it's freewheeling: a concept I'm not thrilled by.

"Let me get this," Henry smiles, reaching for the receipt. "My treat."

I flush with pleasure. "You don't have to do that."

"Oh, but I want to."

"Honestly." I laugh and reach for my purse. "This place was my idea, I asked you out first. It's only fair. Equality and so forth. Start as we mean to go on."

Something strange flashes across Henry's face and my feet go abruptly cold.

"No." He smiles a little too widely. "I would prefer to do this, Margot. It's the way it should be."

And I should leave it, but something inside me twists tight.

Red Flag.

"By 'the way it should be' . . ." I study him carefully. There's something in his eyes I hadn't spotted before, under the warmth—something cold and empty—and my stomach knots a little more. "What do you mean, specifically?"

"You know exactly what I mean." His jaw tightens and he leans forward with narrow eyes. "Stop embarrassing me."

The electricity in the air between us shivers, falters, dies: a broken light bulb.

My mouth drops open. "I don't think I'm—"

"Look." Henry's eyes are flinty. "This is just how it is with me. I'm a romantic, traditional kind of guy. One of the *good* ones. A lion doesn't need to tell everyone he's a lion. He *shows* everyone he's a lion, just by being king of the jungle."

I sit back in my chair and evaluate Henry again, excitement now completely gone. There's a faint noise to my right, and I glance up to see the waiter trying not to laugh: he lifts his eyebrows at me, and I lift mine back.

"Henry," I say calmly. "There aren't any lions in the jungle. They live in the grasslands and savannahs. You're thinking of tigers."

"Ohhhh." Henry rolls his eyes. "Great. Another lesson from Little Miss Too Big for My Boots." He leans forward and almost hisses: "You're way too old to be an Insta chick. Get over yourself. And I make a good wage. A solid wage. I can pay. You're not *better* than me."

Red Flag, Red Flag, Red Flag—

There's a sudden sense of vertigo, as if I had been taking a nice stroll along a sunlit path and abruptly plummeted straight off a cliff. At some point in the last hour, he must have online stalked me while I was glibly reapplying lip gloss in the bathroom, hoping to encourage him to kiss me.

"I have *never* said I'm—"

"But noooooo." Henry straightens his T-shirt and puffs up like a pigeon. "You've got to humiliate me instead, in front of everyone." He gestures around the almost empty restaurant. "Nice one, Margot. Really sensitive. Really *feminist*. No wonder you're still single at nearly forty years old."

As if he's not thirty-nine and on the same dating app as me.

This time, there's no satisfaction at all. I did not see this coming. I guess I can now add *Not Emasculated by My Job* to my ever-growing criteria.

"You'd better not make a video about this," he adds fiercely, narrowing his eyes. "I'm not going to be fodder for your *pathological narcissism*."

Red Flag, but who the hell cares at this point: the whole room is on fire.

Ironically, for a fireman.

"I talk about the weather," I say calmly. "Exclusively. Not dickheads. There really isn't enough space on the World Wide Web for that." Then I reach forward and rip the bill out of his hand. "This has been quite the education." I stand up, feeling as if I've just been popped. That'll teach me to *hope*. "Thank you so much for your time, Henry. I'll pay for myself and leave now."

"Bloody *women*," I hear him hiss behind me as I walk toward the waiter. "All you women on dating apps, you're all *exactly* the same. Stuck-up, entitled cows, the lot of you."

I turn briefly. "I thought this was your first online date?"

"That's what I tell you all." Henry laughs nastily. "Makes you feel special and you're all too stupid to work it out."

RED FUCKING FLAG.

And that's it: the experiment is now over. I've done the research, studied the data and have decided that I'd rather be eaten by otters.

"I'd like this broken down," I tell the waiter firmly. "In detail. Please."

"Of course," the waiter says solemnly as I make my way down the receipt with a pen. "I'm assuming you don't want your date to pay the lion's share, then."

"No." I snort lightly, glancing behind me to where Henry is still glowering, looking hilariously huge now behind the little table, knees bunched up slightly. It's strange how someone beautiful can become so ugly so quickly. His blond hair is sticking to his forehead, and his bottom lip is literally sticking out slightly, as if he's six years old and has just dropped his ice cream.

"Actually," I say, abruptly grinning. Frankly, I've dated worse. Hell, I nearly married one of them. "I'm going to pay the entire bill. Plus tip. Add on a pudding at the end and please include a note that says *I'd like a divorce now, please.*"

Because screw him and his geographically relocated lions.

"Done." The waiter starts to prod the screen in front of him. "So, is it Date Seventeen next week, then?"

Blinking, I look up. "Sorry?"

"Date Seventeen." He continues to calculate the bill without looking at me. His voice is low, with a lovely northern lilt. "That was Date Sixteen, wasn't it? Unless I missed one, but I've worked every Monday for the last four months."

I study the waiter more carefully. He's absolutely right: he's been my waiter for every one of my disastrous dates so far. I just didn't really register it properly because it didn't seem key data to input. Shame suddenly whips the back of my neck. And I claim to be good at noticing details.

"Shit," I say quickly, heat rushing to my face. "I'm not as bad as I seem. Actually, that's a lie. I'm even worse. And my language is atrocious."

"Don't panic." He laughs. "You've been the highlight of my Monday shifts."

The waiter is clearly flirting with me now, so I study his face. His eyes are dark brown and close together, like a wolf's; his nose is large and his eyebrows bushy, pointing down slightly at the inner corners. His hair is black, streaked with silver, like a badger, and he's slightly rectangular and (considerably) shorter than me. It's a face I'd swipe left on, not because it's bad but because it doesn't make my heart hop.

"You're flirting with me," I point out in surprise.

"I am." The waiter looks up and meets my eyes. "Is it working?"

"No." I frown. "Not at all."

"That's a shame." He calmly takes my bank card out of my hands. "I was going to suggest I take Date Seventeen so you can pull my entire character to shreds too. I'm becoming far too big for my boots."

I laugh, surprised, and evaluate him again.

Too short. How old is he? Old enough to have silver hair. He works evening shifts and I work all day, which would create tension and emotional distance. As we've just discovered, the disparity between our incomes might result in resentment. I'd have to stop wearing heels; he'd notice and feel embarrassed, then start to hate me for it. One failed date and I'd have to find another restaurant to eat at and that's a hassle I don't need. It wouldn't work. There's no possible future—he doesn't fit my criteria—and I don't have time to waste.

Also, there's absolutely zero chemistry. None. Brutal, but there it is.

"No, thank you." I try to be as polite as I can. "That's a very nice offer, but I'm not sure we're very compatible."

"Fair enough," he says lightly, holding out my bank card. "All done."

I reach forward and as our fingers touch, I see the letters *LR* drawn in dark blue ink on the back of his hand; the glint of my emerald ring; a flash of orange from my bank card. His fingers are large and tanned and familiar; a bolt of heat shoots straight through me.

"*Fuck*," I say, pulling back and dropping my card.

"Everything OK?"

I bend down and take a few seconds on the floor to compose myself again while I pretend to pick up my card. What the *hell* was that?

"Um. Yes." I stand slowly back up again and stare at his hand. "Sorry, I just . . . How long has that been there?"

"From birth, I think." The waiter glances at his hand with an amused expression. "I don't want to brag, but I've got another very similar one if you want to see it."

My nostrils flare slightly, even in my confusion. "Not the hand. The writing."

"Oh!" He lifts one bushy eyebrow. "Since this morning. It stands for Loo Roll. I ran out and need to pick some up on the way home."

Except he must have forgotten: it was obviously there two days ago—the last time I was here—or at some other point over the last few months. He must run out of toilet roll a lot and doesn't know how to write a proper shopping list. It's a memory, that's all, but one that appears to have stuck.

Except something in me has shifted slightly, and I'm not sure why.

"OK," I say impulsively, before I even know I'm going to. "Yes."

"Yes?"

"To the date you offered. You can be Date Seventeen. But I'll be wearing my highest heels. Just so you know."

"Please do." He grins, his eyes crinkle and faint lines shoot like sunrays through his face. "Who knew that running out of loo roll could be so magnetic. Date Seventeen it is, Margot."

He already knows my name, and I know nothing about him.

"And you are?"

"Oh." The waiter looks over with amusement at my date, still sulking at our table with his big arms crossed. "I'm Henry too."

5

Unbelievable

U R exactly why good men are so wary about online dating.

What's your bank details I'm going to send you my half of last night's cheque right now you don't get to win you silly cow

Hello

Margot reply to me RIGHT NOW

I COULD BLOCK OTHER Henry, but I don't.

There's satisfaction in watching the fireman reveal himself. Every time my burner phone beeps, I get another rush of pleasure. This could have taken weeks to come out all on its own—me, blinded by lust and inordinately white teeth—and what a terrifying waste of time that would have been.

MARGOT BLOODY ANSWER ME FFS

At some point, Henry will rage himself to sleep like an angry toddler.

In the meantime, I continue working.

None of my "job"—as my mother puts it, using her index

fingers as quotation marks—comes naturally to me, which is a brand-new experience. I was comfortable at the Met Office. I examined the data, I processed the data, I made forecasts based on the data. I was good at it. Now I'm running around sourcing interesting content, making videos that take six times longer than they should, replying to DMs with private weather forecasts and answering an influx of emails from brands and potential sponsors who have nothing to do with the topics I talk about but would like to be shoehorned in somehow.

But no matter how busy I am, I somehow find time to stalk Lily. I'll skip lunch, forgo a shower, yet still pick up my burner phone and scan it methodically for Lil's most recent social media updates.

Lily Howard—or @LilSunnyDayz, as she's known worldwide—is a "lifestyle influencer" and prolific in her content creation. She has a life so beautiful it has its very own, slightly tawny filter that makes everything look like a new form of daguerreotype, as if she's a modern Victorian. It's all whimsy and lace and butterflies: a porcelain teacup with a robin on it next to a nibbled croissant; a photo of her in a huge camel coat walking down a beautiful street, red hair all the way down her back. There are "arty" shots where it's just her neck and shoulder; her toes on the edge of a blue lake; cuddled up in an enormous wool knit, knees tucked underneath it as if she's too tiny, too cute, too implausibly adorable to buy a jumper that actually flaming fits her.

There are "real" shots—hiding under a duvet in the morning with her sunset hair perfectly ruffled—and there are mind-numbingly expensive branded sponsor shots: a specific gold necklace, a subtle designer belt, the slow drip-drip of buy it, pay the money, and you can have a glow just like mine.

And it's not a new thing, that's what's so galling. She hasn't fabricated any of this for an exquisite internet persona: she's simply upgraded slightly.

Lily has *always* been this person.

She was the girl at school everyone watched and copied: what is she wearing, what is she doing, how do we somehow bottle her magical essence and spray it laboriously all over ourselves like Davidoff Cool Water? Lily has this mysterious, slightly strange lilt to her voice, but instead of everyone mocking her for it—as I was, having been born in Australia—it inexplicably spread. If Lily bought a backpack that was slightly too small, the backpacks around us shrank as if we were in *Alice in Wonderland*; when Lily cut herself a bad fringe with her mother's kitchen scissors, so did everyone else.

And she was genuinely *nice*—that was the hardest part.

Lily was never judgmental, never sneery, superior or smug. Lily would go out of her way to compliment everyone, just to make their days a little brighter. It was like she had so much of her own natural glow, she could afford to just *leak* it at will. As if the rest of us were jealously hoarding whatever sparkle we could muster while she effortlessly spread in shifting rainbow colors across the sky like an aurora: pure sun energy meeting invisible lines of a magnetic field, making the light dance.

Which made it all the more inexplicable that she chose *us* to be friends with: the gang we'd formed in primary school and which had moved up seamlessly through the years. Eve Williams, with her neon socks, pale, lopsided plaits and tarot cards; Jules Achiuwa, sarcastic and foul-mouthed, with heavy black eyeliner even at twelve. And me: reserved and watching. Observing everything, collecting data, methodical and slightly gray no matter what I was wearing, like a tired owl. Lily brought all her prism-like colors with her and we reflected them and loved her for it.

And now two million random strangers love her for it too.

All she has to do is post a photo of her wearing a crochet dress and smelling a bloody pink rose and it's a lovefest of adoration and approval: *How are you so cute though, Lil you're gorg, what a pure soul you have <3 <3 Keep glowing bb!*

In the meantime, I spend three hours diligently making a video about global warming and underneath will be: *It's a hoax you stupid bint, grow up. Can we not get political plz this used to be a fun account.*

It's hard not to examine the data, to compare and contrast.

Teeth gritted—I'm slowly developing the jawline of a bulldog—I scan her account quickly. There's a brand-new photo (sepia-tinted, always) of Lily on an empty tropical beach in a white dress, palm trees and turquoise, bending down with her hands on her legs, laughing with her eyes shut. It's a real laugh, and I can tell the difference because I know her: I know how her turned-up little nose crinkles when she's really giggling, I know how her eyes disappear into sunny crescents. These are the worst kinds of posts, for me. Because, for just a minute, you become the person taking the photo. You are two people: yourself and the person with Lily. You can feel the affection, the love, radiating from behind the lens toward her.

Worse: you can feel the love radiating back.

Breathing out slowly, I think about what fake @Lucy_Jones7 would write.

Then I hit "like" and type: So beautiful. <3 <3

Ugh. I have become the kind of person who trolls people online with random insincere compliments and it's safe to say I never saw *that* coming either.

A few seconds later—to my intense surprise—Lily "likes" my comment and writes: Thank you so much so are you. <3

"Oh sod off," I snap loudly, throwing my burner phone across the sofa. "I'm a bloody squirrel."

Then I stand up, stretch and glare at my makeshift green screen. I don't get to sniff a flower for money, sadly; I have to actually come up with *information* to impart. Today's scheduled topic: *silver linings.* I am nothing if not a hypocrite. I know exactly what a silver lining is, just not how to find my own.

It's taken a solid hour to get my hair, make-up and top half of my outfit to a point where I feel ready to sit in front of two hundred thousand people. I never used to bother, but I discovered that the "better" I looked, the better my posts did, the more followers I gained, the more money I made. It's outrageous—@Hurricane_Humphrey rarely brushes his hair—but unless I want to go back to the Met Office in Exeter, which I can't, I have to play this game in all its patriarchal horror.

Exhaling slowly, I sit in front of a shade of green that makes my skin look even more corpse-like than normal. Then I switch on the ring light, take a deep breath, smooth my fringe down and hit record.

"Greetings, meteorologists! Margot here." I beam for the camera, even though it feels like making pizza dough: pulling it at the edges until my face stretches and snaps back. "Today I'm here to talk to you about silver linings! We've all heard the expression, which can be traced back to a John Milton poem, *Comus*, or *A Masque Presented at Ludlow Castle*. He wrote, '*Was I deceived, or did a sable cloud turn forth her silver lining on the—*'"

I promptly stop recording.

Yes, that's exactly what the general public wants when they are casually scanning social media for videos of a tiny puppy being washed in a sink: quotes from a poet who died in 1674, after going totally blind. Lily would never.

So I try again: "Greetings, minimintiminologol—"

This time I can't even say my own profession: delete.

"Greetings, meteorologists! Margot here!" I quickly reach for a sweet smile and fail; all I can see is Lily's effortless crinkle. "Now, we've all heard of a metaphorical *silver lining*, but what exactly is it? When light rays travel around the edge of an object such as a water droplet and bend—"

My phone beeps and I grab it with a sharp sense of relief. Saved.

JULES: Did you forget again?

No! I'm on my way! Ten mins!

Then I stare at myself in the video, which is still switched on.

It's a face I'm recognizing less, even as the internet recognizes it more. There are new lines of tension around my mouth, darkness around my huge eyes and something in my pale blue irises that reads as something it never used to: icy, cold, hard. I am becoming a frozen person. My cheeks—angular at best—are becoming gaunt, scooped out like ice cream. My long, dark, pin-straight hair no longer has any bounce or shine but hangs, dull and defeated. Even my collarbones look sharp and angry. There's no light here, no sparkle, no rainbow or aurora. I am gray like a moth without a light to hover around anymore.

"Stop being so bloody self-pitying, Margot," I tell my image fiercely, and it tells me straight back. "It is *deeply* unlikable."

And I switch the recording off.

"FINALLY!" EVE LOOKS UP, swaddled in a too-big white dressing gown like a tiny child freshly out of the bath. "I knew you'd make it!"

Even without valium, Eve retains a slightly wide-eyed, sparrow-like quality: the perky optimism of someone who still looks at clouds and sees ducks and bunnies, where I see only a cumulus that signals a storm coming.

"As if I'd miss it." I look around for Jules. "Where's the other fake baby mama?"

"Hot tub." Eve grins and pats her fluffy stomach. "I'm not going in, just in case. I've got a really good feeling about this time, Maggie."

Smiling, I straighten out my own robe, perch next to her and pat her leg.

My pocket vibrates and I try to ignore it.

As Eve isn't currently drinking, we've forgone our regular pub sessions and have decided to try out other, more sober activities: cinema, cooking classes, bowling, afternoon tea, a horribly expensive spa. I glance over to where Jules has clambered out of the hot tub. She gives me a quick military salute before heading toward the sauna, bored already. If Eve is a sparrow and I am an owl, Jules is a hummingbird: never still, always hovering.

"So how's school?"

My phone goes off. *Buzz. Buzz. Buzz. Buzz.*

"Brilliant." Eve leans her fair head back on the pillow. "The kids are *hilarious*, as always. One boy asked me where poo came from, so I told him. Then he asked if that's where Eeyore comes from too, and I giggled so hard I farted."

I laugh. *Ting.* "It's a bit early to be losing control of your bodily functions."

"Oh." She closes her eyes and beams. "Unrelated to the Maybe Baby. The only edible thing the canteen serves these days is baked beans."

Buzz. Buzz. Ting. Buzz.

Eve is a primary school teacher and her students adore her as much as she adores them, even if I suspect they sometimes see her more as a peer than as an educator. Cotton-wool clouds and crystals hang from her classroom ceiling and she regularly wears jumpers with squirrels knitted into the sleeves. Whenever a five-year-old does something naughty, Eve sits them in a corner on a cozy beanbag, turns on a "sunset" lamp, faces them toward a large photo of the view from the top of a mountain and encourages them to "think about the bigger picture." I meet her occasionally after school and she's always surrounded by dozens of adoring faces turning toward her like shiny buttercups. It is a constant source of amazement to me that Eve, who has wanted children her entire life and is surrounded by them every day, can still stay hopeful when her body is seriously insinuating that she may never have her own.

"What are we talking about?" Jules plonks down next to us in a one-piece, lean and dripping. "It better not be kids again. I'm maxed out."

I give her a sympathetic glance. I could not agree more.

Jules hasn't changed in nearly three decades. She didn't like dolls, especially the baby kind, and she has no interest in any of that now either. She's a top national journalist and she doesn't have time for "that generic societally enforced female shit."

"We were just talking about how we've signed you up to a two-hour-long massage," I grin, feeling my phone buzz in my pocket yet again. "A nice relaxing bit of being rubbed by a stranger."

"Touch me and die," Jules says flatly, stretching out her insanely long legs.

Another *ting* and I finally capitulate and pull out both my phones.

The Flat Earthers have found me again. They tend to come in waves, which ironically they don't know how to explain.

FlatEarther7138: You NEED to get ur FACTS STRATE "Margot" if earth is a ball TEL me why we can't feel it SPINING stop spreading LIES #wakeup #openureyes

This is under a video where I explain the impact of a rotating Earth on daily weather: something you'd think was relatively uncontroversial, but nope.

Frowning, I start typing:

Hello @FlatEarther7138 and thank you for commenting. The reason we can't feel ourselves "spining" is that the Earth is rotating at a constant—

"Oy." Jules prods me with her big toe and then uses it to point at a large sign on the wall. "That says *No Phones Allowed*, does it not? And unless I'm sorely mistaken, that is a phone. If I can manage two grim hours of me time, so can you."

I scowl and put my still-buzzing phone back in my dressing gown. I'll get back to @FlatEarther7138 later this evening, once the globular Earth has, ironically, rotated a little further.

"Fine."

"You're working too hard," Eve says, worried. "You need to think about outsourcing or something."

"*Or* . . ." I pretend to think about it for a few seconds, as if this hasn't been on my mind for hours. "Perhaps what we all need is a *holiday*. You know, like the old days. Just the three of us, a nice beach somewhere, sun loungers, books. Wouldn't that be great? I could *totally* switch off then."

"Oh yeah?" Jules narrows her dark eyes and studies me

carefully. "A holiday? On a nice tropical beach? With, I don't know, maybe a few palm trees? A flowing white dress to giggle in, perchance?"

I look vaguely over at the hot tub while my cheeks start to burn. A couple are kissing vigorously in it, and honestly, this place should spend less attention on who has a mobile phone on them and more on who is fornicating in shared water.

"I don't know what you're talking about."

"Yes, I think you bloody do." Jules's lips are compressed. "You're still doing it, aren't you? You're still stalking Lily. You *promised*, Margot. It's unhealthy. Unhinged. Verging on completely batshit crazy, at this point."

"Actually," Eve jumps in quickly, "I told her. About the . . . thing. Didn't I, Meg? It just kind of fell out. You know what I'm like."

I give her a grateful glance, even though Jules isn't buying it because Eve clearly doesn't know what we're talking about.

"Right. I'm just going to say it." Jules's voice has softened slightly and she leans forward, eyes fixed on mine. "All of this . . ." She waves a damp hand in the direction of my still-buzzing dressing-gown pocket. "Starting up your own Instagram page just to compete with Lily"—I flinch—"following her every move, buying that boxing bag . . . You're losing yourself, Margot. And I'm worried about you."

"I'm not *competing*." I blink, suddenly feeling tiny. "And boxing is *exercise*."

"Try yoga," she says firmly. "You're supposed to be *moving through* grief, that's why they're called *stages*. And you're not. You skipped denial, went straight to anger and just stayed right there, rolling around like a—"

"Badger," Eve offers helpfully.

"Since when do badgers roll?" Jules smiles affectionately. "Seriously, Eve. How are badgers famous for their rolling?"

"They probably roll sometimes," Eve says indignantly. "And I thought it sounded a bit nicer than *pig*, which is where I suspect you were going with that unnecessarily unkind simile."

"Margot, you need to stop," Jules says. Both of them turn to stare at me. "Right now."

I look down, cheeks still red. "OK."

"Is that a real OK?" Jules misses nothing: it's what makes her such a great journalist. "Or is that a fake OK to placate us while you go set up another fake account when we're not looking?"

"The latter." I fiddle with my dressing-gown belt. "Originally. But now it's a real OK. I'm sorry I'm being so . . . weird."

"It's time to move forward. Consider this an intervention." Jules puts her arms around me and Eve as they both press their foreheads against mine. "We love you and we want the old Margot back. Not now, not immediately, but eventually."

Something inside me sinks. I wish I knew how to tell them I'm not sure who the old Margot *was*. It's hard to make your way back to something that was never really there: like trying to hold a rainbow in your hands.

"Noted."

We spend another hour taking it in turns to sit with Eve or sweat it out in the sauna, and then Jules abruptly decides she's done, as Jules is wont to do.

"Right." She stands up and shakes the water off, like a dog. "I think that's enough pathological relaxing for one evening. I don't know about you guys, but I am feeling about as tense as it's possible to get and I've got an overdue deadline to meet."

Eve stands up and stretches, glancing hopefully at her belly.

My phone buzzes again.

"I'll think about getting someone in to help me," I say in a meek voice, as if I'm one of Eve's five-year-olds. "I know *initially* I probably set it up out of spite or whatever"—spite, it was pure spite—"but I don't completely hate it. I get to talk about the weather, at least."

I never thought I'd spend my meteorology PhD convincing strangers that the globe is a bloody globe, but that's apparently where I'm at now.

"That's an excellent idea." Jules kisses my cheek. "I've got connections to some advertising sites, so I'll send them over tonight."

I nod, feeling incredibly relieved. "Thank you."

The three of us waddle in our berobed, flip-flopped glory toward the spa changing room like three huge teddy bears, and I vaguely hear Eve asking if anyone else wants a chocolate milkshake because she—

But everything has suddenly gone hazy, cold, and the world pivots.

HIS FACE IS in profile.

The hawk-like nose, the bushy eyebrows; tanned hands on the wheel. He glances toward me briefly, dark eyes warm, and I feel a rush of something intense, giddy, almost solid. Then he turns back to focus on the road and I realize we're in a small car. The seats are bright red, ripped and worn, our knees are slightly bunched.

On either side of us, it is green and yellow: tiny flowers in hedges, a narrow road.

My hand reaches out and touches the elbow of his brown tweed jacket. There's a large star patch sewn there: pink, tacked on badly with yellow stitching. My fingers touch it lightly, and he looks at me again and smiles, slightly snaggle-toothed.

I feel myself glow at him like a nacreous cloud, illuminated from below.

Then he reaches forward to twiddle with the car radio; the air crinkles with a sand shaker and an electric guitar, he hits the wheel with his palms and says—

"MAGGIE." A HAND on my shoulder. "*Margot.*"

Blinking, I stare at Eve.

"Are you OK?" She peers closely at my face and puts a hand on my cheek. "Is it the heat? Do you need to sit down?"

"Um." I swallow and look vaguely around. "What . . . happened?"

"You just glazed over for a few seconds." Jules frowns.

"Oh." I rub my face, feeling sick. "I think I'm just exhausted, that's all."

Except tiredness, heat and dehydration don't quite explain why the face I just saw was the waiter's. It was vivid, as if I was actually with him. I *felt* him looking at me. I felt the warmth, mirrored and reflected back. I haven't thought about him since I gave him my number last night. I was busy ignoring another, much more aggressive Henry.

Frowning in confusion, I reach in my pocket and pull out my burner phone.

Hi Margot. It's Henry. Not the lion
version. Dinner tomorrow night? X

OK, *that* makes a lot more sense.

Checking between my two phones, I must have caught a glimpse of this while I was being nagged by Jules—that's why he's now on my sleep-deprived mind. It's dehydration combined with exhaustion combined with intrusive thoughts. Which is still a little weird, but not too worrying. I'm reaching the end of my twenty-date experiment, and I'm just excited about not having to do this anymore.

I think I've collected quite enough data for the foreseeable future.

Quickly, I type back:

Sure. Where? X

Four more dates and I can officially leave romance behind me. An immediate *ting.*

Oh, I think you already know. ;)

6

FRANKLY, THE END can't come too soon.

"YOU REALLY DIDN'T have to do this."

With an impending sense of doom, I stare around Pasta La Vista for the third time in one week. Same red-checked tablecloths; same tiny vases, same flowers; same piano music playing. I'm all for keeping the conditions of an experiment the same—it's basic science—but nobody needs to eat *this* much carbohydrate.

"I think I did." Henry gestures solemnly toward my usual table. "You can't compare and contrast hypothetical outcomes unless there's a constant baseline. So here it is. Your constant. Ideally, I would quite like the independent variable to be me."

I stare at him briefly in genuine surprise.

That is *exactly* why I've come to the same place so many times: because I want to know that the data I collect is at least reliable, even if the people sitting opposite me are not. Then I smile faintly. On the table is a little paper sign, scribbled with blue ink: *Margot Date Seventeen—Henry Armstrong, 42, Waiter and Loo-Roll Specialist.*

"Tell me you're at least not working again." I take my normal chair. I'm starting to suspect the small puffy cushion on it is slowly taking the form of my butt cheeks, like sand. "Because that's taking the study a bit too far."

"I've got the night off." Henry gestures down at himself

with a charming little flourish. "As you can tell from my lack of apron."

I study him, waiting for any of the giddiness I felt in my daydream to return.

Unsurprisingly, it doesn't. I feel nothing at all—an emptiness where fire should be—but Henry does look nice: dark blue jeans, a black T-shirt and a chunky gray knitted cardigan because the weather has completely shifted in one day, as it tends to in Bristol.

"Shame," I say, noticing that I tower over him this evening by at least five inches. I didn't wear my *highest* heels, but I didn't wear flats either. "It was the apron I was most looking forward to."

"I suspected as much." Henry sits down too and suddenly we're the same height: he must have quite short legs. "I've got a spare one out the back, just in case things take a downturn."

I smile faintly and look at his large hands. The etched blue *LR* has gone—scrubbed off—and I feel unexpectedly sad, as if there was something important carved into a school desk and suddenly a teacher has gone over it with a sander.

"Not married," he adds, holding up his ringless left hand. "I wouldn't dare."

"Good. I'm still working through the last lot of free food."

"I bet you are." Henry laughs and it's bright but low, like the sun setting. "Put the garlic mushrooms in the oven for twenty minutes with some cheese and serve them on toast. Thank me later. I essentially live off whatever the chef gets wrong. Luckily, he's incredibly forgetful."

All this does is remind me that Henry is a full-time waiter.

And now all I can think is: how would this work? Would we end up constantly fighting about money? More importantly, just how much Italian food can one not-Italian woman eat in a lifetime?

Henry is studying my face calmly, and I'm abruptly mortified.

He can see what I'm thinking. I'm certain of it.

"If you're worried about an income disparity between us," he says easily, "then I'll be honest, Margot. I am too. Frankly, my tip jar is overflowing and I shall need to place one hair over the lid to make sure you don't steal it."

I laugh and relax slightly. Why the hell am I already worrying about what will happen in twenty years' time when we haven't even ordered a drink? Forecaster by profession, forecaster by nature.

I smooth down my navy dress. "Strong gold-digger vibes from me, huh?"

"Overwhelmingly so. Although a generous tipper, so I'll overlook it." Henry glances up and smiles as a waiter approaches our table. He has white hair fluffed out like a koala. "Hello, Frank. How's Mary's poor back? Any better?"

"Nope." Frank taps his pen on his notepad, clearly distracted. "Painkillers aren't really working anymore."

"Still cramping in both legs? Gets worse when she bends over?"

"Yup. They're still saying she's probably sprained a muscle."

"I think it might be spinal stenosis," Henry says after thinking about it for a few seconds. "She may need a lumbar laminectomy if it doesn't improve. Go back and say you need an X-ray and don't take no for an answer."

Frank's face clears. "We will. Thank you. Are you both ready now?"

Henry nods and rubs his hands together. "Please."

The waiter leaves and Henry turns back to see me staring at him with what I now realize is a slightly gaping, goldfish-shaped mouth.

"What the hell was that?" I say bluntly. "Lumbar *what*?"

"Laminectomy." Henry smiles and shrugs. "I've been worried about Mary, so I did a bit of research last night. That's all."

I look at him with a reluctant bolt of respect: a man who researches things entirely unrelated to him is a man I instinctively like.

"So what have you discovered about me?" I sit back a little coldly and assess his face again. His eyes have tiny sparks of amber shooting outward like crepuscular rays, the kind you see at sunset in hazy conditions. "What data have you collected?"

Henry doesn't look away.

Instead, he assesses me quietly for a few seconds while he thinks about it. I wriggle slightly, pinned down, a cell under a microscope. It's an incredibly rare quality: the ability to sort through your own thoughts before you answer. We're all so trained to believe that an immediate response shows intelligence when actually there's more weight to a pause. A beautiful kind of gravity that keeps everything pinned down while we spin.

I feel something inside me go strangely still, as if pulled downward.

"I know your name is Margot Wayward. I know you're thirty-six years old and are absolutely *not* a 'bloody Weather Girl.'"

"I actually kind of am," I admit with a small smile. "I just don't like being told what I am by other people."

"Noted." Henry nods, still observing me gravely. "I know that you can be sharp-tongued and merciless, biting and brutal, but you can also be kind, witty and thoughtful."

My cheeks abruptly hit 90 degrees Celsius. "I don't know about that."

"I've watched you listen to the most inane monologues I've ever heard in my life without interrupting once. Date Thirteen, for instance. A forty-minute rant about exactly how many reps he does at the gym, which muscles he works on, how often he fasts for 'increased energy'—and all you did was ask questions and listen."

I shrug, embarrassed. "If somebody's passionate about something, who am I to tell them it's boring? I talk about clouds for a living."

"Right. Except nobody has asked you. I've watched, and not one date cared."

I clear my throat. "Nope."

"I know that you're a good friend, because you're constantly leaving voice notes and answering texts as soon as your date goes to the bathroom. I know that you adore your grandfather and feel very guilty that you haven't seen him much recently."

I stare at him. "How the hell do you—"

"Because on Date Three, Date Eight and Date Fourteen, you left him voicemails checking he'd eaten and asking if there was anything he needed. And you apologized profusely. You could hear how much you love him in your voice."

I flinch slightly. Date Fourteen: that was two whole weeks ago.

"Everyone loves their grandparents." I start playing with my fork. "That's like saying I don't kick puppies for fun. Nice, but not exactly noteworthy."

"I know that you don't appear to think very highly of yourself." Henry's eyes are suddenly soft and the amber is brighter. "At all. And when you're complimented in any way, you play with cutlery on the table."

I quickly put the fork down. "Oh."

"And, finally, I know that when Date Fourteen gave you 'six out of ten,' I nearly walked over and punched him straight in the gullet."

I look up in surprise. "Did you?"

"Rating women as if they're Amazon purchases." He scowls, bushy eyebrows gathering, his forehead lines deeper. "'I ordered a size ten and got a size twelve instead, very unhappy, want a full refund.' He can go fuck himself."

I laugh, surprised by his sudden cursing.

"Wow." I'm a little confused about why I don't feel more creeped out. This man has been watching me incredibly closely. "So have you been making notes about me, then? In your little waiter notepad?" I flush again. "Sorry, I don't mean *little waiter* notepad. That was incredibly patronizing. I just mean it's small. Physically. Not figuratively."

"It is small." Henry lifts his eyebrows but doesn't seem

offended. "No. I just pay attention. I have a naturally good memory. And I was standing right next to your table for a lot of it. Literally two feet away. Waiting to take your order."

This takes the heat in my cheeks to an entirely new level. "Of course you were. Sorry."

"That's fine. A good waiter is one who disappears so you can enjoy whoever you came here with. Or not, in your case."

I can feel myself assessing Henry again. His eyes are kind, slightly solemn, and they're eyes I recognize. Eyes too old for his face. And I suddenly realize why I don't find his powers of observation "creepy" or odd: because I do it too. We are the watchers, with our tiny figurative notepads, putting together the details, collecting the rain.

Something in my stomach starts to hurt again.

"That's enough about me," I say as lightly as I can, fiddling with my spoon and then wincing and consciously putting it down. "I've not had the chance to research you yet, so what is it that—"

You're passionate about, I want to say, but Frank arrives carrying trays of food.

Many, many, many trays.

"Did we order?" My stomach plummets. "I don't remember ordering."

Because there it is: a *Red Flag*, waving as hard as it can. It had to be something, didn't it? Henry was being so nice, then he orders for me off a menu without asking and says, *Don't worry, I know what you like, trust me, no, you won't be getting the red wine, I've ordered you a salad and vodka soda, fewer calories.*

I glare at him, ready to start destroying.

"We have a secret menu." Henry's nose twitches at my stony expression. "Consisting of special dishes the Italian chef, Emilio, makes while he's experimenting. They're insanely good. So I ordered a little bit of all of them to see if you like any. If you don't, you can get the tagliatelle again. Obviously. Don't kill me."

My anger drains away as I stare at the food. Burrata topped with plums; Parma ham with figs; sea bream with orange and rosemary; mussel bruschetta; roasted beetroot with endives. It's a *bit* of an overreach—a slightly pink flag, at best—but it's also a genuinely sweet gesture.

"Thanks," I say reluctantly. "That was thoughtful of you."

"Hang on." Henry frowns, searching the dishes. "I swear I saw a black truffle in the larder yesterday. I'm going to see if I can find it."

He gets up from the table and I watch him walk away, consciously pulling his shoulder blades together. He lifts his chin just a fraction, and something in my chest squeezes slightly. It's a tiny gesture, but it says so much—nerves, anxiety, a desire to impress—and suddenly I feel another swell of softness toward him: he really wants me to like him.

And—with just that little movement—the ice inside me begins to melt a little.

Jules is absolutely right: it's time to let go.

Taking a deep breath, I pull my burner phone out of my pocket.

Stupid bitch

Noted, Other Henry. You're not entirely wrong.

Smiling slightly, I click on Lucy Jones's social media page. Keeping tabs on Lily is not going to make the loss of her—of us—any easier. I'm not going to repair the pieces of something dropped just by staring at them on the floor.

Glancing up quickly—Henry's still in the kitchen—I hover over the screen.

Then I go to *Delete account* and pause.

A photo has popped up on my timeline, entirely unbidden. It's the final grenade, casually lobbed. On the white sand are pink petals, laid out in the shape of a perfect heart. Around it are dozens of candles wedged into the sand. In the middle of this romantic mess are pale shells—carefully selected, the same size—spelling out . . .

I feel my ears go numb, my cheeks cold; my stomach rolls.

MARRY ME

The restaurant and everyone in it splinters.

Unable to breathe, I swipe to the left: Lily is now laughing. Her hair is wind-coaxed, her face lit by the candles. Pointless candles, useless and "unnecessary" candles; a waste of money, a cliché, a fire hazard. The room tips. There's a loud clatter and my chair falls backward as I stand. Ears ringing, I swipe again. There's a photo of a delicate, tanned hand with a dainty diamond ring. White gold. Unbearably trendy.

Underneath, the caption simply says: I said yes. <3 <3 <3

But all I can think is: no.

Blind, I reach for my handbag, knock the wine over, stagger into the table, send a tray of food flying. The room is too small, too airless, too close, I can't breathe, can't stay here, can't wait, can't—

"Margot?"

I push past Henry and run out into the street.

The question wasn't even a question. It was just *Marry Me*, as if the answer was so inevitable that punctuation was unnecessary. Night air smacks my face like a hand and my stomach spins urgently. I run to a nearby shop, bend over and vomit a semi-digested pot noodle into the doorway.

"Margot!" Henry is behind me. "Are you OK?"

Blinking, I wipe my mouth on my cardigan sleeve.

"Was it the food?" His face is blank but lined, like a piece of paper. "I should have checked for allergies, I didn't even think—"

A hand touches my shoulder and I feel like a lightning rod in the middle of a storm: as if electricity is channeling through me in one brutal line.

"*Get off me*," I hiss, flinching.

"Sorry." Henry puts his hands up like a traffic warden. "I just—"

"Just *back the fuck off.*" My eyes are wet and I wipe them with my other sleeve: two thin trails of mucus now lining both arms. "I don't *want it.*"

Breathing hard, I gesture at the world in general.

"You don't want . . . what?" Henry's eyes follow my hands. "Sorry, Margot. I'm not sure I understand exactly what's going on."

"I don't want *this.*"

Now I point at him, then at me, then at him again.

Because I don't want romantic meals and getting to know each other better and how many siblings do you have and are you close to your parents and what are your hopes and dreams and your deepest fears and all the things you hate about yourself and oh you have beautiful eyes and goodnight texts and good-morning texts and emojis and in-jokes and pot plants and DIY trips and shower singing and *I love you* and *you love me* and our lives entangled together like hair in the wind.

I don't want the etching of ourselves into each other, the carvings in places that won't heal over, the growing before pulling ourselves out at the roots. I don't want the you and me and the us versus them. I don't want someone to invade my head until they're all I think about; invade my life until it revolves around them.

I don't want it.

Henry stares at me for a few seconds, frowning.

I glare back, breathing hard. My teeth are gritted, and any softness in me is gone. I just want him out of here. I want me out of here. I want everyone, everything, put somewhere far away, behind a wall nobody can ever, ever climb.

"Margot," Henry says slowly as my phone starts buzzing. "This is our first date. We've known each other about ten minutes."

Buzz. Buzz. Buzz. Buzz.

Henry is looking at me with new eyes. All the warmth has

disappeared. Gone is the cute, acerbic, slightly guarded woman he asked out, and in her place is a vicious monster with spit on her sleeve. I am the problem, he's finally realized. Not the men I date, and not the infinite flaws I find. Me. It always was.

I am the Red Flag, and I am the one who will burn everything.

At least now he knows.

At least this way we reached the end faster.

"Ten minutes," I snap, turning my back on him as my phone buzzes again. "Ten fucking years. What difference does it make."

7

JULES: Maggie pick up

EVE: We love you, PICK UP

JULES: We're just going to keep calling

Missed call: Eve
Missed call: Jules
Missed call: Eve
Missed call: Mum and Dad

MUM AND DAD: Are you OK sweetheart?
Eve just rang. Call us back. Xxx

But I don't.

Still exploding, I return home to obliterate the hell out of my punching bag, but my rage only escalates, shooting from my clenched fists until the air around me is thick and crunchy, red and bruised.

It's still not enough, so I run around my flat in a fury.

One by one, I pick up cardboard boxes, heave them all through the back door and toss them into a huge pile in the tiny garden, where they crack and break like bones. Breathing heavily, I grab two full bottles of vodka from the top of an empty kitchen cupboard, take a couple of large swigs from one on my way back outside and then pour the rest of it on top. Still drinking from the other one, I grab a pack of matches, strike one and throw it.

It flickers, goes out.

Another match flares and disappears.

Teeth clenched, I step closer—where the hell is fire when you actually need it—bend down and purposefully hold a flame to the edge of a soaked box, watching in satisfaction as light creeps along the edges.

Then I step back to watch as everything I own goes up in flames. The life I packed away, believing that one day I would unpack it. That one day there might be something worth keeping.

"Um." My neighbor—a polished, pretty woman in her forties—pokes her head over the fence. I have no idea what her name is: since moving in two months ago, I haven't bothered asking. "Is everything . . . alright?"

It must be nearly midnight by now, and I have turned the garden bright orange.

We both watch as the flames climb higher.

The box marked "PHOTOS" disintegrates and I watch years of faces turn red, then black, then gray before they disappear. Behind me, I feel my neighbor's sympathy for my clear mental breakdown mixed with a palpable panic that the flames will take the whole road down while she remains too polite to say anything.

"Yup," I say flatly. "All good here."

Because now my flat is finally empty, and so am I.

I SLEEP WELL for the first time in months: no dreams, no nightmares, no late-night sweats or memories crowding around my bed like curious ghosts. When I wake nearly twelve hours later, I feel calmer. Cleaner.

As if I've set myself on fire and erased myself too.

It was dramatic, it was unnecessary, hyperbolic and extreme. It was totally worth it. I feel a sudden, latent flash of guilt—it could all have been donated to charity—before I decide that nobody else wants my memory-soaked items either. Who knows what those emotions could do, carried into unsuspecting houses. It would be irresponsible to send my ghosts to haunt others instead of just me.

Significantly calmer now, I settle down to work properly.

With renewed energy, I blitz through my emails, messages and comments. The sponsor requests are becoming increasingly ridiculous. Margot the Meteorologist is not being offered designer handbags, coffee machines and lifestyle gildings. This morning, while I was fast asleep, I received a large wooden blackboard for children—complete with windsock, thermometer and rain collector, highly inaccurate and overpriced—and an opaque mushroom-shaped umbrella with a cartoon smiley face that renders you dry but essentially blind.

Slightly frustrated, I rip open yet another new package.

It's an adult PVC jumpsuit—pale pink and transparent—that goes over your clothes (hopefully), zips right up to your chin and has a bizarre and extremely wide ruff tied around the neck that sticks out half a meter and makes you look like a kinky triceratops.

Confused, I scan my inbox again for some kind of context.

Dear Miss Wayward,

We here at Rain of Terror have been very impressed with your rapidly building platform, and have been watching you closely for some time.

OK: a little bit creepy.

Our interests appear to align perfectly—it's snow joke!—so we are suggesting a mutually beneficial brand collaboration between us, with you as our Ambassador. We would like you to introduce our Brand-New Thunderwear range, which we will be launching in the next few weeks.

This morning a package containing the I-THUNDER-STAND-3000 should have arrived.

If you could wear this in one of your videos,

Not a solitary snowball's chance in hell.

we will compensate you to the sum of £5,000. An opportunity not to be "mist"!

Love,

Your friends at Rain of Terror xxx

Ugh. I pick up the jumpsuit again and swallow.

That's not money I can afford to turn down, given that I just incinerated all my belongings. No flowing white dresses and gifted tropical holidays for Margot Wayward. Prostituted ridicule it is.

Cursing repeatedly—sorry, Mum—I do my hair and make-up for no apparent reason. Then I sit in front of my green screen, set up the camera and pull the creaky rain suit over a plain navy dress. Sighing loudly, I pull up the hood. The ruff sticks out so widely I look like a fly-fishing Elizabethan. It's supposed to keep your body dry, which makes no sense at all—rain is rarely vertical, so it's just going to collect until I've accidentally drowned myself—but here we go.

Already feeling claustrophobic, I reach forward and switch on the camera before pride and ego get the better of me.

Fuck my fucking stupid life.

"Greetings, meteorologists!" I smile broadly, cheeks squeaking slightly against the plastic. "Margot here! I'm here today with my new weather obsession! This is the I-Thunder-Stand-3000"—kill me—"and it's absolutely *adorable.* So much fun! Now you can truly Stand Out in the Rain!"

That line was my addition, and I'm actually kind of proud of it.

"Now, obviously this is a sponsored post, which I have to say for legal reasons." I wink jauntily at the camera—set me on fire too. "But I genuinely think it's brilliant! So original! And practical! I know what I'll be wearing next time there's a downpour!"

A bag over my head, so that nobody ever recognizes me again.

"So check out my friends over at @thunderwarez and maybe give one of these beauties a spin for only . . ."

I pause so I can check the paper that came in the package. Are they *kidding* me?

". . . a hundred pounds! You'll be striking, just like lightning!"

Then I turn off the camera and peel myself out of the sweaty plastic as fast as I can, sounding like a ripped crisp packet. Yet another flash of intense guilt. I'm not just unhinged and environmentally unfriendly: I'm a fraud, a liar, a peddler of shit goods. Less than a year ago, I was running a team of trained meteorologists in a beautiful glass building with thirty-two and a half days of holiday allowance and a lovely bonus package, plus free coffee. Now I'm a joke in front of two hundred and fifty thousand total strangers and I have to make my own beverages.

My phone beeps:

He lo is

Evry thing

Ok I hop

The rage inside me evaporates, replaced by guilt.

To be clear: I'm pretty sure that in the past I used to have more than two emotions, but at some point in the last eight months I've been filed down into a red spike of anger and culpability.

Love you. I'll be there in ten. Xx

Quietly, I let myself in through the front door.

My grandfather's house—less than a mile from where I live now—is dim and smells faintly of something green, mossy, like a forest. Frowning, I pick up a splayed handful of unopened post from the doormat and riffle quickly through it. A few handwritten postcards—a gaudy one from my parents, featuring a beach—and envelopes with the spidery, delicate handwriting of people over eighty, a couple of official brown envelopes. The back of my neck suddenly prickles: my ninety-three-year-old grandfather is not somebody to let correspondence lie dormant. He is normally by the door every morning, his ornate, bird-shaped letter opener at the ready.

Slipping my shoes off, I walk barefoot through the hallway.

I poke my head into the kitchen, frowning: there are half-filled cups of tea and dirty plates piled next to the sink. When I glance at the calendar ("Garden Birds of Great Britain"), I realize in shock it's still showing July: a photo of a blue tit. The tiny bird is bright eyed and somehow courageous, with its yellow chest fluffed out proudly, bright sapphire head and a black stripe through the eyes that always reminds me slightly of a superhero's mask. But it's been August now for three whole weeks. The turning of the months has always been an occasion in this house. I'd arrive on the first day of every month, straight after school, and my grandfather would meticulously tear off the previous month with amused gravitas.

"What's past is prologue," he'd say, handing me the ripped-out page.

"Cool," I'd say in awe, with no idea what he was talking about.

But now the baby bird remains, the season has not changed; the house is locked in a month that has been and gone. I wipe my finger on the kitchen counter and stare at it: it's gray and powdered. Something feels . . . wrong.

Extremely confused now, I poke my head into the sunlit living room.

My grandfather is sitting in his huge leather armchair, facing the garden. His face is tilted slightly, his pale blue eyes fixed on something in the distance, and it seems for just a minute as if all the light in the world is coming from him.

"If you're here to rob me," he says calmly, without turning round, "I should let you know that my vault full of rare jewels is actually upstairs, so you're wasting your time hunting around the kitchen."

I laugh. "Where's the silverware again?"

"I'm sitting on it." My grandfather chuckles. "Don't forget the gold coins tucked under my mattress. It's getting rather bumpy at night."

With another grin, I cross the living room and kiss his soft cheek.

"Hello, my grandad."

"Hello, my Meg."

I move a pile of folded, unread newspapers from the opposite matching armchair and sit down as my grandfather turns toward me. There is no face on the planet I love more. He's like an ancient tree: rooted deeply and shaped by the years. I love the little white hairs that grow upward and outward, like leaves, and the broken pink veins in his cheeks. I love the wooden strength of his nose, the brown speckles like lichen on his forehead. I love the pale blue of his eyes, a sky between branches; the lines etched proudly like oak rings, collecting over time, marking the seasons. I love how permanent he is, how solid, as if the winds can blow but he will still be there. A place I can return to, always, and sit under, shaded and protected.

I feel him gazing at me as if everything I'm made of is beautiful too.

"I'm so sorry I haven't visited," I say, sounding seven years old. "Things got really . . . busy for a couple of weeks."

Except I still had time to go on dates that went absolutely nowhere, didn't I? I still had time to sit and eat pasta and judge men. I had all the time in the world to spend in the wrong places, with the wrong people.

Somehow, I always do.

"Don't be ridiculous," my grandfather says sternly. "I won't tolerate an apology, Meg. You're an adult woman and we've spent quite enough time together, as far as I'm concerned. Frankly, I needed the break."

He winks and I grin. "Enough Margot for one year, huh?"

"Oh, I wouldn't say one could ever have enough. But an exceedingly old man needs to be left alone with his thoughts now and then. All three of them."

When I left Exeter, I moved into my grandfather's spare room and spent my time hanging out with him like a freeloading flatmate. When I wasn't building my Instagram page in the garden shed—making my first anxious and wobbly videos—we'd get pizzas and watch black-and-white films and discuss the flowers in the garden. I felt like a child again, which is exactly what I needed. There was no part of it I didn't enjoy, no part that felt like I was doing him a favor, even if I did a little washing up and cooking now and then. The generosity—as always—was entirely his.

"Are you doing OK?" I lean forward and study him. "Eating properly? Have you been outside? Gone for a walk?"

Grandad has gone back to staring into the garden. Ever since my grandmother passed away a few years ago, he has spent more and more time here. Sometimes I wonder if he's waiting or if he's actually watching. Looking for something. I just don't know what.

"Of course. How was your date with Henry?" He doesn't look at me. "Did it go well?"

"No," I sigh slightly. I'm guessing Eve told Mum, and Mum told him. Grandad knows all about the Date-a Experiment. In fact, it was his idea. "But it doesn't matter. I've decided that twenty is probably a bit of overkill. I don't need *that* much data, right? I think I'll just stop at seventeen and stay on my own for a while."

A sudden memory of myself screaming *I don't want it* into poor Henry's bewildered face. Suffice to say, I collected the data

I was looking for and the conclusion was: I should not be dating other humans.

Not now, possibly not ever.

"Date Seventeen, hey?" Grandad smiles faintly, still focused on the garden. "Stick at Seventeen, I think. Seventeen is a good, powerful number. It represents change and new beginnings, numerologically."

I smile fondly. "It's numerology now, hey?"

"Oh." He shrugs his thin shoulders. "I got interested. Quite a fascinating topic, if a little lacking in scientific evidence."

My grandfather studies and researches like nobody I have ever met: constantly taking up random topics and becoming an expert in them almost immediately, like a character from a Steinbeck novel. He is always curious and asking questions; he made me my first-ever wind gauge from a plastic bottle filled with sand. Everything I'm most proud of, I got from him. Everything I'm not proud of is entirely mine.

"Have you spoken to Mum and Dad?" My phone starts vibrating and I pull it out of my pocket. "Have they called you from Australia?"

"Oh yes." Grandad nods. "Relentlessly."

Then I glance at my screen: suffice to say, people are not loving my new direction.

You look like a literal penis
Sell-out
Unfollowed

I swallow, put my phone away and thank the weather gods that my grandfather has never worked out how to use social media. His inordinate pride in me is one of the only things left that I actually treasure.

"Margot," Grandad says abruptly. "Is that squirrel OK?"

Frowning, I turn and peer at the large oak tree. "What squirrel?"

"The squirrel. On the grass. It hasn't moved for hours and

I'm getting a little worried. There's a drey up there, and I'm worried a baby has fallen out. Do you think you could pop outside, just check it's OK?"

I stand up in confusion so I can get a closer look.

"Grandad," I say, glancing at him. "It's a sock."

"A sock?"

"It's a sock. A blue sock. It must have fallen off the washing line."

"Ah." My grandfather frowns. "Of course. I see that now. Silly me. I guess blue squirrels are rarer than previously thought."

I narrow my eyes at him again, then look around the house.

That's exactly what it is: this house feels frozen, unused, stale. As if he's not touching anything inside it. I suddenly realize that my grandfather isn't looking at me properly. He's gazing in my direction, aiming toward my voice, but his eyes are unfocused, misty, slightly blank.

"Grandad," I say slowly, getting right up close to him. "You haven't commented on my new nose ring. What do you think?"

"Well." His bright blue pupils vaguely search my ringless face and he beams. "Gosh. Doesn't that look quite the ticket?"

How long has his eyesight been fading? How long has he been pretending to read newspapers, moving bookmarks in books he hasn't read so that I don't notice? My eyes suddenly fill: he didn't tell me on purpose. He didn't want me to know because I'd never have moved out or started over. Of course I wouldn't. I'd have stayed here, with him. He didn't want that, so instead he patiently waits as his world goes dark.

"I'm just going to make a cup of tea for myself." I stand up, trying to keep the emotion out of my voice. "Do you fancy one?"

"I thought you'd never ask," he smiles. "I've run out of biscuits, though."

Wiping my eyes, I pick up his mobile phone from the cabinet where it's plugged in permanently, thus rendering it immobile. Seven missed calls from my parents today, because he clearly can't work out where the answer button is. He hasn't told them either, because they wouldn't have emigrated if they knew. No wonder his texts always look like haiku. They must take him literally hours to construct.

Right: this is going to require a fully-fledged plan.

Seething with anger at myself—what kind of shitty person doesn't notice that the person they love most is going slowly *blind*—I clatter into the kitchen and start viciously washing up: scalding myself with hot water, scrubbing at the plates until they scratch. My grandfather clearly doesn't want me to know, so I have to find a way to help without giving it away. What else isn't he doing? I examine the fridge and dirty plates: it's stocked, he's eating, which is a relief. But was he lying to me? Is he going outside at all?

Abruptly, I go into the hallway, take his favorite shoes from by the door and put them on a shelf. If they haven't moved next time I'm here, I'll know he's not even leaving the house.

"Idiot," I mutter fiercely. "You're a total *idiot*, Margot."

"Did you say something?" Grandad calls. "I just remembered there might be some Jaffa Cakes under the stairs."

At least his hearing is spot on, so that's something.

"Okey-dokey!" I kick the door, pretending it's my own stupid face. "Just grabbing them now!"

Muttering more quietly, I open the cupboard and begin rummaging around—wine bottles caked in dust, my grandmother's coats still hanging neatly, untouched—when cold suddenly sweeps through me. Everything gets darker.

The world tips and—

8

LILAC: THE MOONLIT glow of agapanthus flowers.

I look down. My fingertips are purple too, my hands, my arms speckled with bright flecks, like bejeweled ceramic eggs. Bewildered, I stare at them, turning them over slowly as a trickle of amethyst runs down my palm and over my wrist.

Then I look up again at the wall in front of me with a sway of déjà vu.

"Blimey, Megalodon." A gruff voice from directly behind me. "I have never seen someone make such a mess with paint."

I turn around and stare at the lilac speck on the end of his nose. "Henry?"

"Yes, my sweet Picasso?"

The waiter takes a few steps toward me, leans his forehead gently on mine and kisses my lips. I feel the warmth and when he pulls away there's a smear of purple left on his face like a tattoo. When I don't answer, he grins widely, bops me on the nose with his finger and picks up a roller.

Then Henry turns and continues to paint the opposite wall, humming.

Throat suddenly tight, I watch his gray T-shirt lift slightly as he reaches up: there's a scattering of dark hairs across his lower back, and three small moles like stars at the base of his spine. An abrupt wave of something sweet and hot through my chest; I try to swallow but can't.

"Stop perving at me," Henry says without looking. "I can

feel you doing it. I am not here to be objectified, thank you. I'm here to decorate."

I hear myself laugh as I look around the rest of the room.

It's my guest room, I realize in surprise. It's tiny and the window in the alcove overlooking the garden has a curved, half-built seat beneath it. A purple toolbox is still lying on the ground, covered in floral stickers. The hammer has a glittery purple handle, and the screwdriver is adorned with a unicorn.

Another wave of intense sweetness, and without knowing why, I abruptly cross the room and wrap my arms around him from behind, leaning my cheek against the soft, warm curve of his neck.

Henry smells beautiful: of pepper and lemon. Like a sexy cooked chicken.

"Hey," he says, pausing and leaning his head back against me. "You OK, Meg?"

He called me Meg.

"Yes." I smile and nestle in. "I'm OK."

"Good." Henry laughs, and I feel the chuckle vibrate through his T-shirt. "Then we don't have time for these affectionate shenanigans, I'm afraid. Pick up your paintbrush and work. It's getting dark and winter is coming."

I laugh and squeeze him tighter. "Alright, Jon Snow. But don't forget that—"

The room disappears.

BLINKING, I STARE at my hand. I'm back in the cupboard, and the lilac paint has gone; I'm holding on to my grandmother's coat sleeve, a small pearl button pressing into my palm. When I pull my hand away, the shape it leaves behind is indented and pink. How long have I been standing here? *Have* I been standing here? Or did I go somewhere else? If so, how the hell did I get back?

I say this with zero chill: what the *fuck* is happening to me?

"Margot?" Grandad's voice comes from just outside the cupboard. "Is everything OK in there? Do you need a torch?"

I don't even like purple: it's an uncomfortable color, sugary and whimsical. Why on earth would I paint my own house a color I hate? Why would I even *imagine* doing that? What is this daydream trying to tell me?

Shaking, I climb back out from under the stairs. "I'm fine."

I am so very clearly not fine. Admittedly my brain has been breaking for half a year, but this is the final, crazy straw. Never mind blowing up at strangers, stalking and literally setting things on fire. I'm now so internally dismantled, so completely unhinged, I've begun having full-blown visions complete with audio and sensory input.

My grandfather is leaning on his walking stick, peering at me in the low light.

"Um." I rub my hand across my face, unable to meet his eyes. "Bit of a weird question, Grandad, but I was . . . in there the whole time, right? In the cupboard? I didn't . . . disappear, or anything?"

I sound completely insane, but Grandad takes it in his stride.

"As far as I'm aware, yes. You were." He smiles gently. "Or has Narnia popped back up again?"

A tiny jolt of relief. Somehow, my inner child has resurfaced.

I've always had an active imagination, that's all it is, and I'm still thinking about Henry because I feel guilty about how I left things. Because it wasn't OK. It doesn't matter how upset I was; what I did to him was unkind and undeserved. All he did was ask a stranger out for dinner and I blew him apart. Sometimes I feel like a hurricane: fierce air, spinning in the same direction, destroying everything in its path, empty in the middle.

"You never did tell me what happened to Date Seventeen," Grandad says quietly. "Is it something you want to talk about?"

My grandfather has always known what I'm thinking without being told.

"I screwed up." I blow out, the hurricane inside me slowing down. "Badly. I got . . . upset, and I took it out on him."

I don't want it. *I don't want* this.

"Then you should probably apologize." My grandfather

smiles, firm but kind. "We all make mistakes, Meg, but taking responsibility for them requires courage and strength. They are not qualities you have ever lacked. I wouldn't like to see you start now."

I am deeply unwilling to correct him; I wish I saw myself as my grandfather sees me.

The truth is, I am weak and scared of *everything.*

"You're right." I pull out my burner phone. "I'll send him a text."

There's a silence and I feel my grandfather watching me. He's not judging—he never judges—but I can feel his disappointment in me. Or maybe I can simply feel *my* disappointment in me, bouncing between us like a ping-pong ball.

"*Fine,*" I sigh, putting my phone away again. "I suppose I should go and say sorry in person."

Oh God, this is going to be excruciating.

"Good." My grandad smiles. "That's my girl."

ONE OF THE most dangerous weather conditions is black ice.

As I walk as slowly as possible back toward Pasta La Vista, it feels as if that's what's directly underneath me: a world that seems safe but is secretly coated in a thin layer of something that will result in me unexpectedly lying on my back, out of nowhere, bones broken and skull shattered.

My jacket: that's what I'm going to say I've returned for. I need my jacket and by the way, sorry I'm a demon in stripes.

Henry will say *here's your stupid jacket, now bog off.*

And I will leave, at least knowing that my grandfather is proud of me again.

Except, as I stand outside the restaurant and peek in the softly lit window every few minutes, it suddenly seems too hard. I can't see Henry in there—maybe he has a night off—but I don't want to see the way his face has changed overnight, from like to dislike. I don't want to see the consequences of my actions written all over him.

So instead I stand just out of sight, breathing heavily against a wall.

Like a total creep.

Tomorrow. (I close my eyes.) I'll come back tomorrow, when I've built up enough courage. I just need one more evening to prepare my speech and then I'll—

"Hello, Margot."

I open my eyes: Henry is standing in front of me, holding my jacket.

"Fuck," I say flatly.

"You're here for your jacket, right? I wasn't sure how long you were going to stand out there, peeking in through the window at intervals like Oliver Twist. So I thought I'd bring it out for you. Save you the final step."

I'm studying his face, but there's no like or dislike there.

It's a completely blank expression, and I suddenly realize I miss the face I saw in my daydream: amused and affectionate. How can I miss something I've never had?

"Thanks," I say, taking the jacket. "That's very kind of you."

"No problem," Henry says, turning to leave. "Have a great night, Margot."

He's so formal and something inside me suddenly hurts. I don't want *this* version of Henry. All at once, I want the one who I imagined called me *Megalodon* and kissed me, covered in purple paint.

"Henry," I say quickly. "Wait."

He pauses and turns, face still saying absolutely nothing.

"I . . ." *I'm sorry.* I'm sorry for the way I spoke to you, I'm sorry that I blew this without giving you a chance. "I think maybe I'm a bit screwed-up at the moment."

Which is like saying *it's a bit drizzly* in the middle of a thunderstorm.

Henry nods. "OK."

"That's why I've been doing a date every week, for four months." I'm speaking quickly now, as if trying to pull something dangerous out of my mouth by the tail. "Not because I want to find someone, but because I don't want to. I've picked men I already know are awful, so that I can prove to myself that men are awful. That it's not my fault. I rigged the experiment so I can stay alone."

I think that's the first time I've actually admitted that, even to myself.

Seventeen dates, and all I've found are Red Flags because that's all I've been looking for. I ignored any other information and entered the statistics that fitted the results I wanted. It's basic data bias: a collection of skewed results, with myself as the unreliable external factor. Date One: had a valid excuse for being late. Date Four: had a cold, hence eating with his mouth open, and only stole one mushroom that had fallen off my plate. Date Nine: I was so cold, he didn't want to pay for my olives, which is fair enough. Date Ten: was probably joking, ditto for Dates Seven and Twelve. Date Thirteen: a nervous monologue, and who can blame him? I was sitting opposite, waiting for him to make a mistake so I could destroy him.

Date Six: rude to the waiter? Pretty hypocritical, coming from me.

The other dates should objectively have gone in the bin, but that still left half that were exploded entirely by me.

In short, I have gone through the last four months building a List of Icks and Nos that covers two whole sides of A4, and nowhere in my flat is there a list of things I *do* want. Honestly, I don't need a therapist to tell me that I have a pretty serious avoidant attachment style: it's written all over me in neon letters like graffiti on a wall, no less real for being recently put there.

Henry frowns slightly. "A bad break-up?"

"Yes." I wince. "But that doesn't excuse any of it. You weren't awful. And I needed you to be. So it scared me." I take a huge breath and bring down the barrier between us just enough to lob an apology over the top, as if I'm a neighbor with someone else's lost ball. "I am very sorry. You did not deserve that."

We gaze at each other in silence for twenty seconds.

Suddenly I'm not sure why I didn't find Henry immediately

attractive. Side-lit by the candles in the restaurant, his face is kind, strong, solid. It's an *interesting* face. Extraordinary, even. Maybe I just needed to see it again, in my own head, reformatted by my imagination and covered in lilac paint.

"OK," Henry says calmly. "Thank you for apologizing."

Yet it's also a familiar face: one I've seen over and over again, for months, without really registering it. Henry has become part of my weekly routine, somehow infiltrating my subconscious until he pops up in daydreams too. Because that's what's been happening, isn't it? The waiter didn't climb over the top of the barriers I've built; he wriggled under, and I didn't even notice.

"Anyway." I swallow. "I should probably go."

I turn and begin tugging on my jacket, somehow on the wrong arm. I can feel him watching me, so I swear again—more quietly—and try to find the right armhole instead. *Fuck fuck f—*

"I'm just about to finish my shift," Henry says from behind me. "Would you like to walk me part of the way home?"

I turn, jacket still on my arms. "Part of the way?"

"To the train station." He smiles very slightly. "I live in Bath. I'm not going to ask you to walk all the way to Bath. But you can walk me to the train station, if that sounds like something you might enjoy."

Something tiny in me lights up: one fairy light on a long chain of darkness.

But all I can think is: Bath. He lives too far away. It's on the list. Long-distance. Doesn't work. And I know what I'm doing, but I can't stop it. Inside me, a war is being waged. I just don't know who I want to win.

"A walk?" My cheeks flush and I turn away from the light so he can't see it. "But definitely not a date."

"Not a date," Henry confirms with a small grin. "No."

It suddenly feels like I can breathe, for the first time in months.

"Then, yes. I think I would like that a lot."

9

HENRY AND I walk together across Bristol.

With his jacket slung over one arm, we amble through Clifton Village, past turquoise-painted boutique shops and pink cafés lit from within and crowded with colors like Christmas. We cross pebbled pavements next to Georgian buildings with ornate balconies, and through little squares with gardens filled with trees.

And we talk about nothing in particular: films we like, music, art.

It's not a "date," so it doesn't feel like an interview. There is no secret checklist where we attempt to slip in key questions without the other person noticing. Because it's not just me. Over the last four months, I have noticed my dates doing it too. Running through criteria they may not have written down in a notepad but which exist all the same. *Do you work out?* Translation: will you remain in this exact physical condition for the foreseeable future? *Do you do yoga?* How wild are you in bed? *Are you friends with your exes?* Will you be a nightmare if we split up and/or are there lurking exes I should be worried about? *Are you a free spirit?* Do you like casual sex, and would you like to do that straight after we finish the tiramisu? *Do you want children and if so, how soon?* Are you trying to force a connection as fast as physically possible so you can procreate at nearly forty years old, because—if not—I definitely am?

My answers (no, no, no, no, no) are met with disappointment.

And instead of recognizing how completely *mad* it is, meeting a total stranger based on a few photos and immediately trying to work out if you're going to be with them for the rest of your life, it becomes normalized. Swiping through a selection of humans—left, left, left, left, right—like we're filling an online supermarket cart. Adding items, in the desperate hope of finding something worth buying. Love has changed to a point where we now expect to take a human we've never met before and make them the most important person in our life, starting from that precise moment. *You'll do. Let's go.*

No wonder we're all so full of criteria, questions, checklists.

We're interviewing someone for the job of loving us forever: a career of live-in affection and support, ending with us dying in each other's arms. As if love is just another thing we can check off. Job—tick. Hobbies—tick. Friends—tick.

Lifelong soulmate—tick tick tick, *done.*

And I find myself telling Henry this—monologuing at him—as we wander down Constitution Hill. This outpouring of honesty is an entirely new experience, in dating terms. It's so easy to be honest without being honest: you just have to pick the data you share, even if it's only a slice of the picture.

Henry listens, nods, then drops this bombshell:

"I've never actually online dated before, probably for that reason. It all seems a little . . . clinical." A slight pause, then: "Also, I should probably tell you I haven't been on a first date in twenty years. Present company excluded."

I stop walking halfway across Brandon Hill, where we've taken a bit of a detour, neither of us admitting that we're intentionally making the walk longer.

"I was your first date in *twenty years*?"

Is this a Red Flag? Is he just saying it to try and make me feel "special"?

"Um. Yes." Henry looks directly into my eyes and smiles slightly. He's telling the truth, I can see it in his face. "What a re-entry into the dating pool, huh."

"I'm even more sorry, in that case."

"It's not a problem." He grins sheepishly. "I didn't really know what I was doing, to be honest. Probably shouldn't have analyzed you quite as intensely as I did, straight off the bat. That was . . . weird of me. Should have kept my observations to myself. Lesson very much learned."

I sit down on one of the benches next to Cabot Tower as Bristol glows.

"I actually liked that bit," I admit as Henry sits down next to me. "I do it too. Why has it been twenty years?"

"I lost my wife, Amy." Henry stares at the lights too and I turn to look at his profile: the shape of his nose, curved like a hawk. "Five years ago."

For just a second, I hear it literally: he *lost* her, she's been put in the wrong place and now he's looking for her everywhere, like mislaid car keys.

"You—" The meaning hits. "Oh my God."

"Not ideal," he says faux lightly. "Cancer. But it was a long time ago now. I've just been focused on . . ." He pauses. Frowns. "Getting through that, I guess. It's been a bit of a slog, but I think I'm out the other side now. Finally."

My heart hurts; I reach out and put my hand briefly on his.

Then I stare at my hand in shock: I feel something again. The same thing I felt when our hands touched the first time. An almost audible sizzle, like something dropped in a smoking-hot frying pan.

"I'm so sorry, Henry. Really." I should have remembered that hearts can be broken in so many ways—some far, far worse than mine—and that a lot of us are just walking around still in pieces, pretending to be whole. I'm trying to decide how far to probe, how many questions he wants me to ask—whether it's invasive, whether it's rude—when Henry suddenly shivers, reaches for his tweed jacket, pulls it on.

I stare at it for a few seconds as ice spears through me.

"Sorry." Henry laughs and holds out his elbow. "I know. Absolutely ridiculous, isn't it? Not an appropriate jacket for a man in his forties, I'm fully aware."

But I'm staring at the patch: a pink star, tacked on with yellow thread.

Fuck.

"Were you wearing this the other night?" I say quickly, suddenly struggling to breathe. "On our date? Or . . . in the restaurant? You wear it all the time, right?"

He *had* to have been, right? Or it was hanging up on the coat rack, star facing out, and I've been hanging my navy jacket next to it for weeks without properly registering it. That's what it is. That's what it *has* to be.

"Nope." Henry frowns and looks at the star again. "It's been in the dry-cleaner's for ages because I didn't have time to pick it up. Just got it back this morning."

My cheeks are starting to burn. It's too specific. Too unimaginable. He has to be wrong. There has to be a *scientific* explanation.

"What kind of car do you have?" I say abruptly. "What color seats?"

Henry looks at me with understandable alarm and I don't care: just please don't say something small, please don't say red, please don't say—

"A Mini Cooper," Henry says slowly. "With red seats."

I bend over and put my hands over my face, moaning faintly. This can't be happening. I'm a *scientist*, I study the world for things that are real, tangible, demonstrable; I don't deal in the magic, airy-fairy world of *made-up shit*.

"What kind of screwdriver do you have." It's not even a question now. "What is stuck on it. Specifically."

There's a silence and I can feel Henry staring at my back.

"It has a unicorn on it." His voice is flat. "What the hell is going on, Margot? Are you assessing me for eligibility again? My jacket isn't cool enough? My car isn't big enough? My tools aren't manly enough?"

"That's not what I . . ." My voice sounds strangled. "It's not—"

"Then what is it?" Henry's voice is quiet, but I can hear disappointment rising into frustration. "Why could you possibly want to know what kind of car I drive, out of nowhere like that? What relevance does it have, other than as a way to judge me?"

I try to speak—to tell him—but I can't.

"You know what?" Henry snaps, now fully angry. "Never mind. I don't want to know. You were right. This isn't going to work."

Henry leans forward slightly to stand up, and as he does, I see three moles, like stars, right on his lower back, and I can't move, can't move, can't—

I'M BACK IN my lilac room, but it's different now.

Every wall has been painted purple, and in the middle is a large double bed, covered with a floral lilac duvet cover. A pile of purple cushions are stacked against a fluffy white headboard shaped like a cloud, and propped in the middle is a toy panda: one that presumably used to be black and white, but is now bedraggled and slightly gray, with one plastic eye missing. Purple cushions line the completed window seat, and a mobile of stars hangs from the ceiling, also now painted lilac. A swinging hammock is dangling in the corner, and shelves are covered in small keepsakes of no monetary value: pebbles, shells, dried flowers. There's a small floral rug on the floor, and one of the cupboard doors is slightly ajar. Through it, I can see small clothes.

Hanging over the bed is a strip of purple bunting that spells W I N T E R.

It's a child's room.

"Meg!" Henry says in excitement from outside the door. "She's here! I can see her coming down the path!"

My stomach spins; I put a hand to my face and my cheek is hot.

"OK," I hear myself say faintly. "Coming!"

Cautiously—still experiencing an eerie sense of déjà vu—I open the door into my living room. This is different now too. My brown leather sofa is still there, but it's covered in blue throws and green cushions. My kitchen is now pale yellow.

There are paintings on my walls I don't recognize: a large abstract of bright blues and turquoise with flecks of silver hanging behind the sofa; an antique portrait of a woman I don't know in a gold frame; small black-and-white photos of me and Henry, together. Pot plants fill the room with foliage, and there's a bookcase—I stare at it—full of books I haven't read or bought. A large bouquet of yellow flowers sits in a vase on the coffee table, and when I turn, the kitchen is full: spices on the racks, pans hanging from the ceiling. The fridge has bright paintings stuck to the front of it—a child's paintings—and there's something that smells of aubergines in the oven.

My sensible, chic neutral shades have gone, covered by an explosion of color.

"Why am I so nervous?" Henry says, pacing up and down by the front door like a dog. "She'll like it, right? Of course she'll like it. It's purple. Anything purple is good."

I open my mouth and there's a tiny knock on the door: faint, four times.

"Here goes," Henry says to me with a wry grin, then he bends down to speak through the letter box. "I'm afraid I'm going to need the code word or I might be letting in the wrong daughter."

"*Dad*." A tiny voice, followed by a giggle. "I'm your *only* daughter."

"Then it is even more essential that I get the right one." Henry winks over his shoulder at me as I continue to stare at the door. My stomach is tight. "You only get one go, I'm afraid. It's an exclusive entry policy here. After that, I'll be changing the code word and getting a new kid."

"Vinosauraptor," the voice says with a small sigh. "It's always, always vinosauraptor, even though I know that's not a real thing anymore."

Henry stands up, unlocks the door and holds his big arms out.

In the doorway is a little girl, about seven or eight years old.

She's small, fine-boned, with a sweet oval face that reminds me a little of a fennec fox: heart-shaped, huge hazel eyes—a beautiful mix of green and brown—a pointy chin and large ears that stick out slightly. Her hair is chestnut-colored and messy—fringe almost vertical—and she's wearing a puffy lilac coat that reaches all the way to her little knees in their woolen tights. Her trainers are also lilac, flashing from the soles, and over her shoulders is slung a dark purple backpack. Next to her is a tiny purple suitcase, abandoned in the open doorway.

"You did it!" Henry picks her up and kisses her slightly grubby little forehead three times. "Phew. That was close. Come and see what we've done to your new bedroom. I think you're going to be pretty stoked."

"*Stoked* isn't a cool word, *Dad*."

"My bad. It's *rad*. Better?" Then he calls over her shoulder: "Thanks, Mum!"

I hear Henry's mother go back down the path and I stare at the little girl with a lump in my throat. She has accepted Henry's kiss with the patient regality of a small queen, and is now back on the floor, staring at me with wide, dark eyes.

A child. There has never been a child in my house before.

"Hello, Winter," I hear myself say. "Welcome home."

AND I'M BACK in the park again, as if I never left.

But Henry is already walking away and I manage to recalibrate just in time to run after him, wobbling uncertainly down the dark path. "Do you have a child?" I call after him. The park is shadowy, unclear, rotating slightly. "Henry, please. I need to know. Do you have a daughter?"

He stops walking and turns reluctantly to stare at me.

His eyes are cold and hard.

"Yes." Henry is studying my face, deeply unimpressed by whatever he's seen. "I do. I have a daughter. She stuck the unicorn on my screwdriver. She sewed the pink star patch onto my jacket when I got a hole in it. Is that what this is about? Me having a child? Because if that's a deal-breaker for you, that's fine, but you could have just said that. It's kind of a deal-breaker for me too. Obviously."

It was a deal-breaker for me, yes—it's on the list—but that's not what I'm thinking about now.

What I'm thinking is: I haven't gone crazy.

They're not daydreams, based on my subconscious desires. They're not hallucinations I've built in a vitamin- and sleep-deprived mind. They appear to be *visions*, and they appear to be accurate. Way, way too accurate. There is no possible way I could know all of these details if they weren't.

Except—are they visions of what *will* be or what *could* be?

Can I actually see the future, or are they just glimpses of another possible timeline: something that would have happened if I had taken a different path? An alternative version of myself? I'm not moving about in time, because I never leave. But when I arrive, for just a few seconds, it's like I'm both this version of me and *her.* As if time isn't linear but spotted, like rain.

And I suddenly wish with all my heart that I had gone insane. *Insane* is something I could hold on to: check myself into the right clinics, take the right medication, go through the right therapy. I can't see myself going to a doctor and saying, *Hi, I've randomly started having visions of the future. Is there a pill for that?*

"What's her name?" My breathing is finally slowing down now; there is comfort in data, relief in information. "I know how bonkers I sound, but please. What's your daughter's name? How old is she?"

Her name is Winter. She's about seven years old and her favorite color is purple.

Henry assesses me for a few seconds. "Winter. She's six."

Winter is six. That means whatever I saw—the purple room, the paint, the little suitcase in my doorway—happens (or could happen) in about a year, eighteen months at most. Henry and Winter move into my house. Or they were *going* to, before I knocked it off course. There is absolutely no way of knowing.

I've only had four visions, and only one of them has come true so far, right at the beginning.

But Henry is still staring at me in horror: here is a woman so hard, so cold, she'll attack a widower simply for having a child. And I suddenly need to make this OK, without telling him the truth. I want the expression I saw in the car, warm and affectionate, without saying *Sorry, just casually having visions of a pretty serious future together* on our third proper meeting.

"I . . ." I scrabble to explain myself without explaining myself. "Eve."

Henry frowns. "Sorry?"

"My best friend Eve." I feel a rush of relief, even as the lie forms. "She's a teacher in a primary school. I think I know who Winter is. I've seen you before while I was waiting for her, picking your daughter up from school. In a Mini. With red leather seats."

I watch as Henry's face begins to clear, very slightly. "Oh!"

"Sorry. I was just shocked because . . ." I search carefully for a way to explain the inexplicable. "I knew I'd seen you before, somewhere outside the restaurant, but I couldn't place where. Then I suddenly realized. She's about this big." I hold my hand out vaguely at waist height. "Wavy brown hair. Hazel eyes. Very cute. She loves the color purple. Wears it all the time. Backpack, coat. Everything."

Now Henry's expression completely changes: his relief is palpable.

"Yes!" He visibly lights up and pride pours out of him. "That's her! St John's Primary in Clifton?"

"That's it!" Thank goodness he filled in the gap for me. "I remember noticing her little purple flashing trainers. I asked about her, and Eve said she's brilliant and stuck a unicorn sticker on her dad's screwdriver, so she could make DIY prettier for him."

OK, that's a guess, but why else would a child pimp up tools?

"That's exactly it!" Henry laughs. "She's on a constant mission to make my world more aesthetically pleasing. Even my 'boring' tweed jacket. I tried to stop her and now I just let her embellish everything around to her heart's content. I think it actually works. My world *is* more beautiful now."

The tension has completely gone now—on his side, anyway.

"Shit." Henry looks down, suddenly embarrassed. "Margot, I'm so incredibly sorry. I totally jumped to the wrong conclusion, didn't I? Then I got up and stropped off when all you did was ask me a couple of questions. I get really defensive about my daughter. This is . . . new for me. It's been just the two of us for so long. Please accept my apology. I am absolutely mortified."

Guilt races through me, but what alternative did I have?

I can either lie and gaslight him—which is the path I have clearly chosen—or I can tell this man I barely know that I have been having very clear visions of us meeting for the first time, road-tripping together, moving in together, painting my flat, living with his child. We've only known each other now for roughly two hours, total.

The fear has only just left his eyes; I don't want it to come straight back.

Except now the fear is all mine.

Because it's only just hitting me that if it's the future I can see, Henry and I are going to fall in love. This is someone I'm possibly going to build a life with, a *family* with. And I don't know him. I literally know nothing about him, other than what kind of car he drives and how he roller-paints a room.

He's a stranger, and apparently I'm being told to tie my life to his.

Not because of my emotions, or how I feel about him *now*, but because of how I've seen I may feel at some point in the future. How do you start from the beginning when you've seen chapters of a story, written in the wrong order? How do I fall in love again, knowing that I *have* to?

"So." Henry smiles at me, his sweet face warm again. "Shall we keep walking? Can you forgive me?"

I stare at him, suddenly wanting to cry.

Because I can't do it.

I cannot go into this, knowing that at some point my heart will be on the line.

"Um." Fear swells inside me from the ground, like fog. "Actually, I've just remembered I have a really early start for work tomorrow. So I should probably be getting back to Clifton now. I'm sorry."

Henry looks crushed—blaming himself—and I feel something inside me hurt again.

"Of course." He nods. "I understand."

"This was lovely, though," I say lamely, unable to meet his eyes. "Thank you for my . . . jacket and everything."

"You're welcome." Henry smiles sadly. "See you around, Margot."

I swallow, hard. My eyes are still stinging. Why does it feel like we're breaking up when there's nothing here yet to break?

"Sure. See you around, Henry."

10

MARGOT?"

There's yet another loud bang on my door.

"*Margot.* We know you're in there, so you'd better stop hiding and open this door before we go ahead and kick it in."

A much quieter voice: one I can't hear properly.

"Then *I* will kick it in," Jules says even more belligerently. "I don't need your help. Some things are more important than Georgian trim, Evelyn. We're not just *leaving* her in there."

Blearily—they're not going to go away, this is the fourth round of knocking in four days—I shuffle off the sofa toward the front door, bringing my fluffy cream blanket with me. Then I wrap myself more tightly, swaddled like a caterpillar, and bend down toward the letter box. A flash of memory: *vinosauraptor.* Except it's not a memory, is it? Because it hasn't happened. It's the opposite of a memory, contained neatly inside just one person.

"I'm fine," I lie through the letter box.

"You're not fine," Eve says, bending down too, until we're eyeball to eyeball. "As I tell the kids, nobody is ever *fine.* You haven't updated your Instagram page in four whole days, which is unheard of. Both your phones are off. The lights are all out. We've been conducting surveillance from outside on a daily basis, and that's the only reason we know you haven't given up the ghost."

"Unless your ghost is watching television," adds Jules. "And getting up every few hours to hobble to the loo swaddled like a mummy."

I groan in frustration. If I *wanted* to talk to anyone about this, I wouldn't have made myself uncontactable. This is the problem with having childhood best friends: there are no boundaries, no normal rules that establish healthy, ordinary dynamics between completely unrelated humans. These two helped me work out how to use my first tampon. There is no space they won't barge straight into.

"Open the door," Jules says again. "Now. I mean it, Margot."

Slowly, I unlock the door and then start shuffling back to the sofa, where I lie down in a straight line, face turned toward the cushions. I feel two dead weights sit on my legs, using me as some kind of extra upholstery.

"Jesus," I hear Jules say, and I can tell she's looking around my flat. "What *happened*? Don't tell me you finally unpacked, because it's still emptier than a ship's hull in here."

"You know what happened, Julia." There is a rare anger in Eve's voice, mild but no less whipping for its quietness. "I *know* you know what happened, because you wrote 'Congratulations!' underneath. I saw it. Followed by two bloody love hearts. *Two.* You can be so insensitive sometimes."

"Yeah. Well." Jules coughs. "Margot wasn't supposed to *see* it, was she."

"Maggie." Eve leans forward and awkwardly tries to cuddle me by attempting to get her arms around my neck. "We're on your side. We love you. Don't let this throw you. It's just another stage you have to get through, OK?"

Slowly, I roll around with them on top of me until I'm facing upward.

Both of their lovely faces are now about two centimeters from mine, staring at me intensely, as if they're about to either kiss me or ask me to smell their breath. They're worried about me, as they probably should be. But they're studying my face for answers I don't have.

"What are you talking about?" I say tiredly.

"The . . . you know." Eve takes a deep breath. "The . . . *betrothal.* I can't even imagine how that must have felt."

"Who says *betrothal*?" Jules says in frustration. "Are you a Tudor?"

"It seemed a little less brutal than *engagement*."

"I *told* Maggie not to look. Did I not tell you not to look, Maggie? And yet again, you completely bogging ignored me and looked, and here we are."

Ohhhh. They're talking about Lily's engagement.

So much has happened since then, I'd completely forgotten she even exists. I'd been more focused on my new-found ability to both see the future and then—somehow—prevent it from happening. There have been no new visions in the last four days, but I've still spent all of them curled up in the dark, waiting. Unsure what the next one will be, or if there will even *be* a next one. What else am I going to see? My own death? I don't want to see that. I like knowing what's coming—I've built an entire career on it—but this is taking prescience about nine hundred steps too far.

"I'm fine," I say yet again, wriggling slightly. "It threw me a bit, but I'm OK now. Can you please stop pinning me to my own sofa? I'm not going to leg it. I'm still in my pajamas."

Slowly, my friends climb off me, then regard me for a few seconds, still mummified. Eve sniffs; she pulls a horrified face. Then they fork off in two very determined directions: Jules toward my kitchen, and Eve toward the back door.

"Right," Eve says, swinging the door open before I can say *don't*. "Let's get some fresh—"

With alarmed eyes, she turns to Jules, who—finding all my cabinets empty—immediately grabs the expensive bottle of red wine I carried home at the start of the previous week (along with the glass, stolen) and quickly crosses the room to stare into the garden.

"What," she says, spinning toward me fiercely, "have you done?"

I swallow. "I *may* have . . . burned everything."

In unison: "You *burned everything*?"

"Yes. I just wanted to . . . start again."

Saying it out loud makes me feel even more unhinged than I did as I stood over the illegal garden bonfire with a bottle of vodka. What the hell is wrong with me?

"You're not a bloody *phoenix*," Jules points out sharply, opening the wine. "Right. Apparently, we're all sharing one glass this evening because you incinerated the rest, so you can go first."

She pours and hands it to me with such violence, it spills on the floor.

"So you're just going to buy all new stuff?" Eve is staring around her in amazement. "Replace everything from scratch?"

"I don't see why not," I say with a firmness I don't feel. "People do it all the time."

"Because they *have* to," Jules mutters in a low voice. "Not out of *choice*, you nutter."

"No, she has a point." I can see Eve rallying to find a way to support me, whatever mental gymnastics it takes, and I love her for it. "It's a great idea! It's just a shame you didn't burn all your clothes too."

Jules and I both stare at her in synchronized surprise.

"Rude," states Jules, presumably so I don't have to.

"I don't mean it like that!" Eve flaps her hands apologetically. "You're very stylish, Mags. I just mean . . . it would be so nice to see you in something other than navy. Just once. Something brighter. I'm sure even *French* people wear other colors sometimes."

"Rude," I say this time, because how dare she question my non-Frenchness.

"So if this isn't all about the engagement," Jules says, taking the shared wine glass off me and swigging, "what's going on? Is this about that video you posted? Because I'm going to be honest with you—if I was wearing a giant condom on the internet for all eternity, I'd probably be hiding in here too."

I grimace—I'd forgotten about the catsuit too—and wonder if I can tell them.

So . . . I've been having hallucinations about things I can't possibly know the details of. They may or may not be the future. They may or may not be warnings. It may or may not be an Alternative Me: a split somewhere, a different universe. There's no way of figuring it out, and I'm incredibly confused. And scared. If there is anyone in the world to whom I can tell the truth, it's these two women.

Ladies, I have made the switch from forecaster to possible soothsayer. Let's call it an upgrade.

But the concern on their faces is already too naked, too painful. I'll tell them what I can, and hope that it's enough.

"I went on another date," I say slowly. "I . . . didn't see it ending well."

More specifically: I didn't see it ending at all.

"OK . . ." Eve looks even more confused. "But you never see it ending well, Maggie. That's literally your entire dating strategy."

"And that's a good thing," Jules says quickly. "You're protecting yourself."

I can feel myself limbering back into the truth now—a part of it, at least.

"Exactly. He just wasn't right for me." I shrug. "All wrong, in fact. Too short. A waiter. Doesn't earn much. Very little free time. Lives in Bath. Also, he has a kid. So . . ."

Eve and Jules glance at each other. "So?"

"So . . ." I take the wine—my turn—and speak into the glass. "I'm no good with children. You know that. I don't have . . . the maternal urge, or whatever. I'm just not . . . It's not for me, that's all. It's at the top of my Criteria List for a very good reason."

I have a sudden flash of Winter's little face as she stood in my living room with her suitcase: the grave, concerned way she was staring at me. Looks like Other Margot is pretty terrible with children too. That's comforting, I guess. No change there.

Then I notice that Eve has quietly taken the wine off me.

"Eve," I say quietly. "No."

"Yeah." She sips, then looks up, smiles brightly. "Didn't work again. But hey-ho! One more round. What's a bit more debt and a lot more hormones? So I'm having wine tonight. That's all."

Jules reaches forward and touches Eve's arm gently.

"I don't want to talk about it," Eve says with a hard, bright fierceness. "We're here to talk about Maggie's giant meltdown."

I open my mouth to object, then realize I can't.

"Nothing to say here either." I grin too cheerfully. "No point in investing in something that won't work, is there? I've saved myself a whole bunch of time. Consider it a narrow escape."

Plus, I don't want to paint my flat *purple*. I don't like *purple*.

Eve and Jules look at each other for a few seconds, eyebrows raised, then back at me.

"*What?*" I sigh. "Just say it."

"You say it," Jules says to Eve finally. "Go. You'll do it more sensitively than me."

"Right." Eve clears her throat and thinks about it, searching for her most subtle and encouraging words. "Margot. You are fucking up your entire life."

"Wow." Jules blinks. "That wasn't what we rehearsed."

I stare at them as if I don't know what they mean, when I know exactly—to the microdata—what they mean. "What do you mean?"

"The Criteria." Eve gestures at the coffee table, where my little notepads are still sitting. "The lists. The dissection and analysis. All the Red Flags. The copy-and-paste dates. How *hard* you've become. You never used to be like this, Maggie. Never. I mean, you were always a *little* analytical and judgy—"

"But in a good way," Jules interjects. "In a clear-sighted way."

"Absolutely." Eve nods fervently. "Weirdly spot on, every time. But now it's turned into something else. You've become a little . . . mean. Not to us!" Her eyes widen at my expression. "Never to us! But to . . . others."

"Men," Jules confirms chirpily. "So no judgment here."

"And it's breaking our hearts," Eve interjects. "Seeing you close yourself up. We hoped it was just a phase, but you're getting worse."

"Which makes *sense*," Jules says quickly. "Of course it does."

"But we need to say something now, because you're becoming bitter when you used to be so much *fun*."

My throat clenches. "I'm not fun?"

"That's not what I meant." Eve quickly back-pedals. "You're fun! Sure you're fun. But . . . you used to be light. Funny. Joyful. Slightly acerbic, but in a playful way. In a *kind* way. And now you're . . . not."

"Fucking hell, Eve," Jules mutters. "Grab a spade and keep digging."

"And this guy?" Eve leans forward. "This last one?"

"Henry," I admit reluctantly.

"Too *short*? When have you ever cared about *height*? You lusted after James Turner in Year Ten, and he was the size of a bollard. Waiter? So? Totally respectable job. The world needs waiters. Maybe he enjoys it. No spare time? You'll *find* time, if you like each other. Lives in Bath? What does that even *mean*? It's twelve minutes on the train and it's a lovely place to visit."

"Historical." Jules nods faintly. "Full of places to sit in water."

"As for the child . . ." I feel Eve wince slightly, and I instinctively put my hand on her knee. "Where did you even get the idea that you are 'no good with children'? *Jules* is no good with children. Jules is bloody horrible with children."

"Unquestionably," she grins. "Little underdeveloped humans, the lot of them."

"But why on earth do you think you are?"

There's a silence while I blink in confusion. It's just a fact that I've accepted about myself—*I'm no good with children*—like the blue eyes I inherited from my grandfather, or a chin so pointed it looks like a lethal weapon.

"Aaron," I say slowly, suddenly realizing. "Aaron told me I was no good with children. Every time we saw his friends' kids, he'd say, 'Don't leave them with Margot! She won't know what to say!' Then he'd laugh and pinch my cheek. And every time I brought up the topic of starting a family, he'd say, 'Do you really think that's for you, Margot? Do you think you're *cut out for it*?

Let's put a pin in it for now, while you really think about what that *means*.'"

"I fucking *knew* it," Jules bellows, abruptly standing up. "I *knew* it was that asshole, getting in your head again. Jesus Christ." With wild eyes, she looks around the empty room. "And there's nothing left to *smash*."

She picks up the TV remote control and lobs it hard onto the sofa to no effect.

Eve watches it bounce onto the floor and turns back to me.

"You need to let Aaron go," she says softly. "Not just the life you had together. That's just the *detritus*, Margot. You need to let go of everything he's put inside *you*. Or, more importantly, taken away."

My cheeks suddenly feel hot, and my eyes sting.

They're right: they always are.

There's no point burning my belongings, moving city, quitting my job, starting a new one, changing my entire life, if Aaron is still inside my head: undoing me, piece by piece. Still telling me who I am and who I am not. Still deciding my fate for me. Still breaking me apart in every way possible.

"Did you *like* Henry?" This, surprisingly, is from Jules. "Forget the Criteria. Did you *like* him, as a human? A man, yes. But that's not his fault."

I stare at them both, my chest hurting. "Yes."

Because I did. It wasn't love at first sight—or seventeenth sight—and it wasn't fireworks. It wasn't chemistry that set my organs on fire. It wasn't like a romance novel, colors suddenly saturating, and it wasn't lust, the kind where you can't stop looking at them, touching them, staring at your phone in the hope that they call.

But I did, absolutely, *like* him.

I've had the other kind of love, and look what happened to me.

"Then maybe give him a shot." Eve firmly hands me my mobile and nudges me toward the bedroom. "And if it goes wrong, we will be here."

"With wine." Jules nods in approval, holding up the glass.

"And snacks. Where are your snacks, by the way? Did you burn them too? I haven't had dinner yet."

"But . . ." I stare at my phone, suddenly terrified. "What do I say?"

Eve smiles patiently, and I feel like one of her five-year-olds: just needing a little prod in the right direction, without even knowing I've been prodded.

"Well, Margot. Here's an idea." She puts a soft hand on my face and kisses my cheek. "You could always try telling him the truth."

11

I STARE AT MY burner phone while it rings.

The truth.

Where do I even start?

"HI." THIS SEEMS like a good place. "This is Margot."

"Hello, Margot." Henry sounds faintly surprised but not angry. "I didn't expect to hear from you again."

I sit on my bed. "I didn't expect you to either, if I'm being honest."

Henry laughs and I hear a small voice saying, "Who is it?"

"Just a friend," he says, sounding a little further away. Something in my stomach tightens: Winter sounds exactly as she did in my vision. "Winnie, can you do me a favor and pick up all those toys before I end up with a broken ankle? Then I'll order us a pizza to say thank you. Pepperoni with extra-spicy meat. *All* the meat."

"*Dad*," I hear in the background. "I'm a *vegetarian*."

"Except for when it's ham sandwiches," he chuckles. "Super-veggie, extra-veggie pizza it is. Just give me five minutes, OK?"

I hear a little squeak of confirmation, and Henry is back.

"Hello again," he says into the phone, and I hear a door close. "I am truly sorry, Margot. I'm not sure I'd have wanted to speak to me again after I walked off like that. So thanks for calling."

"Please don't apologize," I say quickly. "This isn't about that."

I'm not allowing myself to think about the visions just yet, or what they could mean: I can only take one mind-melting step at a time.

"So." It sounds like Henry has sat down and I briefly imagine both of us on a split screen, perched on the edge of our beds. There's something sweet about it, like a film from the 1950s. "Margot. What can I do for you?"

I smile slightly: he sounds exactly like a doctor, as if I'm about to tell him what's wrong with me in laborious detail, hoping he can make sense of it.

Which, in a very real way, I am.

"I want to tell you why I've been such a dick, Henry. Not as an excuse, because there isn't one, but more as an explanation. I haven't told anyone this. Mainly because I didn't need to. Everyone close to me already knows."

You think it's bad wearing a pink plastic ruff in front of the world? Try not having to explain your humiliation to your nearest and dearest because they already have front-row seats. It suddenly feels as if inside me there's something dark and sharp—a splinter the size of a ship's mast—and I'm trying to pull it out as gently and as slowly as I can without doing too much damage.

There's silence; I can feel him listening.

"Eight months ago, I was getting married. To a man named Aaron."

Henry grunts to affirm that he's still listening.

"We were together for ten years, and lived together for eight. We met at the Met Office, he's in Human Resources, and it was . . . magical. At the beginning, anyway. It was like Aaron had *chosen* me, and that was it. Gifts, declarations, constant texts and phone calls. He wanted to know everything I thought, everything I had ever wanted, and I found myself giving it all to him. Everything I had. It was . . . intense. Fireworks, movie romance, the works. I was totally swept away, which was somewhat out of character for me. I'm not really a *sweeper.* I'm more of a . . . strategic tiptoer."

I take a deep breath and wonder what Henry's thinking: *moron*, probably.

"But I loved him. Enormously. The kind of breathless love where you can't stop thinking about them, where you just want to be with them all the time. Where it physically hurts when you're not. But when we moved in together, things kind of . . . changed."

I think about Aaron's face the day we moved into our flat together.

His clear irritation at my excitement.

"He was suddenly there, but not *entirely* there. He turned up in fragments, as if he'd somehow become two people. Except my feelings for him were still exactly the same, and I just wanted that first version of Aaron back. But I also felt like a child for wanting the 'honeymoon' period to last. So I did everything I could to get glimpses of it and I didn't notice I had changed in the process. Shaped myself around him. It was . . . more of a slow-dripping tap, when before you know it, you turn around and the sink is overflowing."

I clear my throat. Ten *years.* Ten years of water, soaking everything.

And everyone noticed but me.

"Anyway. I kept waiting for him to propose. Pathetic, isn't it? Six years, seven years, eight years, and I should have walked away. But he always said that a 'ring doesn't mean anything' and we already had a marriage 'in real terms.' And I tried to believe him. I had to. Because as the years ticked on, as I was climbing the ladder in the Met Office, I'd already invested so much *time.*"

"The bus theory," Henry says quietly. "You've spent so much time waiting, you have to keep waiting or you might as well have walked."

"Exactly." I smile. "Plus, I loved this bus. This bus was the one I wanted."

Aaron was—is—charming, funny, bright, handsome: the world and everything in it rotates around him effortlessly. I felt like the moon quietly orbiting his sun: absorbing his light and trying to reflect it back whenever I could.

But when the sun disappeared, my light disappeared too.

It could get so incredibly cold.

"Anyway. Eventually, nine years in, he turned to me in the middle of watching *The Godfather* yet again and said, 'What about it? Shall we lock this shit down?' Right in the middle of me eating a piece of sweet and sour chicken. And that was it. We were engaged."

"Romantic," Henry says quietly.

"I know." I laugh bitterly. "He explained afterward that he kept it *low-key* because he knows I'm a logical, cool-headed, data type, and I wouldn't want 'all that jazz.' So I told myself he was right, and he knew me so well, really *saw* me, better than I did, and I didn't want it. I didn't *need* it. But I think, actually, I did want all that jazz. I wanted the whole bloody band."

"No shit."

"So I threw myself into arranging the wedding. I had a pretty substantial pot of savings I'd managed to squirrel away from my job and I plowed through it all. Probably because it felt like if the romance was going to come from somewhere, it had to come from me."

I take a deep breath.

"But Jules, Eve and Lily were amazing about it. My best friends, from school. They came to the dress fitting, they helped me choose flowers, they went with me to see venues. They were so excited for me. At least, I thought they were."

I have looked for the signs so many times over the last eight months. It's my job—it's what I'm supposed to be good at. Noticing the details and working out where they will lead; seeing what other people miss, and forecasting the future as accurately as I can.

And I still can't find any, even now.

Maybe a few moments where Lily was quiet, a few tiny laughs that came a little bit too late, or a mood I couldn't fully read. Nights she couldn't meet us because she was "working on her Instagram page." But how was I supposed to put that data together? I would have needed to be looking at an entirely different map.

"During the rehearsal dinner, the night before, we all got carried away. There was a bit of dancing, some silliness, everyone scattered. I was slightly tipsy, and I decided to go outside for a quick smoke."

"Fucking hell," Henry says in a low voice. "You're not—"

"A smoker? God, no. Not anymore. I quit ages ago—it was just a final cigarette. You know, nerves and whatnot."

"Margot. That is *not* what I was going to say. Are you telling me that—"

"Oh." I nod, suddenly feeling flat. "Yeah. Aaron and Lily. I caught them together outside. Heard the whole thing. Apparently they'd been sleeping together for a year. Since just after the engagement."

Apparently, the only shit being locked down was *me*.

"I don't know what to say," Henry says after a pause. "Bloody hell."

I'm not going to tell him about standing in the dark of that blisteringly expensive garden I had paid for, blowing smoke into the air, worrying that Aaron would smell it on my breath—wondering where I could steal a mint from—when I heard the voices. "*We need to tell her,*" followed by: "*We can't tell her. We're going to stop, right?*"

A pause, and then: "*We're not going to stop, Lil, and you know it.*"

And the bit that fully broke my heart was that the person who didn't want to tell me the truth was Lily.

"What did you do?"

"I confronted them calmly. I got the information I needed. Then I left."

I was the one who had to formally text everyone: So sorry, but I'm afraid the wedding in thirteen hours has been canceled. Please let me know if there is any way I can compensate you for funds already spent. Margot xx

Which nobody took me up on, because by then everyone knew: the groom had run off with the bridesmaid, that old chestnut. And a part of me still wonders if some already suspected. Jules and Eve swear they didn't, and I believe them—I have to—but Mum? Dad? My grandfather? He never liked Aaron, and I should have paid more attention to his opinion.

"Did they reach out to at least apologize?"

"They both tried, but I wasn't interested in hearing it. It was way too late for excuses. So I quit my job and moved back to Bristol, which is where I grew up. And now I'm an angry, bitter, hard woman who destroys men for fun. And punches things. And burns my belongings. That's it. That's my story. All ten years of it."

"Wow. What happened to Lily?"

I think about all the *time* I have invested stalking her online.

Watching as Lily plays out her perfect romance, soft-launching, no name, no face, without telling anyone how she got it. And I knew it was bad for me—that I was simply hurting myself more—but how could I not look? How could I not collect data, knowing I should have been doing it the whole time? Ten years, and my best friend walked in and took the exact life I'd been waiting for. Got given everything I had begged for over and over again, without even having to ask.

"They're still together," I say bluntly. "They just got engaged."

"Already?"

"It's been a year and eight months." My voice is calm. I have screamed enough, burned enough. "That's how long they've been together, if you don't include me. He took her to a beach and made a heart out of petals and candles. Apparently, Lily is not a *data* type of girl. Apparently, Lily deserves *all that jazz*."

Because that's what has really been eating me alive, isn't it? That I didn't get any of it because I wasn't worth enough, wasn't valuable enough, didn't have enough of my own glow.

But the person standing right next to me did.

"When you say *just*?" Henry's voice is slightly husky. "When exactly did they get engaged?"

"At the start of our restaurant date."

"Ah. I see."

Henry is silent, so I curl into a ball inside my blanket, ready to slip into the dark. Because it's less about the love I lost and more about the time. It's always, always the time that I missed. Ten years I could have spent with my friends. Ten years of taking up new hobbies. Ten years of learning who I actually am, and what I want, and how to love myself properly, instead of using all that love on someone else.

I will never get those years back.

A hundred and twenty months ripped off my calendar forever.

"I didn't see the Red Flags," I say quietly. "I didn't see them at the beginning, and I didn't see them at the end. And worse, I didn't see them all the way through either. A decade, and I just . . . wasn't looking."

I wasn't paying attention, so my entire life was set on fire.

"That explains pretty much everything," Henry says as I close my eyes, too tired to say anything else. "And I'm so grateful you told me, Margot. You didn't do anything wrong, you know that? Right?"

I nod, eyes still closed. "Mmm."

But I don't know that, because I stayed when I should have gone.

Henry's voice is soothing, deep, and I suddenly remember the warmth I felt when I watched him from across the purple room. The way he kissed my lips and I left paint spattered on him like a tattoo.

"I completely understand if you're not ready to date yet," Henry continues quietly. "Hell, I don't think I'd ever date again. But I like you, Margot. I think you're something pretty special. And I think there might be something here. I'm not sure what it is, but I'd really like to get to know you better. Whenever you're ready. We could start again, from the beginning. If that's something you might want."

The room is starting to drift: I feel light, empty.

And the visions of me and Henry together suddenly don't seem quite as scary anymore. If anything, they're comforting. Are they actually us, or an alternative version? Are they something that could be, or will be? What, if anything, are they trying to tell me? That somewhere out there, in the future, my heart might be ready to restart? At least they made me feel connected enough to tell him the truth.

And for that, I am simply grateful.

"OK," I murmur as sleep finally takes over. "That sounds nice."

Because all I know is that in every vision, I have wanted to be there.

Perhaps that's all I needed to see.

12

WHEN I WAKE the next morning—gently covered by a duvet placed over me by now-absent friends—it feels as if the glaciers inside me have melted, my underground reservoirs are tapped. There's nothing trapped inside me anymore. It's all released and finally moving again: pure, rushing, fresh.

Stretching, I open my eyes and smile at the ceiling in surprise.

Then I get up and wander around my flat with brand-new eyes, making notes of what I want to do with it. What colors, what shapes, what little bits of myself will I start to collect, treasure, strew around the house until it feels like somewhere I belong? An exposed brick wall, some yellow paint. Plants. Some old rugs I'll forage from antique shops gradually, over time; "sentimental" nicknacks that aren't just "collecting dust"; fairy lights I can keep up all year instead of being forced to take them down on January 1.

This isn't going to be like my last home, with me as a permanent guest. It's not going to have me making myself as small as possible so that I somehow fit. I'm not going to shrink until all I do is orbit, gray and dull and only reflecting somebody else's light.

Aaron even tried to turn me against my friends, planting tiny seeds and waiting for them to sprout. "*Jules thinks she's better than everyone else.*" "*Eve is baby-obsessed, yet she calls herself a feminist.*"

"And Lily is . . ."

I pause. What exactly did Aaron say about Lily? "*Lily is a stuck-up cow who isn't as hot as she thinks she is.*"

Well, there you go. Enjoy the next decade, Lily.

WITH A SUDDEN GRIN, I sit down in front of my green screen.

All at once, I can feel my love for meteorology rushing clear and pure. I don't want to make a video out of spite, or competition, or out of a bitter, instinctive need to prove myself *equal.* I want to share the world, in all its moods and magic. I want the weather to fascinate people as it has always fascinated me.

Clearing my throat, I breathe deeply and turn on the camera.

"Hello, meteorologists!" I beam, and for the first time in a very long time it feels like a real smile. "Margot here. I'm back! Today we're going to talk about *rainbows,* which I have a feeling we all love. How could we not? As William Wordsworth said, '*My heart leaps up when I behold A rainbow in the sky: So was it when my life began; So is it now I am a man; So be it when I shall grow old . . .*'"

My grandfather had this poem etched on my very first weathervane, a birthday gift when I turned eight, and I want to share it. I think briefly about Winter, and whether she loves rainbows too.

Crystals. Maybe I'll hang crystals in her bedroom.

"But what *is* a rainbow?" I hold my hand out to where I'll edit a rainbow into the green screen behind me. "What you're actually looking at when you see a rainbow is falling rain at its most beautiful. So why does it happen?"

I feel all the excitement I felt when I first learned what a rainbow was.

"When the sun hits drops of falling rain, the light is bent and bounced back in the same direction. Light is made up of many colors. This means that shorter wavelengths like blue, violet and green are bent more than longer wavelengths like red, orange and yellow. This splits all the colors that are already in light, and spreads them out in the sky according to the lengths of their waves. And here's the best bit."

I feel myself glow, just as I did when my grandfather explained it.

"Even if someone is standing right next to you, they're seeing the light from different raindrops at a slightly different angle. Which means that what you're seeing is your own rainbow. Nobody has ever seen that rainbow before, and nobody will ever see that rainbow again. That rainbow belongs entirely to you."

I hear my burner phone *ting.*

Without turning off the video—I can edit it later; I may have gotten a little too gushy—I launch myself across the sofa and grab it as fast as I can.

Hey Margot. Henry here. Hope
you got a good sleep. ;)

He doesn't seem to have taken me falling asleep mid-conversation too personally, which is a good sign.

I was just wondering: would you like to meet Friday
night? And if so, would you prefer a low-key second
First Date, or something a bit more amped up?

Taking your lead on it. Xx

I think about it, briefly.

My impulse is to say: Keep it low-key. Casual. Non-scary. But:

All that jazz, please. X

Ting.

Then you shall get the whole band. :) xx

I look up to the camera again, and only then do I see my expression.

It's bright, lit from within: my eyes are warm, my cheeks are pink. I don't look as hollowed out as before. And it's not Henry.

Or it's not *entirely* Henry, anyway. It's more as if whatever Aaron took is starting to slowly come back, drip by drip.

"And remember," I say, shining at the camera, "you don't have to wait. Take a hose into the garden, put your finger over the end and stand with the sunshine behind you. Just go ahead and make your very own rainbow."

Still smiling, I stop recording.

Trying to decide what to call this video—"Hue Wants to Talk About Rainbows?"—I turn my real phone on and blink as it starts beeping like a van reversing. What the—

Four days without turning it on, and apparently the entire world has something to say about it.

MISSED CALLS: 28
TEXTS: 39
INSTAGRAM NOTIFICATIONS: 15,589

Holy *fuckballs*.

Holding my left hand slightly over my eyes, I wince and click on MargotTheMeteorologist.

Scammer
You should be ashamed of yourself
Unfollowed
Unfollowed
AND YOU CLAIM TO LOVE THE ENVIRONMENT
I think the Met Office will probably have something to say about this. FRAUD.

What the hell is—

Oh no. No no no no no no—

As I quickly scroll down the thousands and thousands of comments on my last video, it becomes clear that I didn't just "humiliate" myself with a laminated catsuit. I also accidentally sent hundreds toward a scam account to have their information harvested. The @thunderwarez account has been deleted, and when—in escalating panic—I search for them elsewhere, it's all videos talking about legal action.

Why the *hell* didn't I do my own research?

Was I really that desperate that I didn't think through the consequences of what I was doing properly? I think through the consequences of *everything.* It's literally my defining characteristic. Apart from when it actually matters, apparently.

In less than a week, my count has plummeted—87k people left—and every time I refresh, it drops another hundred. More furious comments on my page are appearing every second, and I don't really blame them.

You will be hearing from my lawyer

In full panic, I quickly fire off a beseeching email to Rain of Terror. How exactly did I think I was going to get paid, anyway? I normally do everything by the book—check it all carefully, arrange a payment plan, a contractual agreement—but the *one* time I'm too emotional and exhausted to remember, I single-handedly destroy my entire business. What is *wrong* with me? My inbox is now full of potential sponsors and advertisers curtly retracting their offers.

Unsurprisingly, my email bounces straight back, undelivered.

Rain of Terror indeed.

"Fucking fucking fucking SHITBALLS," I yell at the ceiling, glow totally gone. "Fucking fucking fucking fucking *MORON, MARGOT.*"

Shaking, I pace quickly—still swearing—to my empty kitchen and reach into the back of a cabinet. Fumbling, I find the little hidden cardboard box. Statistically, each cigarette takes eleven minutes off your life, and frankly, these are minutes I would very much like to erase if possible.

"You're an *idiot,*" I hiss at myself as I fumble at the back-door lock. "A stupid, life-destroying *idiot.*"

Did I do it on purpose? Did I set my *entire* life on fire? Was there a part of me, having burned everything I owned, that was trying to burn down what remained of my meteorology career too? I'd prefer to think my subconscious went full phoenix—as Jules might put it—because otherwise I am just *that* stupid.

"Margot the Miscreant," I hiss as I light the cigarette and stand with it in the garden, staring at the bonfire I still haven't cleared up. "Margot the Malevolent. No, Margot the *Megalomaniac.*"

Because it was hubris that made me start my own page, wasn't it? A need to prove myself in some way: that I was still *someone*, that what I said or thought *mattered*. That somebody—anybody—could *see me*. And this is the result.

"FUCK," I yell again at nobody in particular, taking a huge puff and immediately starting to cough. "FUCKING FUCKING FUCK—"

"Um." A calm voice from the next garden. "I'm so sorry, but do you think you could maybe . . . scream something else instead?"

Blinking, I turn and look over the fence.

"Fudge, maybe?" My neighbor looks incredibly uncomfortable. "Or . . . FRIDGE?"

Next to her are two fair-haired children—twins, about three years old—staring at me with plate-sized blue eyes. They're sitting on a brightly colored picnic blanket, with letter blocks laid out in front of them. One of them—clearly a genius—has just pulled out the F and the U and laid them proudly in front of her.

"Fuck," I say again, then wince. "Sorry."

"It's not that I want to control what you're saying," my neighbor says, clearly mortified. "At all. Curse to your heart's content! But I'm teaching them to spell today and they appear to be picking it up quite quickly."

The cleverest twin has already picked up a K and is working out where to put it.

"Sorry," I say quickly. "My language is really terrible. My mother is constantly on at me about it. I'll try to retrain my vocabulary."

My neighbor smiles, then looks at me with more concern.

"I didn't realize you smoked."

"I don't." I try to inhale again and begin coughing. "I just . . . thought it might help and it doesn't."

"Bad day?"

"It started well." I grimace, stubbing out the cigarette on the ground. "Then it fell off the top of a mountain."

"You're Margot the Meteorologist, right?" My neighbor is looking at me more carefully. "My kids love your page. We watch every video together."

I wince again: yup, add *Destroyer of Children* to the list.

"I am so, so sorry about that." I try to smile at them over the fence. "Hi! How are you? They're very nice . . . bricks you have there."

Aaron was right. I really *don't* know how to talk to kids.

They both stare blankly back at me.

"I'm Polly," my neighbor says, holding out an elegant, fine-boned hand across our garden fence. She's tall, naturally white-blonde, beautiful, even in leggings and a T-shirt. "I don't think we've met properly yet. I was going to introduce myself earlier, but you seemed a little . . . focused. And I didn't want you to think I was just, you know. Into the celebrity thing."

A little focused. That's a very nice way of saying *bitchy and distant*.

"I'm not a celebrity," I say quickly. "I just make content in my living room. About things I already know. It's nothing to be impressed by. And it looks like it's a short-lived experience anyway."

You know what? Maybe the total destruction of my entire meteorology career is the perfect ending to the last decade.

"Is it . . ." Polly frowns and clears her throat. "Are you stressed about that last video you posted? Because we saw it and it didn't seem . . . very Margot." She looks alarmed. "Not that I know you! Sorry. Just . . . it didn't seem on-brand."

"I don't have a brand," I admit bluntly. "I was too busy having some kind of mental breakdown." I wave vaguely in the direction of my bonfire. "Which I think you caught a glimpse of, actually."

"I did wonder." She nods. "I'm not sure saucepans are really built to burn."

The cardboard box of "KITCHEN SHIT" has eroded away and now it's just a charred pile of Aaron's cooking equipment: none of which he needed, apparently, because "Lily has her own branded line."

"I'm all over the place," I admit. "I don't know what I'm doing."

How do I explain that I haven't known *what I'm doing* for so long, I can't remember what it even feels like to *know*?

"Actually," Polly says thoughtfully, "I'm looking for work."

I stare at her: weird segue.

"Oh!" I try to smile. "Cool! Well, good luck with that."

"No, I mean—" She laughs. "I think I might be able to help you. That's what I used to do, before the kids came along. Brand management. But I stopped when Posy went to school, and then Perry and Paige came along and . . ."

I blink. Polly, Posy, Perry and Paige? Blimey.

"Oh, I know." She smiles, embarrassed. "The names were my husband's idea. Peter. He thought it made us a *cute set*, so I reluctantly went with it. He works a lot. Comes home very late, normally when they've gone to bed. And we can't afford childcare. So I can't really go anywhere until they've started school too."

I blink in surprise: husband? I have *never* seen a man in their garden.

In fairness, I only normally come outside to burn things in the middle of the night or swear into the sky, so I wasn't paying a lot of attention. Add that to the list of things right in front of me that I don't notice.

"Right." I'm thinking about it. "You think there's anything you can do?"

"I could try." She nods. "And we could delay payment until

you get back on your feet? I'd be sad to see Margot the Meteorologist disappear. The kids look forward to your videos before bathtime every night. It really is such a lovely page."

At the word *page*, the child I assume is Paige looks up hopefully.

"Not you, darling," Polly says, stroking her head affectionately. "Go back to spelling FUDGE. There's no J. That's your first clue."

I pretend to think about it for a few seconds, but there's really nothing to think about. If nothing else, it might at least make me feel slightly less alone and encourage me to improve my posture.

"Yes," I say before she changes her mind. "*Please.*"

"Great. It's a deal."

Polly grins at me confidently and I feel instantly reassured. She is poised, calm. Completely invincible.

"Is tomorrow too soon?" I wince slightly at my desperation. "Obviously, if it is, then that's fine, but I'm just asking because—"

I nod to where my work phone is beeping incessantly in the house.

"I'll come to yours first thing tomorrow." Polly smiles, unruffled.

I feel her serenity seep over the fence toward me. I nod gratefully, wondering when the last time a cigarette saved lives.

And I didn't even smoke it.

I may have just found my very own rainbow.

13

POLLY ARRIVES ON my doorstep the next morning with an armful of folders, twins holding anxiously on to her legs like sailors in a storm.

"First things first," Polly says as she gently nudges Paige and Perry toward my living room with a pair of iPads. "Behave, you two. Margot, we're all about Damage Limitation right now. We can think of ways to rebuild your brand afterward."

I watch the twins settle themselves without a word.

God, she's impressive.

"Right," I say faintly. "I'm not sure there's going to be much to rebuild."

I've spent yet another night awake, watching my business dismantle itself with the speed of the wind that hurtled over Barrow Island in 1996 at a rate of 253 miles per hour: the fastest ever recorded. Angry comments are growing, and followers are still dropping by the thousands. They "always knew" there was something "dodgy" about me, apparently. I don't touch anything—Polly has told me not to—but instead I simply watch as what I built over nearly a year dismantles. There's a strange sense of familiarity: here we go again. *Poof.* Gone.

Believe it or not, Barrow Island actually had no casualties.

This time, it's just me.

"I did tell you not to look at what was happening," Polly says with a wry smile, studying my deflated expression. "But something tells me that *not looking* is not in your DNA, Margot."

She sits herself at my dining table.

"I've written a script for you," she says, pushing forward a piece of paper. "And don't worry about memorizing it—I can get it on a prompter."

I pick it up and swallow. "Do you think it will help?"

"It can't hurt." She nods. "After that, we'll need to make a plan to regain followers, get back sponsorship deals, reach out to new ones. Maybe brands that actually exist, for starters."

She smiles and I try to smile back. "I'm an idiot."

"People have been forgiven for far worse than being an idiot," she says, putting on glasses. "After we've managed the damage, it might be a good idea to start expanding past Instagram. You're a highly trained meteorologist, Margot. Your passion is infectious, and it helps that you're gorgeous. I think there could be some really exciting areas you could branch out into. Media, radio, even television."

"Mmm." I look up from the script I'm studying intensely. "Sorry, what?"

"You must have thought about using your skills elsewhere," she says in surprise.

"Um." I think about what prompted my sudden career shift. Heartbreak, panic, jealousy, competition. "Not really."

"Well. One step at a time." Polly stands up and starts surveying my flat. "Let's fight this particular fire first."

I watch her study my bleak and empty living room and feel a sudden intense urge to explain that I'm not a woman with no personality: I'm just working out what it actually *is* before I start distributing it everywhere.

"We don't want this in front of a green screen," she says firmly. "It needs to feel personal. Remind people you're a real person."

"I am." I follow her gaze and guess what she's thinking. "At least, I think I am."

"I know you are," she laughs. "Do you have a book collection? Anything we can put on the shelves behind you so you seem more personable?"

I shake my head: all my books stayed in Exeter. I assumed I'd return at some point to collect them, but it would mean seeing Aaron again, and frankly, I'd rather stab 2B pencils up my nose until I can draw lines on my eyeballs.

"That's fine." Polly evaluates the room and her obediently engrossed children, watching some kind of cartoon on the iPads. "We'll just pop you on the sofa and I'll go grab some art from my house to jazz it up a bit in the background. Back in a minute."

"Wait, no, I—"

She's gone. *Shit.*

I stare at the twins, who—as if by magic—are no longer absorbed in cartoons. I take a deep breath and try to stay calm. This is going to be fine. It's two minutes, three, max. I can entertain children for three minutes. Right? I am *not* "no good with children." I just haven't had a chance yet, that's all.

"Hello." I perch myself in front of them. "I'm Margot. Fuck. You already know that, don't you?"

"Fuck!" Paige agrees solemnly.

"Fuck." Perry nods. "Fuck fuck fuck."

"No, no!" I wave my hands around frantically. "Not that! No! Shit."

"Shit," Paige tries out experimentally, rolling it around in her mouth. "Daddy says *shit* sometimes. Not *fuck*."

"Not *fuck*," Perry agrees. "Fuck is one of the *bad* ones."

I look in desperation at the front door, waiting for Polly to return, hear that I've broken her children with my potty mouth and promptly leave again, taking the twins and what remains of my career with her.

"Hey!" I quickly jump up and grab the weather station blackboard from where I've stashed it at the back of the living room. "Look what I've got! Doesn't this look fun!"

The twins stand up and move toward it, eyes huge.

"See?" I point at the illustrated dial. "This one is showing us the *season*. Do you know what season it is now?"

They stare at me. "Sunny."

"Well, no. Because that's not a season. Summer would be the

picture of the tree with all its leaves. Then there's winter, which is the tree with no leaves. Spring, with blossoms. And autumn, with orange leaves. That's what it is now. Just."

I self-consciously move the dial while they stare at me.

"And do you know *why* we have seasons? It's because the Earth is tilted on its orbital plane, and sometimes that's toward the sun. That means longer days and shorter nights. Then it tilts away, so there are shorter days and longer nights."

Orbital planes might be a little too much for three-year-olds, but they're still staring at me with wide eyes, so I crash on.

"When the days get shorter, hormones in the plants are triggered, which changes the colors of the leaves and causes them to die and drop from the tree."

Paige's eyes grow very wide. "They're dead?"

"Yes," I confirm happily. "Super dead."

Then I watch in horror as her little face screws up and her blue eyes start to fill.

"They're *dead*," she starts to wail. "Perry, the leaves are *dead*."

"But they come back," Perry says, trying to comfort her by wrapping his arms around her neck. "When it's sunny. Don't worry."

"They don't," I say without thinking. "I'm afraid they're *different* leaves."

Now Perry starts to cry too.

"Gosh," Polly says from behind me as the twins sob incoherently into the air. "Chaos. How long was I gone?"

"Mummmmyyyyy," Paige sobs, lobbing herself forward to cling to a leg again. "Margot says leaves *die* and they *don't come back* and they're just orange because they're *saying goodbye*."

"Well," Polly says calmly as I try to stop Perry from ripping the windsock off the blackboard in a fit of anguish. "Isn't that lovely, darling? They turn orange to tell you they've lived a happy life and now they're done. Thank you for explaining it so nicely, Margot."

Paige's wails grow slightly softer, and I turn around.

My blood freezes.

In Polly's pale hands is a giant painting: bright blues and turquoise with flecks of silver. I know this painting. It's the unfamiliar painting in my vision of a future with Henry: same size, same colors, same details. In shock, I watch as Polly walks it round the room, pausing by the fireplace, over the television, by the window. Breath held, I wait for her to take it to the wall behind the sofa—which she does.

"There," she says, holding it up. "Doesn't that look perfect?"

I suddenly feel dizzy.

Is it the future? Is that what I'm seeing? Am I going to be watching my life build, piece by piece, like a Lego house with a picture on the front of the box, knowing exactly how it's going to look? If so, is that a good thing?

"You know what?" Polly smiles at me. "This painting doesn't really fit our color scheme, but it was a wedding gift, so I can't get rid of it. Why don't we leave it there, just for a little bit? Bring some life into the room."

I swallow. It'll be here at least a year and a half. "OK."

The painting goes on an empty nail on the wall and I find myself looking around the room, wondering when everything else will start turning up: the black-and-white photos, the cushions, the antique portrait of the lady. It's a sense of déjà vu, except now working backward. *Jamais vu.* Never seen.

"Are you OK, Margot?" Polly grabs the camera and settles the twins back down again in one seamless movement. "You look like you've seen a ghost."

I suppose I've spent so long haunted by the past, it's extremely bewildering to have the future following me instead.

"Not quite," I smile. "I'm fine. Let's do this."

I sit on the sofa, trying to refocus, then pick up the script again and clear my throat.

"Right." Polly looks up at the camera. "We're going to keep this short and sweet. Just say the words and we'll edit later. Action."

"Action?" My nostrils twitch. "Is this Hollywood?"

"Sorry." She laughs brightly and her entire face changes: her composure shatters slightly. "I wasn't sure what other word to use. You know—*go*."

Smiling, I breathe out and quickly scan the paper again.

"Hello," I say, looking up and into the lens. "This is Mar—"

A familiar wave of cold rushes through me.

Fuck. Not now, not here, not—

"This is M—"

The room flickers, blurs, and I'm hanging on to the present by my fingertips.

"This is—"

And I'm gone.

CAUTIOUSLY, I OPEN my eyes.

This time, I have no idea where I am: it's a totally unfamiliar location. I look around with a slightly nauseous spin, a sensation of vertigo, as if I'm on a boat. I'm lying under a thick mustard blanket, on—I pull it slightly to the side—a dark green velvet couch. It's nighttime, and in front of me is an ornate Victorian fireplace covered with lit candles, and there's a bowl of something green on the coffee table in front of me. Surprised, I prod it slightly: soup. It's soup. A stale piece of cold toast is perched next to it with a faint air of disappointment.

I cough hard, suddenly feeling unbearably hot.

Everything hurts and my forehead is damp. I run my hands through sticky hair and realize with shock that it's a short bob. Where the hell has my hair gone? Whatever I'm wearing—I look down, it's a pair of yellow pajamas with stars on them—is completely soaked with sweat. With a horrified lurch, I clumsily pull the blanket off me and try to stand up, feel woozy, sit down again.

What the hell is happening to me this time?

"*Henry*," I try to say, but I can't form the word: my throat is raw, lined with pain. It comes out as a frog-like croak. "*Henry*."

Because he has to be here, doesn't he?

He is always in my visions, and I suddenly realize I need him to be. I don't want to be stuck here, wherever I am—*whenever* I am—on my own. I look desperately around the unfamiliar flat, but it's just me. Tall windows, intricate cornices, dark gray walls the color of a pavement in the rain. There's a large indoor tree in the corner, and a huge painting of a ship on the wall. Where the hell am I? Panic whips the back of my neck. What if I get stranded? What if I'm trapped in this strange place indefinitely? In pain, foggy and confused? I could be any time, any place, and then how do I get back?

"*Henry*," I say huskily again, trying to stand up. "Are you here?"

No answer.

My head hurts, it's an empty vision, a blank time-hop, and I don't understand, I don't want it, I need to get out, I need to—

Wobbling, I reach the front door and start rummaging at the lock. *Out. Out. I need out, I need—*

A voice behind me: "Meg?"

I promptly start crying.

"Oh *shit*." I feel Henry's hand rest briefly on the back of my neck. "You're burning up, Margot. I *told* you to stay on the sofa. You need to stay warm, not be wandering about at random, sweating your balls off."

Still crying, I turn around.

Henry is here, he's here, I'm not on my own, I'm not stranded.

"I thought you'd gone," I say, sobbing fully now. "I thought you weren't going to be here. I thought I was on my own."

"I was just checking on Winter," Henry laughs, wrapping his big arms around me. He smells the same: pepper and lemon. "I haven't gone anywhere, I promise."

Still sniffling, I tuck into Henry's neck and feel myself quieten. It feels normal, as if I do this regularly. As if he somehow calms me, every time.

"Is Winter OK?" I murmur, suddenly needing to know. "She's not too sick?"

Because I'm sick: I've suddenly remembered. I don't know

how I know, but I do. As if Other Margot and Me Margot are momentarily the same person. I look around me again—I'm in Henry's flat. This is Henry's flat, in Bath. I know it, even though I'm not sure exactly how. The past, still the future, is starting to flicker in and out. Déjà vu, except working in two directions.

"It's just the flu," Henry confirms, brushing my fringe out of my sweaty face and studying me carefully. He looks tired. "And she's fine, Meg. You've got it far worse, I'm afraid. It'll be gone in a few days."

I nod, staring at his face. His stubble is slightly longer, more clearly silvery. It suits him, and I suddenly feel overwhelmed, still weepy. I'm so grateful he was here: that I wasn't waking up on my own.

I don't want any visions that don't have him in them.

"Henry," I say. "I think this is—"

"MARGOT? IS EVERYTHING alright?"

Blinking, I stare blankly into the video camera and then at Polly, still standing behind it. The pain in my body has gone. The heat has gone. I touch my forehead: it's dry. Tentatively, I clear my throat: it doesn't hurt anymore.

"Mmm," I manage faintly. My voice is clear, normal. "Yes."

"Is the script OK?" Polly frowns at me. "Do you want to practice it again?"

I look down to where I'm still holding the piece of paper, then up at the camera again. The green light is still on, it's been recording the whole time, and I suddenly need to know, for sure, what is actually happening to me when I leave.

"Can I just see something?" I stand up, no longer wobbly. "The recording?"

Polly nods, faintly surprised, and I get behind the camera and rewind until I see myself sit down on the sofa. I watch myself straighten myself out, looking anxious, then say, "*Action? Is this Hollywood?*"

"*Sorry*," Polly's voice says behind the camera, followed by a laugh. "*I wasn't sure what other word to use. You know*—go."

I watch myself smile, breathe out, look at the paper.

"Hello. This is Mar—"

My face starts to empty, go completely blank.

"This is M—"

I can see myself struggling, trying to stay present.

"This is—"

Like the flip of a switch, my eyes become completely vacant. My face slackens, and I stare straight ahead: unmoving, trance-like. It's eerily normal. I just look like someone who has forgotten what they're about to say.

I count: one meteorologist, two meteorologist, three meteorol—

The life abruptly returns to my eyes, I blink a few times and Polly says, "*Margot? Is everything alright?*"

I'm gone for just under three seconds.

Except I'm not "gone" at all: I'm still exactly where I'm supposed to be. It appears that no matter how long the vision lasts, it takes mere seconds in real terms. Which is comforting. I was scared that I was gone for minutes at a time, either vanishing into thin air, juddering like a washing machine or projecting some kind of vision into the air in front of me like in a cinema.

It was going to be hard to cover *that* up in the local supermarket.

Relaxing slightly—this should at least be easier to manage and hide—I run my hand through my hair: it's back to being long again. Why do I chop it all off? There's no way of knowing when that vision happens, or if it's *going* to happen. Perhaps I could start asking questions when I get there—what's the date? The year? Our relationship status?—but I don't seem to be able to control the future version of me. She is doing her own thing, while I do mine. We are two separate people, somehow existing together.

Sort your shit out, Other Margot. Ask for details.

"Do you want to continue?" Polly looks a little bewildered as I turn off the recorder and breathe out. "Or do you need a break?"

My brain is still spinning: what happens if I *don't* cut my hair?

Just one tiny change and that vision is no longer accurate, right? Does that work for all of it? What if I move the painting? What if I paint the kitchen a different color, instead of yellow? What if I *don't* get sick? What if I replace Henry's screwdriver, or hide his star-elbowed jacket? Just one, almost imperceptible difference and it's not the future anymore, by definition. It's an alternative universe, branching off immediately. So what does that mean? Are the visions clues I'm meant to be following? Do I wander through the present, trying not to touch anything so that I get to them safely? Or do I just accept that they're futures that *could* happen, but they're not set in stone?

This is exactly why humans aren't supposed to see the future.

It is *extremely* discombobulating.

"No," I say slowly, "I can do the video again."

"If you're sure." Polly studies my face, which I'm assuming has the expression of a woman steadily losing her grip on reality. "Do you want to . . . talk about anything? You seem . . . a little disjointed."

I blink. She can say that again. I am so *disjointed* that it appears I am literally in two chronological places at once: two *people* at once.

Both me and Other Margot, whoever she is.

For a second, I consider telling Polly the truth: get some outside perspective, maybe get driven to a hospital for a quick brain scan. Except . . . how would hallucinations caused by a medical issue tell me what color screwdriver Henry owns? That doesn't make sense either.

"I'm good," I say, nodding. "Let's do this."

I look at my watch: it's nearly midday already. My date with Henry is this evening and I'm almost painfully excited to see him again. Even though I just saw him. *Because* I just saw him.

Would I even be going on this date if I hadn't had these visions? If I hadn't seen the letters on his hand, the flash of orange card, would I have said yes? In which case, am I seeing the future, or is the future creating itself by showing itself to me first?

Time, like a rainbow, is apparently not a straight line at all.

"Right." Polly waits until I sit back down on the sofa. "Are you ready to start again, Margot?"

I look at the camera, feeling as if I'm in two places at once.

"Yes," I admit. "I think I am."

14

I MAKE MY INCREDIBLY earnest, boring apology.

While the video is being uploaded—to a slightly mollified public response—Polly takes to my inbox to deal with sponsors, brands, advertisers. When I ask if there's anything else I can do to help, she looks faintly surprised: why would there be? That's her job.

Except it was *my* job, and now I don't know what else to do.

At a total loss—I haven't had spare time in over half a year—I hit Google. I've been ringing my grandfather regularly, just to check in, but he essentially told me—as gently as possible—to get a life. ("I'm *fine*, Margot. Surely you have better things to do than call me every seven minutes.") So I leave the poor man alone and start on The Plan instead: booking a cleaner and a delivery of food thrice-weekly, along with a variety of gadgets for the visually impaired. When that's all done, I leave a short, guilty voicemail for my parents, apologizing for not calling them (again). I order flowers for Eve to cheer her up, sent directly to her school, and a large bar of chocolate for Jules so she doesn't feel left out.

I buy a few random cushions, to match Polly's loaned painting.

Finally—feeling lighter than I have in months—I don my stripes, sort out my hair and make-up and try to suppress what I now realize is fast becoming a bit of a crush on Henry. It feels as though it's come out of nowhere: a giddy sensation, much like I had on James Bollard in Year Ten. One I'm going to have to hide as vigilantly as possible, because I'm not sure that *I've had random visions of us in the future and it's making me fancy you like crazy* is completely suitable for this stage of our relationship.

"You look lovely," Polly says as I lurk by the clock on the wall, watching the minutes count down. "Going somewhere nice?"

She's packing up her stuff: folders, children, all impeccably neat.

I stare at her for a few seconds.

"I don't know," I admit, still processing this question. Months of controlling, analyzing, collecting, examining. Months of knowing everything. "Henry hasn't told me."

I don't know where I'm going, or what's going to happen, or what the plan is.

I don't know anything.

And I have to be honest—it feels absolutely amazing.

HENRY IS WAITING for me on the bench on Brandon Hill. He doesn't see me approaching from behind, so I take the opportunity to assess him again. He's wearing black jeans and a different coat—large, gray, almost army-like—and his hair is almost entirely silver from the back, like a wolf. His shoes are old neon trainers, battered, wrong for his outfit. They're shoes that Margot of the Seventeen Dates would probably judge, immediately. Do I really like him? Are these simply fabricated endorphins, created by visions I shouldn't have actually had? Have I been tricked by the future? Shouldn't I be starting from the beginning of love: chronologically, the way everyone else does?

As I walk toward him, I note that Henry's hands are resting on his thighs, and every few seconds he wipes them almost imperceptibly. He sits up a little straighter and tilts his chin upward, preparing himself for my arrival in the opposite direction. I see him take a few deep, conscious breaths. Just like in the restaurant, there's such a sweetness to his nervousness. It doesn't seem to fit him properly—he seems so confident, so assured—but these flashes of anxiety, of disquiet, are beautiful to me. Delicate, vulnerable, raw. Human. Weirdly sexy as hell.

Then I step on a twig: it snaps, he turns, his face lights up.

I feel mine light up straight back.

Fuck.

Yes. I do, one hundred percent, have a big crush on this man.

"Sneaking up on me, huh?" Henry is very clearly trying not to grin too hard. "Good thing I wasn't picking my nose."

I laugh. "Is this where you come to do that?"

"Yup." He meets my gaze briefly and then grins at the floor again. "This is my nose-picking bench, Margot. Each bench in this park is allocated to a different disgusting habit. Just be glad we didn't meet on the one down by the small pond."

He stands up to kiss my cheek just as I try to sit down next to him.

We bump into each other and laugh again.

"We're not staying here," Henry explains quickly, grabbing a large bag. "I just wanted to kind of . . . undo the other night. The stomping and so on. I thought we could rewrite that memory, in this place."

"Consider it rewritten," I say quickly. "Nose-picking bench it now is."

"Well, that backfired horribly," Henry grins. We can't seem to stop smiling at each other, like two people with a secret. "I'm not sure if this was the right thing to do, but I brought you a little something."

As we begin walking down the hill, he reaches into his pocket and I feel a tiny twist of fear: Aaron and his extravagant *gifts*. What did Jules say, repeatedly? *Beware the Love-Bombing, Margot*. But did I listen? No, I did not. I took the romance—the flowers and the jewelry—and I twirled with it in a giddy circle, like Rose and Jack downstairs in the *Titanic*, unaware the ship was about to sink and one of us was going to drown.

Bewildered, I stare at the small blue glass ball Henry's holding out.

"Wow," I say. "I don't think I've been offered a marble by a human male over the age of seven before."

Henry, I realize with another bolt of affection, is a massive dork.

"It's a reject." He smiles with a small wrinkle of his nose. "Wrong color, apparently. Not purple. And look . . ." He points at the little swirl of white inside it, looking inordinately proud of himself. "It looks a bit like a cloud, doesn't it? I thought you might like that. Kind of . . . weathery."

I take the marble and hold it up to the light. I'm pretty sure it was supposed to be a white flower—it's just not particularly well executed—but if Henry says it's weather, then weather it shall be.

"Lenticular." I peer at it. "Altocumulus lenticularis, to be specific. It's a cloud caused by mountain waves in the air, and it looks like a saucer. A lot of people think that's where many UFO sightings come from."

"All my hopes and dreams of aliens shattered in one go," he says with a sigh. "Thanks very much, Margot."

I wink at him. "Consider this just the beginning."

We both laugh, Henry's wide shoulder grazing my upper arm. I'm still quite a lot taller than him—a good three inches, even in flats—but suddenly I'm not sure why I ever cared. Why was it on my list in the first place? Do I really need to see up a man's nostrils to find him attractive? Can't he just look up mine for a change?

All I know is that the second we touched, I felt . . . something. I'm just not sure *what.*

"So." Henry's voice is light, but there's a slightly ridged texture to it: an undercurrent of anxiety, like a thin thread of silver in the sky. "I know you wanted *all that jazz*, but I also didn't want to give you too *much* jazz. More of a three-piece, rather than an orchestra. It's a very fine tightrope to walk, knowing almost nothing about you."

I glance at Henry's face and feel a sudden swell of pity for him. This is what happens when you constantly blow up at random for no apparent reason: everyone around you starts acting like they're playing Statues. One wrong move and *boom*—they're out. Then you wonder why they're all edging their way across the room, staring at you with wide, terrified eyes.

"I'm not sure orchestras play jazz," I point out in amusement.

"Valid objection." Henry looks at me more carefully. "What I mean is—just say the word and I'll rein it in. I don't want you to feel overwhelmed, that's all. You've been through quite enough this past year already."

I abruptly stop walking and put my hand gently on his arm.

This man is amazing. He lost his *wife* five years ago, he hasn't dated since, yet all his focus now is on making sure that *I* feel comfortable. No wonder Other Margot adores him: she clearly has great taste in men. Much better than this Margot has had historically.

I feel weirdly grateful to her: *Well chosen, girl.*

I mean, fully grown woman.

"Henry," I say quietly, "I am very happy to be here, whatever it is we're doing."

He visibly relaxes. "Excellent. Because I may have screwed up again."

Around the corner, I can now hear faint music and a *lot* of people laughing and shushing and whispering, "They're coming." It's dark now, and there's a glow of light coming from behind a rather large bush.

"Did you throw me an enormous surprise First Date party?" I ask. "Is everyone I know going to jump out of a cake?"

"Not quite." Henry laughs. "It's just . . . well, Frank had tickets, but Mary's back is too bad, so I grabbed them this morning. I thought it was . . . fitting."

As we turn the corner, I see hundreds of fairy lights strung everywhere, and people sitting on blankets on the grass, angled toward a small empty stage in the center. Henry swings his large backpack off his shoulder, pulls out a purple blanket with pink hearts on it and a couple of mismatched glasses. It is sweetly, earnestly disorganized, and I feel another wave of warmth toward him.

With an elaborate flourish, Henry flicks the blanket onto the ground and gestures.

"Your seat, madam. I borrowed this too. Obviously."

"Lies. It's your favorite blanket and you know it." Laughing, I take my position on the ground. "What are we watching?"

"Your surname is Wayward, right?" Henry plonks down next to me and pulls a dusty bottle of Prosecco out of his bag, along with what are clearly the remains of last night's restaurant shift: cold lasagna, some mozzarella and tomatoes, slightly stale garlic bread. "So . . ."

I stare at him blankly. "So . . ."

There's the sound of a trumpet, the music dies down and floodlights hit the stage. From behind us, through the crowds, tiptoe three women in long velvet cloaks, hunched and claw-handed.

I frown. "I'm afraid I am not following the logic of this thread."

The women reach the stage, where they kneel down, form a triangle and throw their hoods back to reveal faces wizened and haggard with make-up.

"When shall we three meet again?" The tallest one looks at the sky. "In thunder, lightning, or in rain?"

"Hey!" Henry nudges me. "She likes weather too!"

"*Macbeth*?" I paid no attention in English class, but I only know of one very famous play with three witches in it. "I don't get what this has to do with me."

Henry looks at me in surprise. "The Weyward Sisters?"

I stare at them again. "That's what they're called?"

"Are you kidding?" He laughs. "You didn't know you're named after the most famous witches in English literature?"

An older lady in front of us whips round and hisses, "*Shhhhhh.*"

"*Sorry.*" I make an elaborate zipping motion across my

mouth, and then—when she has turned round again—I throw the imaginary zip at the back of her head. "I didn't know, no. Nobody said anything."

Huh. Isn't this exactly the sort of fact my grandfather should have been informing me of from birth? Enthusiastically and in sweet but frankly unasked-for detail?

"Well." Henry nods at the hunched, decrepit women. "Pretty sure they're your ancestors. Much better-looking, obviously. Improved posture."

I laugh and push the top of his arm. "Sod off."

Another flash of fury from the woman in front of us, and we grin at each other conspiratorially like two naughty kids at the back of class.

"Weyward," Henry whispers, looking so sweetly triumphant. "It was an alternative spelling of weird, by the way."

I nod, looking at the stage.

"Yeah," I say faintly. "That tracks."

FOR THE FIRST ten minutes, I don't have a clue what's happening.

My entire focus is on Henry: how close he's sitting, his hand resting on the blanket right next to mine, the smell of him—different to my visions, slightly sage-like—and the freckle just behind his right ear. Every few seconds, I surreptitiously flick my eyes in his direction so I can study him, totally absorbed in the play. It's so lovely, watching emotions shift across his face like sunrays. Like sitting in front of scenery that keeps changing, oblivious of how beautiful it is to those watching.

"What's going on?" I whisper finally. "I'm a bit lost."

Probably because instead of listening, I'm waiting for him to hold my hand.

"The witches have prophesied that Macbeth will become king," Henry whispers back, still focused on the actors. "So now he's plotting with his wife to kill the king so that it comes true."

Suddenly interested, I stare more closely at the stage. "Isn't that cheating?"

Henry grins. "That's kind of the point."

Much more interested now—and with a faintly creepy tingling sensation at the back of my neck—I pay more attention. "*If chance will have me king, why, chance may crown me without my stir.*" And there it is: the ultimate question. To sit back and let "fate" do its own thing, or actively participate in its completion? Because, when it comes to prophecies, doesn't time become circular? Once known, the prophecy itself becomes part of the future: you essentially become trapped by your own knowledge. Everything you do or do not do—to avoid or chase that vision—leads you to the vision. A vision that wouldn't have happened without the vision itself.

My breath is suddenly strained and tight. I feel incredibly claustrophobic.

But what about free will? What about *choice*?

More importantly—as I watch with mounting horror as Macbeth goes from an apparently nice, normal guy to a mass-murdering sociopath within the space of half an hour, fulfilling the prophecy through force and bloodshed—which am I? The witches or Macbeth? The seeing or the one being seen?

Because it's starting to occur to me I'm *both*.

Which is possibly even worse.

Appalled, I watch as Lady Macbeth goes mad and kills herself, as entire families are murdered offstage, and then as Macbeth—apparently unbothered by all of the above—is brought down by his own complacency and inability to understand what the visions actually *mean*. He thinks he's safe, bubble-wrapped by fate, when actually he's already in pieces—he just doesn't know it. Until finally some dude strolls onto the stage with Macbeth's chopped-off head under his arm.

Well . . . *shit*.

I take a long, deep breath. What a nice, uplifting story about the brutal consequences of knowing too much while also nothing at all.

"Well?" Henry finally turns to me, eyes glowing. "What did you think?"

I think I'm screwed.

"Very interesting," I say as lightly as possible. "Quite a lot of dying."

Henry laughs. "For our next romantic venture, I'll bring you to see *Titus Andronicus*."

I smile faintly, still trying to recalibrate.

Because the *weight* of this gift—curse, whatever it turns out to be—is only now starting to hit me. If my visions are actually true, then every single word I say now, every decision I make, is predestined. I'm nothing more than a breathing chessboard piece: shuffled around by a giant hand I can't see. I have no control. No autonomy. Looking down, I lift my hand slowly, staring at it in awe. Was I always going to do that? If so, was that gesture even *mine*? If not, who does it belong to? Even Banquo couldn't escape the visions—even if he didn't actively chase them—and he died anyway. No wonder Lady Macbeth went batshit. It is a *lot* to process.

"So," I say as casually as possible. "What would you do? If you were in Macbeth's shoes?"

You know, just conversationally. No personal relevance here.

"I'd have nothing to do with any of it." Henry grins easily. "Nope. I bump into three old crones dancing in a circle in the middle of a storm? I'm out of there. No thanks, not for me. Enjoy your Saturday night, ladies."

I laugh, relaxing slightly. "It would be a very short and less famous play."

"A three-minute wonder, and then everyone goes to the pub." Henry fills my glass as the rest of the audience begin to pack up, then he holds out a piece of garlic bread: we're clearly going nowhere. "I have absolutely zero interest in knowing what's going to happen to me. Finding out is the best bit, isn't it?"

"Right." I take the bread and chew on it thoughtfully. "Even if it meant you could prepare for whatever's coming?"

"Ever the meteorologist, huh." He nudges me with an affectionate expression. "I'll forgo my metaphorical umbrella and just risk getting wet, I reckon."

I look at where our shoulders have touched, warmth suddenly radiating.

We are so incredibly different—in outlook, in temperament, in verticalness—but I like it. As if we are on either sides of a scale, balancing each other out. Where I am anxious, he is calm; where I look forward, he is always present.

Henry puts his hand on top of mine and I feel my fingers curl around his.

"And if Winter grows up to become a professional base jumper, which is her current plan," he grins, "at least I'll hopefully be ready to put her back together again, if needs be. Thanks for brainwashing my six-year-old daughter, YouTube."

"Oh yeah?" I study his fingers. "You going to be a magician in the future?"

"Pretty much." He laughs and holds both his hands out. "Although I think they're called surgeons these days."

I blink at them, then up at him. "Wait—what?"

Oh God, here we go. The inevitable Red Flag: forty-something waiter thinks he's going to be allowed to operate after watching two episodes of *Grey's Anatomy.*

"I start back at medical school next September," Henry says easily. "So I'm currently trying to catch up, revising everything I missed."

It feels like I've been joining the dots of Henry, thinking it's a picture of a kitten when it's a bloody spaceship. I did not see this coming either.

"Missed? What do you mean?"

"I was three years into my medical degree when . . ." He pauses, his eyes softening. "We'd just had Winter, so when Amy died there was no chance of me going back. I had a baby to look after, and a lot of shock and grief to deal with, and I needed to be there for Winter all day and also work in the evenings. Now she's finally at school, I've been taking extra shifts at the restaurant while my parents cover the gaps when needed, which is a lot. And then revising when she's in bed."

I suddenly can't quite swallow. "That's . . ."

"Exhausting." Henry smiles with a shrug. "No wonder Winter keeps coming home with drawings of me with wrinkly lines all over my face, the little rotter."

I was actually going to say *amazing. That's amazing. You're amazing.*

"But you're going back?" I can't quite wrap my head around the dedication it takes to go through all of that trauma, pick yourself back up and start studying again in your forties. "And you're training to debut as a surgeon? In your . . . fifties?"

"I'll be fifty-four when I qualify in my specialized area of surgery, yes." Henry laughs. "I was already by far the oldest student on the course when I started the first time round." He sticks his fork in a piece of lasagna. "Worth it, though. I've been playing Operation obsessively since I was four years old, and I don't want to brag, but I win *every* time. And yes, I will be telling my patients that just before the anesthetic kicks in."

I guess that explains the *laminarectomy* conversation, or whatever it was.

"Do you even have *time* to date? Physically?"

"Nope." Henry laughs. "Not at all. I'll have to squeeze you into loo breaks."

"I can be the human equivalent of one of those fact books that gets left on the back of the cistern."

Henry smiles, puts his hand on my cheek and leans forward.

"You weren't part of the plan, Margot," he says quietly as he studies my face. Something in my chest catches, leaps, and there it is: fire. Except it's a different kind, this time. Warm, not burning. Healing, not destructive. No red flags; just a glorious, contained heat. "And that is *exactly* why I prefer not to have one."

Suddenly, I understand why Macbeth went all out to fulfill the prophecy: to do what had to be done to make it happen. Because when you've seen a glimpse of something you really want, it's impossible not to run toward it as hard and as fast as you can. Not to grab for it and hold on tightly. It's difficult to just leave it up to chance, to fate, to the whimsical decisions of a massive, unseen hand.

Not when you know something beautiful is just within your reach.

So screw the consequences; screw the warnings.

Because, as Henry leans in to kiss me and I feel myself light up in a way I haven't for years, all I can think is: this is what I want.

15

THE STAGE EMPTIES, but we stay where we are.

It feels effortless, and it slowly dawns on me that it never really has before. With Aaron, I always had to *try*. I tried so hard, I didn't even realize how much effort I was making until it slowly wore me out. Or perhaps wore me down: smoothing the edges of who I was like water over rocks, until I only realized I'd become a different shape when I finally emerged, totally unrecognizable.

Henry is witty, erudite, sharp—all attractive qualities, big tick—but it's his *kindness* I am blown away by. Compassion seeps from him: not in labored anecdotes about what a "hero" he is, but in the way he grins when I get excited about a cloud and subtly pulls the blanket over my toes when it gets cold and asks questions he can't possibly want the answer to (why, yes, the first thermometer *was* designed by Santorio, thank you for checking). His brown eyes soften when I talk about my grandfather; they shine like light bulbs when he talks about Winter.

And as night falls and we keep talking, I realize I'm not studying Henry's face for subtle shifts—the tightening of a jaw muscle, a dark flicker in the eyes. Signs I grew so used to reading because they signaled danger. One wrong word and the ground would rumble: Aaron's mood would shift, and everything would tilt with it.

With Henry, the world is still and calm but slightly giddy.

Admittedly I'm also pretty tipsy now, but for that I'm blaming the Prosecco.

"DAMN." HENRY GLANCES at his watch. "It's nearly eleven."

I look around in surprise: the park is dark and cool, and we've now been sitting on the ground for four hours.

"You need to go?" I sound tangibly disappointed. "Already?"

"It's the last train back to Bath in half an hour, so I really need to get to the station." He grins at me. "Logistics only, and no shade at all on your company, which is delightful."

I grin back and glance down, cheeks glowing with pleasure.

"I could . . ." don't be too keen, don't be too keen ". . . walk you to the station? You know, like I offered to last time?"

"Ah, before I stomped off like a hormonal teenager." Henry grimaces. "That would be lovely and extremely gentlewomanly of you. Thank you, Margot."

His formality is so sweet, a little archaic: Jimmy Stewart vibes.

Beaming, I help tidy up. It's embarrassing how eager I am to squeeze out my time with him. I feel like a small kid who knows it's way past bedtime but is attempting to quietly disappear between the sofa cushions so that nobody notices.

We start wandering back toward the lights of the city.

"You're working this weekend?" I can't figure out why I'm not slightly out of breath, and then I realize it's because Henry isn't walking three paces ahead of me, rolling his eyes, pointedly urging me to catch up. "At the restaurant?"

"Tomorrow night." He nods. "My parents have Winnie. They adopted a new puppy and I suspect she'll be putting in an application to move in permanently. She spends enough time there as it is. I honestly don't know what I'd do without them. You?"

I think briefly about the sheer mess I've made of my career.

"Actually," I admit, slightly evasively, "I think I'll be taking some time off."

"You run an Instagram account, right?" When I look questioningly at him—I've deliberately avoided this topic—Henry laughs. "I'm just basing this information off what Fireman Henry was yelling in the restaurant."

"Ah." I nod. "Yes. It's . . ." I take a deep breath and decide to tell the humiliating truth. "I was happy where I was, at the Met Office, but . . . I couldn't stay. Not after everything. Exeter is too small, Aaron still works in the same building, and I couldn't risk running into him daily. Lily has a very successful Instagram account, and . . . some dark, obsessive part of me felt a need to compete with her. How humiliating is that?"

"It sounds pretty human to me," Henry says calmly.

"That's only the start of it." I feel a sudden need to unburden myself, as if I'm testing fate: prodding at it, to see if it buckles. "I have a fake online profile, and I've been leaving comments. Nice ones, but still. I'm a nearly forty-year-old woman, trolling my ex–best friend with compliments under the guise of a squirrel."

Henry laughs. "It's not working, Margot."

"What's not working?"

"Trying to put me off you. We all do weird shit when nobody's looking. For instance, I'm a bit of a hypochondriac."

I grin at him in surprise. "Aren't you, like, a doctor-in-waiting?"

"That's the problem. Every time I read about a rare condition in a textbook, I convince myself I have it. Last year, I spent half an hour absolutely positive I had acquired methemoglobinemia because I'd woken up short of breath, with a blue tint to my hands and chocolate-colored blood on the bedsheets. I was so certain, I panic-ordered a blood count kit so I could test myself in the living room."

"And it wasn't, I'm assuming?"

"No, Margot. I did not have methemoglobinemia. I finally looked in the mirror and realized Winter had decorated me with blue face paints while I was asleep. And the chocolate-colored blood? Chocolate. She'd been eating Christmas pennies next to me while watching cartoons. And leaning on my chest."

I laugh loudly. Under the streetlamps, his face radiates with pride.

"You won't be laughing when I'm convinced a shaving rash is shingles." Henry grimaces. "I'm a grown man who checks his own temperature every night, just in case he has sudden-onset hyperthyroidism."

I feel another wave of warmth toward him. Is it really so surprising that a man whose young wife abruptly died is a little vigilant about health conditions? I feel a strange flicker of surprise. And is it *totally* irrational and crazy that a woman whose fiancé ran off with her best friend on the night before her wedding is a little hung up on (OK, obsessed with) both of them for a bit while she processes the situation? I think that's the first time I've given myself some compassion for the way I've reacted. Somehow, Henry's kindness is making me be kinder to myself too. His total lack of judgment toward everyone is making me judge myself less as well.

I stop walking: we've reached the train station without me noticing.

Damn it. That was way too fast.

"So . . ." I awkwardly stick my hands in my jacket pockets and realize the marble is in there, cold and reassuring. I roll it around between my fingers. "I've had a really nice night, Henry. Thank you so much."

When what I mean is: kiss me. Kiss me, kiss me, kiss me, *kiss me.*

"I have too." He takes a step forward, then pauses awkwardly. "Shall we do it again? At some point? Maybe next week?"

"Yes." I feel punctured: next week is too long. "I'd love that. Or . . ."

I open my mouth, shut it again, frown. Fuck it.

"You know, there's a walking path along the railway line. From Bristol to Bath. It's about twelve miles. I looked it up. When I was . . . casually researching local routes."

Henry lifts his eyebrows. "Twelve miles? That's about three hours to walk."

"Just over three hours." I nod. "Which would take us to . . . past two a.m. I've actually been meaning to stay more active. You know, get the blood pumping."

He laughs. "Pumping blood is good. Important. Living-wise."

"This is purely an opportunity for some impulsive exercise," I say as we both start beaming at each other conspiratorially. "That's all. Just a casual midnight stroll to improve my cardio levels and get my steps up."

"Well." Henry pretends to think about it. "As a doctor-in-training, I think that sounds extremely sensible. Necessary, even. For your health."

I laugh. "So, shall we do it? You don't think I'm being too keen?"

"I think you're being embarrassingly keen." Henry holds his hand out and smiles. "And I absolutely bloody love it. Let's go."

HENRY AND I walk all the way to Bath.

Holding hands the whole way, we stroll along the dark railway line, chatting the entire time. I find out that he comes from a town just outside Manchester—hence the delicious accent—and that he has an English degree and worked as a teacher until his early thirties.

"Fifteen years of medical training just seemed way too long when I was younger," he explained. "Too much of my life to invest. Then I turned round one day and realized I was the age I would have been if I'd just done what I really loved in the first place. Time was going to happen with or without my input, so I might as well spend it wisely."

Just like that: as if he understands the answer to a question the rest of us don't even know how to ask.

"And you wouldn't go back to teaching, just temporarily?"

Henry shakes his head. "I can't risk giving myself an alternative route in case I get stuck in it by accident."

Every layer of Henry just makes him more extraordinary. I

want to know everything about him: what food he likes, what makes him laugh, what sets his world on fire, what makes him anxious, and it feels like I'll never run out of questions to ask.

And Henry wants to know all about me: about my unplaceable accent (a strange hybrid of Bristolian and Australian), my relationship with my grandfather and how I feel now my parents live so far away, about Eve's baby journey and the articles Jules writes and the way my friends feel part of me in some integral way, like organs.

By the time we arrive in Bath, Henry feels like somebody I have always known.

Somebody I will always *want* to know.

But mainly what I feel is gratitude to my visions, for forcing me to give Henry a chance. Because if that's all they've done, I'll take it. If they don't come true? It's still enough. I can take it from here, Universe. Signs acknowledged, I've got it.

"So." Henry stops outside a regal, decaying period property. "This is me."

"You're very old," I observe, looking up. "With extremely big windows and ornate moldings."

"Tricky to heat is what everyone says about me." Henry smiles and takes a step toward me. This time, there's no hesitation. "I like you, Margot. You're scary but kind of impressive."

"Like a box jellyfish."

"No." He grins and puts his hands on either side of my face. "Like a shark. Ha—I think I shall call you Meg the Megalodon."

My stomach glows. That's exactly what he called me in my vision, and I can literally *feel* the future fitting into place like a perfect jigsaw. It's just another piece of evidence that I can't have imagined: it's all coming true.

"Aren't they extinct?"

"Well, I just found one. With a bite that could crush a car."

"Just kiss me," I grin with an eye roll. "And stop talking about fish."

As Henry kisses me, the fire leaps from my stomach through my chest and into my arms until they wrap around him like two magnets. I feel fifteen again: as if this is my first kiss, my last kiss, and everything in between.

"Should I call you a cab?" We separate reluctantly. "To get you safely back to Bristol?"

I study Henry's face, wondering how I ever found it anything other than beautiful. It is a perfect face: a face I want to swipe right on, as many times as I possibly can.

"No," I say firmly. "I'm coming in."

IT'S AMAZING HOW quickly I've adjusted to the extraordinary.

In less than two weeks, I have gone from bewildered by my visions to taking them in my stride. As Henry shows me with sweet pride around a flat I've already seen before, I note with bizarre complacency the dark green velvet couch covered in a thick mustard blanket: the very one I will (possibly?) be sweating and shivering under at some point in the future. I note the same ornate Victorian fireplace—candles unlit this time—the oil painting of a ship and the dark gray walls still the color of a pavement in the rain.

With a sense of slight bemusement—something is off—I frown and study the room, suddenly realizing that the large indoor tree is in a different place. I feel a lurch of my stomach: what if the tree stays there? If that one thing changes, does the future peel away like cheap wallpaper? And if so, how do I stick it back up?

"Oh," Henry says, following my gaze. "Hang on."

Without another word, he walks over and lugs it to the exact spot in the window alcove where I saw it in my vision.

"Henry." I stare at him. "Why did you do that?"

Time feels flickering and delicate, like a candle about to blow out.

"Oh." Henry scratches his beard. "That's where it normally lives. I only moved it because Winnie was doing some kind of dance routine in front of the window yesterday."

With a bewildered nod, I gaze around the room, taking in

details I was too sick to notice last time. Henry's flat is full of character, just like him. Trinkets collected and books with broken spines; paintings, plants and lights. I nod in appreciation: *this* is what a home should feel like. It just begs the question of why we move into mine, not his. Surely it would make sense the other way round?

There's a collection of framed photos organized on the mantelpiece, and I pause to study them. One is clearly of Amy—laughing with a baby Winter in her arms—and my chest hurts: I cannot conceive of that great a loss. Poor, poor Henry. Poor, poor Winnie.

My stomach suddenly drops. "Who is this?"

It's a large black-and-white photograph of a beautiful lady dressed in a flapper costume with arched eyebrows and a wry smile. More significantly, it's the unknown portrait in the gold frame that I saw on the wall in my vision of my flat.

"That's my grandmother," Henry says with warmth. "She died when I was little, but I still miss her. You're so lucky to still have your grandfather."

"I am." I smile: another piece of the puzzle slots into place.

"So . . ." Henry puts his arms around me and I feel myself soften into the solidity of him. "What do you think? Are my crumbling original features a deal-breaker?"

"Well," I laugh. "Actually, I think they're something I could—"

A familiar chill runs down my spine: time is shivering through me like sand in an hourglass, moving me from one place to another.

WE'RE ON A windswept beach, and Henry's arms are still around me. I'm swaddled in a woolly hat and scarf. I feel myself immediately relax in Henry's arms: whenever or wherever I am now, he's still here. It's no longer frightening because I'm now certain that all my visions will have him in them; I will never have to be here on my own.

"You've gone again," he says in a low voice.

"Oh." I blink, then stare at the sea in an attempt to ground myself: choppy, gray, it looks like winter. "Yes. Sorry. Where are we?"

Somehow, this version of me has managed to infiltrate Future Margot in order to ask a basic geographical question; I think I'm slowly gaining a tiny bit of control over her. Even if it makes us both sound stupid.

"Weston-super-Mare." Henry takes my question in his stride—I'm clearly forgetful in the future—and kisses the side of my suddenly cold, runny nose. "I treat you to all the most exotic locations."

"You certainly do."

Instinctively, I lift my hand to wipe the dribble from my nose and feel something sharp catch the side of my nostril. With a pulse of shock, I pull my hand away and stare at it. There's a gold band on my ring finger: small, dainty, with the world's tiniest diamond.

"Holy fuck," I say out loud.

"Yes, it's pretty impressive." Henry grins and squeezes me tightly. "Thanks for the sweary validation."

I stare at the ring in amazement. Bloody hell.

This relationship just went from first proper date to engaged in literally thirty seconds: it's the fastest courtship known to man. Apparently I don't just move in with Henry, I'm going to *marry* him, or at least agree to. For a second, I feel a twist of fear—not another bloody wedding—and then it abruptly disappears. Henry is not Aaron. Our wedding will not be that not-wedding. Even this ring feels exactly as it should: comfortable, small, sweet. It fits my hand in a way the other one never did. More importantly, I can *feel* my contentment, or—more specifically—Other Margot's contentment: a sense that everything is *right*.

She's happy. So incredibly, unfeasibly happy, and I'm suddenly grateful to her for letting me share a few moments of it.

"I love it," I say quietly. "It's perfect."

"*I* think it should have been amethyst," a little voice behind me says breathlessly. "When *I* get married, it's going to be a bright purple amethyst or I'm saying no thank you very much, I'll marry someone with better taste."

Henry chuckles, and as I spin round, Winter zooms off again toward the ocean and my breath catches. She's taller, lankier. Her hair is darker and much longer, knotted by the wind. She must be about nine years old.

Three years. We get engaged in three years.

"Henry," I feel myself say quietly, "I want you to know that—"

AND I'M BACK.

Except . . . what did I want him to know? It suddenly feels like it was Future Margot slipping in again and taking back the reins. Trying to tell him something important from the future; I just don't know what it *was*.

"Hey." Henry frowns and pulls away slightly, studying my face. "You OK?"

We're back in the living room: my clothes are different, my nose is no longer running. I look down briefly. My ring finger is empty again. A thread of happiness tugs through me, like a bright gold string: not at the ring's absence, but at its potential arrival.

"I'm good." I nod. "Sorry, I just . . . got lost for a second there."

Because when I'm there, in the future, I can feel exactly what Other Margot feels: her emotions momentarily become mine. Which makes logical sense to me. If it *is* the future, then I am *all* the Margots. I am the Margot to come and the Margot of now, but I'm also the Margot that remembers the vision when she gets there, so I simultaneously become the Margot of the past too.

For those few, confusing seconds, I am all the different versions of me in one place.

And all I feel when I'm there is . . . love.

Not just for Henry—that's pretty clear by now—but for Winter too. As I watched this little girl I've yet to meet run to the edges of the waves, squeaking at the cold and hopping up and down, I felt an almost painful kind of love: one I've never experienced before. It's fierce, almost feral, as if I would fight the entire ocean if it tried to even touch her feet. It's a lot to adjust to, in three seconds: that much brand-new love, in one go.

"So . . ." Henry smiles. "What do you want to do now?"

The love is still there. Not in the same intensity—I haven't got to it yet—but I can feel the spark of the beginning, glowing in my chest.

"I want to stay the night," I state simply. "With you. If that's OK."

Henry laughs so loudly I flinch slightly, moderately concerned he may have burst one of my eardrums.

"So direct," he says with a chuckle. "I think I'll allow it."

16

MARGOT? MARGOT, WAKE up."

"Nope."

A short laugh. "I mean it, Margot. You have to go."

"Already?" With gritty eyes, I roll backward and smile at Henry over my shoulder. "For a wannabe doctor, your bedside manner is terrible."

Henry grins and kisses my shoulder blade, his silver fringe tufting upward at the front like a cute duck. All I'll say is that last night was exactly the kind of sex I'd hope for with a man I'm planning on potentially spending the rest of my life with. Sex that is statistically only going to get better, which at this point seems physically impossible, but I'm very much looking forward to giving it a go anyway.

"What time is it?" I rub my eyes. "Have we slept until evening?"

"It's seven a.m.," Henry says, grabbing a sock and hopping round the room, trying to pull it on. I watch his lovely back with a slightly smug cat smile on my face, staring at the star-constellation moles on his back. I am *much* more familiar with them now. "My mum just texted. She's on her way with Winter."

All smugness and any remaining sleepiness evaporate immediately.

"Wait—what? *Now?*"

"Now." Henry's clearly panicking too. "Winnie had a bad night and she insisted on coming home first thing. It's Sod's

Law—she normally angles to stay over there as long as possible. Where's your bloody jacket gone?"

"Winter's coming *now*?" I repeat, frozen to the spot.

"I *know*," he says desperately, spinning in a circle around the bedroom. "No offense, but it's *way* too early for you to meet her."

Absolutely no offense taken. It's *way* too early. I need to prepare properly before I meet the tiny human who's potentially going to play such a huge part in my life. I have a rather nasty habit of trying to shake the hands of children before desperately handing them loose change from my pocket.

Henry's phone beeps and he glances at it with wild eyes. "Five minutes!"

"Oh *crap*," I say, snapping into action. "I need to *go*."

Panic spreading, I grab my jacket from behind a curtain and we both run like chickens around his apartment looking for my handbag. It has apparently evaporated, much like any of the residual sexiness from last night. Nothing punctures giddiness quite like two people screaming *shiiiiiiittt* while looking under the sofa.

Henry looks up hopefully. "Can you go without it?"

I stare at him for a few seconds. "Not unless I want to be homeless, penniless and uncontactable for the foreseeable future, no."

"Sorry." He grimaces. "Got a bit carried away there."

"The fridge!" I shout, standing up and running into the kitchen. "I put it on top of the fridge! Got it!" With a cry of triumph, I grab my handbag and hold it aloft as if I've just won an Olympic medal. "Score!"

"Oh, thank God." Henry breathes out. "Right. To be clear, I had every plan of making you a coffee and then taking you out for an elaborate brunch, but we're going to have to put a pin in that because I do not want to explain to my six-year-old why a stranger is in her house for the first time ever at seven a.m. on a Saturday."

"Really?" I glow at him. "The first time ever?"

"Focus, Megalodon," he laughs, grabbing me and giving me a very quick kiss. I feel myself instinctively lean in for another one. He goes with it for a few seconds, then sighs and breaks away. "And when I see you next, I'll tell you what an amazing evening I had and how great I think you are. But right now you have to *go*."

"I'm gone," I say quickly, giving him a third kiss. "I'll look forward to a full evaluation of our time together when I see you next. With a grade, ideally."

"It's a solid A-minus," Henry grins. "This has brought us down from an A-plus."

He gives me another quick peck, as if we're magnets and can't seem to stop touching each other, and a wave of warmth pulses through my face: I've never been so happy to be unceremoniously booted out of someone's home.

"Shoes!" Henry shouts as I open the front door.

"Got them!" I grab them from the welcome mat and take a few steps backward, barefoot. "I'll text you when I get—"

There's a small noise behind me and I freeze.

Fuckity fucking fuck—

Slowly, I turn round. Winter is standing directly behind me, at the top of the iron staircase that leads up to Henry's flat. Her hair is in the wonky plaits traditionally given by grandparents. This may be my first real-life sighting of her, but she looks—and by this point, there's no surprise at all—exactly as I knew she would: just slightly smaller, and with a missing front tooth. Behind her, a lady who looks astonishingly like Henry is staring at me in bemusement: silver hair, same brown eyes, same strong albeit unbroken nose.

One more minute: that's all I needed to get away unseen.

One minute, and I spent it kissing Henry four times. Can't say I regret it, if I'm being fully honest.

"Who are you?" Winter's voice is high-pitched but sweet, a little bird singing. "And why aren't you wearing your shoes?"

Henry's mother looks me up and down, seeing everything: just like her son.

I turn to where the front door is opening again and Henry is now standing with a shell-shocked expression on his face.

"Um," Henry says, rubbing a hand on top of his head. "So, this is—"

"I'm your new cleaner," I improvise quickly. "I like to clean very early in the morning. You know, before everyone wakes up." I look down with a wave of inspiration. "And I take my shoes off so I don't muddy up the floor! Saves time."

Henry's mother isn't buying it, and neither—sadly—is Winter. The little girl glowers at me suspiciously, and I have to bite back a smile: she has the exact same expression as her dad when he's concentrating.

"So if you just got here, why were you leaving? And where's all your cleaning stuff?"

I thought children were supposed to be easy to lie to: the entire industry of Christmas is kind of based on this premise.

That, and bribery.

"I'm, uh, just cleaning the welcome mat first." I quickly bend down and pick a bit of mud off it, then randomly toss it into their neighbor's garden. "Done! And I'm going to use your cleaning equipment. So it smells the same."

I glance back at Henry and see he's trying very hard not to laugh.

Thanks for the support, buddy.

"OK . . ." Winter's face relaxes slightly. "But you mustn't touch my teddies. They're arranged in the *exact* right order."

"Noted," I say with a small wave of warmth for her. "No teddy touching."

"Well." Henry's mother is still studying me intensely. "It's very nice to meet you . . ."

"Margot," I say quickly, apologizing to her with my eyes.

"Margot." She nods with a small smile. "Henry, Winnie will tell you what happened. Let's just say the puppy peed somewhere he should not have peed."

"On my *bed*," Winter says fiercely, still clearly outraged. "Daddy, he peed on my *bed*. It got on my *dinosaur pajamas*."

"What a rotter," Henry says, amused. "No more water for him. Thanks, Mum. You're a lifesaver, as always. I'll call you tomorrow."

He ushers Winter through the door and then mouths *thank you* at me.

"So are you coming in, then?" Winter turns around and looks at me expectantly with her strangely direct hazel eyes. "You can clean the kitchen first. Daddy is really, really messy when he cooks."

Henry flinches slightly. "Cheers, dude."

I stare at both of them for a few seconds, unsure how to get out of this. Suffice to say, I did not think this impulsive lie through properly, because it now looks like I'm going to have to go back in and *clean*.

"Great," I say, giving up. "I'll start with the kitchen."

OK, THERE'S NO way my visions of my future with Henry are accurate, because at this rate I'll have murdered him by lunchtime.

"Here's the antibacterial spray," he says, plonking it on the worktop. "Some cloths. A nice scouring pad. Do you clean ovens, perchance?"

Then he stares at me, shaking slightly with suppressed laughter.

"No," I say through gritted teeth. "I do not clean bloody *ovens*."

"Blood doesn't actually get in our oven," Winter chirps up from where she's standing next to him, still watching me carefully. "We're vegetarian in this house, aren't we, Daddy? We don't murder animals."

"We don't," Henry agrees. "Unless they pee on our beds."

Winter shoots him a horrified glance. "*Dad.*"

"*Joking,*" he adds with a laugh, pushing her slightly with his hand. "Come on, Winnie. We've talked about jokes."

"Jokes are supposed to be funny," she informs him imperiously.

"Yes," I say pointedly. "They are."

"Aren't you supposed to be cleaning?" Henry grins back at me, clearly enjoying himself way too much. "Underneath the fridge could do with a good sweep."

"I'll sweep *you*," I mumble under my breath, picking up the cloth and tentatively spraying the worktop. "I'll sweep you right into next week."

"I'll go get the vacuum then," he says cheerfully. "Speed things up."

Henry leaves the room with a small chuckle and I feel my nostrils flare slightly: I will find a way to avenge myself, even if it takes years.

I start half-heartedly scrubbing the kitchen tap.

"Are you named after Margot Fountain?" Winter is following me around like a little shadow, watching everything I do. "And have you always wanted to be a cleaner? I want to be a vet so I can save animals, but I don't want to make them sleep forever, so Daddy says I have to be really good at it."

I pause from where I'm uselessly wiping a cabinet. "Fountain?"

"Margot Fountain," Winter explains patiently. "The ballerina. I've seen videos of her. I like ballet. I think I might be a vet during the day, and a ballerina at night. Daddy says like Superman but with a tutu."

"Margot *Fonteyn*." I look at the little girl in surprise: the famous prima ballerina retired from dancing before *I* was born, let alone before Winter was. "I am, actually. Yes. My mother had high hopes that I'd be a dancer too."

"Not a cleaner?" Winter asks innocently. "That's sad."

"Nothing sad about being a cleaner," Henry says firmly, coming back into the room, notably minus a vacuum. "Your dad is a waiter, remember? Very upstanding professions. You know, Margot, as this is your very first session, I thought maybe we could just use it to show you the flat? Forget the cleaning this one time."

He winks at me. I try not to grin back but fail miserably.

"Oooh!" Winter jumps up and down. "Start with my bedroom! I want you to see my rock collection so you know how to clean it properly!"

She races off and Henry puts an arm around me. "What are your rates like? Because you don't seem very well trained."

"Sod all the way off," I laugh. "Or I'll pee on your bed."

"Come quickly!" Winter yells. "We have a *lot* to get through."

"Welcome to my life," Henry says dryly as we walk toward the room. "You will now be forced to make teddies perform elaborately staged plays where only my daughter has the script and everything you say is inexplicably wrong."

It's extremely strange, how *normal* this all feels. As if I've slotted straight into a place I was supposed to be. I feel weirdly proud: I've spent so long avoiding children, believing I lacked *the mum gene*, but maybe I'm not as bad as I thought. Granted, Henry's child thinks I'm staff, but I'll take the win where I can.

"Daddy!" Winter pokes her head round the door just as Henry whips his arm from my shoulder. "Do you know where I put my stereoscope, so we can listen to the teddies' heartbeats?"

"It's a stethoscope," Henry says warmly. "And it's mine, Winnie, as I've told you multiple times, but I think it's under the—"

"I *HATE* YOU."

I blink in shock at a completely empty living room: one I don't recognize at all.

Where the hell am I this time?

A door slams somewhere above me. Turning, I spot a wooden staircase. Lying on the bottom step—stretched out luxuriously—is the biggest cat I have ever seen. It's bright orange with giant triangular ears, and it takes up so much space its paws are up the wall on one side and hanging over the edge on the other.

The cat looks at me, yawns like a tiger and promptly goes back to sleep.

"Winter!" I hear knocking upstairs and Henry's voice, firm but clearly furious. "Young lady, get your arse downstairs and *apologize*."

"No! I won't!"

"You will or I'm going to ground you until you're sixty."

The door opens and I watch in bewilderment as a young woman thunders down the stairs toward me, jumping right over the still-unconscious cat. Her hair is cut into a jagged bob and she's wearing a black crop top and baggy jeans. She's angular, tall, lean, all elbows and collarbones, and she's radiating pure rage: directly at me.

"Winter?" I say in bewilderment. In literally thirty seconds, Henry's little girl has become a teenager. A very, very angry fifteen-year-old. With a lot of mascara and a pair of blunt scissors at her disposal.

"*What?*" she snaps at me. "What do you want *now*?"

I blink as Henry comes down the stairs, also stepping neatly over the cat, who seems totally accustomed to all the drama.

"One of these days you're going to get stepped on, Cheds."

Henry looks older too, but it suits him: his hair is now entirely silver, and I feel a sharp, hot pang in my stomach.

"What did I do?" I ask him in amazement.

"You didn't *do* anything," he sighs tiredly. "It's like having an active volcano in the house. Winter, say sorry to Margot right now!"

"I will not!" She whips round and glares at me. "This is *your* fault."

I open my mouth. "I—"

"You're so *embarrassing*," Winter continues without taking a breath, lava erupting everywhere. "With your stupid *costumes* and your stupid *catchphrases* and your *stupid cloud*. Why did you have to turn up looking like that? I am *mortified* and I will *never, ever recover.*"

Um, what costumes? What catchphrases? What cloud? What did I turn up looking like, and where? What have I done to this poor girl?

"Stop being so dramatic," Henry tells her sharply. "All Meg has done is pick you up from school at the last minute straight after work. In other words, go out of her way for you. As always."

"I didn't *ask* her to, Dad. She's not my *mum*."

"How *dare* you?" Henry now fully erupts too. "After everything that— Right. Your big sleepover next weekend? Canceled."

"Dad—"

"Rosie's birthday party? You're not going."

"*Dad!*"

"In fact, say goodbye to all your parties for the next month. You can't socialize with other humans until you've learned how to do it at home."

"Oh my God!" Winter glares at me with pure venom. "Thanks very much, *Margot*."

Crushed, I stare at her. "I'm so sorr—"

"MARGOT? ARE YOU alright?"

I'm standing in the hallway of Henry's flat again, but it feels like I've just been hit by a truck. A teenage-girl truck composed of hormones and anger and what appears to be roughly nine years of built-up resentment toward me.

Scrap all my hopes of a positive relationship: Winter is going to *hate* me.

"Oh." I nod at Henry, totally devastated. "Just a head rush, that's all."

"Again?" He frowns in concern. "Is there something going on with your blood pressure? I'm going to have a look. Hang on while I grab the Hypochondria Kit."

"I'm fine," I say quickly. "Just tired."

That's the furthest forward I've seen, and it's a lot more draining: it appears to take considerably more energy to jump ahead that far.

"Look!" The tiny version of Winter appears at the doorway and grabs my hand so she can drag me into her bedroom.

"I've put them in order of my favorites. This is number one. It's called amethyst."

I stare at her neat little box of semi-precious stones as she chatters away, excitedly pointing out what they all are: tiger's eye, jasper, agate (she pronounces it a-gate). All of the glow I felt has abruptly disappeared. This sweet, happy little girl evaporates at some point, but am I the cause of it? The vision indicates that Henry and I are in it for the long run, but also that I'm going to be the world's worst stepmother.

Also, in the future I apparently live in a carpeted house and wear "costumes" and use "catchphrases" and do something with a *cloud*—technology, maybe? Which proves my Instagram page is doomed. What do I eventually become? Please don't let forty-five-year-old me wear an inflatable hot-dog costume and stand on the street spinning an advertising banner, because that would be the cherry on the humiliating meteorological-career cake.

Plus, we have a cat called *Cheds.* What kind of stupid name is *Cheds*? What is it even short for? Cheddite? Have we named a pet after a French explosive device? I hate cats. What is Future Margot *doing*?

"Hey." Henry puts a gentle hand on Winter's fluffy head, watching my expression carefully. "Winnie, I think we might be overwhelming Margot. Shall we leave the rocks for another time?"

I blink, trying to pull myself together.

I'd begun to hope my visions were accurate, and now I'm suddenly not so sure. Is this what I want? To enter Henry's life and destroy Winter's in the process? Is there not some way I can keep the *good* bits of the future while erasing the *bad* bits? Can I not retain *some* kind of control over what's going to happen, like an overly expensive pick 'n' mix? Take out the horrible ones, keep the ones I like? Lovely ring and lovely Henry: yes, please. Furious stepdaughter who hates me: no, thank you.

With a quick glance at Henry's gorgeous face—and a quick flashback of last night—I decide that I can at least *try.* Slightly desperately, I try to work out how to set this thread straight as fast as physically possible. How can I make this little girl warm to me? Reverting to form, I impulsively reach into my pocket and pull out some change.

"Hey," I say, holding out thirty-five pence in shrapnel. "Do you want money?"

Bribery and corruption: I'll start there.

17

BUT THE VISION has deflated me, as if the cloud I've been floating on has condensed into rain. By the time I leave the house (equipped with handwritten instructions for how to clean Winter's shell collection and a £5 "tip"), I just feel sad. And I know it's ridiculous—I can't expect *every* vision to be a lovely one—but this feels like a big deal. I don't want to spend the next nine years being hated. I definitely don't want to wear a "costume" or have "catchphrases."

I one hundred percent don't want any kind of pet.

Plus the sheer *frequency* of these visions seems to be speeding up, and it's a concern. What happens next? Are they going to start crowding together until I'm just sitting in an armchair, staring into the distance, dribbling into whatever the hell I've started wearing? I don't think that's a gift I want; no wonder *Macbeth*'s witches look so haggard.

I've just returned home for a long bath—attempting to ignore yet another concerned call from my mother—when the doorbell rings. I rack my brain with all the possible options of who it could be: Eve or Jules. Blimey, I should really start expanding my social circle.

"One second!" Dripping, I grab the first towel I see. "Hang on!"

The doorbell goes again. Slightly panicked, I shuffle with wet feet a lot faster, very aware that my towel is not really doing what it's designed to do, in either drying or covering.

Doesn't matter; they've already seen everything.

"*Wait*," I say as the bell goes again and I drop the towel while attempting to open the front door. "Jesus Christ, *patience*, people."

Barely covered, I stare at Polly standing on the welcome mat, polished and smart in a crisp white shirt and black leggings. She laughs and I abruptly realize I'm still wearing the bright green face mask I thought I'd be enjoying in private.

"What an impressive early-morning routine," she grins. "I thought you'd be asleep."

"And yet you're here," I retort, instinctively prickly. I pull my towel down a little and end up exposing too much on top. "On a Saturday. Ringing my doorbell without sending a text first and waking me up, should I actually be asleep."

"Sorry." She doesn't look sorry. "I couldn't wait."

All Polly's Zen-like calmness has gone. I look down in surprise: she's bouncing on her tiptoes like a small kid turning up at a birthday party. Any residual irritation evaporates. It's not her fault I'm grumpy—it's the visions, and also probably too much sex and not enough sleep.

"What's happened?" My stomach spins. "Is it my Instagram page?"

They've blocked me for reprehensible behavior; they're suing me for fraud. I'm minutes away from being dragged out of my new flat in nothing but what appears to be a hand towel.

"Nope!" Polly smiles. "You've stopped losing followers."

I blow out in relief. "That sounds good?"

"Oh yes." She nods. "We've put a halt to it, stopped the leak, so to speak. Unlike my bladder after kids. But that's not what I'm here about."

I lift my eyebrows. "Is this the kind of conversation I want to have naked?"

"Probably not." Polly laughs again. "Sorry. Put some clothes on and come next door." She starts bouncing down the path, then pauses and turns. "You know what, I haven't felt this excited about work for ages. See you in a minute."

"Right," I say faintly. "I guess I'll get dressed, then."

"HELLO!" POLLY SWINGS her door open and beams. "Come in! I've made coffee. You look like you need one."

"Rude," I say flatly.

"You're welcome." My neighbor grins, and I grin back: she gets me. "Sorry for the mess," she adds automatically, gesturing at her ridiculously spotless kitchen. "Three kids under nine, it's practically a circus."

I look around curiously: the room is sophisticated but full of warmth, not unlike Polly herself. Beautifully daubed children's paintings are stuck to the fridge in colors that exactly match the decor of pale greens and pinks. I briefly wonder if she gave the children a color palette before they got too creative, or whether they're so well trained that they created tonal pictures of their own accord.

"So what's going on?" I take the seat she's pulled out. "My curiosity is piqued."

"I went for dinner last night with an old friend from university," Polly says, taking the seat opposite me. "And I mentioned you."

"You told them your insane neighbor is having a mental breakdown and is starting random fires in the garden at illegal times of night?"

"Well, yes." She smiles. "But then I told her who you were."

I blink. "Who am I?"

"Margot the Meteorologist," she says slowly, excitement mounting. "I said I'd taken on a bit of freelance work to help your brand and she got *really* excited. Her kids watch your videos too. They're obsessed and have become weather fanatics, making their own little weather stations out of plastic bottles and pointing out cloud names and whatnot."

I nod, slightly embarrassed: the plastic bottle was an early video. I was having a particularly wobbly day and the adult comments were not very kind.

"Right . . ." I say slowly. "That's cool. But I'm not sure what—"

"Margot, she's really high up in the BBC."

Polly sits back and watches my blank face in amusement as I struggle to join the dots.

"To be clear, I already knew this." She grins at my confusion. "Hence arranging a dinner with her straight after seeing you. I'd been thinking about your page, and your next step seemed obvious. Charlie—that's her name by the way, Charlotte Taylor—she agrees. We both think there's a hole in the market for a children's weather show fronted by a highly trained meteorologist with a gift for making it exciting and fun."

I frown. "Which would be . . ."

"You," Polly confirms. "Potentially, yes. Obviously you'd have to meet her, we'd have to discuss how it would work. I'd come on specifically to build your brand, which would be super exciting for me too. But this is just the first step."

I stare at her. "I can't be on television."

"Why not?" She calmly pours me more coffee, which I immediately swig as fast as physically possible. "You're already making videos. It's just a different format."

"But . . ." I frown. *I only did it out of vengeance and spite* doesn't sound very professional. "I'm not very *good*."

"You are," Polly says firmly. "Sod the adults, it's the kids who love you. Your excitement about the weather is contagious, and you explain meteorology in a clear, bright way that really seems to catch their imaginations. Don't you want to ignite the minds of an entire generation of budding meteorologists?"

I scowl slightly. "Not particularly, no."

Polly laughs. "Yes, you do. Bet you didn't see *this* coming, huh?"

For a second, I wonder if she knows about my visions, then realize she's talking meteorologically, which is a relief.

"I need to think about it," I say slowly, standing up so I can anxiously start circling the kitchen like a tiger in a cage. "I'm not sure that it's really . . . me."

I'm not entirely sure what *me* is, but I'm pretty sure it's not *that*.

"I think it could be." She smiles as I turn and circle back

in the opposite direction. "At least think about it. Think how *fun* it could be."

I swallow: think how many *kids* would be watching me screw up.

"Does she know about . . ." I pause by the fridge and stare blankly at the beautifully color-coordinated daubing. "You know. My fraudulent behavior and huge loss of followers and sponsors?"

"Oh," Polly flicks a hand, "it's no big deal, Margot. Seriously. You got conned too. The internet just overreacted, as usual."

I frown, still staring at the fridge paintings. I'm not going to go back to the Met Office, and I'm definitely running out of steam on Instagram, if I ever really had any to start with. "I suppose that—"

I stop. My stomach goes cold.

In the bottom corner of the freezer door, wonky and presumably stuck there by very small hands, is a photograph. In it, Polly is beaming at the camera in a green Barbour jacket and wellies—very aspirational—and is covered in three pretty, fair-haired children as if they're climbing a tree. Next to her is an extremely handsome man, smiling for the camera. It's a man I've seen before. A man I had dinner with a couple of weeks ago.

There is no *possible* way this is happening: the statistical odds are just too low.

"Oh!" Polly gets up to stand next to me. "Not the best photo—look how windswept I am. I think one of the kids stole it from Pete."

I blink at the man again. "Pete?"

"Peter, my husband. Really rare to get a photo of him—he's normally behind the camera, directing us like he's David Bailey, not an accountant."

Peter—or *John,* as I know him—smiles guilelessly back at us, as if he's not writing LOL all over his online dating profiles while his wife makes his house beautiful and single-handedly holds their lives together. Bristol is a relatively small place: this man has balls of steel. The absolute *audacity* of him.

Also, I was wrong: "John" doesn't have two children.

He has three. My bad.

"Um." I'm breathing way too fast. *What the hell do I do?* "So, he's . . . an accountant?"

I'm stalling, but at least it appears *everything* Peter said wasn't a lie.

"Yup." Polly becomes abruptly aware that I'm having an existential crisis right next to her. "Are you OK, Margot? The news about the show was too big, wasn't it? I'm so sorry to lob it at you like that. It's just . . . when I think about how happy it makes me when my kids get excited about something other than cartoons . . . We could do that but for *millions.*"

Nope: this is all too much.

I'm desperately trying to do the math. Nearly half a million people live in Bristol, but only 13,000 in Clifton. Roughly halve that for men, then narrow that pool down to those online dating, in my age range, and suddenly it's not that improbable I'd accidentally go on a date with my married neighbor.

But why have I never *seen* Peter before? I've only been here a few months, but still—we'd have crossed paths at some point, right? Except I rarely go outside, I never look out of the window, and if he works late, and I'm hiding in my bedroom . . .

"Ah." I take a deep breath and step backward. "I just need to process, I think."

More importantly, I need to work out what I'm going to do. I need to tell her, right? That's the right thing to do. The morally upstanding thing to do. But how do you casually drop that kind of life-changing information into a conversation? *Hey, so I know we've met twice, but your husband tried to have sex with me last week. Biscuit?*

I don't think our budding friendship and/or work relationship could survive.

Plus, I really *like* Polly. She's sweet, calm and polished in a way I have always known I will never be, even in infinite shades of navy. It's been so lovely connecting with someone new for the first time in years. I don't want to hurt her.

"Of course!" Polly opens her hands out. "Just promise me you'll think about it?"

"Oh," I say slowly, tightening my dressing-gown belt until it feels like I'm being cut in half. I feel grotty. Sullied. That bad, bad man. This poor, poor woman. "I'll be thinking about it, I can promise you that."

18

CAN'T GET RID of you, can I?"

With my feet, I try to close the front door behind me, a pile of boxes propped precariously under my chin. Glancing to the right, I see my grandfather's walking shoes still perched on the shelf where I left them.

Right. He lied about leaving the house. Good to know.

"Nope." I lumber through to the living room and put the boxes down. "Sorry."

"Looks like I'll have to tolerate your presence again then." Grandad grins at me from his chair. "It's a chore, but somebody has to do it."

"Ever the stoic," I say warmly, checking the room. "Did the cleaner come?"

She was supposed to turn up this morning, while I was being unexpectedly thrown into further inner turmoil by a married man with lovely hair and zero morals.

"Oh yes!" Grandad lights up. "What a nice lady. So sprightly! We had a lovely long chat about you."

"I bet you did," I laugh. With highly complimentary and inaccurate editing, I'm guessing. At least *this* situation is something I can start fixing immediately. "So, I was thinking . . . You like learning new things, right?"

"Of course." My grandfather nods and eyes the boxes curiously. "What have you got for me?"

"I'm glad you asked." I grab the bird letter opener. "I think it might be time for you to start embracing technology. You know, so you can keep up with the kids, as befits a young and nimble-minded spirit like yourself."

"I am nimble like a mountain goat." My grandfather cocks his head slightly. "With similarly wobbly knees."

"Indeed." We grin at each other. "So I thought I'd drag you into this century."

"No dragging necessary," he smiles. "I will accompany you willingly."

"Great." I breathe out as I cut open one box, hoping he doesn't get upset or embarrassed. I put the small round gray object on the table. "Let me introduce you to a young lady called Alexa. You can talk to her and she'll play you music and tell you the time and the news and the weather, and even read you books. You just need to tell her whatever it is you want."

"Goodness gracious," Grandad says with amused blue eyes. "Can she make me a lamb hotpot?"

"Probably," I grin. "Maybe let her settle in first."

Pleased with his reaction, I impatiently rip open the next box: a Kindle, which I program so it has roughly two words per page. Together, we download Steinbeck, Trollope and Dickens while I explain it all to him. Then a kettle, a magnifying glass, a contraption for cutting vegetables, a new mobile phone and a TV remote control with buttons the size of strawberries. His eyes widen with each new box, and I feel so much happiness at his expressions that for a moment I'm not sure where to put it. True to form, I focus on cursing the letter opener instead.

"Margot," he says finally, just as I pull out a new camera. "Halt."

Surprised, I look up and realize his bright blue eyes are glistening and wet. Guilt flushes through me. I didn't want him to feel embarrassed or as if I think he's weak. "Grandad, I'm so sorry, I just—"

"I know what you're doing," he says firmly. "You have hidden it poorly."

"Oh. I thought I was being incredibly subtle and nuanced."

"Meg, I love you, but subtlety is not one of your strongest qualities." He lifts his bushy eyebrows. "You are the human equivalent of a bullet."

"Accurate." I nod. "But I just thought that . . ."

He reaches forward and takes my hand.

"My world is never going to be completely dark as long as you are in it," my grandfather says quietly. "You don't need to worry about me."

I make a choking sound and try to swallow. "I—"

"Having said that," he grins cheekily, squeezing my hand and staring at all his new gadgets with what looks like genuine excitement, "I am *very* much looking forward to revisiting books again, and maybe casually chopping a few carrots. I suspect Alexa and I shall get on famously. What a gift you have given me. What *gifts*. You just happen to be my favorite, that's all."

I feel my eyes well up and quickly wipe them on my jumper.

"Shut up, Grandad."

"I absolutely shall not, Margot."

We beam at each other as my phone beeps.

You got the job. X

For just a second, I assume it's from Polly and think: blimey, that was fast.

Then I see it's from Henry and laugh loudly.

The cleaning job? Yesssss x

A beep.

Obviously not, you were rubbish. You got the considerably harder job of another date with me, if you want one. Tuesday? X

My entire body lights up as I laugh again.

Deal. As long as I get another
fiver at the end. X

Glowing, I put my phone away and realize my grandfather is watching me. He looks ridiculously pleased. Nay, smug.

"Henry?"

"Henry," I confirm. "He forgave me."

"Ah." He nods. "I thought he might."

"Anyway." I change the subject so I don't have to dissect this relationship in gory detail before it's ready for that level of analysis. "I have *one* more surprise for you, Grandad. And I'm sorry in advance. We're opening Pandora's box, and there'll be nothing either of us can do to close it again."

I help Grandad to his feet and walk him slowly into the family room, where I attach a camera to the enormous smart TV and hit a few buttons. Luckily, his television is pretty much brand-new: it's the one thing of value I stole from Aaron, *mwahahaha.*

"This is exciting." Grandad sits carefully on the sofa. "What adventure shall you unleash on me now, Meg?"

"Total chaos." I pick up my phone, hit the right button and cast the image onto the screen. The little camera attached to the front glows blue. "We won't be able to take this back, I'm afraid. So . . . apologies. Again."

There's a loud ringing sound and suddenly my mother's nostrils appear in HDTV, the size of dinner plates.

"Maggie! Finally! Are you . . ." Mum frowns and leans forward. "Where are you? Is that . . ." She inhales. "*George!* Get your bottom here right now!"

"Ugh, can a man not water his rhododendrons in peace?"

Dad appears and his face lights up so fiercely I have to swallow a lump in my throat again.

"Dad! What are you doing on our phone?"

"Well, hello!" Grandad's entire body is radiating happiness. "George! There you are! You're huge! I can see you! Gosh, don't you look tanned? What's the weather like over there? Is it unwelcomely warm?"

I laugh: here we go, straight back into vague weather discussions.

"I'll make you a fresh coffee, George," Mum says, giving me an approving little glance. "Looks like we'll be here awhile."

Something tells me my parents will now be harassing my grandfather daily until he begs me to throw the television out of the living-room window.

"*Well*," Dad grins, settling down comfortably, "it's inordinately hot, but not in a humid way, you know? Do you remember that holiday we had in France when I was about ten? It's pretty much like that, but . . ."

As I smile and leave my grandfather and his only child chatting—thousands of miles between them evaporating—it suddenly feels like nothing else matters that much. For just this moment, my Instagram account, Winter's fury, the visions, Polly's looming heartbreak . . . my worries seem to fade away into a faint gray fog.

After all, what is more important than seeing, and being seen?

BY THE TIME they finish talking, it's dark outside.

In the meantime, I've pottered around, setting up various gadgets. I also make sure I rip off the calendar month, and discover an impatient little robin waiting to be revealed. With a small smile, I put the month of the blue tit in my bag.

The month has turned and it's a new start, for all of us.

Finally, the weather has been discussed to its fullest extent, so I tentatively return to the living room.

"So, Dad, you'll just be able to press that button whenever we call!"

"So I will." Grandad smiles as Dad goes back to his plants. He glances at me: there goes his remaining time with his three thoughts. "What a joy and a revelation."

"Maggie!" Mum appears just as I'm showing Grandad where the Go Away switch is on the remote control. "Can I have a moment with you?"

"Um." I'm immediately wary. "Sure."

No doubt she wants to talk about Henry and his potential as my future husband. I'm doing quite enough of that myself without my mother jumping in too.

"I'll go and introduce myself to Alexa," Grandad says quietly, standing up with visible effort. "I suspect it shall be quite the interaction."

I smile at him, nod and take the warm seat he's just left.

"Thank you," she says. "I don't think you realize how much that meant to your dad. Or to me. He's been putting on a brave face, but I don't think he's adjusting well to being so far away from his father. Or you, actually."

"Oh!" I nod, surprised. I wasn't expecting that. "It's no big deal."

"It is," Mum disagrees gently. "He's homesick, he's gardening *way* too much, and this has really helped. So thank you. You're a good girl, Maggie."

I feel myself flush with pleasure, and I wriggle uncomfortably. "Nah."

"I know I sometimes push you a little too hard, but it's only because I want you to be happy. You know that, don't you?"

I frown. "Obviously."

"And you know how much I love you?"

"Of course." Now I'm really confused. "What's going on?"

"Nothing, darling." Mum is visibly struggling with the expression of her emotions, as always. Like mother, like daughter. "It's just . . . all this distance. I think we'd spent so long focused on what our retirement would look like, being back in Australia, that we didn't really think about what we'd be leaving behind."

"Mum." I lean forward. "Nothing exciting is happening without you, I promise. You guys just need to focus on having fun and relaxing."

I miss you horribly and I want you to come home immediately seems far too selfish, even for me.

"I suppose." Mum scratches her eyebrow. "All this sunshine is doing my head in, Maggie. I've started fantasizing about gray skies, constant rain and wet feet."

I laugh. "Don't worry, that's all still here too."

"And my God, your Aussie grandmother is *driving me up the wall.*" Mum grins sheepishly. "I'd forgotten what a total pain in the arse she is."

"Mum! Language!"

"Sorry." She puts a hand over her mouth. "I guess I inherited it from you."

We smile at each other fondly, and I miss her with a sharp, tugging pang in my chest.

"I *may* have met someone," I say, throwing her a bone. "A man."

"Oooooh!" She looks offensively surprised. "Who is he? What does he do for a living? Is he kind? Is he handsome?"

I laugh—she must be faking it, because I'm certain Eve has already told her everything—then pause: I can hear my grandfather in the living room having the world's most ridiculously polite conversation with a non-sentient being. He's thanking Alexa so much that she's starting to get audibly confused.

"I'll ring you in a few days," I say, standing up. "And tell you *all* about it, I promise. I've just got to go make sure Grandad doesn't start becoming Alexa's butler instead of the other way round."

"Good idea." Mum frowns. "Listen, Maggie—"

Everything suddenly goes woozy and here we go *again*—

BLINKING, I STARE at a television.

Somehow, I appear to have landed in front of another telly: slightly smaller, set against a dark gray wall. Confused, I peer at it. Quickly, I put my hand to my head: short hair again. Then I look at my finger. No ring. These seem to be the only clues I have to try and roughly pinpoint myself in time: I'm less than three years in the future, but further away than whenever I cut my hair.

"Henry?" Frowning, I turn slightly. "Is that you?"

"Mm-hmm."

It's really dark in here, and I abruptly realize I'm back in Henry's flat, but what I thought was a painting of a ship is actually a television. His face is flickering in front of what appears to be a cooking show: they're making a raspberry pavlova.

"Sorry." I quickly try to make amends, make Other Margot sound less stupid. "I dozed off for a second there."

"Aha."

Henry doesn't even glance in my direction and—confused—I look back at the television. They're whipping the cream, but it doesn't seem quite mesmerizing enough to require quite so much focus.

"Where's Winter?"

"Mum and Dad's."

Then Henry grabs the remote control and pointedly turns up the volume. I stare at him in shock. What the hell is going on?

"Um." I lick my lips. "Henry, are you OK?"

"Yup." He's still not looking at me. "Just let me watch the show in peace for a minute."

My eyes widen: have I just landed in the middle of a *fight*?

In which case, what are we fighting about? I quickly search Other Margot's emotions for a lingering clue of what the hell is going on. Somewhere under *my* confusion and hurt, Other Margot is . . . Ooh, she's angry. Seething, in fact. Other Margot wants to bite Henry.

"We're fighting," I state matter-of-factly: I need to know what's going on. "So can we talk about it? About . . . you know."

Yeah, that's all I've got.

"Not right now." Bristling, Henry gets up from the sofa. Ooooh, he's super mad too. "I'll go watch them finish the pavlova in the bedroom."

Shocked, I jump off the sofa and follow him. I think this is both of us now: me and Other Margot, wanting exactly the same thing, at exactly the same time. I can feel my anger rising to meet hers.

"Don't you dare!" I call. "Don't you bloody dare just walk away!"

He closes the bedroom door and I feel another powerful wave of fury as I bang on it as hard as I can.

"Oy! Henry Armstrong! Get your butt out here so we can fight properly!"

I don't know what we're fighting about, but I do know that both Other Margot and I want to have it out as loudly as possible.

"I don't want to fight right now, Margot! I'm tired!"

"Well, too late," I yell back. "Because we're fighting, so you just get on board and fight me back. You will *not* keep avoiding confrontation, mister."

Breathing hard, I stare at the door in surprise.

Where the hell did *that* come from? Does Henry avoid confrontation? How did I know that? But something in me, in this version of me, somehow knows he does. Is it a Red Flag? Is this a sign I should be paying attention to?

Teeth gritted, I watch as the bedroom door swings slowly open.

"Mister?" Henry says with his eyebrows raised. "Did you just call me mister?"

"Yes," I say belligerently. "You're being a dickhead."

"Enough of a dickhead to be called mister?" Henry's nose twitches. "That's a large gauntlet to throw down, *missy*."

The corner of his mouth is twitching and now I'm even more infuriated. Don't you dare just throw me into a random fight in the future and be mad at me when I don't even know what's happened. I bet this is all his fault anyway.

"This isn't funny," I hiss.

"It is. A bit."

"No."

"On a scale of one to ten, Megalodon, how funny would you say this fight is?"

Annoyed, I feel my nose twitch too.

"Tell you what," Henry says, his face clearing. "Why don't you come and watch the pavlova with me and *then* we can fight. I'll have an energy drink so I can shout back at you properly. But first I need to see what kind of shape they put the raspberries in, Margot, because it's a goddamn cliffhanger of a show and I must see how it ends."

Both Other Margot and I soften as Henry gestures with an ironic bow toward the king-size bed. I make a mental note: we get new bedding, with little blue flowers. It's nice. I like it. I bet I chose that. Good job, me.

"*Fine,*" I say with dignity, stalking toward the bed. "But you're still a dickhead."

Probably.

"Takes one to know one," Henry grins, picking me up and lobbing me onto the bed with neither ceremony nor effort. "Now shut up or we'll miss the bit where they dust it with icing—"

"—WEEK?"

I blink and stare at my mother's face.

"Um." I'm sitting on my grandfather's tweed sofa. I must have stood up and abruptly sat down again. "Absolutely. Or . . . not? Sorry, what was the question?"

"Are you alright?" Mum peers at me. "It might be a bit of a—"

"Oh!" I scratch my eyebrow, still dizzy. "I'm fine! Just a little head rush. Need to take some more vitamins. Don't worry about me."

She nods, watching me with the careful, astute expression of a mother who is vaguely aware her only child is still existing on carbohydrates.

"Anyway, love you." I give a little wave while I try to recalibrate. "Speak soon. Bye."

"Maggie—"

Too late: I've switched her off.

I LEAVE GRANDAD contentedly asking Alexa what the capital of Slovenia is and return home to spend the night worrying. It's one thing watching for Red Flags in the present, but what about the future? Can smoke signals be read accurately from this kind of distance? I don't want to have to chase Henry down every time we have an argument. It seems like an exhausting way to potentially spend the rest of my life.

Just after midnight, still unable to sleep, I give up and slam out a quick text:

You up??

A few minutes later:

JULES: That's a fuckboy text if ever I've seen one

EVE: Hahaha

JULES: What's up?

Fighting is normal, right?

JULES: Who are you fighting this time?

Henry

EVE: Already?? That doesn't sound good.

I pause, unable to say: *Nope, at some point in the future.*

Kind of.

EVE: What about?

Not sure exactly.

There's a small silence, then Jules starts to type. Here it comes: *Get out while you still can, he's clearly an asshole, I never liked the sound of him anyway.*

JULES: Go to sleep, Margot. You're an idiot.

Oh. Right, then.

EVE: Stop analyzing for half a second and give him a chance. ;) Night night xxx

I breathe out heavily, relieved.

Not only do I have no idea what we were fighting about, but the fight clearly didn't last very long. In fact, Henry started laughing right in the middle of it. That seems good, right? Healthy? Or . . . not healthy? Avoidant?

It's hard to know because Aaron and I never really argued.

Breathing out, I sit straight up in bed: actually, we never argued at *all*. Aaron would get icy and mean and I would apologize until he was nice to me again. Maybe the shock of my argument with Henry was less that we were having one and more that *I* was having one.

An actual fight, where I felt comfortable enough to yell at him. Huh.

Thanks, guys. You're the best. Night. Xx

Lying back, I stare at my ceiling.

Another vision with something to teach me.

Another future, with a lesson to learn.

And I suddenly can't help wondering if that's why I'm getting them: not just so I can see the future, but so I can see the past too. Like light passing through a drop of water, changing all the angles and splitting into colors that weren't visible before. For the best part of a year, I've been convinced that I lost my great love—that Lily got the life I wanted—and it's becoming increasingly clear that it's not true. The life I want is ahead of me, not behind me.

Impulsively, I grab my phone and text Polly.

I'm in. Let's do this TV thing. Xx

Then I wriggle happily into my pillow and close my eyes. Maybe I didn't realize what my life could be until I saw it.

Until I started realizing who I was, and who I could possibly be.

19

I SPEND THE NEXT three days frantically preparing for my interview.

"It's not an interview," Polly says yet again as I go through my notes.

I nod—it's an interview—while attempting to cram fifteen years of collected meteorological knowledge into a fifteen-minute slot.

"Margot." Polly laughs and takes my notepad off me. "Relax. This is a casual chat over a cup of coffee, and I shall be there as a buffer. Charlie is lovely. She just wants to say hi, spitball a few ideas, see if there's a click."

Then she pauses and looks at the front of my purple notepad with her eyebrows raised, flipping through it slightly.

"Oh!" Flushing, I grab it from her. "Don't look at that."

"Margot's List of Dating Criteria?" She cocks her head, like a curious Labrador. "That seems very . . ."

"Sensible." I bridle slightly. "Sage and informed."

"I was going to say *meticulous*." She looks at me calmly. "Has it helped?"

"Absolutely." I'm weirdly protective of the data I've collected. "Very much so." But she's still watching me, so I clear my throat. "Mostly." Polly's eyes are locked on mine. "Not really, no. Not at all. Happy now?"

"I was genuinely curious," Polly grins. "I've never approached love like that, I guess. I just wanted to know how it's panning out."

My stomach twists: this is the perfect bloody segue, and I know it.

I've not only been making lists of ways to impress a total stranger tomorrow, I've also been making a list of the pros and cons of telling Polly about Peter, and frankly, it's not been very helpful at all. On the pros list, I have: the right thing to do, compassion for Polly, friendship, female solidarity, exposing the bastard and straight-up honesty.

On the cons list, I have: *I don't want to.*

It probably didn't need its own notepad, which I'm really glad now I left in the bedroom, because Polly seems to have no problem reading other people's private information.

"So . . ." I feel sick. How to gently introduce this topic? "Peter. Is your husband."

Yup. My famous lack of nuance is very much still intact.

"He is, yes."

"Yes. Peter is your husband."

"Yes."

I clear my throat: this is going well. "You met . . ."

"At Oxford," she fills in for me, smiling. "Freshers' week. I was inexplicably attracted to the handsome guy standing on a table in front of all his rugby friends, downing a pint with a boiled egg at the bottom of it."

"Wow." OK, so Peter's always been a dickhead. "That's . . ."

"A terrible meet-cute, I know." Polly stands up and walks to my closet. "It got better, though. We just kind of . . . grew together. Time and three kids will do that to you. Gosh," she says, slightly bemused, as she opens my closet door. "What an awful lot of navy and black."

"And . . . you're happy?" I don't know why I'm foraging for information like this: *just say it.* "With Peter? And the kids?"

"Sure." Polly smiles. "It's marriage, you know how it is."

"I don't know, no. I was dumped at the altar."

Where did *that* come from?

"Gosh!" Polly turns to me with a horrified expression. "I'm so sorry, I didn't realize . . ."

I grin at her, suddenly realizing that I feel nothing for myself anymore: no sadness, no self-pity, no heartbreak, no rage. In fact, I now appear to find the whole situation quite funny.

"Not at the altar itself," I laugh. "About fifteen feet away."

That always seemed to be the ironic cherry on the whole wedding cake: when I caught Lily and Aaron, he was wearing a suit and she was wearing a long satin dress, and they were standing so close to the perfectly arranged floral bower I'd chosen and paid for that *I* felt like the one getting in the way of a big love story. Which I suppose I was, really.

"It's fine," I say with a smile. "I'm just saying I don't really know much about what it's like to be married. Not really."

Because what I had with Aaron wasn't "practically a marriage": not even close.

"It's . . . complicated." Polly frowns. "But . . . good."

I open my mouth to say: *It isn't good—he's trying to sleep with women on the internet using photos that presumably you took.* Then I catch myself. That is not how to do it, Margot. This is Polly's *life,* not a dramatic plot twist. Do it sensitively and compassionately or don't do it at all.

"Great." I smile at her encouragingly. "That's . . . great!"

It is so not great. *Not only is your husband a cheater, he has lied about his age to manipulate younger women.* Nope, that's not it either.

"Thanks." She smiles, distracted. "I'm *really* excited about tomorrow. I've got so many great ideas for branding, marketing, setting up a new page and—"

For fuck's sake, Margot. Just *say it.*

"Um, while we're on the topic of dating and whatnot, I need to—"

My phone beeps and I stare at Henry's name, my insides torn. Ignore the phone, Margot. Just prioritize: tell her and put yourself out of your misery—simultaneously throwing Polly straight into hers.

"Henry?" Polly glances at the phone I'm still staring at. "You going to answer?"

I bite my lip. *No. Instead I'm going to tell you that your entire life is a lie and then watch as you fall apart, unable to do anything about it.*

"Ah." I swallow. "I guess."

I'm a coward, a wuss, a total let-down of a woman. I pick up the phone.

Still on for this evening? I am
IMPATIENT to see you again. xx

I love that Henry isn't playing it cool or pretending he's not interested just to try and invoke my deepest and darkest insecurities, thereby manipulating me into liking him more. He likes me, he lets me know he likes me, he lets me like him back, no mind-molding games here.

Glowing in spite of myself, I quickly type back:

VERY MUCH ME TOO. Xxx

Another beep.

No grammatical sense there but I'll
take the caps lock as a yes. ;)

Meet you at mine at 6:30 and dress
up—I have A PLAN. xx

When I look up, Polly is watching my bright expression with a warm, sweet smile. It makes it worse, somehow. That I'm so smitten and happy while her relationship is about to implode with the force of a supercell thunderstorm.

"So I guess the dating list worked after all?"

I think about it briefly: without my list, without my data

experiment, I wouldn't have been in that Italian restaurant, I wouldn't have met Henry, I wouldn't have realized that I didn't give a flying crap about my list.

"Actually," I smile back, "I suppose it did."

I TRY TO tell Polly three more times and fail. Because I'm weak, because I truly like her, but mostly because I know exactly how it feels when the life you've built abruptly crumbles. So I let her return home and attempt to push the guilt aside for one more evening. I'll try again tomorrow. For now, Henry has A PLAN and I need to give it my full attention.

Spurred on by Polly's visible disappointment at my sartorial choices, I dig around in my closet until I find the only visible bit of color: a bright red dress I bought for Jules's wedding and which went unworn because she impulsively ran off to Las Vegas without telling anyone. It's exactly the right combination of sexy and fun and puffs up when you walk, as if you're a 1950s film star. I put it on and turn in circles in front of the mirror, trying to see what I look like from multiple angles. Then I try to walk past and catch myself unawares, to get an idea of how Henry will see me.

I am genuinely surprised by the change in me: the *brightness.*

With a tiny wink at myself (hoping nobody saw that through the window), I give a happy little wriggle, grab my jacket—my Henry jacket, the one that gave me another chance with him—and slip on my shoes.

The future is coming, I can feel it.

And I am finally racing toward it with both arms held out.

"SHIT!" HENRY GREETS me at his door. "Didn't you get my text?"

I blink in disappointment: this is not the reaction to my dress I was hoping for. I actually took my jacket off just so he could see it in its full glory, and now I'm bloody freezing for no reason at all.

"Comment on my dress first," I say bluntly. "It's very pretty and I made an effort—and now I'm going to put my jacket on because you ruined it."

"Sorry." He laughs. "You look beautiful. That was very impolite of me."

"And no, I didn't get a text." I pull my phone out of my bag and stare at it. "Oh, wait. Yes, I did."

So sorry but can we take a rain check? xx

Presumably, I got it while I was twirling around in front of my mirror: that'll teach me to be so inordinately pleased with myself.

"We're rain-checking?" I frown. "Do I have to go home?"

"I'm ridiculously sorry." Henry pulls on his coat with a guilty grimace. "The restaurant called me an hour ago. Literally *all* the staff have rung in sick. There's nobody left but me and the chef, and the place is fully booked. Plus—"

"Oh!" Winter appears behind him. "Hello! Are you here to clean while we're out?"

"Mum and Dad were supposed to take her, but they're feeling rotten too." Henry looks stressed. "So you're coming with me tonight, aren't you, Winnie? A nice five-hour shift of sitting with an iPad in the corner on your own, asking for more garlic bread and Diet Coke and eating us out of profit."

"I can stay here," Winter says emphatically. "I'm big enough now."

"You're not."

"I am." She crosses her arms. "I'm nearly seven. I'll be totally fine. If there's a problem, I'll just scream really loud."

Henry looks at me with flared nostrils, then back at her.

"Comforting, but no. Put your coat on. We're already late."

I put my jacket back on too and assess the situation. Yes, I'm slightly disappointed that I don't get my swanky date with Henry—whatever it was going to be—but it's just another example of him being a decent person. And isn't this an *opportunity*?

To try and correct things before they go wrong? A chance to . . . bond? Or is it too soon? Does he even trust me enough? *Should* he trust me enough?

"I . . ." I clear my throat. "I can take her."

Henry pauses and stares at me. "What?"

"I don't mean *take her*, like I'm a child-snatcher," I correct quickly. "I just mean . . . you know. Look after her for a few hours." Winter is staring at me curiously too, so I add: "Babysitting is actually on my list of . . . jobs I do. As well as cleaning, obviously."

"I can't ask you to do that, Margot." Henry is firm. "Absolutely not."

"You don't need to. I'm offering."

He hesitates and I suddenly realize he hasn't seen what I have seen: he doesn't know what our future potentially holds. I'm just some woman he barely knows, offering to take his precious offspring without a background check.

"Unless," I say, panicked, "you don't think that I—"

"I *trust* you," Henry says quickly. "It's not that. It's just . . . she can be a bit of a handful sometimes."

"I *cannot*!" Winter is indignant. "Dad! *Please* can the cleaner stay with me? I don't want to sit in your restaurant. It's very boring and smells like chicken."

Henry smiles at her and then looks toward me. "If you're sure?"

"I'm sure," Winter says in a clear voice.

"I didn't mean you, you little plonker." He faces me and I nod to let him know that I, too, am sure. "I should be able to get out at about half ten, if I convince the chef to cash up for me. Actually, I stole his very expensive black truffle to try and impress you, so he may not be up for that. But I'll try my hardest."

Henry doesn't notice the little line appearing between Winter's eyebrows, but I do.

"You're amazing," he says, leaning forward to give me a quick, distracted kiss on the lips. "*Thank you.* Behave, Winter!

I mean it! And show Margot where the snacks are, but don't eat too many, because you won't sleep. See you guys in a few hours."

Realizing the time, Henry jumps down the iron staircase and starts jogging along the road toward the train station.

Slowly, I turn to Winter. I can't believe Henry just did that.

Yup: that's the face of a six-year-old who is neither blind nor stupid.

"You're not really the cleaner, are you," she says clearly.

"No."

"Because Daddy doesn't kiss our cleaners on the lips."

I should hope not. "No."

"Or steal things to try and impress them."

"Probably not."

I watch her process this information, her entire face moving as her brain desperately attempts to piece it all together. Who am I? What will happen to her life now? Her face settles on a scowl, and I feel a sense of doom in my stomach.

I cannot believe Henry just accidentally landed me in this mess and then ran away.

"So if you're not the cleaner," Winter says, crossing her arms and glaring at me, "then you're just a big fat *liar,* aren't you."

I take a deep breath. "Yes."

"Don't touch my rocks," she says, stalking back into the flat with her shoulders tight and bristling. "You're not even properly *trained.*"

And so it starts.

20

This is going about as well as I thought it would.

Aware I'm watching, Winter pointedly opens the snack drawer, takes out an entire armful and shuts herself in her bedroom. Just in case I hadn't got the message, she opens the door again and says, "You are *not* welcome," then closes it again, much more loudly.

"OK," I say faintly. "Sorry."

Anxious, I lurk in the corridor, worried that she'll accidentally choke on a biscuit wrapper and I'll have to explain to her father that I didn't realize because I was trying to "respect her space."

"Winter?" I knock on the door quietly so as not to scare her. "I'm very sorry we weren't honest with you. It's . . . really, really early days, and we just wanted to be sure we liked each other before we said anything."

"Go *away*," she shouts at the door. "I am *busy*."

"OK." I move away from the door. "I'll just be . . . out here, if you want to talk."

I suppose I could go and sit on the sofa to wait for Henry—watch some telly, read a book—but I feel too guilty. This is a *lot* of information to throw at a child all at once. It's been just her and her father her entire conscious life. Plus, I'm not really sure what babysitting entails. Do you have to be directly next to them the whole time? Probably. It just seems dangerous to leave them to their own devices.

God, I feel like a warden at a very small prison.

Overwhelmed, I slide down the wall until I'm sitting on the floor outside Winter's room: close enough to hear if she starts coughing in a worrying way. I have no idea what she's doing in there, just that I can hear drawers being opened and closed with alarming speed.

"My namc really *is* Margot," I tell the door, hoping she can hear me. "And I really *am* named after the ballerina." A bolt of hope. "Actually, I think we can get you your very own tutu online if you just come out here and help me pick a color—"

The door opens to my side and I breathe out: bribery worked!

But it clearly hasn't. Because Winter is standing in the corridor, clutching a small floral purple suitcase. A suitcase I've seen before: the one she uses to move into my house.

"I'm running away," she tells me imperiously. "I do not want to live with liars."

My nose twitches slightly—she's so incredibly sweet—and I have to use every bit of facial control I have not to smile.

"That's fair," I say gently. "And logical."

"So I think I will go and live with someone else." She considers her options. "Granny and Grandad. Or Isabella. She's my best friend at school. And she has a hamster—and we're allowed to hold it."

Then she looks outraged at herself for sharing this intimate information.

"So I shall be leaving now." Winter starts wheeling her case across the living room. "Don't try and stop me. I'm leaving forever."

I stand up and wait for her to reach the front door. I'm not entirely sure what to do: I can't exactly explain to Henry that his daughter flew the nest and is currently wandering around Bath with God knows what packed in a case: shells and dried flowers, probably.

"OK," I say, trying to hold my nerve.

"*Don't* try and stop me," she repeats, eyeing me coldly. "It won't work."

"I can see that." I nod. "You've got to do what you've got to do."

Winter puts her little hand on the door handle and pauses, gathering all of her courage. I watch her shoulders straighten and I feel an intense pang of warmth toward her.

"So here I go," she announces, pushing the handle down.

"Safe travels," I say behind her.

She whips round, now absolutely incandescent. Little chestnut curls are sticking out around her ears, which just makes her rage even more adorable.

"You're going to let me *go*?"

"You seem quite set on it," I reply calmly. "So I respect your decision."

"You can't just let me *run away*!" Winter holds her arms out. "I am a *child*. I am only six years old!"

My nose twitches again. "Nearly seven, remember."

"That's still a child!" She looks infuriated by my stupidity. "You have to look after me! It's the *law*. And you promised Daddy you would!"

"I did." I nod. "That's very true."

"And you're *not* looking after me if you just let me run away! You're a liar again!"

"I'm sorry." I try even harder not to smile, but I'm failing miserably. "You're right. Please don't leave, Winter. I'm sure we can work this out together."

"OK." She softens in relief—homelessness averted—and holds her pointy chin up. "Yes. Well. That was *very* close, you know. I was nearly gone. You are a very bad babysitter. If that's what you *actually* are."

This time I laugh loudly and she eyes me suspiciously.

"Tell you what," I say, grabbing my phone. "Why don't we *both* run away for a bit? We can go on an adventure, one that maybe even runs slightly past your bedtime."

Winter thinks about this for a few seconds. "OK. But I will probably tell my daddy that you let me stay up too late."

I grin while texting. "That's your call."

Taking her for a little walk, is that OK? She has a lot of energy. Xx

A beep:

Doesn't she just. ;) Go for it. THANK YOU AGAIN. xx

"Is there anything in your suitcase you need?" I help her put on her purple puffer coat, but she seems fixed on doing her shoelaces herself. "To take with us, just in case?"

"Oh." Winter eyes her suitcase with zero embarrassment. "No. It's mostly teddies and seashells."

"Got it." I smile at her. "Then perhaps we'll leave them here."

WINTER IS THAWING, snowflake by snowflake.

She's trying very hard not to—and bristles when she remembers she hates me—but in the spaces between I gently ask questions until she starts to chatter: about her best friend Isabella (she loves dolphins, but Winter is not convinced—they "look angry"), her grandparents' new puppy (she's forgiven him, just) and what her favorite game in the playground is (tag, apparently still going strong).

As we wander through Bath, I wonder briefly if this is going to be my new life: walking and talking around the West Country with members of the Armstrong family.

I don't hate it.

In fact—I realize with surprise—I'm enjoying it immensely.

Bath is unquestioningly beautiful, and while admittedly I've never spent any time with a six-year-old—apart from when I was a six-year-old myself—Winter is a funny little thing. She feels strangely old for her years, with exactly the same clear, formal way of speaking Henry has. At one point—while telling me that somebody took the last jacket potato at lunch and she was considerably upset by it—she uses the phrase "Alas, my potato," and I stare at her briefly.

"Alas?"

"It means 'Oh no,'" she explains patiently. "Like 'Woe is me' but not as sad."

"Where are you getting this from?" I think I know the answer before I ask it. "Who taught you that?"

"Nobody *taught* me," she says, giving me a sharp look. "Daddy reads me poetry at night and I just *pick things up*. I am very clever like that. Daddy says I have the memory of a pair of pants."

I laugh. "Elephant."

"No, Margot," she sighs. "You must focus and improve your constabulary."

We make another loop around inner-city Bath. It's a small place and we've essentially just gone round in circles, but I'm desperately trying to distract her, get her talking and also wear her out, like a small dog. It's not working. Her energy levels are considerably higher than mine. Although, in my defense, I'm wearing high heels and a red dress and she's not.

"Hey," I say, trying to work out if anywhere sells ice cream at this time of night. "Do you fancy a—"

Winter has abruptly stopped walking and is staring straight ahead.

"Winter?"

She says nothing, but her body has stiffened and her face is struggling: bottom lip moving, nose wrinkling, eyebrows clenched.

"Winnie?" I bend down until I'm kneeling on the ground. "Sweetheart, what is it?"

"It's my mummy."

Alarmed, I look up: where? What the hell is she talking about?

"There." Winter lifts a pale finger and points at a slim red-haired lady standing on the grass in the little square we've paused at. "She's right there."

Horrified, I stare at them both. The woman smiles at us, and my stomach flips over: this can't be happening. Has Henry *lied* to me? Is his ex-wife, mother of his child, actually living locally and taking casual evening strolls around the neighborhood? That's not a red flag: that's as flammable as it gets.

"That lady?" I feel nauseous. "She's your mummy?"

"What?" Winter looks at me in confusion. "No, my mummy is dead. Did Daddy not tell you?"

The red-haired lady suddenly whistles and I jump as a tiny terrier leaps out of a bush behind us and follows her jauntily onto the path, ears bouncing. Bloody hell. Why do I always jump to the worst possible conclusion? What is *wrong* with me?

"Oh!" I breathe out. "Sorry. Yes. I knew that."

"It's the tree." Winter points again, and I suddenly realize she's pointing at a huge oak. "That's where Mummy is. Daddy put her there, after she was gone. He thinks I don't remember, but I listen when he's talking to Granny. He got planning permission and everything."

I nod faintly. "That's good."

"It's not her, though." Winter frowns. "She's gone. But maybe a little bit of her is still there? Because Daddy makes us walk the other way."

My heart suddenly hurts for Henry, for this lovely girl, for Amy. I can't blame Henry for avoiding this part of town. I moved an entire city to get away from what had hurt me, and this is a completely different level of pain.

"Do you want to go and see?"

Winter looks up at me with such fierce gratitude it knocks the wind out of my lungs.

"Can we?"

"Of course. Let's go and say hello."

As we start walking across the grass, I feel her hand slip into mine: fingers so delicate and soft, like the stems of a plant. She doesn't even realize she's done it—she's focused on the tree—but my heart does something new: swells so fast it feels as though it's straining at the edges of my chest and leaking, like a sponge.

"Right." Winnie gets close, lets go and puts her hand tentatively on the tree trunk. "Um. How do I do this?"

I bend down next to her. "I think you just say whatever you want."

"OK." She takes a deep breath. "I miss you, Mummy, even though I don't remember you because I was a baby when you went. I have all your photos, though, and you were so pretty. We don't talk about you very much because it makes Daddy sad, but I want you to know that my favorite color is purple too."

My eyes suddenly go all wet and misty: this answers that question.

"So . . . that's all I have to say." She coughs lightly. "Oh! And Granny has a puppy and it peed on my bed. But it's OK. I'm not mad anymore. We washed my pajamas. They have dinosaurs on them."

She glances at me and I nod sagely: important information to impart.

"And maybe I'll come back?" She's cautious, clearly feeling guilty. "One time? If Margot brings me?"

I dip my head in acknowledgment, unable to speak.

"Then that's it for now." Winter puts her hand back in mine and uses the other to pat the tree. "Bye, Mummy. Sleep well."

Quietly, we walk away.

But something in me feels changed, has shifted, like the opening of a flower.

"I'M SORRY!" HENRY rattles through the door at nearly midnight. "Sorry, sorry!"

"Sssshhh." I flap my hands. "She's asleep. I bored her into unconsciousness by reciting every type of cloud I could think of."

He puts his arms around me. "Show me your magical ways."

"Lenticular," I murmur as he kisses my neck. "Altostratus. Stratocumulus. Altocumulus. Nimbostratus. Mammatus . . ."

"A whole new type of sheep," Henry says, kissing my mouth. "I'm into it."

"Good." I kiss him back. "Because that's how I plan on boring you into obedience too."

"I am ready to do whatever you tell me." He laughs, then pulls back. "Margot, I realized what I did while I was on the train home. I'm such an idiot. Is Winnie OK?"

I lift my eyebrows. "She tried to run away, actually."

"Of course she did." He sighs. "If it helps, she does that when I won't let her stay up late to watch cartoons, so don't take it too personally."

"I didn't." I laugh. "I like her a lot. You have a very sweet, very precocious and clever child on your hands."

"Ha." Henry physically expands, as if I've just blown air into the top of his head. "I really do, don't I?"

"Yes. You should be proud."

"Honestly," he shrugs, "I think she just turned up like this, fully formed. I'm not sure how much of it I can take credit for. God, that shift was a nightmare. It was just me, and suddenly *everyone* wanted lasagna."

Henry sits with a plonk on the sofa and rubs his eyes.

"Henry . . ." I say slowly, trying to find the words. "Do you realize that . . ."

Winter knows exactly where you put her mum's ashes and she really needs you to take her there sometimes, so she can connect to her.

Not now. I'll bring it up at some point in the future: he's way too shattered to be discussing the delicate topic of his complicated grief process now.

I pause and he looks up. "Do I realize that . . . ?"

"This is our third official date." I smile at him warmly. "And I had a lovely time, thank you. It turns out you don't actually need to be there for it at all, which is handy to know."

He laughs loudly and I widen my eyes and look pointedly at Winter's bedroom.

"Sorry." Henry puts his hand over his mouth. "You're right. This is only our third official date and I ran off and left you with my verbose little daughter. On a scale of all the dates you've ever been on, how bad was this one? Give me the truth, I can handle it."

With a wave of affection, I stand in front of him. "Oooh, bad."

"Really bad?"

"So, so bad." I gesture downward. "I wore a brand-new dress and you have *barely* commented on how lovely I look, which makes you very, very impolite and no gentleman, sir. You haven't even noticed that I *swish*."

To demonstrate, I swing side to side and rotate slightly so that my skirts spread out.

"Wow." He widens his eyes. "You really do."

"It's wasted on you."

"Not wasted. Never wasted. Wait—can you do a full circle?"

"I believe I can." I grin and turn slowly, like a rotisserie chicken. "Yup, look at me go."

"Blimey." Henry leans forward and grabs my hand. "I have never, and I say this with all sincerity, seen a swish *that* impressive. You did not tell me that you swish professionally. Nay, at an Olympic level."

There it is: *nay* can go with *alas* and *woe is me.* I think we know why Winter is Winter, and she didn't just turn up "fully formed" at all.

"I know, right?" I grin. "I am quite the catch."

He pulls me onto the sofa and kisses me firmly, hands on either side of my face, and I feel my insides go gooey like marshmallows held over a flame. The way he's holding me is like he's found something infinitely precious in a charity shop and can't risk letting it go in case someone else picks it up and takes it away from him.

"Good thing I caught you, then." Henry smiles into my face and flexes a hand in front of me. I see his large, tanned hand, the hand in my very first vision, and realize it is already so incredibly dear to me. "Told you I was good with my hands. Would you like to stay the night, or have you had enough of this family for one day?"

I look around the lovely flat, with its gray walls and its photos and its warmth and its beautiful, big-hearted occupants, one now snoring sweetly into her purple pillow.

I have not had enough. I'm not sure I ever will.

"I'll stay," I reply as calmness spreads through me. "But if you make me clean the oven in the morning, you'll be bloody paying me overtime."

"Deal." Henry laughs. "Best cleaner I ever didn't employ."

I SLIP OUT in the morning before Winter wakes up.

While my budding friendship with her is going better than I'd hoped, I don't want to push it. Or, frankly, explain to a six-year-old why I'm still wearing the same clothes and my hair looks like I've been caught in a tornado and whipped around like spaghetti.

"Good luck," Henry says while he's collating Winter's school packed lunch (more leftover lasagna). "Not that you'll need it."

I stare at him. "Good luck for what?"

"The interview." He lifts his eyebrows in exasperation: no wonder Future Margot's constant questions about where we are and what we're doing don't throw him. I've clearly never been the sharpest tool in the woodshed. "You know, the one you kept interrupting sex to tell me about, which was *highly* erotic. Just before you popped in that blindingly attractive mouth guard."

"Oh!" Oops. "Yes. I'm quite the seductress."

"Very much so." Henry smiles and bops me on the nose with his finger, which I find bizarrely validating coming from him. "Just go and blow them all away with your amazingness, Meg."

"Like a hurricane."

"Exactly." Henry laughs and kisses me. "The sexiest hurricane I have ever seen."

EXCEPT, JUST LIKE a hurricane, by the time I reach home I'm coated in a thin layer of water. The motion of the train has made me feel nauseous, my underarms are drenched, the back of my neck is running with sweat and it even feels like my toes are soggy, which is inexplicable but true nonetheless. I'm boiling and also shivering all over. With inconceivable effort, I manage to get into my house after three attempts of smashing my key against the lock and then try my hardest to make it to my bedroom.

It suddenly feels a billion miles away and moving further off with every step, like some kind of mirage.

Giving up—too hard—I lie down on the sofa with a pillow over my face.

Far away, I hear my phone beep.

Beep again.

Too far.

I close my eyes and promptly pass out.

"MARGOT?" THE DOORBELL rings. "Meg? Are you in there?"

Blearily, I try to lift my head.

It's dark and I let out a small squeak: it feels like I've been dipped in a vat of acid and now my entire body is disintegrating, organ by organ.

How long have I been home? A while. Hours or days? I'm still wearing my red dress, no longer either swishy or puffy. I can faintly remember getting up to pee and instead vomiting before lying on the bathroom floor for a nice long while with my face pressed against the tiles.

"Mmmmm," I groan, trying to get up three times and failing.

"Open the door, Margot. Come on. You can do it."

I finally manage to roll onto the floor and lift myself up by holding on to the coffee table. Desperately, I aim for the front door and realize I have never tried this hard at anything in my entire life.

Shivering, I finally manage to heave it open, already out of breath.

Henry takes one look at me, grabs a navy coat off the hook by the door and wraps me up in it. I don't have the energy to ask questions like how is he here? What day is it? Did I even give him my address? None of this makes sense. Honestly, I don't really give a crap at this point: I might actually be dying.

"Shit," he says, holding a hand against my forehead. "You're burning up."

I nod weakly: yes, I do appear to be on fire.

"Right." He picks me up. "You're coming with me."

21

I OPEN MY EYES.

I'm lying under a thick mustard blanket and I pull it to the side: I'm too hot, too sticky, too scratchy. Cautiously, I look around. It's still dark, but I appear to be in Henry's flat. The fireplace is covered in lit candles, and there's a bowl of something green on the coffee table in front of me. Surprised, I prod it slightly: it's soup. A stale piece of cold toast is perched next to it with a faint air of disappointment.

I cough hard, still feeling unbearably hot.

Reaching up, I run my hands through sticky hair and realize with shock that it's short. When I look down, I'm wearing a pair of yellow pajamas with stars on them. I'm covered in sweat and the large indoor tree is in the right corner by the window and the television is a ship and am I having the same vision again? Have I somehow slipped into the exact same part of the future? Then I cough hard and oh my God, it's not a vision, I'm here, it's happening.

I have finally become Other Margot.

Nauseous panic rushes through me: what if it isn't the same? What if everything I've seen isn't true? What if I say the wrong thing, do the wrong thing, somehow send my destiny spiraling in a different direction? What if—somehow, with one stupid move—I lose Henry?

"*Henry*," I croak, my throat raw. "*Henry*."

No answer.

What if he's not here? What if he's gone out, doesn't hear me, doesn't respond, what if everything I want falls apart, and what the hell has happened to my *hair*?

"*Henry*," I say again, trying to stand up. "Are you here?"

Maybe he's outside, maybe he's coming back. I need to reach him, need to make sure he's still here. I don't want to lose him this way, don't want to change anything, don't want to go back to my life the way it was, I don't want to be alone again, I need to see him, need to get to him, need to—

Wobbling, I reach the front door and start rummaging at the lock. *I need to find Henry.*

A voice behind me: "Meg?"

He's here, just like last time, and I promptly start crying.

"Oh *shit*." I feel Henry's hand rest briefly on the back of my neck and it's the same, it's the same, I don't know how, but I'm both Margots, I'm two of us, I remember this, and I feel her and I feel me too, and we're both here and we're the same.

Still crying incoherently, I turn round.

"I thought you'd gone," I say, sobbing. "I thought you weren't going to be here. I thought I was on my own."

There's an intense, almost physical wave of déjà vu, and even as I hear the words, I realize I've said them before. Or heard myself say them before, except this time they mean something different: for Other Margot, for this version of me. It's the same, but also not the same, and it's happening whether I try to control it or not.

"I was just checking on Winter." Henry laughs, wrapping his arms around me. He smells of pepper and lemon, and I suddenly realize this is the first time he's smelled like this in the present. "I haven't gone anywhere, I promise."

Disorientated and confused, I tuck into Henry's neck and feel myself grow calm.

This is it: this is how it feels now, the calmness, the safety, the sensation of being suddenly home. Past Margot felt it, and now I feel it too.

"Is Winter OK?" I murmur. "She's not too sick?"

Because I now remember the last couple of days: me, incoherent on the sofa, Henry bringing glasses of water, soups, smoothies, and gently coaxing me to eat. I remember crying randomly because I couldn't swallow properly or make the ache go away. I remember Winter being poorly too, and I remember why: it's the flu that was going round at Henry's work. He must have passed it on while remaining completely fine himself—the world's healthiest hypochondriac. But suddenly all I care about is that little girl, and whether she feels as horrible and as frightened as I do.

"It's just the flu," Henry confirms, brushing my fringe out of my sweaty face and studying me carefully. He looks tired. I remember now: he's been up for days, looking after both of us. "And she's fine, Meg. You've got it far worse, I'm afraid. It'll be gone in a few days."

I nod, staring at his face. His stubble has grown and so seems slightly more silvery, just as it did in the vision—it wasn't as far in the future as I thought—and I feel a sudden sense of overwhelming relief and gratitude.

I don't want a future that doesn't have him in it.

"Henry," I say. "I think this is . . ."

Proof.

It's proof that my visions are real, that somehow me and Other Margot will continue being the same person, blending together in a weird state of now and then. We are not two distinct people, as it seemed at the beginning. We're just one person. And much like Macbeth, I can't change anything. What I have seen will happen, and any effort to avoid it or bring it about is useless because it will just lead me there anyway.

". . . where I need to be," I finish in an emotional voice.

Because the déjà vu is over and Past Margot has gone: it's just me left now, and I silently say goodbye to her. See you next time, Other Margot.

"I know," Henry grins, kissing my hot cheek softly. "When Winnie started getting sick, I realized you were probably super sick too, and you weren't answering your phone, so I freaked out, as I tend to do."

I stare at him, suddenly needing answers to questions I've had for a while.

"Where the hell is my hair?" I frown. "Where has it gone?"

Wait—no. I don't need an answer to that. I suddenly remember. Somewhere, in the foggy mists of really bad flu, I chopped it off in the bathroom so I could feel air on my neck. But I didn't do it on purpose: that's what's so weird. I didn't remember the vision at the time; I was too ill. I just . . . did it.

"You went full Britney," Henry smiles. "Something about 'letting go of the past,' and more very long speeches that didn't make a lot of sense but were quite impassioned. It was dramatic and I did try to stop you, for the record, but it was too late, you'd already done the back. So I did the front, to try and even it out."

I nod in amazement, running my hand over my hatcheted hair.

"Does it look OK?" God, I'm so vain. I've now confirmed I can actually see the future, but hell to that: am I pretty? "Do I look horrible?"

"It doesn't look *great*," Henry admits. "You look quite a lot like a Barbie that Winter got tired of. But I'm sure it'll look amazing once we've taken you to a hairdresser. You could be bald and still look gorgeous, Margot."

I roll my eyes: I don't have time for these compliments, I have stuff to ask.

"Whose pajamas are these?" I point at the yellow pajamas with stars all over them. "They're not mine."

"I couldn't let you sweat your life out in satin, could I? So I ordered them online and they turned up yesterday. You weren't happy. You started crying and saying you wished they were pink. I had no idea you were so passionate about the color pink."

"Nice." Neither did I. That's embarrassing. What else? "Wait—how did you know where I live? You've never been to my house before, have you?"

"Ah." Henry rubs his face. "You know how weird I am about sickness, and when I couldn't reach you for two days, I panicked and messaged Margot the Meteorologist on Instagram. I had to pass quite a rigorous security check, along with sending screenshots of our last conversation to prove I was who I said I was, but luckily you'd told Polly about me and she eventually told me where to find you."

My eyes open wide. "How very stalkerish of you."

"I *know.*" He looks mortified. "But, Margot, you were *really* sick. I don't know if you remember this, but you vomited in my car on the way home. All over the dashboard. And it was my fault you had the flu in the first place. I couldn't just *leave* you there to deal with it alone."

My eyes sting. Last time I was this sick was about seven years ago, and Aaron did leave me there to deal with it alone. He certainly wasn't applying cold flannels to my forehead every ten minutes and apologizing for buying me pajamas in the wrong color.

"Thank you," I say, leaning up to kiss him and sneezing instead.

"You're very welcome." He wipes my snot off his cheek without twitching. "Look. I know this is all . . . moving pretty fast. What with all the unexpected babysitting and the sweating and the coughing and the sneezing and the vomiting."

"And the crying," I add. "About nothing."

"And the crying about literally nothing," he agrees with a warm smile. "So if you're feeling like you need to pull back, slow things down, I *totally* understand. I was mostly stepping in from . . . a medical perspective. You know, as a wannabe doctor with a lot of guilt about making you ill. Just say the word and I'll leave you alone for a while so we can go back to normal dating."

"You mean sitting in random restaurants, politely asking each other if we have brothers and sisters."

"Exactly. I don't, by the way."

"Me neither. Only child."

"Same. I don't love it."

"Me neither. That's why I adopted Jules and Eve."

"Who rang multiple times, incidentally. They were getting frantic, so I eventually picked up and told them you were super ill and that you'd call them as soon as you surfaced. Then Jules asked me a *lot* of interrogatory questions and Eve told me I sound hot, which was nice of her."

I laugh: that sounds about right, for both of them.

"Well." I pretend to think about it, even though I know exactly what I'm about to say. "Now I know you have no siblings, where you work and how adept you are at hunting people down on the internet, and you know how I feel about yellow pajamas, what my puke looks like and how invasive my friends are, I think we can probably fast-forward to the next bit of this."

Henry grins. "And which bit is that?"

"The bit where you call me your girlfriend."

"Too late," Henry smiles, kissing my nose. "I already told Polly."

IT TAKES ME a full week to get any kind of strength back.

I stay with Henry and Winter for all of it. I don't leave, they don't ask me to, and as the days pass, I realize how *right* it all feels. Wandering about in my star pajamas, watching terrible films while I recuperate, making pancakes for Winter when Henry goes to work and waking up every morning to him checking my temperature with his funny little bedside-table thermometer.

I sit quietly next to him, reading a book while he studies, watching cooking shows (no pavlova yet, thank God) and—when I'm feeling better—giggling every time he grabs me for a kiss while Winter's out of the room. I discover that the lemon-and-pepper scent is a new aftershave he bought "to impress" me, but apparently I told him when I was sick that it makes him smell like a "sexy chicken," so he's a little disappointed.

Henry was also right that Winnie didn't get the flu anywhere near as badly as I did—she probably doesn't live off pot noodles—and after a couple of days she bounces back and very sweetly tries to "nurse me back to health": copying her dad by conscientiously patting my forehead with flannels she's found under the sink and which I don't have the heart to tell her are meant for cleaning the oven.

"Sssshhhh," she tells me, hauling some fresh ice cubes out of the freezer and vigorously rubbing them all over my face. "You'll feel better soon, don't worry."

One of the ice cubes sticks to my cheek and she rips it off: *ouch*.

"I think I'm better now," I say as firmly as possible.

"Ssssshhh," she says again, having none of it. "You're very, *very* sick, maybe dying, so you just lie down and be quiet. I'm a trained vet, you know."

Alarmed, I watch her wander off, presumably to find a cone for my head.

By the time I've regained my health, I can't remember a time when I didn't know these two beautiful humans—when they weren't an integral part of my daily life—and when it's finally time, I don't want to go.

"You can stay longer," Henry says for the third time as I gather my belongings, which consist of a phone, a coat and a ruined red satin dress. "There's no rush at all. In fact, as your new not-quite-doctor boyfriend, I highly recommend staying. Vague safety reasons and so on."

"I really do have to go home." I smile at him. "I have a life I need to get back to."

"Fair." Henry pauses. "You know, it feels like I've known you a really long time, Margot. I'm not sure how, or why, because it makes no sense, but it feels like I have."

I feel it too, and wonder if my visions have left a mark. As if, somehow, a part of him knows what's coming for us too, just without having to see it first.

And it *is* coming. For the first time, I'm sure.

"Soppy bastard," I smile, throwing my coat over my arm. "Thank you for taking care of me. I'll text you when I'm home."

EXCEPT I DON'T.

Because just as I'm walking up the path to my flat, I see Polly. She's climbing out of a blue car in her driveway, followed by three small, giggling blond children, and—panicked—I instinctively pretend I haven't seen her. She's been leaving long voicemails all week, and I've been far too mortified to listen to them. It took me three whole days of vomiting to realize I'd accidentally ghosted the interview, and I'm guessing our budding friendship is now firmly over.

"Margot!" Polly waves at me as she opens her front door. "Hang on! Kids, get in, grab an orange juice carton each out of the fridge and I'll be there in a second."

Then she crosses toward me and I look for an escape route.

Shit. She knows where I live.

"I'm sorry," I say quickly, holding my hands up as if she's about to shoot me. "I disappeared on you, there's no excuse, but I was really—"

"Oh, hush." Polly shakes her head in exasperation. "Are you alright? Henry told me how sick you were and I've felt awful about it all week. I assumed you'd freaked out, but I should have realized you wouldn't just evaporate without a good reason. I'm so sorry."

"No, *I'm* sorry," I say in relief.

"No, *I* am."

"I am."

"How about we're *both* sorry," Polly laughs.

"And Charlie?" I wince slightly. "Does she know I was ill?"

"Ah." Polly clears her throat. "Charlie's not picking up my calls. She came all the way to Bristol from London for that interview, and I don't think she was super happy about it just being me and a stale piece of cake."

I deflate further. "So what do we do now?"

"I'm not sure," Polly admits, at a visible loss for the first time since I met her. "I've been approaching all my media contacts but haven't had any bites. Apparently there's 'just no market for a show like that.'"

We stare at each other for a few seconds, both willing each other to remain hopeful but failing.

"This is it," I say flatly. "Isn't it? The end of my meteorology career."

My voice catches slightly.

"I'll think of something," she promises me, rubbing my arm. "Just leave it with—"

Behind her, a blue car door opens. I stare at the man leisurely climbing out of the driver's seat: ridiculously handsome and well dressed, all five foot ten of him.

"Pols," he says flatly, still looking at his phone, "do you want me to take the car seat out of the—"

Peter looks up and locks eyes with me.

His face changes color, and his eyes widen so abruptly he looks like one of those fluid-filled toys that's just been squeezed. I hold his gaze without looking away. His LOL-ing days are now very much numbered, and he knows it.

"Oh!" Polly smiles at him, distracted. "Don't worry about it, Pete. Leave it in there. I've got to take Paige to the dentist's in an hour anyway."

She looks back to me, apparently not noticing anything amiss.

"This is Margot," Polly adds easily, gesturing toward me. "She moved in not very long ago. I was just saying hi."

"Hi," I say through gritted teeth.

OK: that's slightly weird. She hasn't mentioned me before? Not even once? Hasn't she been making copious notes about branding me for the last two weeks?

"Hello, Margot." Peter lifts a hand, trying to control his face. "Nice to meet you."

"Mummy!" a small voice screams from the house. "Perry took the last orange juice and it's *not* fair because *he* likes apple juice too and I *don't* and he says I *have* to have apple instead and you have to come in and make him give it *baaaaaaack*!"

Polly closes her eyes briefly and pinches the bridge of her nose. It's nice to know her children are normal and not the well-behaved little clones I initially thought they were.

"Bloody hell," Polly sighs. "God forbid they share an orange juice."

Then she opens her eyes and smiles brightly—"Coming!"—before hurrying toward the house and lobbing a farewell wave at me. "I'll text you, OK?"

I nod, slightly bewildered by the vagueness. "OK."

Then I turn back to Peter. He looks even more alarmed—what are we texting each other about?—and presumably is also trying to work out the odds of this happening, much like I did. He's an accountant. I'd imagine he can do the math quicker.

"Um," he says slowly as soon as Polly's gone. "Ah."

"*Margot.*" I point to myself and jab my collarbone a few times. "Mar-got. M, A, R, G, O, T. And how do you spell Peter? Is it J, O, H, N?"

Peter flinches and I suddenly want to smack him: did he actually think I was just going to let him get away with it?

"You're . . ." He takes a deep breath. "Not going to tell her, right?"

Oh. Yes. Apparently, he did.

"Of course I'm going to tell her." I scowl at him, now absolutely furious. The sheer *audacity* of this man. "You bought an Italian dinner, not me."

And I turn and slam back into my house.

22

But a fire has been lit.

I'm not sitting around any longer, waiting for the great hand of fate—or Polly—to fix my life for me. I will not be lulled into a false sense of security, like Macbeth, but I won't be defeated by visions of failure either. And I sure as hell will not allow *men* to decide the pattern my life takes, yet again.

Who I become will not be decided by Other Margot, or anyone else. I am going to choose what I want, make a decision and carve my own route: shaping the landscape around me by force, like a strong wind. I will not be just blown around by the breeze of other people, even if that person is my . . . future self.

Still furious—fucking *Pete*—I pull out my notepads.

With venom, I go to the back of my cupboard and find one forgotten photo album: the only one that didn't get burned with everything else. Impatiently, I rip out every photo of me and Aaron—drunk, giggling, hiding the truth behind happy selfies—and throw them in the bin. Then I grab my laptop and printer and set to work. I start with extreme weather conditions, always exciting. I note down physical demonstrations, where possible: the size of the largest hailstone ever recorded—bigger than a melon—and how quickly the hottest temperature on Earth could cook an egg. Blood rain (caused by microalgae spores); the strongest wind; the biggest tornado. I remember that the longest recorded lightning flash was an unbelievable 790 kilometers, which is roughly the distance from London to Zurich, so I diligently draw that on a map too.

I print out images and scrawl notes about how the moon affects tides and how the planet is lopsided; that you measure snow accurately by melting it down.

Then I move on to seasons, climate change, rainbows and satellites.

Fogs and fires, floods and heatwaves.

The scope is never-ending—the world is full of infinite content—and as I bury myself in my work, I can't remember the last time I was this fired up.

Finally, exhausted and covered in paper cuts, I turn on my video camera.

"Hello, Charlie," I say in a clear and steady voice. "This is Margot the Meteorologist. I can understand why you think I'm not the right person for this show, but I want to prove to you that I am."

I pause and hold up the scrapbook, now stuffed full, and point at the huge words I've scribbled across it: *Weather or Not.*

"In this book, enclosed, I have included detailed ideas for our weather show. I want it to be interactive, where kids can ask as many questions as they want. Perhaps with a little mascot, some kind of cartoon. A lightning bolt, or a raindrop."

Winter would like that, wouldn't she? I shall take her as my guide.

"Why am I right for this? I have a decade of experience working as a meteorologist, plus almost a year of creating successful video content for social media. But, more importantly, I have an entire lifetime of loving the sky and everything that comes from it. This is the job I was meant to do."

I can't go back to the Met Office, but that's OK: I don't want to.

I want to move *forward.*

"So if you give me another chance, I will bring everything I have to help you make a show that captures the imaginations of children all over the world. I will bring the fresh ideas you were looking for. And I will—"

Cold runs through me.

For God's sake, not now, I am *concentrating*—

I'M STARING AT Henry.

His face is all I can see, all I want to see, and it is so beautiful, so warm, so incredibly kind; the little silvery hairs in his beard are shining like metal. I smile at him—hello, you—then realize with alarm that his eyes are slightly wet, as if he's about to start crying.

"Are you OK?" I whisper, taking his hand.

"Yes," he whispers back, squeezing my fingers.

I squeeze back, then become faintly aware that we're still staring at each other and there's piano music playing, except it sounds like it's coming from a real piano, and it feels as if I'm supposed to say something?

Blinking, I pull my eyes away from his face and look down. What the—

Bloody hell, am I wearing a long white dress?

"Henry . . ." I say in shock, then hold out a foot so I can check what kind of shoes I'm wearing. Yup, they're white too—flat, with beads all over them. Now I glance up at Henry more carefully. He's wearing a dark gray tux, with a little purple flower in the buttonhole, and when I look slightly down I see Winter—taller, about ten years old, hair beautifully plaited—beaming at me, wearing a matching purple dress.

She gives me an encouraging nod and my heart squeezes.

"I think it's your turn," Henry whispers. "Take your time. No big deal."

Nodding—I was going to, thank you—I turn to my side and see Polly standing there with Eve, both in lilac with yellow bouquets. Eve has clearly been crying (her nose is all pink), but Polly is standing steadfast, as always.

Amazed, I look upward: we're outside, under a bower of lilac and yellow flowers—wow, we really went hard on the purple theme—and huge trees stretch all the way around us. Huh. I'm getting married in the middle of a wood. That seems very unlike me: did I put up a fight? Did I complain about the mud? I look at the fairy lights hanging in the trees. It's so beautiful. No, I do not think I put up a fight. Everything is absolutely perfect.

Still bewildered, I turn to look at the crowd—a sea of faces I don't recognize; Henry must have a lot of friends—when there's a tug on my dress.

Amazed, I look down.

A little boy with brown curls, about four years old, is trying to talk to me. He's so gorgeous, so completely beautiful, and I can *feel* the fierce love I have for him rising up like a tide. I bend down slightly and put a hand on the top of his fluffy head. Oh my God—is this *my* child? Is this my child with Henry?

My eyes fill and suddenly I can't speak.

"Not just yet, Gus," I hear Henry whisper gently. "Hold your horses."

"OK," the little boy says with visible disappointment, putting two rings back in his pocket. Gus. Gustavo? Angus? Who is he named after? Or did we just like the name? So many questions, but now is not the time to ask them.

Overwhelmed, I look up at my beautiful nearly-husband and now I can feel Other Margot's frustration with me. She remembers this, she remembers *me*, my confusion, and she knows we're just standing, gormless and weepy, in front of everyone we've ever met.

Just get on with it, I can almost hear her saying, sharp but amused. *Yes, you've been here before, it's the vision, congrats, just say yes so I can marry this man.*

Smiling, I pull myself—ourselves—together. We both want the same thing: it doesn't matter if I'm not ready to marry Henry right now, I *will* be by this point of our relationship and I know it.

"Yes," I say clearly, my voice wobbling.

"I think the classic response is usually *I do*." Henry grins widely. "But I'll take it. No backsies."

The crowd laughs and I feel my grandfather's eyes on me, full of love.

Thanks for that, Other Margot whispers.

"I mean, I do," I say quickly. "Obviously. And so on."

The priest, celebrant—whoever he is—smiles warmly.

"And do you, Henry Armstrong, take—"

I can feel the vision fading, but this time I'm holding on as hard as I can: I want to stay here, I want to hear him say *I do*, I want to see our little boy again, I want to give Winnie a cuddle, I want to enjoy the party with my friends and my family, and most of all I want to stay in the blissful, intense, all-consuming *love* I feel: for Henry, for my life, for everything that has brought me to this point.

You'll get here eventually, but it's my turn now.

With a twinge of sadness—and a weird sense of love for myself, for a version of me I haven't become yet—I nod and say goodbye to her, to me, to us.

And I leave myself in the future we have built together.

WITH WET EYES, I stare at myself on the screen.

I've only been gone three seconds, and everything has changed. I'm going to be a wife and there's a chance I'm going to be a mum, and it feels nothing like I expected. I don't feel scared, or anxious, or convinced that I'm going to screw it up. I don't worry about what it "*really* means" for my life. I'm not terrified of change or if I'll do it right, because somehow I know I will. I'm just . . . happy.

Ridiculously, overwhelmingly happy.

I will choose this future too, I abruptly realize. I'm not being forced down this path by an unseen hand. This is the path I *want*, the landscape I want to carve, and I don't need to even think about it.

I want it *all.*

Smiling, I wipe my eye: I can edit my little trance out of the video in a minute.

"So please consider me for the job," I finish with a tiny, emotional nod. "Because I want this to be my future."

23

So have you heard back?"

I shake my head: I sent the scrapbook to Charlie—plus the video on a memory stick—in a big box covered in little clouds and lightning bolts and sunrays. It looked quite a lot like a school project done by a six-year-old (I suspect Winter would have done a better job), but I vaguely hoped Charlie might think I was harnessing my inner child.

But that was days ago now, and I still haven't heard anything.

Not that I'm surprised: my visions have strongly suggested that I'm going to be wearing an oversized hamster costume and serving burgers. But I had to at least *try*, right?

"Nope." I clear my throat. "It's fine. I'll sort something out."

Henry gives me a piercing side glance and squeezes my arm. He's been amazing—totally supportive, encouraging, one hundred percent full of belief in me—but there isn't a lot he can do. He's got enough going on, trying to fix his own career.

"And have you told Polly?"

I wince. My future husband is alarmingly invested in the minutiae of my life, which is lovely but also kind of annoying. *My future husband.* A thrill runs through me: it feels so safe, so comforting, like a tiny break in a storm I'm carrying with me.

We wait for a van to pass, then we cross the road toward the pub.

"No," I sigh. "Not yet. I've tried like six times, but she always has the kids with her when I see her, and this isn't information I want them overhearing."

"You'll do it," he says comfortingly. "When the time is right."

We stand together outside the pub.

That's the problem, isn't it? The time. All those years stretching out in front me, and I don't know what order it all goes in.

"Yes." I nod. "Are you ready?"

"No." Henry laughs. "Is anyone ever ready for this?"

"Nope," I grin, kissing his cheek. "Good luck. You're going to need it."

"*HENRY!*" EVE LEAPS up from her seat with her arms out. "Finally!"

My best friend leaps over a pub stool and flings herself at poor Henry, wrapping herself around him while he blinks in surprise.

"Oh you're *lovely*," Eve adds, tightening her grip. "I like you already."

"Eve, I'm guessing." Henry smiles. "Hello."

"How did you know?" She retracts her arms and pats frantically at his jacket lapels with her hands. "Sorry, I think I've got crisp crumbs all over you."

Jules nods at him, lifting her eyebrows. "Hey."

"And you must be Jules," Henry says, his nostrils twitching slightly. I warned him that Jules would not be easy to win over, and he was totally unfazed. "It's a pleasure to meet you. The column you wrote a few weeks ago was wonderful—you know, the one about the statistical happiness of women who don't marry or have children. It was so beautifully done. So fair and compassionate. Eye-opening, in fact."

I stare at him proudly: good homework, Henry. A*.

"Oh!" Jules wriggles slightly, struggling between her innate need to remain on guard and her love of creative validation. "Thanks."

"The comments section was horrifying," Henry adds sincerely. "So many people furious at the life choices of total strangers."

"*Right?*" Jules lights up. "You wouldn't believe the quantity of hate mail I got. Pages and pages of it. Apparently, I'm an angry, bitter lesbian, and that's only sixty-six point six percent true, thank you very much."

Henry laughs and Eve glances at me in triumph: he's smashing it.

"Can I get you both a drink? Same again?" Henry glances at the table, notes what Eve and Jules are drinking—white wine, Guinness—then looks at me with a small twinkle in his eye. "And you can have one too, I guess. Freeloader."

"Go on then," I smile as he briefly kisses me. "Gin and tonic. When are your friends turning up to interrogate me?"

"In about ten minutes." Henry glances at his watch. "I gave us a little breathing room so that it wasn't total chaos straight away. And I apologize in advance. I met them at uni and they're bloody idiots. Doctors, all but one of them."

Eve beams at him, approving of literally every word out of his mouth, like a besotted child. I wonder briefly if any of Henry's friends are hot and single, and whether I can set them up with her. Though maybe I should leave that until after I've actually found out whether I pass The Test myself.

"Well." Henry puts his jacket down on the booth seat. "I shall go and order from the other side of the pub so you can discuss your first impression of me in private."

He leaves and Jules and Eve immediately turn to me.

"Oh my God," Eve breathes. "I *love* him. *Absolutely love him.*"

I nod: that kind of went without saying. Henry could be wielding a machete and Eve would still think he's *a truly sweet soul.*

Biting my lip, I look anxiously at Jules. "And you?"

"I can't make an accurate assessment after three bloody sentences, can I?" She sees my tense expression and relents slightly. "But so far, yes. I approve."

My entire body relaxes. "Oh, thank God. Yay! Can I have a crisp?"

I take a crisp before anyone answers because it was a rhetorical question and they've spent the last twenty years raiding my fridge.

"So how long has it been?" Eve sits back and I look again at her wine with a wave of sadness. "A month? It seems to be moving fast. Meeting the friends already? That's a big step."

I shrug slightly. "It doesn't really feel it, weirdly."

After all, I was with Aaron an entire decade and I think he sat down properly with my friends a total of four times. For every single one of those he was dragged there with vague promises of "reward" afterward, like a dog with a biscuit. Henry actually *wanted* to meet them, because if they're important to me, they're important to him too. I had no idea how much that would mean to me until he said it.

"What do we know about these friends of his?" Jules glances curiously at the door. "You can tell a *lot* about someone from their friends."

I smile. "Exactly, so be on your best behavior, OK?"

"Is there anything you want us to ask him?" Eve looks warmly over at the bar where Henry is patiently waiting as promised, facing away so he can't secretly lip-read. "You know, things you want to know about him but haven't been able to ask yet? Like has he ever cheated, does he have a bad temper, does he sniff his socks and turn his boxers inside out to avoid washing them, that kind of thing?"

"No," I laugh as Jules's phone pings. "I'd rather find that out the normal way. You know, by slurring random questions at him when I'm drunk."

Jules makes a strange squeaking noise.

Eve and I both look at her in surprise—that was a very not-Jules noise—and she quickly puts her phone back in her pocket.

"Just work," she says tersely. "Sorry, what were we talking about?"

Yeah, that's not going to fly with us. I study her: her face has tensed up, her shoulders are tight. Something is very, very wrong.

"Bullshit," I say sharply. "What was it?"

"*Work.*" Her jaw clenches. "Like I said."

"Oh, come *on*," Eve says, launching herself to the side and grabbing Jules's phone out of her pocket. "I swear if it's yet more hate mail, I'm going to send them a reply myself, and I will *rip* them to—"

She looks at the lock screen and pauses. "Oh."

Eve hands the phone back to Jules, then focuses intently on the nearly empty packet of crisps. "So Henry's training to be a doctor, right? That must be hard work, very impressive. I've always wondered what it would be like to be at uni as a mature student—"

I stare at Eve as she gabbles, then back at Jules. "Tell me."

"No."

"Tell me."

"No."

"Fucking *tell me.*" My voice is rising. "You're my best friends, *tell me what it is.*"

Wincing, Jules hands her phone over to me in silence. On the lock screen is a message from Lily:

Hey J! I've told the world! Thanks for all the support, babe. Love you. See you Friday! Xxx

Below it is an Instagram alert: *@LilSunnyDayz has posted.* I can only see the first few words:

I am beyond delighted to announce that

Teeth gritted, I hold the phone up to Jules. "Open it."

"Margot . . ."

"Open. It."

Jules breathes out and opens Instagram, holds it up to me.

I am beyond delighted to announce that Aaron and I are expecting our first baby! So the wedding will be on hold until next year, but we are so so so excited about starting our beautiful family together! True love is everything. <3

Underneath are thousands and thousands of comments:

OMG! Congrats! You deserve the world!
Sooooo happy for you.
You're GLOWING you ANGEL.

I look back at Jules, who is avoiding eye contact. I feel almost nothing about this new announcement, no jealousy, no pain, no hurt. Aaron and Lily can do what they like, it's none of my business—but what I absolutely do feel now is incandescent *fury*.

"How long have you known." My voice is flat, no question marks. "Jules, how *long* have you known."

"A couple of weeks," she says in a small voice.

Weeks, and she didn't give me a heads-up: she just told me to stay away from Lily's social media pages.

"And what did she mean, 'see you Friday'? How often do you see Lily?" I'm getting louder and louder, but I don't care. "How *often*, Jules?"

"Every few weeks," she whispers. "She's quite far away, and they're renovating the new house, so she needed—"

I take a deep breath. "You *told* me you cut her off."

"I—"

But that's not it: that's not the anger I'm feeling. It's bad enough that she's stayed close with Lily after what she did and has deliberately lied about it. It's bad enough that she's secretly traveling all the way to Exeter every month to help them redecorate. No, it's the thought I've had since that night, since the wedding, the thought I've been pushing away as hard as I possibly can, and now it's right at the front of my brain and I can't keep pushing.

"Did you know." I stand up. "*Did you fucking know.*"

In my peripheral vision, I can see Henry tentatively approaching with three bemused men and this probably isn't the best first impression I could make, but I don't care, I don't give a shit, I am going to rip this pub up from its goddamn roots.

"Jules!" I scream. "*Did you know that Aaron was with Lily before I did?*"

She looks down. "Yes."

I close my eyes in pain and it suddenly hits me: Jules isn't in my wedding. I'd been so focused on Henry, the little boy, the happiness, I hadn't paid attention to the fact that my best friend wasn't standing next to me at the altar. She's gone, and this is why.

"Margot—"

And it feels worse.

Somehow, after everything Lily and Aaron did, *this* feels like the biggest betrayal.

"What about you?" I turn my fury on Eve. "Did you know too?"

"No!" Eve's green eyes widen and even in my anger I feel a nauseous wave of relief. "I swear! I didn't know anything! And I really *did* cut Lily out. I haven't spoken to her since, I wouldn't, I *swear*, Maggie."

"She didn't know," Jules says quietly. "It was just me. And I am so, so—"

"Don't talk to me," I hiss, grabbing my handbag as my eyes fill. "Julia, don't *ever* talk to me again."

And I push past a bewildered Henry into the street.

24

"MEG! WAIT!"

I continue stomping, fully aware that the second I stop feeling furious the real pain is going to start and I am not ready for it.

"Don't," I snap hoarsely as Henry catches up. "Don't tell me to calm down, don't tell me I'm overreacting, don't tell me not to be so dramatic—I don't want to calm down, I am *allowed* to feel fucking angry, it is my *right* as a *human*."

Henry touches my elbow. "I wasn't going to."

"*Good*," I snarl, not at him: at the world. "Because I have *never* been this angry. *Ever.* She went with me to wedding-dress fittings, she helped me choose my flowers, she sorted out my stupid updo for me when, when—"

I was shaking too hard to do it myself.

She asked me if I was certain Aaron was the person I wanted to marry.

"Aaaarrrghhh!" I scream, kicking a bin as hard as I can. "Owwwww, *fuck*! Why is that made out of metal, what the *fuck* is wrong with this city, why can't it be *plastic*? I'm going to write to the council, I'm going to email the mayor, I'm going to—"

Henry wraps his arms around me and I burst into tears.

"She's my *best friend*," I sob into his neck. "I've known her since I was five years old, I don't remember a time when Jules wasn't my favorite person, and *she chose Lily*."

Except it doesn't come out like that: it comes out in a garbled roar.

"I know." Henry strokes my head. "And you're allowed to be bloody furious, Meg. You're allowed to feel it."

Except now I don't know how I feel: rage is morphing into sadness into shame into pain into fear and back again. Because now I haven't just lost Lily, I've lost Jules: two of my best friends, gone. A foursome, cut in half.

"I'm sorry," I mumble, starting to cry again. "I ruined meeting your friends, they think I'm nuts, they *hate* me, and I've ruined *everything*."

"Actually," Henry says, pushing my fringe out of my eyes, "I think they found it all quite exciting. An iconic first impression. Either way, I don't give a crap. I'm dating you, not them. They'd be rubbish girlfriends."

I laugh and a bubble of snot pops out of my nose. "Sorry."

"I've seen you do worse," Henry smiles. "Margot, you're not dramatic, you're not overreacting, you don't need to calm down. I'm not sure why you think you do."

Because Aaron wouldn't let me feel emotions, I abruptly realize. Every time I was angry, or upset, or scared, or uncomfortable, or sad, he'd tell me to *calm down* and to *stop being so dramatic*. I was *too much*, until I reduced myself to the only emotion he wanted me to have: admiration for him.

It feels like all the rage that has been building for nine months now has reached its pinnacle and I'm looking down from it, at a great height, ready to burn. Except it hasn't really been building for that long, has it? It's been building for ten years. An entire decade of suppressed emotion. More than a quarter of my life.

"I'm still angry," I say, pushing myself away and wiping my face. "I'm still angry, I'm still hurt, I still want to kick things."

"Or throw things?" Henry asks gently.

"Yes," I confirm. "Or throw things."

"In which case," he says, taking my hand, "I have an idea."

"I'm *not* bowling," I sniff sulkily as Henry leads me down a back street. Jules has rung so many times in fifteen minutes, I've had to put my phone on silent. "I appreciate that it might take my mind off things, but I don't have any energy left to pretend to be excited about skittles."

Henry laughs as we take a corner. "It's not bowling."

We're standing outside a large black industrial building covered in red lettering: *Urban Axe Throwing.*

"Axes?" I say in surprise.

"Axes," Henry confirms. "Think you could throw an axe right now?"

I search myself for the rage I felt and still feel it bubbling at the base of my stomach, hot and red. I've tried punching, I've tried setting things on fire, I've tried screaming, I've tried moving house, I've tried collapsing my career, I've tried being a bitch to everyone I've ever met, I've tried taking down every man in a thirty-mile radius.

Throwing deadly weapons at a wall: not so much.

"Absolutely," I say firmly.

HENRY SEEMS TO know the people at the axe-throwing place—they manage to squeeze us in, last-minute—and when I look at him in surprise, he simply shrugs.

"We all get angry sometimes," he says simply.

Then they usher us into a large cage and give us a pink-haired, heavily pierced instructor named Gary, who also seems to know Henry.

"My dude!" Gary slaps him on the back. "Long time no see!"

I look at Gary suspiciously: he has a cartoon frog tattoo on his neck, and I'm not sure that's the kind of person we need overlooking a potentially lethal activity.

"How's it going?" Henry grins at him. "Moved up to manager position yet?"

It is astonishing to me how this new boyfriend of mine manages to make friends with everyone who crosses his path. Probably because he asks questions and genuinely cares about the answers.

"Last year," Gary chuckles, handing him an axe. "Thanks for the advice, mate. Super helpful. Obviously, I need to be here for legal reasons and whatever, but you know what you're doing."

Henry laughs and hands the axe to me. "It's not for me, this time."

I look down at my new weapon, brightening at the weight of it, the sharpness of it, the solid potential fatality of it. Oooh, I think I'm going to enjoy this. I can't believe I've been punching a bag in my living room like an amateur.

"Um." Gary has noticed the dangerous gleam in my eye. "I'm going to need to run through the guidelines with you, in that case. Keeping it safe, people. Hahaha."

Clearly, he can see I am not here to play.

Nodding, I half listen to what Gary's saying (throw it at the board, follow through with your shoulder, stay facing forward, hold on tight, don't let go too early, please don't kill me by accident, woman with crazy eyes) and focus instead on the wall in front of me. I can feel the fire in me flickering, and I'm suddenly worried it's not hot enough anymore: just embers and glowing coals and sadness.

As Gary finishes a quick demonstration—making it look a lot easier than I suspect it is—I turn the axe round and round in my hands.

Then I look at Henry desperately. "I don't think I can do this."

"You can." He grins warmly. "You have to. I just paid, like, three nights' worth of tips."

"Right." I nod, and stare back at the wall. "So I just . . . throw it?"

"Just throw it," he agrees.

"OK. Here goes."

Lamely, I pull my hand up and attempt to chuck the now ridiculously heavy axe at the wall. The side of it hits with a thud and it bounces straight onto the floor, looking disappointed.

"Good first try!" Gary says behind me encouragingly.

"I don't feel anything," I say, turning to Henry in frustration. "It's not working."

"How about you try talking to the board?" He smiles. "Tell it what you're angry about. *Then* throw the axe. Say whatever you want to say, no judgment from me. Or Gary. Right, Gary?"

"Trust me," Gary says darkly. "I've heard it *all*."

Swallowing, I nod and turn back. "Um. Hello, board. It's nice to meet you."

Henry laughs. "So polite."

"I . . . um." I take a deep breath. "I'm angry that my best friend Julia has lied to me and that she took Lily's side over mine." I feel an abrupt need to contextualize this, for both Gary and the board. "Lily was my best friend too, by the way. She ran off with my fiancé the night before our wedding."

Gary nods—gotcha—and the board has zero reaction, as expected.

Lifting my arm, I throw the axe.

This time, it hits the board with a beautiful, deadly *thud* and a thrill runs through me.

"I'm angry that my friendship group has been destroyed by a *man*," I say more loudly, lifting another axe with a lot more energy this time. "That *thirty years* together has crumbled because of a pretentious, black-T-shirt-wearing, guitar-not-playing, lying, cheating idiot."

I throw another axe: it lodges itself in the wall.

"I'm angry that Aaron treated me terribly for years and I didn't do anything about it because I thought it was what I deserved." Another axe. "I'm angry that I never had it out with him, or her, that I just *walked away*."

There goes another axe.

"I'm angry that my parents left when I needed them, and I'm angry that they didn't even *ask* me to go with them, and I'm angry that a part of me is glad they're not totally happy there because it means they miss me, and I miss them, and I'm so selfish sometimes it makes me *furious*."

Another axe.

"I'm angry that my grandfather is old and I can't do *anything* about it."

Another axe.

"I'm angry that Eve can't have a baby."

Axe.

"I'm angry that I keep *seeing* shit and am expected to handle it all on my own, puzzle it all out, as if I don't have enough to bloody worry about."

Axe.

"I'm angry that my neighbor's husband hit on me and now it's down to *me* to sort it out when it should be down to *him*, and yet *another* friendship is at risk because of a *man*."

Axe.

"I'm angry that I worked my entire adult life for a career I loved, which I threw away out of pettiness and *spite*."

Axe.

"I'm angry that I wasted most of my twenties and my thirties and I will *never* get that time back."

Axe.

"I'm angry that now I have an amazing boyfriend and I wasn't ready for him to be amazing, wasn't sorted out enough, wasn't healed enough, but now I have to heal and be OK as fast as I can so I don't *screw it up*."

Axe.

I'm shouting now—and sweating profusely—but I don't care, it needs out, I need these emotions *out of me*, I need that board to be *full* of axes.

"And most of all," I say, wiping my forehead on my sleeve, "I am angry because I'm not angry anymore. I'm happy. I'm so fucking happy. And it feels wrong, because I've forgotten what that even feels like and that makes me *angry*."

I throw the axe and hold out my hand.

"We've run out of axes," Gary says faintly.

"Oh." Blinking, I stare at the wall. "Right. Sorry about that."

Slightly out of breath, I turn to face Henry, expecting to

see some kind of horror and repulsion as he realizes what he's letting himself in for.

It's not there. He just looks . . . proud of me.

"I'm going to need an axe," he calmly tells Gary, who is busy collecting all the axes I've already buried. "Just one, this time."

With a nod, Gary hands it over.

"I'm angry too," Henry says simply. "I'm angry because I feel things for you that make me feel like I've lost Amy all over again, and I feel guilty and worried and ashamed that I'm moving on and scared that I'll lose you like I lost her, and most of all, I'm angry that I'm happy too."

He throws the axe and it lands perfectly in the middle, in a way that tells me Henry has been very, very angry many times before. Angry that his beautiful young wife died, that he lost his beloved medical career, that he had a tiny child to look after all on his own, that he has a brain the size of a small planet and he spends this power asking people if they want Parmesan on their tagliatelle.

We stand and stare at each other in silence for a few seconds.

"You need to take Winter to see her mum's ashes," I say quietly. "She needs to be able to talk to her. To talk about her. Even though it hurts you. She needs to know who her mum was."

Henry's face colors. "I know."

"You can't avoid things because they're hard, Henry. We have to be able to fight. Properly, *really* fight. Because if we can't fight, then it means this isn't strong enough. It means what we're throwing isn't an axe, it's a vase. I've had the vase, and it broke. I need the axe."

A nod. "I know."

Henry doesn't ask how I know he avoids fighting when we've never really had one. He doesn't even ask how I know about Amy's ashes, although something tells me Winter may have given him a clue.

"So . . . you want extra time?" Gary steps in awkwardly. "Or . . . are we all done?"

I smile at him. "I think I'm done. Henry?"

Henry nods. "Me too."

Holding hands, we walk out of the axe-throwing cage room, and I now realize groups of people are yelling, laughing, screaming, celebrating: it's a place for joy, for fun. Or maybe they just have punching bags at home: it's difficult to tell.

"Hey." Henry pauses. "Margot, what you said . . ."

I flinch slightly. "Which bit?"

"About 'seeing shit.' And . . . puzzling it all out on your own."

Nice one, Margot. What a way to reveal that you can see the future: screaming, with a deadly object in your hand.

"Oh!" I frown. "It was more . . . you know. Metaphorical."

Henry looks at me carefully. "Right."

"Not *real*. Not like, uh, visions or whatever." I laugh and it sounds forced, like air squeezed out of a bottle. "I'm not having *visions* of the future or anything, and then trying to piece them together in the right order. That would be *crazy*."

Henry frowns. "Yes. I guess it would."

I stare at him. "You guess?"

"No, it totally would. I'm just saying, if there's ever anything you need to talk about, I'm open-minded."

Yeah, I am not taking him up on that. Nobody—bar maybe Macbeth and his wife—is *that* open-minded. If I wasn't experiencing it myself, I'd be calling the nearest hospital and having the Prophet locked away, highly medicated. Plus, at no point in any future vision has Henry indicated that he knows about my visions, and I have never mentioned them. And one of us surely would have by this point, right? Which obviously means I don't tell him, and I'm good with that decision. It seems like the smartest move.

"Cool," I say as my phone vibrates in my bag. "Good to know."

Missed call: Jules
Missed call: Jules
Missed call: Jules

Biting my lip, I scroll down, a long way down.

Let's just say that while I was throwing axes, Jules was lobbing a very different but equally sharp weapon at me in turn. Guilt, predominantly, along with three decades of history, i.e. emotional blackmail.

Please talk to me.

Teeth gritted, I text back:

GO. AWAY.

"You sure you don't want to hear what she has to say?"

I glance up at Henry with a scowl. "Nope."

"Ah." He lifts his eyebrows. "Because you would never avoid something just because it's hard, right?"

"Touché." I scowl at him a bit harder. "Shut up."

"No." Henry smiles. "I will not."

I smile too, but he doesn't get it. This isn't about fixing something chipped or slightly cracked around the edges. And there aren't two sides to this story: there's the whole story, and then there are the people who only knew half of it. Jules was supposed to be on my side, with me. Oblivious and stupid.

And I don't want to hear what she has to say, because I know how this ends: I've seen it, with my own eyes.

What we had is already broken.

25

IT TAKES ME two days to realize I'm a hypocrite.

It's not always easy to look inward instead of raging outward; it is far easier to blame other people instead.

"HI." I STAND on the doorstep, hands in my pockets. "Can I come in?"

It's early in the morning and Polly is mid tying her hair up in a perfect blonde bun, grips sticking out of her mouth like insane beige teeth. She cocks her head slightly. It's sweet how often she does that, like a curious beagle.

"Mmmnneeugh!" She takes the pins out. "Sorry, I mean—of course!"

I follow her into her spotless, glossy house, feeling nauseous.

"Is anyone else at home?" I swallow and look around. "Like . . . uh . . . small people with big ears and whatnot."

"No, no small people, no inordinately large ears." Polly smiles. "I've finally got the house to myself. School and nursery and work, respectively. I'll let you guess which one is at which, but Peter was furious when they handed him Lego."

I force a smile in return.

This is it. No more excuses.

I've been ignoring all phone calls and essay-length messages from Jules—not even reading them, just muting and leaving them in archive—except now I wonder if this is how she felt too.

Every time we sat down together, was she desperate to tell me and unable to work out how? Did she feel sick all the time? All I know is that I can't fling numerous toys out of the proverbial pram while doing almost exactly the same thing to someone else.

"I need to talk to you about something pretty serious," I say bluntly. "And I'm not good at the whole . . . sensitive conversation thing. I'm the human equivalent of a bullet. So please forgive me if it comes out wrong."

Polly frowns. "OK."

"And by *pretty serious*," I amend, "I mean very, very serious. Like, life-shatteringly serious. Like, nothing-will-ever-be-the-same-for-you-again and you-may-hate-me serious."

"Gosh." She frowns. "Hang on—do I need coffee? I'll get coffee."

Polly stands up and walks over to the coffee maker, pauses and looks back at me with her eyebrows raised.

"It's a gin conversation," I admit flatly. "At ten a.m. I'm sorry."

"Right." She opens the larder. "I've got vodka. Will that work?"

"Yep. Pour me one too."

With a steady hand—we'll see how long that lasts—Polly pours two enormous glasses of vodka. Then I continue to watch with growing amazement as she cuts a large fresh orange in half, patiently squeezes it on top of each glass and carves little orange peel curls to pop on top. When she starts searching for sugar and cinnamon to dust, I let out a loud groan.

"For fuck's sake, Polly. Stop procrastinating and just bring the bottle."

She nods and sits down. "Right. I'm ready. Go."

"Your husband is shagging about on the internet," I say, staring her directly in the eyeballs. "Or, at the very least, trying very hard to. I unwittingly went on a date with him about a month ago, in a nearby Italian restaurant, and he was calling himself *John*. He tried to go home with me, but I wasn't interested. I guessed he was married, but also I just didn't like him.

As a man. Or a human. Sorry. Actually, I ordered everything on the menu and made him pay, as revenge, which isn't really relevant at all, but I just wanted to clarify that I did *not* have sex with your husband."

Perhaps unsurprisingly, Polly's face is a total blank.

"I've known for a fortnight," I add hurriedly. "Since I saw the photo of him on your fridge. But it was . . . never quite the right time to say something."

My mind skitters back to all the times Jules could have said something.

Is there *ever* a right time to hurt the people you love?

"Oh! And I have evidence. Look."

With no satisfaction at all, I hold out my burner phone. John's profile—sorry, Peter's profile—disappeared about three minutes after we ran into each other in their driveway, but I got there quicker and screenshotted everything. Let's just say you don't need to have visions of the future to have seen *that* coming.

There's silence from Polly as she takes a huge swig of vodka and orange.

"I'm sorry," I say earnestly. "I am so, so, so sorry. I could have told you sooner. Are you OK? Do you want me to confront him for you? He knows I know, by the way. We obviously 'met' when you came home the other day."

Swallowing more vodka, Polly takes my phone off me.

Cheeks bright pink, she studies the screenshots.

"Six foot? You're *still* saying that, Pete? You weren't six foot twenty years ago and you haven't grown since." She scrolls down, reading intently, then makes a face. "He *is* a Gemini, but he knows *exactly* what that 'means' because he reads his horoscopes daily. Long walks on the beach, my ass. He usually drives and meets us at the other end. Never smokes? Our garden is *littered* with poorly hidden butt ends."

I reach out and attempt to put a compassionate hand on top of hers, even though it's holding a now almost empty glass of vodka.

She's clearly having a very polite meltdown.

"'*Hear* to talk'?" Polly keeps reading. "Jesus. How embarrassing, Peter. Posy can spell better than this already."

I'm watching her face, but I don't fully understand the reaction.

Surely she should be crying, pacing, staring out of the window, dramatically evaluating where her youth has gone and so on? Calculating how many women he has met, how far it has gone, whether their marriage is salvageable?

"That is a really horrible photo," she says, pointing at the final one. "See how the sun is shining straight down? You can tell he's losing his hair. What a rookie."

"Um." I take my phone back. "Pol—can I call you Pol?"

"I think once you've been on a date with my husband, love of my life, father of my children, you probably should, yes."

I blink. "OK. Pol, are you, perchance, in shock?"

"I am in shock, yes. Absolutely." She nods and finishes the vodka. "I'm in shock that his profile is so *humiliating.* Why did you even go on a date with him in the first place, Maggie? The man wrote LOL at the end of three sentences and he's nearly fifty years old."

"I . . . uh." This time, I blink three times. "Not important. Self-destructive mode. Can we circle back to your bizarre reaction now, please?"

"Margot," Polly says patiently, as if I'm one of her kids, "I know."

"What do you mean, you *know*?"

"I know. I've known for ages. Over a year, actually. You think you can have an online dating profile in a city this size and get away with it? I've had two single girlfriends send me screenshots already, although by the looks of it, he's actually made his profile *worse* since the last time I saw it. I don't think he's having much luck. The man needs a decent copywriter."

"You know," I repeat in amazement. "Of *course* you know."

How could Polly, the most together and polished human I've ever met, *not* have worked it out? It's just me, the gullible idiot, who doesn't have a clue what's going on right under their nose when their partner comes home late at night, unwilling to kiss them before they've brushed their teeth.

"And you're OK with it?" Now it's my turn to swig my drink. "You're fine with Peter . . . dating other women?" A sudden thought: "Wait, is this one of those super-modern marriages where you both date other people and come home and tell each other about it for fun? Is it, you know, an *open marriage*?"

All my anxiety has completely evaporated. *She knows.*

Maybe they take alternate evenings, organizing their schedules properly so they don't have Italian two nights running.

"Of course I'm not OK with it," she says in exasperation. "He's barely enough of a husband when he's here, let alone when he's wining and dining other women. Clearly, neither of us is happy. But I'm not in a financial position to leave. Not yet. So I've been putting all my ducks in a row, sorting out separate bank accounts, talking to my lawyer friend about joint custody arrangements, trying very, very hard to find a new job without him noticing. Which is surprisingly easy, because he pays absolutely zero attention to what I'm doing."

She looks at me pointedly over her glass.

"Oh!" I inhale in surprise. "Right! OK, that explains why you were more excited about the telly job than I was."

And also why she didn't tell him about me.

"One giant step toward freedom," she says with a shrug, pouring both of us more vodka. "If I can get a job that lets me work from home, doing something I love, I don't have to wait until the twins go to school, as was originally the plan. That would mean I can leave much, much sooner. But I do also believe in this project, and in you, Margot. Truly. I'm not just using you to, you know, get out of my shitty marriage."

"I know." I laugh, so incredibly relieved I feel a bit sick again. "You don't have to say that. And I'm not using *you* to save my shitty meteorological career."

"It's a mutually beneficial relationship," Polly says with a grin, cheeks now all glowy and rosy. "Like clownfish and anemones."

"Is it?" I burp lightly. "What do they do?"

"Well, the anemones protect the clownfish with their stinging tentacles and the clownfish clean the . . . Actually, it doesn't really matter. Posy was talking about it yesterday, that's all, and I'm a bit drunk now. We help each other. That's what I mean."

"Sounds quite a lot like a friendship to me."

"It does, doesn't it?"

Polly and I beam at each other, then hold up our glasses.

"Here's to new friendship," she declares loudly to nobody in particular. "And moving forward, and starting again, and spelling *here* correctly."

"And actually laughing instead of saying LOL."

We both laugh loudly, now pretty tipsy.

"Did you *really* order everything on the menu and make him pay for it?" Polly leans forward. "Because that explains why he came home in an inordinately foul mood a few weeks ago, with breath that smelled of crab and Posy's flu snot still on his shoulder."

Not a baby: just a sick eight-year-old. What a douche.

"I did, yes." I nod. "It did not go down well. Fed me for three days, though."

"Good." She smiles widely, reaches forward over the dining table and takes both my hands. "Thank you, Margot. For telling me and for spending our joint-account money on . . . garlic bread?"

"Garlic mushrooms."

"Even better. Let's get out another bottle to celebrate."

And as I watch Polly go back to the larder and start rummaging around, humming and clearly pretty hyper about her future—her imminent freedom, her brand-new beginnings—I see her lovely face at my wedding, grinning at me.

"Hey," I say impulsively, feeling an intense wave of warmth toward her. "Pol, how do you feel about wearing purple satin? Like, a kind of lilac shade? Floor-length? Nothing too fancy. With sparkly shoes?"

She turns. "Oh, I'd look excellent in that. Why?"

"Nothing." I grin at my vodka glass. "I was just wondering."

BY THE TIME I get back to my flat, I'm extremely drunk.

It's all of fifteen steps, and it takes me a solid ten minutes to make it: holding on to various impeccable rose trellises (Polly's) and slightly crumbling brick walls that I really need to sort out if I'm going to be staying here (mine). Polly asked an extremely miffed Peter to "take the kids somewhere fun" for a few hours after school, so that we could continue celebrating her imminent freedom from him in private. It's getting dark now, so I presume we've put the world to rights; I *know* we finished her alcohol cabinet.

I feel warm and giddy and at peace with the world, with myself.

Actually, I'm lying.

Jules is still haunting me, asking why Polly can forgive me but I can't forgive her.

Because it's not the same, I drunkenly shout at her in my head. *Polly was already married, for starters. It wasn't time dependent. I wasn't going with her to wedding fittings, fully aware that the wedding shouldn't happen. I hadn't known her thirty years. I didn't tell the truth because I got caught. I wasn't lying to protect someone I loved more.*

I don't love Lily more, I hear Jules say back calmly.

You must do, because you chose her over me.

"You know what?" I slur crossly, slamming my key into my front door multiple times. "I'm not having this argument with you now, Jules. I'm drunk and you're not actually here and you're being *really* annoying."

Wobbling, I manage to slip off my shoes by holding on to the wall and then stagger to the kitchen, where I desperately look for some kind of sustenance. There's nothing here: just an empty fridge, empty larder, empty life. God, I can't wait for Henry to move in and bring his saucepans and roasted aubergines and lovely lemon-pepper scent with him.

Then I catch myself: I'm doing it again. Waiting to build my life around a man, my entire identity around someone else.

Not going to happen, Margot. Not this time.

With extremely drunken fervor, I manage to find a handful of dried pasta and some tinned tomatoes. Then I wobble out to the garden, where I retrieve the least burnt saucepan, and back into the kitchen to fill it up with water.

Inordinately proud of myself, I sway in front of it and wait for it to boil.

It takes me fifteen minutes to realize I haven't turned on the hob.

"Tomorrow," I promise it firmly. "Cook tomorrow."

Standing on my tiptoes, I retrieve my final pot noodle from a top cabinet and apologize to my cells for giving them zero nutrients, yet again. I manage the kettle, just about. Then I take my precious snack to the sofa, where I briefly check the time on my way: 9 p.m. Nice one, Margot. This is what having no job does to your schedule. You are one short, slippery slope from standing outside a pub at 11 a.m., shouting at it to open already.

I'm just waiting for the powder to turn into mush when the doorbell goes.

"No!" I shout. "No, Jules! Sod off! I don't want to speak to you!"

The doorbell goes again.

"I said NO," I yell into my pot noodle. Huh: there's only one dried pea. This is outrageous. Do they think they can just get away with this? I have been *conned*. "GO. TO. HELL."

"Meg?" A much more welcome voice. "It's Henry."

Henry! Lovely, lovely Henry. When did I last see him? Three days ago? Two? Ugh, it's been so long. He's so lovely. Is he here to cook me dinner? Is he going to physically pick me up like he did last time? Because I don't need him to, but if he *wants* to, he can.

"Hang on!" I get woozily to my feet and try to find somewhere to put the pot noodle. Quickly, I stuff it under the sofa. "Coming!"

Accidentally bumping into the wall, I make it to the door.

"Hellooooo," I say, throwing it open. "Are you here to make passionate—"

Love to me goes drunkenly unsaid—thank goodness—because I now see there's a wailing Winter standing next to him: cheeks streaked with tears, little chest racked with sobs, eyes closed.

"Oh my God." I instinctively get to my knees. "Sweetheart, what is it?"

I will *murder* whatever—or whoever—has hurt her.

Winter throws herself into my arms with such ferocity she almost knocks me over, and I look up at Henry in surprise as she clings to me like a small tentacled sea creature, incoherently trying to explain in between wet little hiccups.

"What she's trying to say," he translates with a small smile, "is that we need your help. Also, you have a noodle stuck to your chin."

26

I AM BLAMING POLLY for this.

She could have just shouted at me for going on a date with her husband, chucked me out of her house and refused to let me drink all her alcohol on a weekday. But noooooooo, she had to be amazing about everything and now here I am: totally screwed.

"Uh." I stand up with difficulty. "Absolutely. Of course."

As elegantly as possible, I remove the noodle from my chin, quickly consider where to put it, give up and pop it in my mouth.

"Nice." Henry nods as I chew and swallow.

"Make yourselves at home!" I wave vaguely in the direction of my pot noodle. "Sit down! Make yourselves comfortable! I . . . um." I look desperately at Henry. "I've had a bit of a *long* day already, if you know what I mean."

Over Winter's head, I make the universal mime of *I'm drunk*, followed by a finger pointing in the direction of Polly's house.

Then I mouth, *I'm so sorry*.

"You told her?" Henry beams with pride at me. "Well done you! How did it go? Either very well or very poorly, judging by your, um, merriness."

Winter wails at the ceiling. "Daaaaaaddddddyyyyyy, tellllll heerrrrrr."

"Sorry." I pat her head and miss slightly. "What's going on?"

We sit on the sofa together and I suddenly realize that Winter is bundled up in an extraordinary way for relatively mild weather. Her purple coat is all puffed up, her arms are held tightly across her stomach and—as I stare in horror—I realize something under there is moving, struggling, trying desperately to get out.

Bloody hell, it's like a scene from *Alien*.

"Henry!" I look up at him in inebriated alarm. "What is—"

"It's a *baby kitten*," Winter sobs, opening her coat dramatically. "She's all on her own and she hasn't got a mummy and she's sick and cold and Daddy says we *can't take her* because he is *mean* and doesn't *love animals* like I do."

At this, the sobs kick up a gear.

"Now, be fair," Henry says gently, with a faint air of frustration. "That is *not* what I said, Winnie. What I said was that legally we're not allowed animals in our flat, our landlord lives upstairs, we'll get kicked out immediately, there's no garden, and what with you being at school and me being at the restaurant, *he* would get lonely."

He looks up at me with eyebrows raised.

"It's a boy," he adds over her head. "I've explained how I know this, with all my advanced medical training, but she's having none of it."

But I'm still staring at the little head now poking out of Winnie's coat.

It's tiny and adorable and . . . orange.

"*Dadddyyyyy*," Winter wails. "We can't just *put her back* there!"

"We were never going to just put *him* back there," Henry says patiently. "I've explained that multiple times, Winter. I'm not a total monster."

He looks at me again, clearly desperate.

"He was behind one of the bins for glass at the back of the restaurant. Winter found him while she was with me for a shift, and the other waiters were like, *hell no, thank you*. I'm guessing the mummy cat was . . ." Henry pauses sensitively ". . . otherwise occupied at that time."

With his hands, where she can't see, he makes a series of

hand gestures that presumably mean *hit by a car*, somewhat less sensitively.

"Goodness," I say in horror, looking at the animal in front of me. It's staring at me with big, round green eyes—and almost incomprehensibly huge ears—and my heart suddenly hurts for it. I do not like cats, I do not want a cat, I have never wanted any kind of pet, but this is the cat from my vision, I am certain of it. This is the cat, it appears, I am getting. Because it is going to be *my* cat, I can feel it.

"I'm not asking you to take him permanently," Henry says quickly, guessing my thoughts. "I was just hoping you could maybe look after him for a day, maybe two, while I ring the local shelter, find somewhere else for him to go."

"Margot will take her forever!" Winter looks up at me with a wobbling little chin. "Margot is *kind*. Margot will be her mummy now, won't you, Margot?"

I had no idea my chest cavity could feel like this: so broken and so whole, all at once. Henry flushes deeply and flinches, aware of what his daughter is really saying, even if she doesn't realize it herself.

"Meg . . ." he says slowly. "This is a lot to—"

"I'll take him." I nod and pick the kitten up. "For now, anyway."

It'll be eight years, at least, and there seems no point in fighting it: another part of my future locks irrevocably into place. This is why they move into mine rather the other way round—they're not allowed pets. The orange kitten stares at me gravely, then puts a paw on my cheek and licks my nose experimentally with his little Velcro tongue, presumably as affirmation that we're now a lifelong unit.

"Thank you, thank you!" Winter lobs herself at me again, nearly knocking the kitten off the end of the sofa. "She's only *little*, she'll be no trouble at *all*."

I look at the orange ball of fluff with my eyebrows raised, feeling rather sober. This is going to become the largest cat I have ever seen in my life: capable of hanging over both ends of a stair at the same time, legs up the wall, while serenely weathering an extremely vocal teenager who *will* be trouble. Maybe we move into a house just to give our giant cat extra room.

"Something tells me he won't be little for long," I observe somewhat dryly. "So what shall we call him?"

I already know, but I don't want to say it, don't want to put that piece of the puzzle there myself.

"Cheese!" Winter hops up and starts to dance, all sadness vanished in the way that sadness vanishes when you're six. "She's the color of cheese!"

I frown: nope, that's not it.

"He's the color of American *Cheddar*," Henry corrects gently, picking him up. "The really crazy neon-orange stuff."

My new flatmate squeaks in confirmation and I see Henry struggle with an intense wave of reluctant love for him, fully aware that he's been thoroughly seduced already.

I nod faintly: Cheddar, which eventually becomes "Cheds."

There it is.

"Hello, Cheddar," I say as the kitten struggles to get back to me. "Or Cheddite when you're naughty, like a French explosive device."

Henry laughs, and as the kitten climbs into my lap, squeaking like a rusty door, I feel another wave of love. Would I have said yes if I hadn't already seen that Cheddar would belong to me? I think so. He's too cute, too alone, too fragile to say no to. This was going to play out exactly the same way even if I hadn't known it was coming. It's impossible to know which bits of my future are caused by the visions—with me fulfilling them knowingly—and which are simply shown. Time is a never-ending circle that can't be pulled apart.

"Welcome to the extremely weird household," I add softly.

Henry gives me a look of such pure gratitude, such softness, such affection, that I don't quite know what to do with it.

So I smile at him, and he smiles back.

"Do you want us to stay while he settles in?" Henry abruptly glances at his watch. "Winter's bedtime was an hour ago—don't look at me like that, Winnie, it is, you don't get special dispensation for being a hero this evening—but I'm obviously not just lobbing a baby animal at you and disappearing, Meg."

I yawn widely, all my drunkenness switching abruptly to exhaustion.

It's been quite the day.

Quite the days, with many yet to come.

"I think I need to sleep," I say as Cheddar climbs up my sweater with considerable effort and courage, like a tiny mountaineer. "I think we probably both do."

"*Thank you*," Henry whispers as Winter sulks toward the front door, rubbing her eyes. Then he leans in to kiss me gently. "You are nowhere near as scary as you pretend to be."

"Tell anyone and I'll kill you," I whisper back.

And my future—the rest of it—disappears into the night.

I DON'T SLEEP.

Instead, I lie in my bed and stare at the ceiling as a tiny ball of Cheddar-colored fluff climbs all over me, investigating every inch of my room until he's satisfied that, yes, this is where he belongs, before promptly passing out in the nook of my arm.

As I stare at his little sleeping face, I am overwhelmed with emotion.

My life—the one I thought lay in one straight, unknowable line—is shining like a silver river, pulling me forward. There's so much I still don't know. Still so much I have left to find out. After all, my visions would total approximately fifteen minutes if Sellotaped together, and there are all the days, the weeks, the years in between that remain invisible.

But those moments are there, and when they catch in the light, they flash.

And I don't understand where my visions have come from, or why I'm getting them. I don't know if it's just me and if I'm alone with this gift, or whether there's some kind of secret underground Premonitions Anonymous club I can join to discuss its complications and maybe swap badges. I don't know if I can tell anyone or whether this is a secret I'll have to carry with me permanently.

I just know that if these visions stopped right now—if I never had another one again—they will have changed my life.

Not just changed but lit up my life like a ray of sunshine.

In such a short time, I have started to become someone I didn't know I could be: unraveled and unwound, unguarded and unlocked. I'd thought I loved Aaron—so much, for so many years—but now that love seems . . . contained, somehow, like a storm inside a bottle. When inside me was all the weather—all the rains and the fires and the hurricanes and the clouds, the rainbows and the dews and the tornadoes and the halos—waiting to be unleashed. I just had no idea, until I was shown how much of everything I could be.

"Thank you," I whisper to Other Margot, wherever she is now.

Cheddar looks up briefly, makes a small mewing noise—*you're welcome*—and goes back to sleep. I curl up on my side, stroking his little head.

And when my phone starts ringing, something tells me it's another part of my future, falling silently into place.

"Hello?" It's an unknown number. "Margot Wayward speaking."

"Hello, Margot. This is Charlotte Taylor, from the BBC."

I sit up in shock and glance at my bedside clock: 9:49 p.m. Oh God, I *cannot* sound drunk right now.

"Oh, hello, Charlotte." Nice. Sober. "How are you this very beautiful evening?"

Slightly less sober.

"I'm sorry to call you at this time," Charlie says. "But I wanted to say that I received your package. The little confetti raindrops inside exploded all over my office. It was a bit of a clean-up job."

I put my hand over my face.

"I'm sorry," I say quickly. "I didn't think that one through."

"Actually, I liked the enthusiasm. It might be the most important quality for a children's television presenter."

There's a pause and I sit up straighter. "What do you—"

"I loved it," she confirms. "I loved your ideas, and you have a natural passion that comes across so well on screen. I've taken the scrapbook to my board and they loved it too. We're keen to get you in for a test shoot as quickly as possible."

There's a silence while I continue to stare in inebriated shock at exposed brickwork.

"Any thoughts?" Charlie prompts. "At all?"

"Oh!" I blink. "Yes, please. Thank you. Please. Thanks."

Stop.

"Good." I can hear Charlie smiling. "And we'd like to bring Polly on as well, to help build your brand. The woman is annoyingly efficient. Always was."

I feel myself light up a little more. *Polly.*

"Can I tell her?" I grin. "I'd like to tell her."

"Of course. Then I'll sort out the details with her. Just a quick question—how do you feel about costumes?"

I frown. "A costume?"

"You know, rainbow boots, raindrop earrings, maybe a lightning clip in your hair—something instantly recognizable and fun for the kids?"

With a bolt of shock, another piece of my puzzle clicks into place. I'm not dressed as a cheeseburger when I pick Winnie up from school: I'm dressed as a children's TV presenter.

"I can do a costume." I nod, eyes welling up.

"Fabulous. I'll get Polly on that too. Have a lovely evening and I'll see you very soon. Bye for now, Margot the Meteorologist."

"Bye, Charlie."

I end the call and stare at my phone for a few seconds. My future wasn't a passive offering at all. It was there because I went after it like a tornado in the rain.

Hitting a few buttons, I wait a second and say: "Polly?"

"SUP!" She hiccups. "My new bestie! How's it *go-ing*, pretty lady?"

I grin: she's still hammered. "Charlie called. We got a test shoot for the show."

"What?" Polly hiccups again. "Why? *How?* Why? Oh God, the room is spinning."

"I'll explain when I see you," I smile. "Sleep off the vodka and I'll come round in the next couple of days so we can prepare."

When she's gone, I make another call and it goes through to voicemail.

"Hi, Grandad. I just wanted to say . . . I love you. That's all. I don't say it much, but I do. I'm sure you know that already. But I love you, a ridiculous amount. I've got a new job opportunity, so I'm going to be snowed under for a few days, but then I'll come round and tell you everything. Sleep well."

I put the phone down and take a few deep breaths.

"Excuse me," I say politely to Cheds, picking him up and moving him gently onto my pillow so as not to disrupt his well-earned slumber. "There's just something I have to do."

I stand up, brush myself down, stabilize myself.

"YESSSSSSS!" I shriek, punching the air and then kicking it like a ninja. "FUCKING YES! YESSS, MARGOT! YOU BLOODY DID IT, YOU DID IT, YOU TOTAL BLOODY LEGEND!"

With a quick hop, I cross to my wardrobe mirror. Cheddar looks up and stares at me in bewilderment.

"Get used to it, buddy," I tell him jubilantly. "There's a *lot* more of this kind of nonsense coming, and nobody will see it but you."

And eventually Henry, once he's in love with me enough to handle it.

I point at myself in the mirror and realize I am, in fact, still very drunk.

"OTHER MARGOT," I yell at my reflection. "HERE I COME."

27

MY SMUG GIDDINESS lasts throughout the next morning. In spite of the fact that by the time I finally wake up—hungover—Cheddar has already successfully launched himself off the bed like a base jumper, made his tottering way to my closet and ripped apart at least three pairs of trousers.

"Oops," I trill lightly, picking him up. "Naughty boy."

Cheds squeaks in response—*whatever*—and struggles out of my arm. I watch him with an ache of affection as he looks for something, anything, he can ruin.

"Good luck," I chirp sarcastically as he frantically claws my leather sofa. "That's going to have a blue blanket on it eventually, and I think we know why."

Then I unsuccessfully search for something to feed him. I'm studying my uneaten pot noodles—pretty sure it's not going to double as kitten food—when the doorbell rings.

Opening the door, I stare at the delivery man in front of me, holding a large paper bag.

"Here," he says abruptly, handing it over and leaving.

Blinking in surprise, I open the bag: it's stuffed full of kitten food, toys, treats, litter, and a box that I assume is for him to poop in, but—as a new cat mum—I can't be perfectly sure. Still stinking of vodka, I run back to the door and watch the delivery man drive away. Angel? Is he a clairvoyant too? Could he see this coming?

Then I look at the little paper receipt stapled to the bag.

Thank you again. Henry.

PS Fancy a sexy weekend away as a gesture of my intense gratitude? xxx

PPS Call Jules. Don't waste your time being angry.

I let out a grunt of gratitude, pleasure and irritation.

Mind your own business, Henry Armstrong, you sweet, thoughtful, incredibly sexy man.

And yes—I would very much like a sexy weekend away, please and thank you.

I grab my phone and breathe out.

Missed call: Jules
Missed call: Jules

JULES: Please talk to me, Margot. I need to explain.

JULES: Eve, are you OK?

JULES: Eve.

JULES: EVE PICK THE FUCK UP.

I blink at our group chat, where Jules is getting increasingly panicked.

It's only then that I realize she has been messaging *both* of us and Eve hasn't responded. Which is, and I say this with three decades of knowledge, unprecedented. Eve responds when it's 2 a.m., when she's ill, when there's nothing to respond to. When we got our first mobile phones, Eve spent six whole weeks constructing laborious LUV U 4EVA <3 <3 messages that must have taken her about three hours each to type out and got responses like K and U2 and PLS STP ND JST CLL S because vowels were too much of a faff for thirteen-year-olds to bother with.

Panic bubbles in my throat as I dial Jules's number.

"I'm not talking to you," I say fiercely when she picks up. "I'm still very fucking angry with you."

"I know," Jules says. "I get it. Have you spoken to Eve?"

"No. Have you spoken to Eve?"

"If I had spoken to Eve," Jules says with a small sigh, "would I be asking you if you'd spoken to Eve and leaving messages like EVE PICK THE FUCK UP?"

"Really?" I snap. "You wanna get all smart-arse with me, Julia? That's the life path you've decided to take?"

"I'm really worried," she continues, gamely ignoring me. "She's not picking up, she's not responding to texts, she's not at home or in the library. I went to her school and she's called in sick."

"She's called in *sick*?" Another wave of panic. "Eve doesn't call in sick."

"Why are you telling me that? I bloody know. So where the hell is she?"

Cheddar doesn't care where Eve is: he's meowing at me very loudly.

"Ugh." Holding the phone under my chin, I quickly open a bag of kitten food and pour it in a cereal bowl, then put it on the floor. "There you go. Eat and be quiet."

"Who, me? Who are you talking to?"

"I've got a new . . ." I pause. Nope, she's not getting round me that easily. "None of your goddamn business. So what the hell is—"

Oh my God. I am the worst, most selfish person on the planet.

We *both* are.

"The baby," I say, putting my hand over my eyes. "Lily's baby."

"Shit. You're right."

The guilt is overwhelming. I thought that news was *my* news to kick off about, but it wasn't. Because Eve was sitting there, quietly falling apart too. Three days of no texts or messages from Eve is completely out of character. And we didn't even *notice*, we were so busy making it about us.

"We are horrible, horrible friends," I say, grabbing my coat and putting on my shoes.

"I'm worse, if that helps."

"You're *definitely* worse," I seethe. "But I'm not talking about this with you right now. I'm still too angry. We have Eve to worry about."

What the hell am I going to do with Cheddar while I'm out? I don't have time to google *Can you leave a kitten on its own or is that irresponsible parenting*, so I pick him up and tuck him into my coat. "You're coming with me."

"Me?" Jules says.

"Not you." I scowl at the phone again. "I don't want to see you. I'll find Eve and then I'll tell you where she is, and then you can go *separately* and talk to her too. After I've been."

"Right. OK." Jules pauses. "Margot, we really need to—"

"Nope," I say. "Conversation over."

JULES WAS RIGHT: Eve isn't at home or at school.

As I stomp with growing frustration around Bristol, all I feel is anger at myself. It's an unpleasantly familiar feeling. *There she is*: Furious Margot-who-hates-herself is back, just as aggressive and as in charge as ever.

"You're an idiot," I hiss at myself, checking the local park: Eve's not there. "You're a self-absorbed, self-obsessed idiot."

With Cheddar in my pocket, still fast asleep, I stomp around the city, visiting all of Eve's favorite haunts.

"You've got to *be better*," I mutter at myself. "Stop being so incredibly selfish and—"

Thank God: I see her.

There's a wave of relief so strong I have to pause while my chest tightens, my eyes fill, my fists clench into balls. I was on my way to her house, but I should have realized where she'd be immediately. Eve is sitting on a low wall, opposite the IVF clinic. She's wearing a dirty gray tracksuit—which I didn't know she owned—and staring woodenly into space as couples emerge from the doors every now and then, kissing each other and beaming in hope.

Quickly, I pull out my phone:

Found her.

Oh thank God.

Holding my breath, I approach quietly.

Eve doesn't hear me coming, isn't aware of anything going on around her, and I can *feel* the sadness arching out of her, the heartbreaking defeat. I hurt for her so badly, and suddenly I realize I would give *anything* to make her feel better. To take it all away.

Without a word, I sit next to her on the wall.

She turns to me, her face blank. She's been crying: her green eyes are all pink and veined, like one of her beloved pieces of expensive stone, and her blonde fringe is sticking upward.

"Why?" she says simply. "Why, Maggie?"

"I don't know." I pull her into my arms as she starts crying. "It's not fair and it's not right and I don't know and I am so, so sorry."

"I just . . ." Eve looks up at me with wide, bewildered eyes. "I can't keep trying. I can't. I'm so *tired.* All the hormones, all the hope, all the disappointment. It wasn't supposed to *be* like this, Maggie. I was supposed to fall in love, to be a *mum.* That's all I wanted. I know it's not modern or whatever, but it's what I've always wanted and it didn't feel like too much to ask from the universe. But it is. I've asked for too much. I've done it six times now and I'm so *tired.*"

I nod, smoothing her damp hair out of her face. "I know."

"And then Lily . . ." She takes a deep breath. "I'm a horrible, horrible person. I am, Margot. I know I am. Because I didn't feel glad for her. I should have been glad, I should have been happy because she's happy, she was my friend for so long, but I *wasn't.* All I could think was . . . why is it all so *easy* for you, Lily? Why don't you have to try as hard? Why don't you have to *ask* for it? And now she's taken the life we *both* wanted, and I *hated* her for it."

I frown. "That doesn't make you bad, Eve. It makes you human."

Somewhere in the back of my head, I can hear Henry telling me the same thing, and I wonder how many of us spend our lives hating ourselves for the ugliness inside us that we tell nobody.

"It does, it makes me bad. And selfish and unkind and . . . and . . . If I was one of my students, I'd be putting me on a time out in the corner to think about my attitude." Eve looks again at the IVF clinic door as another couple walk out, holding hands. "I'm so, so, so grateful that you and Jules have been with me the whole way, but I wanted *that*, Maggie. I wanted a *family*."

I put my arm round her. "You *have* a family, sweetheart. *We* are your family."

"You're not because you're *fighting*." She starts crying again, and I suddenly see my sweet best friend as she was: with her lopsided plaits and her missing front tooth and her backpack covered in floral stickers. I am so, so angry that little girl didn't get everything she wanted. She deserved all of it. "And I already lost Lily, but I still love her. I haven't spoken to her because what she did was awful, and you were so hurt and angry, but I still love her and I miss her so much and I feel so *guilty all the time*."

My stomach clenches tight. "Eve . . ."

Because I'm only now realizing that in my anger, in my rage, in my hurt, I had asked for too much from the people I loved. Without ever saying *never talk to Lily again*, I had implied it with the noisiness, the sheer thunder of my pain. I wasn't at fault for what happened, but I *was* at fault for how I handled it. For the way I let the lightning shoot through me and hit everything else around me on the way down.

"You can still see Lily," I say quietly. "Of *course* you can. She's your friend, you don't have to take sides."

"But I'm angry at her," Eve sobs wetly. "For me, as well as

for you. I don't understand how she did that. A whole *year* of lying, of cheating, of deceiving us all. Apart from Jules."

"Apart from Jules." I nod, my chest aching. "She's always been the cleverest of us."

"I just . . . I can't switch off like that, not after so long, not after we grew up together, and I can't *believe* that—"

I STARE AT an enormous cake.

It's a ridiculous cake—covered in little toy cars, jammed into clearly handmade icing, candles aflame—and somehow, I'm not sure how, I know that I made it. Some part of me, the future me, knows, remembers, understands. Unbelievably, in an enormous departure from my current personality, I have become . . . a cake-maker.

Blinking, I look around. Where is Henry?

A wave of relief: he's standing next to me, arm around my shoulder. He's singing loudly but with an astonishing lack of skill, totally tone-deaf. In fact—I look more carefully—the room is packed with people and *everyone* is singing. With a curious expression, Henry glances at me—*you OK?*—and I suddenly realize I'm supposed to be singing too.

But I can't, because I don't know who we're singing to.

Then I look down.

On a small wooden chair sits the gorgeous little curly-haired boy from my wedding. Except he's not the same: he's younger, smaller, even cuter, if that's possible. I breathe in sharply—the intense love I feel for him is overwhelming—then crouch down next to him. He's staring at the cake, trying desperately hard not to stick a chubby finger in it. As I instinctively reach my hand out to hold his, I abruptly realize I don't have a wedding or engagement ring on—just my grandfather's emerald—which puts me roughly between now and three years' time, if I've calculated correctly.

The blue candle sticking in the cake is a big, slightly melted TWO.

Two. Our little boy is two years old.

"Happy Birthday, dear Gu-uss," everyone finally finishes, Henry attempting some kind of harmony and failing. "Happy Birthday to youuuu."

They all break into applause and I look up at Henry.

His face is full of exactly the same emotions I can feel pouring out of me, and I know that this little boy, this tiny human, is going to make us so unbelievably happy.

"OK, baby boy," Eve says, stepping forward and crouching down. "It's time. You can blow out the candles now. Just one big blow. You can do it."

Nodding bravely, Gus breathes out and spits all over the cake.

Everyone laughs and Eve beams at me: her face radiant, her pride shimmering. And I realize, all at once, as if I already knew: this is not my child. Gus is not my son, and he is not my future. He belongs to someone else. And it hurts like an axe in my chest, but I also feel Eve's happiness as if it's mine too: the two of us, permanently woven together.

My eyes fill: I look at Henry and realize his eyes are full too.

We don't have children yet, but we desperately want them.

I know because I see in his eyes the same pain, the same joy, the same heartbreak, the same sadness, the same acceptance. I know, because there are no other children at our wedding. Yet somehow, when I smile at him and stand up, he puts his arm around me and kisses the top of my head and it all feels bearable.

Everything—whatever it will be—feels bearable.

"Gus!" Winter is back—more gangly, not yet a menace—and both Henry and I laugh as she pushes herself to the front of the crowd. "Open my present first! It's the *biggest* one and I made it myself, so you need to—"

AND I'M BACK.

Disorientated, I stare at Eve's face as I recalibrate. It's still tear-stained, but I've seen her future happiness, I know where she'll end up, and *this* is the gift I can give her.

"Are you OK?" She puts a hand on my forehead, just like the sweet-souled mother of our group she's always been. "Are you hot? It's not that flu again, is it? Shall I call us a cab and get you home?"

I smile and put my hand gently on top of hers.

"I'm fine," I say, trying to keep the emotion out of my voice. "I just . . . Eve. Look. I know you're tired. I know you don't think you can do this again, and I know you don't think you're strong enough. But you can, and you are, and you will."

Because I'm doing the math—luckily not that hard as I'm pretty exhausted now—and this time the IVF will work. If Gus is two years old in less than three years' time, that means Eve is going to get pregnant very, very soon.

"I'll pay for it," I say quickly as she opens her mouth to object. "I've got a new job, nearly, and I'll have the money, so don't even think about that. And I will be there for all of it. We will *all* be there. Every injection, every appointment, every late night. You're not going to be alone. It might not be the way you planned it, but I *promise* you, you will have the family you want."

It may not be the standard, traditional family, but it *will* be a family.

I have seen it, and I have felt it.

"OK." Eve nods bravely, straightening her spine. She always trusts what I say: it's one of the most bewildering things about her. "If you really think so. One more time. I think I can do just one more—"

She blinks and looks down.

"Maggie," she says quietly, abruptly holding my arm. "I don't want to alarm you, but there appears to be a ridiculously cute cat in your pocket."

I'm nearly as surprised as she is: I'd forgotten Cheddar was in there.

"Oh!" I pull him out and hold him so he can wriggle and sniff the tears on Eve's face in a way that should be creepy but is frankly delightful. "Yeah. I got a cat. He's alright, I guess."

When what I mean is: I am fully in love with him already.

"Wow." Eve blinks. "A cat. Big day. How beautiful are you?"

With the soft expression of somebody already smitten, she kisses the end of Cheddar's fluffy nose and tickles the top of his head. My cat, I realize, is going to be another part of the family we build together.

Then she hesitates slightly.

"Maggie, do you . . ." A cough as she attempts to be the peacemaker while simultaneously not setting me off again. The joy of being friends with Make a Mess Margot, I guess. "Do you think that you and Jules will be fighting for a *very* long time?"

I stare briefly into space. Jules.

"I don't know," I admit softly, because she's not in the vision, she's not singing, she's not eating cake, and I feel a different kind of pain, sharper and edged with fear. Where is she? Why isn't she with us?

More importantly: is it all my fault, *again*?

28

THE LOSS OF Jules feels like a missing organ.

She texts and calls multiple times a day—begging me to speak to her—but I am still archiving her messages and silencing my phone.

It doesn't work—I'm still furious—so I spend the next few days with Polly, preparing for the test shoot. Perry and Paige—now permanently camped out on my living-room floor—spend the entire time energetically trying to hug Cheddar with an enthusiasm he's not at all sure about.

"*Gentle*," Polly says, still peering at her folder. "Be *gentle* with the kitten."

"Mummy, I *love* him," Paige squeaks as Cheds tries to climb on her lap, using her knees as scaffolding. "I *love* the baby."

"Can we have him?" Perry asks. "At home?"

"Please, Mummy, *please please please* can we have him?"

"No, darlings." Polly looks up and smiles gently. "Because he's not your cat, and also you know Daddy is allergic. Maybe at some point in the future you can have one."

When they've gone back to trying to torture my pet, she grimaces at me.

"It's the only thing I'm freaking out about," she whispers, leaning forward. "How the kids will react when we leave. How hurt they'll be. But I'm going to make sure he gets equal custody, and we'll stay close. No fighting, no drama. Just . . . not together anymore. Not a couple. I still love him, in a tired, defeated way, and I have no need to punish him. I'm not a monster, right?"

"No," I say firmly, remembering how Peter stared at my breasts and gave me a mark out of ten, like I was an Olympic gymnast he wasn't particularly impressed by. She is *so* much kinder and more dignified than I would be, in her position. "You're not a monster, Polly."

She nods in relief, then brightens again. "So, we've done a few run-throughs of the script, I've made sure they've got the right props, and they've sent me a rough version of your little cartoon familiar. I think it's adorable. What do you think?"

Polly pushes her laptop over to me and I stare at it.

It's a cloud.

A small, adorable, fluffy cloud with huge eyes and a quizzical little mouth.

Your stupid cloud, I hear teenage Winter yell at me.

There's a sharp wave of relief: any remaining doubt over whether I'll get this job or not abruptly vanishes. I'll get it, I'll be wearing a *costume* for the next decade, talking to an animated cloud and "humiliating" my stepdaughter on national television, and—I've got to be honest—I am so ridiculously happy about it. Sorry, Winnie. I'll make it up to you, somehow. And maybe, when you've passed through the awkward teenage stage, you'll actually be quite proud of me.

"I love it." I nod. "It's perfect. Perhaps we could call it Lenny?"

I think of the blue marble Henry gave me on our second date, now sitting on my bedside table to remind me that I have a man who gives marbles as gifts and how lucky that makes me.

Polly looks confused. "Lenny?"

"It's short for lenticular." I smile. "My favorite type of cloud. Although technically he looks more like a cumulus cloud—they're the fluffy ones—but I don't think we want to be abbreviating that for an audience of children."

It takes a second for Pol to get it, and then she leans back and shrieks with laughter.

Perry and Paige are so shocked, they look up in tandem. Something tells me that however *together* Polly seems to be now, it has not been the easiest year for her—to say the least—and she probably hasn't laughed that much in a while.

I grin at her. "Unless—"

"No," she says quickly. "Let's not call this cloud Cumulus, please."

"Deal. Lenny it is." I lean over the paperwork. "So it's tomorrow morning, twenty minutes in total, we've got the costume ready . . ."

We both glance simultaneously at the "costume" Polly has sourced. It's certainly a deviation from my beloved navy, that's for sure. It was never my dream to appear in front of thousands looking like a giant toddler, but I'll take the win where I can.

"Yup. I'll pick you up in the morning by yelling at you from the driveway."

"Fab." I nod as my phone beeps. "And I'll yell back much more—"

I stare at the screen.

Maggie, where are you?

It's from my parents.

What do they mean, *where am I*? I'm in my own flat, exactly as I have been the last fifty times they've contacted me.

"Hang on," I say, jumping up. "Just got to sort this out."

I'm at home. Why???

My mother or father is *typing* for what seems like four years.

Go to your grandfather's ASAP!!!!

I have literally never felt panic like it.

What's going on? Is he OK?

The message doesn't deliver. I try to call and it goes straight to voicemail.

WHAT IS GOING ON? REPLY PLEASE

"I've got to go," I bleat as Polly frowns at my expression. "Right now."

I'm desperately trying to call my grandfather while simultaneously slamming my shoes on, but he's not picking up either. Fear is bubbling at the base of my throat. He never responded to my drunk voicemail, but I'd assumed that he just couldn't find the voicemail button. I was planning to go round this evening, but—oh my God, is it too late? *Why* did I leave it? *Why* did I think I had all the time in the world?

"What's happening?" Polly says in alarm. "What can I do? How can I help?"

"My grandad," I manage, but that's as far as I get.

I can't say anything else—can't speak the words, in case they become real—so instead I throw open the door and start running.

"GRANDAD!" I THROW myself through the front door so hard it smacks against the hallway wall. "Grandad! Where are you?"

In my peripheral vision, I notice that the house seems spotless, tidy: there's no post on the floor, no shoes on the side. But these unimportant details are absorbed on an almost unconscious level, because all I feel is pure terror. There's a lump in my throat, my heart is banging and my eyes are full of tears again. Please, please, no, no no no—

"GRANDAD," I yell, running down the hallway.

I smash through the door into the living room and see my grandfather: sitting motionless in his armchair, facing the window. Everything in me starts breaking and the lump in my throat travels up, into my mouth, until I let it out in a guttural sob. He is what roots me, I abruptly realize. He's the tree I have sat under, the shade I have sought, the one thing that was solid when the world shook.

Nothing feels safe or constant without him.

"Meg?"

I blink as the room starts rotating.

"Margot, what's wrong? Are you unwell?"

My grandfather's head turns slightly, and I start crying in earnest now: loud, ugly sobs as I hang on to the doorknob for support, clutching my stomach.

"Gracious." He tries his hardest to get up, fails, tries again. "Meg, sweetheart, talk to me. Is it Henry? Has it happened? I mean . . . what has happened?"

Grandad gets to his feet, grabs his walking stick and starts ambling toward me as fast as he possibly can.

"I am going to *kill my parents*," I shriek at the ceiling. "*Kill them*."

"Do you need help with that?" He puts a gentle hand on my shoulder. "Usually I'd be against murdering my own offspring and his wife, but for you, Meg, I'll make an exception. What did they do this time?"

My *bloody* parents. They could have written "*Hey, have you been to see your grandad this last week because we can't reach him and we're worried*," but noooooo. Let's leave cryptic messages that indicate there's an emergency and then turn our phone off.

"You didn't pick up the phone," I sob, sounding a lot like Winter with a kitten under her sweater. "You didn't pick up the phone and I didn't know what to do."

"Oh, my Meg. I'm so sorry. I couldn't reach it in time. I kept telling Alexa to answer it for me, but she's being extremely belligerent."

"You *scared* me," I bleat at him pathetically. "Don't *do* that."

"I'll try," he smiles, patting my shoulder. "My sweet girl, you mustn't worry about me like this. I am an old, old man and when it's my time, it's my time."

"You're not *old*," I squeak irrationally. "Stop saying that."

"Nearly ninety-four isn't exactly a toddler, even if it sometimes feels like it. I need you to promise you'll stop worrying about me all the time, Meg. Fear and anxiety are not the emotions I want to bring into your life. I want to bring only good things, like you have brought me. Promise me?"

"No," I sniff. "I'm going to keep worrying."

"Your heart is too big," he says, taking my hand and kissing it. "That's always been your biggest problem, Margot."

"Really? Because I could name like five hundred others that are considerably bigger."

My grandfather smiles and pats the top of my head, like I'm still a child waiting impatiently for the months to turn over.

"I'm not going anywhere just yet," he says quietly. "So try not to panic. OK?"

"OK," I sniff, suddenly remembering his eyes on me—full of love—at my wedding. That gives us at least three years together, possibly four, depending how long my engagement to Henry is. I should have remembered that when I was pelting down the road with my shoelaces undone. "As long as you live forever, I suppose it's a deal."

"I'll try my very hardest." Grandad smiles and glances up at the little gray ball sitting on his mantelpiece. "Alexa? What time is it?"

"The time is four twenty-seven p.m.," she says politely: clearly finally trained.

"Ah." Grandad nods knowingly. "At least we won't have to wait too long to exact our cunning revenge on your parents. How shall we do it? Do you have any specific murdering requirements, or do you want me to trip them up with my walking stick?"

I stare at him with a flush of sadness. He's losing his memory now too. I suppose it was inevitable, eventually: the senses all fading, one by one, until time doesn't really mean anything anymore.

If it ever really did mean something.

"Grandad," I say as gently as possible, while also wiping my wet nose on my sleeve and then rubbing my sleeve on my hem like a grotty kid. "Mum and Dad don't live here anymore. Remember? They went back to Australia."

"Yes." He nods. "They went back to Australia. I remember."

He continues to regard me calmly, so obviously I need to make this painful situation a little clearer.

"So, they're in Australia," I clarify as softly as I can.

"No." He shakes his head. "They're not."

"They are."

"They're not, Meg."

And I really don't want to fight with my grandfather about geographical locations, but it feels like this is an important distinction to make. "Grandad, I'm very sorry, I know it must come as a bit of a shock, but—"

"Hellloooooo." A chirpy voice from the hallway. "In come the conquering heroes from their Antipodean adventure!"

My mouth opens and I stare at my grandad, who looks a bit smug.

"This is not good security," I hear another voice say, less chirpily. "Joanne, why is the door wide open like this? Anyone could walk in."

"Anyone *did* just walk in, George."

I'm still staring at my grandfather in shock.

"Told you," he says with a wide, triumphant grin.

I turn to transfer my stare to my parents, who walk into the living room and stand there grinning tiredly at us both, as if they hadn't just magicked themselves out of thin air from the other side of the world.

"What the f—"

"Margot Jane Wayward," my mother reproves quickly, holding up a hand. "Don't swear in front of your grandfather. Have some respect, for goodness' sake."

"What the *fridge*," I amend quickly so I can get to the point, "are you both doing here?"

"I told you," my mother sighs, as if she is a long-suffering guardian cursed with an idiot charge. "I sent you a very thorough email with the flight details, and we—"

"What email did you use?"

"Margotthemeterologist . . ." Mum frowns at me. "You didn't get it?"

"Mum," I sigh in frustration. "I'm a *meteorologist*. Not a *meterologist*. Meteors. Not meters. You spelled it wrong."

"Oh!" She makes a little brushing-off hand gesture: unimportant. "I *told* you, *and* we texted you from the train, although you did not see fit to pick us up, your poor, exhausted parents, after a twenty-one-hour flight."

She knows I don't have a car: did she expect me to piggyback them here?

"Um. No, you didn't tell me."

"I *did*." Mum glances at my dad, who lifts his eyebrows. "On the phone. I said we were homesick and coming back for a bit to try and shake it off, and you didn't seem particularly thrilled about the prospect, so I left you alone." She sniffs lightly. "I won't say it wasn't quite hurtful, though. To your own mother."

"I said she wasn't listening." Dad rubs his neck and winces slightly. "I said something was going on with Maggie and it didn't feel quite right. I felt it in my bones. Bones that are now in quite a lot of pain, may I add. That country is very far away."

"Something isn't 'going on'"—it is—"and I *was* listening," I say indignantly. "So I *think* I'd remember if you—"

Wait. That phone call, a few weeks ago: the vision of the fight with Henry. I cannot believe I only visit the future for three seconds at a time, yet I appear to have missed some pretty pivotal information. What the hell else have I missed while I'm gone? It hadn't even occurred to me that while I am Other Margot for those few moments, I am also not . . . me.

"You hung up on me," Mum sniffs in confirmation. "So we figured something else must be going on with you, which only solidified our plans. Didn't it, George?"

I'm going to ignore "something else": now is not the time.

"Hmm?" Dad is still rubbing his neck. "I'm telling you, never, ever get on a twenty-one-hour journey without a neck pillow."

"I wouldn't dream of it," says Grandad. "Good to have you both back."

They grin at each other—both visibly emotional—then go in for a hug.

My mother and I regard each other warily: we love each other, but *hugging* is not one of our love languages. Once, when I was fourteen, she greeted me after a school play with a *Well done, darling* and a handshake.

"So you're back," I say, struggling to suppress a grin. "For how long?"

"Oh . . ." Mum waves a hand airily, also attempting not to smile too hard. Like mother, like daughter. "Not too long. Just a few weeks, while we check in on both of you. You can't survive without us, it seems. Also, your father's incessant gardening is driving me doolally."

When what she means is: *We miss you and we need to be where you are.*

Then I remember—or whatever the opposite of remembering is—my mother and father, both singing at Gus's birthday party in three years. There's a comfort there, a solidity. They're not visiting. They know him. They see him regularly. My family, the one I thought was gone, is expanding by the second.

"You're staying, aren't you?"

"I think so." Mum looks at me carefully. "That OK?"

"Yes." There's another lump in my throat. "That's OK."

29

BY FRIDAY MORNING, I am fully prepared.

Not just for my test shoot, but also for my weekend away with Henry. I got a proper haircut and have been shopping and panic-bought a lot of items that—now I'm thinking about it with a slightly clearer head—are probably a little too keen for a casual getaway. Lace, silk, things that float, things that cling, things that lift, things that do barely anything productive at all. I appear to think I'm going to be starring in some kind of '90s pop video, wafting around a four-poster bed while I delicately eat macarons in heels and lingerie.

It's not an image I hate, if I'm being honest.

Luckily, Henry seems equally excited because he's giving me a countdown:

FOURTEEN HOURS!

BARELY THIRTEEN HOURS MARGOT!

Twelve! I turned caps lock off.

Nine! Are you impressed by how
well I can assess my clock?

With every single text, I feel my insides rise a little.

Last time I went on a "sexy weekend" in Scotland with Aaron, he spent half of it watching football on the fancy hotel bath telly on his own, so, no, I will *not* be managing my expectations this time, thank you very much.

Grinning, I text back:

You really do seem to have an extraordinary grip on time.

I CANNOT WAIT :) xxx

Beep.

I'll pick you up at 7. Go smash your big audition and get ready for ALL THAT JAZZ. Xxx

I grin at the tiny emoji of a saxophone as Polly starts bellowing outside.

"Maggie, I'm yelling!" she shouts. "I'm outside and I'm yelling! Get out here, Margot the Meteorologist, so we can take the world by storm!"

Smiling, I briefly pause in front of the mirror.

I am, without any doubt, now wearing a "costume." Rainbow-striped tights and a little denim pinafore dress with big shining suns embroidered on the front and back, both made by Polly. In my ears are raindrop earrings, around my neck is a raindrop necklace, and there's a big, sparkly lightning-bolt clip in my hair. My shoes have been personalized with glitter and little fluffy clouds, and Pol even made a matching handbag, though I told her that I have never, ever seen a television presenter with a handbag on set. "It completes the look," she said with a shrug. "Also I got a bit carried away with the kids' glue gun and it was fun."

I should look ridiculous—I probably *do* look ridiculous—but I also feel more like *me* than I have for a long, long time. Eve was right: navy really *does* wash me out. Jules was also right: I have never successfully "looked French."

"Take the world by storm," I say as I open the front door

and carefully pick up Cheds, who is marching out to come with me. "I like that as a catchphrase."

"Oooh!" Pol thinks about it, wearing a very sophisticated gray suit that definitely doesn't have glitter stuck to the front of it. "Yes, I do too. Let's put it on the list and try it out."

"Great. Not today," I add firmly as Cheds makes another desperate bid for the great outdoors. "You're too little to go wandering the streets on your own just yet, I'm afraid. You'll have to leave cheating on me with the neighbors for another few weeks."

With infinite care—as if he's a precious Amazon package with FRAGILE written on top—I place him down in my hallway and fondly watch him march off jauntily on wobbly little legs.

"Wait!" Polly is regarding him carefully. "I see no reason why you can't have a cat."

"That's good," I say dryly. "Because I do, as you can see, have a cat."

"No." She laughs. "I mean, this is children's television, right? We've seen how much my kids love Cheddar. If we want to be *truly* dastardly and manipulative, we could try to win over the children of the country with a ridiculously adorable animal too. If they get bored of you, they can just watch whatever Cheds is doing."

"Rude." I look at his face: it's cuter than mine. "But fair."

Cheds squeaks loudly and makes another attempt to get past me into the street: I suspect I'm going to spend the next decade sighing, "*Now* who's bloody fed my cat?" and "Why does he stink of Nina Ricci?"

"That's a yes, then." I pick him up and gently wrap him in a scarf I grab from the hallway hook. He immediately falls asleep. "I think we've found something we can do with the handbag."

CHARLIE IS MORE excited than either of us.

"Margot the Meteorologist!" She greets us at the door of the studio with a wide smile, two coffees and an assistant behind her with two slices of cake. "Don't you look incredible? This is *exactly* what I had in mind. Nice embroidery, Pol."

"Thanks very much." Polly grins. "You mocked it at uni, but I see you're not mocking it anymore."

"My tastes have broadened." Charlie gestures us through reception as she hands out passes. "Everything is ready, and it's looking even better than we hoped. We took your ideas and ran with them, Margot."

She opens the door with a proud flourish.

Polly and I both gape at the set, which looks like some kind of magical Dalí-inspired hallucination. Rainbows painted everywhere, hanging raindrops, sunset lamps, an entire wall dedicated to the seasons, and bright pink chairs that look like clouds. Scattered around the biggest one—mine, I assume—are tiny yellow beanbags with sunrays stitched into them, and the carpet is covered in little blue stars as if somebody flipped the sky upside down.

Charlie didn't *run* with my ideas: she got in a rocket ship and shot into space.

"That's where the kids will sit!" Charlie points at the beanbags with unbridled excitement. "My kids have demanded to be first, but I've said that we don't do nepotism in this family, so they'll just have to apply on the internet like everyone else. And there will be a *lot* of applications, I assure you."

I'm still staring at the set: suffice to say, it is *quite* the upgrade from a dyed green bedsheet hanging on my wall, held up by two drawing pins I hammered in with a saucepan.

"This is . . ." I say faintly ". . . way bigger than I had in my head."

"It'll be bigger if we get commissioned! This is just for an initial test shoot." Charlie grins. "But I wanted to get the *feel* across. Your vision was so fun—a bit Willy Wonka, but with weather instead of—"

"Casual child abuse," I say without thinking.

"Quite." She laughs. "Now, before we start, I'm just going to pop you over to make-up to get a few extra flicks of powder— Oh!"

My kitten chooses this moment to pop his head out of my bag and start yelling.

"We thought . . . a cute sidekick?" This suddenly seems like the world's most unprofessional plan. "To, uh, go with Lenny? But who probably asks a lot fewer questions and might also sometimes pee on the carpet?"

I look around the room again as it hits me how *momentous* this all is. There are dozens of people in black wandering around, enormous cameras, lights, fluffy squirrel things on sticks (microphones?). It's not just me anymore, sitting in my bedroom. I'm part of a *team*, just like I was at the Met Office (albeit with fewer labored puns about "getting the drift" or being "a bit under the weather").

"Hmm." Charlie and Cheds regard each other warily before one of them—not the cat—gives a nod. "Let's give it a go, see how it pans out. They did it on *Blue Peter*, after all. I don't see why we can't try it too."

With a pleased little yawn, Cheds disappears again: job done.

After a few quick flicks of powder and a lot of bronzer, I'm settled down on my big comfy pink cloud chair like a Grecian goddess. The kitten is asleep on my lap, and I've been told exactly where Lenny is going to pop up whenever he wants to ask a question. My script is on the prompter, so I don't have to remember not to swear. But possibly the best, *most* exciting thing about this whole situation is that @J8571823405 isn't going to be able to write *nice tits shame about the nose* under the video when it's done.

"Right." Charlie and Polly both stand behind the big camera positioned in front of me. "Are you ready, Margot the Meteorologist?"

Nodding, I breathe in and stroke the cat's head like a furry little stress reliever.

"Quiet on set! Sound?"

"Set."

"Camera?"

"Set."

"Roll sound."

"Sound rolling."

"Roll camera."

"Marker."

I jump as a guy in a black T-shirt claps his little board thing together like I assumed they only did in the movies, but apparently it's a real thing.

"*Weather or Not*, test shoot, roll one, take one."

"Action."

A wave of calm washes through me. I can do this. I *will* do this. Because I've seen that it will happen. I suddenly wonder how many other parts of my life are going to be infinitely easier just because I know the outcome from the beginning.

"Greetings, mini meteorologists!" I beam into the camera. "I'm Margot, and this is the very first episode of *Weather or Not*. This is Cheddar"—I hold a sleepy cat up to the camera and he gives a tiny squeak—"and this is Lenny, who is here to ask any questions you might have. Details of how to contact us are right here, and we would *love* to see any drawings or projects you make, if you're feeling inspired."

I point chirpily at the area to my right where my little cloud friend will be digitally added in afterward, then at the bottom of the screen, where there are various social media handles, as well as a postal address for the less technologically inclined five-year-olds.

"So, let's start with the most important question. What *is* meteorology? Well, it's simply a fancy word for the science of weather, and it comes from the very famous and very cool ancient Greek philosopher *Aristotle*, who was alive thousands of years ago." I point to my right, where there will presumably be a photo of a marble statue with a nose half missing. "He called it meteorology because in his language *meteoron* meant 'high in the sky' and *ology* meant 'knowledge.' So what we meteorologists do is *study the sky*."

I did check with Polly and Charlie whether ancient Greek etymology and Aristotle were a little too much for children, but they both agreed that this sort of detail is exactly what adults find irritating and kids desperately want. In which case, I fall into the latter category, not for the first time.

Pausing, I smile up at the space where Lenny will be inserted.

"Good question, Lenny. So what is *weather*? Well, it's all around you, all the time, even if you don't notice it. Weather is what makes sure that *you* exist. Without it, none of us would be here. It's the oxygen we need to breathe, and the water we need to drink. It's the sun we need for heat, and it grows the plants we need to eat. And this all happens in something we call *the atmosphere*."

I point at another digitally added photo.

"The atmosphere is a bit like a big cuddly blanket wrapped around the world. It keeps us from getting too hot or too cold, and it keeps the things we need where we can use them, so they don't disappear into space. Which means we have to protect it, just like it protects us. Don't we, Cheddar?"

I lift Cheddar up to my face and he squeaks in his cutest possible voice and puts a tiny soft paw on my cheek, quite the environmental crusader. I hear one of the cameramen go *awwwww* not quite under his breath and I flush with pride: my boy nailed it.

Although I suspect Cheds is going to become a total diva.

"Weather is *powerful*." I feel my eyes light up. "It's hurricanes and tornadoes and storms and lightning and thunder and it can be scary, and dangerous. But it's also incredibly *beautiful*. Rainbows and auroras and sunsets and sunrises and specters and iridescent clouds. It is everything in the world around us, it changes all the time, and every week I'm going to tell you all the things I love about it so that you can love it too. I'm going to teach you how to study the sky for yourselves. We'll look at how fast the wind can move and how big raindrops can get, and why. We'll study snowflakes, jet streams and fires. I'll even teach you how to measure the wind with a sock."

I pause and look to my right.

"Why, yes, Lenny. A *sock*. What do you mean, you don't have any socks? Ah. Clouds don't have feet. I see. I'm sorry."

Polly chortles softly behind the camera and I grin at her.

"So what we're going to do is explore this magical world in all its different moods, so that we can make sense of this incredible planet we live on. And maybe make a little more sense of ourselves, too, while we're at it."

A flush of happiness: *this is my job.*

It's everything I loved about Instagram and it's everything I loved at the Met Office and it's everything I would never, ever have believed I could do if I hadn't been shown it was possible.

"So sit with me, mini meteorologists, and together we will—"

Oh *fuck.*

"We will—"

No.

"We—"

Everything fades and just as Polly lifts her eyebrows—

THE PAIN IS indescribable.

It's a deep, physical agony, spreading from my chest and radiating outward into every cell in my body: through my shoulders, into my arms and hands, my throat, my face, my knees. I ache all over, and my first thought is: flu. I must have the flu again. Except way worse than last time. I appear to be shaking violently, as if my body simply cannot contain the strength of it.

I try to open my eyes, but can't: everything stays black.

Panic builds.

A loud, weird noise pops out of me and I suddenly realize I'm crying: crying with such rawness that it sounds like a seagull screeching. I press my face further into the darkness and realize I can't open my eyes because I'm up against fabric, which is moving slightly. It's warm and wet—I've clearly been crying awhile—and I suddenly realize: Henry. I'm sobbing against Henry's chest; I can hear his breath through his jacket.

Relief pulses through me—he's here—but I still can't stop crying because now my fear is blending with Other Margot's. She's scared too: I can feel it. Scared, and lost, and empty.

"Sssshhh," he whispers, stroking my hair. "It's OK. It's OK, Meg."

Hiccuping, I realize my hand is in my pocket and it's clutching something: a piece of paper or card, slightly glossy. Experimentally, I feel little serrated edges and a weird half-circle cut out. What is it? Why am I holding on to it so hard? It's warm, damp, crumpled; I must have been holding it for quite a while.

And I'm not sick, I realize. This pain, it's not illness. I recognize this feeling, but not at this intensity. Never as strong as this, but a lesser version? That, I know.

It's heartbreak.

"Henry." I try to lift my head a bit, but he's holding me too tightly and I'm slightly trapped. "What's happening?"

Instinctively, I lift my free hand to my hair: now my touchstone in time. It's pretty much the same length, and when I run my fingers across each other I realize I'm not wearing any rings. So this is soon. Wherever I am, whatever is happening, this incredible pain is not far away at all.

Fear rockets through me again: newer, fresher.

"Henry." I struggle to get away now. "*What is happening?*"

I don't care if I sound mad, don't care if I scare him: this pain is absolutely terrifying and I need to know where it comes from before I lose it completely. Except all I see is Henry's face—so sad, so compassionate—and when I look down, I realize he's wearing a black suit.

With a searing bolt of terror, I look down at myself: I'm in black too.

Black coat, black dress, black tights, black shoes.

We're sitting on the bench, the nose-picking bench of our Second Date, and the lights of Bristol are shimmering around us. With growing horror, I realize that there are too many colors. The lights are red, green, blue, pink, white, yellow. When I turn my head slightly, I see the huge Christmas tree that goes up in the park every year. The park is freezing cold, and all the branches are bare, like skeleton fingers.

It's Christmas. But is it *this* Christmas?

"Who—" I'm starting to sob again. "Who is it, Henry? *Who?*"

Because this pain, this feeling of being totally lost, of being stranded, of being alone, this is the kind of heartbreak you only feel a handful of times in your life. For one of the few people who are part of you. I don't know what to do with this feeling, where to put it, and for the first time, Other Margot doesn't either.

We're both lost, together.

Henry frowns and I suddenly realize: whatever is in my pocket, that will tell me, that will give me a clue—maybe it's a program, maybe it's from the funeral, maybe it'll have a photo and an epigraph and a—

Panicking, I rummage for it and realize I'm fading.

No.

Ten more seconds.

Just ten more seconds.

With effort, I pull the piece of paper out of my pocket and—

"MARGOT THE METEOROLOGIST?"

My cheek is wet, and when I lift a hand I realize there's a tear streaking down my face. The pain is still there, like the moments after you wake up from a nightmare. Somehow, this hurt was so great it managed to filter through to this version of me too.

I quickly wipe my eye.

"Sorry," I lie as calmly as I can. "Just got a lash stuck on my contact lens. Let me just run to the loo and get it out—"

"Actually," Charlie interrupts, "we're pretty much at the end now, Margot. You've done amazingly. Maybe you could just wrap it up, and then we're done?"

My entire body still aching, I nod blankly.

"So sit with me, mini meteorologists," I bleat with as much chirp as I can muster, trying to smile, but my chin is wobbling and my eyes are filling again. "And together we will take the world by storm."

Then I stand up, shaking.

"I'm so sorry, but I've realized there's somewhere I urgently need to be. Can you take the cat?" I thrust Cheddar at Polly. "I'll pick him up later."

"Sure." She takes the squawking kitten. "Is everything alright?"

"No. It's not."

Because I've done the math, and if this funeral happens this Christmas—which all the signs point to—then I am about to lose someone I love deeply in the next few months. And I've already seen Henry, Eve, Winter, Mum, Dad, Grandad and Polly in future visions. Which means there's only one person left: one person I love who has been absent from all of them.

I assumed it was a choice, but now I'm not so sure.

And every single shred of anger, resentment and hurt has abruptly disappeared, as if ripped from the ground by a tornado: none of it exists anymore.

All that's left is love.

30

JULES!"

I continue to smash at her door as if I can in some way prevent what's coming by the sheer strength of my fists.

"JULES! Are you in there? JULIA?"

There's a small pause, then I see a shadow hesitate behind the frosted glass in their Cotham front door.

"Sim? Simran, it's really important. Please, I need to see Jules."

The door opens and Jules's wife looks at me apprehensively: I imagine it looks like I'm about to do to my best friend's face what I just did to her property. I quickly unclench my fists and try to look a bit less desperate.

"I'm not angry anymore," I say quickly. "I just need to see her."

"Oh!" Sim coughs and glances warily down the garden path. "She's . . . uh . . . out, I'm afraid. Doing . . . writing stuff, I think."

"'Writing stuff'?" Jules says from behind her, appearing in the hallway in black, paint-splattered dungarees. "Seriously, we have got to work on your lying skills, babe. Absolutely atrocious. The FBI will never come calling for you at this rate."

I stare at Jules as my chest starts to feel tight and painful. This can't be happening. It's a miscalculation, that's all. She is too lovely, too funny, too smart, too young to just . . . No. I'll stop it somehow, whatever it takes. Lock her in a room and prevent her going anywhere ever again. She can curse at me as much as she wants, but I am now going to be her forever guard dog and there's nothing she can do about it.

Jules gives Sim a quick kiss on the cheek and together they assess my intense expression and exchange confused glances.

"What's going on?" Jules frowns at me. "Why are you being super weird? And what the holy *hell* are you wearing?"

"Do you want me to, uh . . ." Sim looks concerned at my outfit too ". . . stay for this?"

"No." Jules grimaces. "You get back to the . . . thing."

"Right." A nod. "The thing." Sim gives Jules a supportive little squeeze of the shoulder, then smiles faintly at me. "It's nice to see you, Maggie!"

But she sounds wooden, false, like a badly made MDF kitchen cabinet, and my stomach starts to hurt.

They both glance over my shoulder again and I'm starting to get the message now.

Fuck.

There is no *time* for arguing.

There is no time to do anything but love everyone as hard as I can, while I still can, and I shouldn't have needed a vision to tell me that.

"I'm sorry," I say quickly as Sim turns and heads back to their sunny little kitchen. "I am so, so, so, so sorry. Please forgive me. Please."

Jules leans against the doorway and rests her beautiful head on the frame.

"OK, you're starting to freak me out now. Talk."

My throat is tight, my voice wobbly. But I can't scare her—this is not something Jules *ever* needs to be told—so I do my best to gain some semblance of control.

"This fight," I bleat pathetically, starting to cry. *What was in my pocket after the funeral? Why couldn't I see what was in my pocket?* "It's nothing. I don't care. I don't care about Lily and Aaron. I don't care if you visit them, I don't care if you helped them hide it, I don't care if you bloody set them up on a blind date behind my back and gave them a bouquet of condoms. You're my best friend, I love you more than anything on the planet, and I *know* you love me and *nothing* will ever change that."

Jules continues to regard me with wise, dark eyes.

"Seriously," I sniff adamantly, wiping my nose with my hand, "I'll stay right here and I'll say sorry and sorry and sorry and sorry and sorry—"

"A bouquet of condoms?" Jules's nose twitches. "A *bouquet of condoms*. Is that a thing? Like, is that a thing straight people actually do?"

"Yeah." I nod. "They put them all together like flowers and then they wrap it in tissue paper and sometimes they put sweets in too, so that—it doesn't matter. Can you just forgive me, please? Right now. Immediately. I cannot spend one more second with us not talking."

Not *one more second* of whatever we have left.

"Why are you apologizing, though?" Jules scratches her nose. "What exactly are you saying sorry about?"

"I . . ." I think about it for a few seconds. "Yelling at you?"

"Right." She nods dryly. "You're normally so logical, Margot. What is wrong with you at the moment?"

"That is very much a topic for another day," I say flatly. "I'm apologizing. So let's just forget about all that and go back to normal. Please."

"No." Jules frowns at me. "Absolutely not."

A wave of horror: I am not giving up that easily.

"Right." I sit down abruptly on the doormat, facing her. "Then you're going to have to step over me to get out of the house, and you'll have to step over me to get back in, and I'll read *all* your post before it gets delivered and I'll ring the doorbell every few minutes while you're asleep."

At this, Jules laughs loudly. "How passive-aggressive of you." Then she sits down on the doorstep opposite me.

"Maggie," she says, briefly leaning her forehead against mine.

"You total rainbow-legginged numpty. I'm not letting you apologize because you did nothing wrong. I fucked up, and I need to explain what happened."

A wash of relief: I don't need an apology, couldn't care less, but this means we're one step closer to being put back together.

"OK. But I forgive you in advance. Just so you know."

"Handy." Jules smiles slightly and takes a deep breath. "So . . . I had suspicions about Lily and Aaron for a while, because something felt . . . off. Every time I challenged her, she denied it. But I found out for sure a few hours before the rehearsal dinner, when we all got to the venue. I caught a text from Aaron when it popped up on Lily's phone. And I went absolutely apeshit. Like . . . fully nuclear."

I nod: that sounds like Jules. If I'm a bullet, she's an atomic bomb.

Then: "Wait—you only knew a few *hours* before?"

"Yeah." Jules winces and glances over my shoulder at the garden. "It's not an excuse and it doesn't make it better. I should have told you what I suspected months before. But if I'd been wrong . . . Fuck, it didn't even bear thinking about. I'd have blown apart a friendship group. By the time I had evidence, we were at the bloody venue, you'd already lost your deposit, everyone was arriving, you were so excited, and I was . . . stuck."

I feel myself soften slightly: a few hours is *very* different to months.

"I was obviously never going to let you walk down that aisle, but Lily said she'd been trying to end it for ages and begged me to let her tell you herself. Except . . . she didn't. She was terrified, Mags. She'd made a huge, life-shattering mistake, she couldn't take it back and she knew she was going to lose you. Us. She was going to lose everything."

I frown: but Lil didn't lose Jules, hence this entire conversation.

"Then you found out in the worst possible way, and . . ." Jules's voice hitches slightly. "Fuck, Margot. You were so broken. All your walls came straight up, barriers as high as the sky, and there was a good chance that if I told you the truth, I'd be on the other side of them. I needed to stay with you."

My stomach twists, because Jules is right. In my anger and pain, I suspect I'd have cast her out of my fortress too.

"But you didn't," I say in a small voice. "You didn't stay on my side. You pretended to, but you kept seeing Lily in secret. You kept lying to me."

"I know." Jules takes a deep breath. "For the first few months, I wasn't lying. I cut her out too. I was so bloody angry with her. But . . ."

She pauses, glances over my shoulder at the lawn.

"All Lil has ever wanted is to be loved, Maggie. Loved by everyone. By *anyone.* You know that, you know what her shitty parents were like. It's why she started that bloody Instagram page in the first place. There's this gaping hole inside her that nothing ever seems to fill. And I think suddenly Aaron . . . did."

"Because he made sure of it," I say weakly, remembering all his intense conversations, his grand romantic statements, his poetic gestures. Remembering the *force* of how hard he chased me, bombarded me, refused to take no for an answer.

I couldn't resist it either: it was overpowering.

"*We're going to stop, right?*" I suddenly believe what I didn't believe before: that Lily *had* tried to get out. Many, many times, without success.

"Exactly." Jules nods. "For a whole decade, I watched that man love-bomb you, control you, demean you, discard you, put you down. I watched him grind you into pieces, and there was *nothing* I could do. He is a handsome *bulldozer* of a dickhead. And those Instagram posts—she didn't sound like Lily anymore. I realized he was going to do it to her too, if he hadn't already. That's who Aaron *is.*"

I stare at her, because that hadn't occurred to me before.

Lily looked so *happy* in those posts, but I should know the difference between reality and a curated version of ourselves: I was jauntily chatting about waves and storms while my entire world imploded.

"He's not going to change," I realize quietly. "And all she had left was him."

"Lil made a terrible life decision, and she knows it. I should have told you, and I'm so sorry. But . . . the more I watched you struggle to put yourself back together, the more I realized I couldn't just leave Lil to the same fate. Despite what she did. She's still Lil."

Jules glances up at the path again and I feel faintly irritated: can you please do the gardening in your head at another, less crucial time, woman? We have my entire romantic history to dissect right now.

"I'm happier now than I have been in . . ." I pause in surprise. "Ever, actually."

"I know." Jules grins and puts her arm around me, kisses the top of my head. "You're finally back to being Maggie."

My eyes fill and there's a lump in my throat.

I am. I'm back to being me.

All the emotion that has been simmering in my chest for nearly a year rises to the surface like oil on water, and I abruptly realize it's not just anger and betrayal. It's also sadness for Lily, for where she's ended up. I wouldn't wish Aaron on my worst enemy, let alone my best friend of three decades.

"I didn't mean to pick a side," Jules says softly. "But I did, by watching everything unfold without doing anything. And I am so, so sorry. I will never be that weak again."

I also spent most of this year watching other people. It wasn't until the universe started showing me my *own* life, playing out like a film, that I was finally able to let go of them and see myself.

"You could have just *told* me all this," I sigh, putting my head in my hands.

"Well I did try." Jules grins. "Repeatedly. But *somebody* kept refusing to return my calls or read any of my laboriously long and eloquent essay-sized texts."

"I *may* have muted you," I admit sheepishly.

"I thought you might have." Jules lifts her eyebrows. "Fucking numpty."

We both laugh—she sounds like Jules again—and I feel the pieces of us click back into place, more beautiful for being broken. Then my eyes abruptly fill with tears again. I don't *know* it's Jules that my vision was about. That was a knee-jerk reaction, born of guilt and sadness. It could be anyone else, maybe someone I don't even know yet.

Please, universe, let it not be Jules.

"You're feeling OK?" I reach over and grab her chin so I can study her skin and her eyeballs and her lips. "Healthy?"

"What?" Jules whacks me away. "Yeah, I'm great."

"And you're not planning on, I don't know . . . base jumping or motor racing or wild horse riding?"

"What, on a whim? No. Sim wants us to sand down the floorboards."

"Don't," I say sharply: big machines, lots of dangerous dust.

"Alright, nutter." Jules laughs and assesses me again. "Seriously, what *are* you wearing? Did Eve do this to you?"

I laugh. "Nope. It was Polly. For the TV job."

"You got an audition! I *knew* you would. How did it go?"

"Amazing." I nod and wipe my face, feeling another rush of pleasure. "I really loved it, I think it's going to make me really, really hap—"

Jules glances up at the garden again. "Shit."

This time I properly lose my patience. "Julia, I love you, but this is a very emotional and pivotal moment for our relationship and I would appreciate it if you could stop checking out the state of your bloody lawn for two—"

Something in her face makes me turn round.

"Shit," I say.

"That's what I just said," Jules confirms, standing up. "Shit."

Breath held, I watch Lily and Aaron come up the road, heading toward the house, Aaron three steps ahead—on his phone, as always—as if the sheer masculine muscle of his long legs cannot bear to be contained by a more reasonable pace.

"Wait!" Lily hops delicately after him. "Aaron, can you just please wait for—"

They turn onto the path and both abruptly notice me at the same time, sitting on the doorstep like the world's most awkward garden gnome.

"Shit," Lily says, freezing.

We both look at Jules with a whole lot of questions, and she grimaces and holds out both of her hands like the shrug emoji.

"Surprise!"

31

MAYBE JULES DISAPPEARS from my visions *because I kill her.*

CLUMSILY, I GET up from the floor and brush down my denim bottom.

"Did you do this on purpose?" I look from Lil back to Jules and back to Lil again. "Is this your lame attempt at a reunion?"

"Yeah." Jules rolls her dark eyes at me. "I invited Lily and Aaron over weeks ago, then I sent out really strong vibes with my spider mind to make you turn up, unannounced and dressed like a toddler, to park your rainbow ass on my welcome mat."

"Good point," I note briskly. "Forgiven."

I can't quite make eye contact with Aaron, so I look at Lily, still standing like a statue on the path. This must be why Sim and Jules seemed so on edge: they knew she was on her way. I've spent the last nine months wondering how I would feel when I saw Lil again—*if* I saw her again—and now she's here . . .

Well, Jules was right: Instagram has been heavily edited, that's for certain. Lily's still in that huge gray jumper, but when it's not perfectly styled with toes peeking out of the bottom, it's bobbly and misshapen and kind of hideous. Her jeans are baggy at the knees, her red hair is in a high, slightly greasy ponytail with one stray piece sticking out like a rhino's horn, and her face is tired. Pale, a little splotchy. Her eyelids are pink, and when

I glance down at her fingernails, they're chewed to shreds. Lil upgraded from chewing her own hair to chewing her fingernails when she was eleven, and it looks like she's now just slowly eating herself in tiny pieces.

Every single cell in me suddenly aches. *Lil. My poor Lil.*

What the fuck has he done?

"Hi, Maggie," she whispers, green eyes huge. "How . . . are you?"

This is the first time we have spoken since that night in the wedding garden. I have spent *so* many hours over the last year thinking of all the things I want to say to her. All the things I didn't say at the time. Sometimes it was pathetic, sometimes hostile, sometimes weepy, sometimes desperate, sometimes outright cruel. In my darkest moments, I would script hour-long monologues that were as nasty as I could possibly make them: pulling her apart, causing her as much pain as I physically could. I would picture her crumbling, the way I had. I would take glee in it.

Sometimes it was the only way I could fall asleep.

Now I don't want to say any of it.

Because it's hitting me all at once that *so* many of those monologues were aimed at Lily instead of Aaron—because she was the one I had loved more.

"I'm well," I say gently, still looking only at her. "How are you?"

"Yeah." Lil squirms uncomfortably. "You know. Good. Thank you for asking."

I glance down at her belly: she's not showing yet. Although, frankly, in that jumper she could be eighteen months gone and there still wouldn't be any visible sign.

"Congratulations," I say genuinely. "Are you excited?"

Lily flushes guiltily, but I see a fire light up in her eyes and I'm so, so glad that something good has come from this mess.

"Yes." She nods in embarrassment. "I really am."

Aaron pointedly clears his throat next to her, clearly furious that he's now being ignored by both of us.

"I mean, *we* are." Lil coughs, glances to the side—unable

to make eye contact with him—and I realize it's some kind of weird loyalty to me: as if just looking at him when I'm here too would be the ultimate betrayal. "Aren't we, sweetie?"

Then she winces, as if she's just realized that accidentally adding *sweetie* to that sentence was an insult to me, but all it has done is prove I no longer feel anything at all.

With breath held, I finally force myself to look at Aaron: as if he's still the sun and I need some kind of special gadget to see him without doing considerable damage. He's still beautiful, unfortunately. If anything, Aaron looks better. Tanned from his exotic holiday. Slightly blonder. Still chiseled. Still incredibly tall. Henry can get so much more human into so much less body.

"Yeah." Aaron gives Lily one of his famous little crooked grins: the one I used to find so charming. "We're excited. We're properly adulting now, hey, Lil."

I'm assessing him carefully for any kind of emotion.

There is some discomfort—I guess that's something—but underneath a faint, thin layer of performative shame and humility, he's . . . *smug.* Pleased with himself. As if the surface of him is carefully painted, like a lovely piece of furniture that once you get home and sand down you realize is not real wood underneath, just laminate. He's actually *enjoying* this. His new fiancée, his old fiancée, his ability to impregnate, the fight over him as if he's the one Ken at a multi-Barbie wedding.

It might also be because I'm wearing rainbow leggings and a sunshine smock: dude has to be hyper-aware now that he traded up.

I search myself for any of the remaining pain, and realize it's gone.

This man was the person I brushed my teeth next to for ten years, and now he's just a stranger I don't like, standing on a lawn.

"Hello, Mags." Aaron attempts to look humble and ends up looking like he's just trod something sticky into a carpet. "You've cut your hair. It suits you."

He's clearly expecting the same grace with which I greeted Lily and he is going to be sorely mistaken, because fuck him.

"Yes," I say curtly. "I bloody know."

"Um . . ." Lily anxiously switches her weight from one foot to another and curls her jumper down around her hands. My heart hurts again: she looks exactly like she did in the dinner queue at school. "Maggie, are you having dinner with us too?"

I glance at Jules, who lifts her eyebrows: *you can if you want.*

"No." I clear my throat. "Thank you. I have plans."

"Ah." Lil nods. "Of course. OK."

There's a silence.

A long, extremely heavy silence, because now what the hell do we say to each other? The weight of our shared past is making polite conversation impossible.

"Actually." I frown. "Aaron, there *is* something I want to say to you."

He shuffles slightly, his sense of enjoyment at the situation waning.

"Of course." He nods sheepishly, taking a deep breath and lifting his chin: a warrior of compassion and courage. "Anything."

I open my mouth and he quickly adds, as if holding up a shield:

"But before you do, I'm sorry that I fell in love with Lil, but it just happened, it wasn't my fault, the heart wants what the heart wants and—"

"Nope." I hold up my hand: what an incredible non-apology. "Don't give a shit."

Aaron blinks. "Oh."

"All I want to say is can you please fuck off inside so I can talk to my best friends without you?"

Aaron's entire face falls—he's rendered irrelevant—and Jules snorts next to me.

"Ummm . . ." He runs a hand through his fringe in annoyance. I can see him wondering where my tears are, where my pain is, where my sadness and hurt have gone. Because how the hell is he supposed to feed off my emotions when there aren't any left? "Yeah. OK. If that's what you want. Sorry. Again. For everything. See you in there, Lil."

Aaron leans over and gives her a quick kiss on the lips, as punishment for me.

Lily's eyes are still locked on mine, and she flinches.

Then Aaron disappears into the house, where we hear Sim do her absolute best to sound thrilled to see him.

The door closes and finally—*finally*—the three of us are alone.

"Margot." Lily's whole body has just relaxed, and I don't think she knows yet that this is how it will be now: tense, every time he's near. "Please let me talk first, even though I know there is *nothing* I can say. I've written so many letters and texts and they've all gone in the bin because you made it clear you didn't want to hear it, and every time I try to say sorry, it just sounds so . . . pointless. What good can an apology do? You say sorry when you break a teacup, not someone's entire *life*."

Her eyes are full of tears and her pointy chin is wobbling.

"But I *am* sorry. I didn't even know I had it in me to do that. I honestly didn't. I used to think I was a *nice* person, that was my entire *identity*. Jules was the clever one, Eve was the fun one, you were the fierce one. So I told myself I was *nice*. And that was enough, my one strength. And maybe I got tired of being nice, or maybe I was never really nice to start with, or maybe I'm just looking for an excuse because I'm selfish and horrible, because it turns out I'm not *nice* at all."

She's saying the word *nice* way too much, as if it's become a mantra for her, and I wonder how long she's been building herself around that word.

My chest aches and I take an instinctive step toward her.

"No." Lil holds up a hand and moves away. "Don't. Don't be kind to me. I can't bear it. I need you to hate me, Maggie. I need you to, because that's the only way it feels fair. I can't have you be kind to me on top of everything else."

Her entire face crumples and she sticks a fingertip in her

mouth and starts aggressively ripping apart her one remaining nail.

"But I'm not nice anymore," she bleats desperately. "I'm *bad* and I know it, all the time, every second, and I'm carrying it with me and I can't put it down. I can't get away from it, and I don't know who I *am anymore*."

Lil puts her hands over her face and starts sobbing.

Is this what we all do? Just *hate* ourselves, constantly, for not being perfect? For making mistakes? For somehow not living up to whatever identity we've created in our own heads? Are we all just walking around, living in our own guilt and shame and flaws like snails in houses we've made from ourselves?

Jules makes a move toward Lily, but I get there first.

"Stop," I whisper, wrapping my arms around her and pulling her tiny, ridiculously woolly body toward me. "You're not *bad*, sweetheart. You have never been *bad*. You screwed up, that's all. It's not the same thing."

Because it's just hit me who else is missing from my visions: Lily.

There is no Lily and, while there is no way of knowing *why*, it doesn't matter anymore. The realization that I will soon lose someone I love makes everything else seem so insignificant. As if I thought I was living in a town with normal-size houses and normal-size trees and normal-size crockery and then Gulliver turns up and you realize that it's all so miniature, it's ridiculous. Maybe if I'd had that vision sooner, things would have been different.

I should be living my entire life as if an unknown giant is looming, because it is.

"Please don't hate me," Lil sobs into my denim smock, completely reversing her previous statement. "Please, please don't. I can't bear it. I understand we can't be friends, but please, don't hate me."

I glance over her at Jules, who looks emotional but is not joining in the hug because Jules doesn't do hugs.

"I don't hate you," I tell Lil truthfully. "Not anymore."

"She doesn't hate me anymore either," Jules chirps up from behind us. "Something weird happened to Maggie today and all the hate appears to have evaporated for no apparent reason, but she won't tell us why. It's all very suspicious. I suspect she was visited by the Ghost of Christmas Past."

"Or future," I say dryly. "That would work too."

Lil wipes her eyes and steps back.

"I wish Eve was here too." She gazes sadly around the garden. "I miss her, so much. It doesn't feel right without her here. Like a table with three legs."

"Good point." Jules gets her phone out of her pocket and makes a video call that takes one second to connect. "Evelyn? Why are you picking up your phone? It's three twenty on a Friday. Aren't you supposed to be at school?"

"Oh!" Eve beams at the screen. "Yeah. Say hi, kids!"

She turns her video to face a classroom full of five-year-olds, who all cheer and wave.

"One of them will probably confiscate my phone from me now," Eve grins amiably, returning to the screen. "What's up?"

"We just wanted to say hello, that's all."

With the triumphant air of a magician pulling a bunny out of her hat, Jules swings the video round so that the three of us are in it.

"Oh my God." Eve blinks and leans forward. "Oh my *God*. Are you . . . It's *all* of you! Lil! Hi, Lil! Maggie! What are you— Oh nooooo, are you all *hanging out without me*? This is so *unfaiiiiir.* Why am I at *schoooooool*?"

Jules laughs. "That'll teach you for pulling a sickie on the wrong day."

Eve looks so happy to see us all together it breaks my heart again: she's like the youngest child after an acrimonious divorce.

"Right." Jules is back into business mode. "I'll fill you in later. Go teach sprogs and whatnot. I've got to go save my wife from whatever shit that ridiculous man is spouting at her now."

Then she blows a kiss at Eve and we hear *byyyyyeee* from thirty school children.

"Aaron's bought an electric guitar," Lil says with a faint air of embarrassed loyalty. "He's honestly pretty good at it."

I bite my lip: no, he isn't.

"Have fun tonight, OK?" Jules kisses my cheek. "Let me know how your big romantic weekend goes—Eve told me all about it. I've got a wedding to argue about." She glances at Lily. "I'm not doing it, Lil. I'm sorry, but it's a hard and permanent no."

"But—"

"No. I'm not doing it. Full stop."

I frown at both of them. "Doing what?"

They pause, looking guilty, and I roll my eyes.

"I don't bloody care about the wedding, guys. Honestly. What are you talking about?"

"Lily wants me to be her bridesmaid," Jules says sharply. "And I've said not again in a hundred years, not if you let me play my own entrance music, not even if you have Guinness pouring out of the little church fountain. I don't do *bridesmaid* anymore. Not after last time. Me and Sim got married in Vegas on our own with strangers for witnesses, as it should be, and I'm not wearing satin now. Not for anyone."

I inhale sharply: something's just occurred to me.

"You wouldn't be a bridesmaid?"

"Not a snowball's chance in hell." Jules folds her arms belligerently. "I'll be at the back of the church somewhere, cheering you on in spirit, with spirits."

"So . . . you wouldn't be a bridesmaid at *my* wedding?"

"Sorry, but—no."

The relief is so huge I nearly burst straight into tears again.

"What about birthday parties for small children? Would you go to them?"

"Hell, no," Jules says firmly, looking at me with even more suspicion now. "I'll send expensive and inappropriate gifts from whatever lovely tropical vacation I'm on at the time. What is going *on* with you, Margot?"

I don't think I've ever been this happy.

It might not be Jules at all. There is a very solid possibility that I haven't seen Jules in my future visions because she's busy zip-lining around Costa Rica with vodka in her hip flask.

"Nothing," I grin at her. "Absolutely nothing."

Jules takes a few moments to assess me—she's not buying it—then pats my nose with her finger and escapes back into the house, where I can already hear Aaron droning at Sim about *amps* and *plectrums*.

"Well." Lily coughs awkwardly. "It was *really* nice to see you, Margot."

I nod. "And you, Lil."

"I guess I'll . . . see you around. I'm sorry. Again. I'll never be sorrier about anything in my entire life, and I need you to know that."

Lily walks toward the front door and I can see the sadness in her shoulders, the red flush on her neck, the little strand of hair sticking vertically from her ponytail. All I want to do is prod it back in again, smooth her out, make her happy.

"Lil," I say abruptly, before I can analyze it all too carefully. "Would you like to go for a coffee sometime?"

Lily freezes and turns round slowly.

"Are you sure?"

"Yes." I nod. "I am sure."

"Then, *yes.*" Her entire face lights up. "*Please.* I would absolutely *love* that."

"Good. I'll text you."

Lil puts one foot in the house, then hesitates and turns around again.

"Maggie . . . are you the squirrel?"

I stare at her for a few seconds, then burst out laughing. "Yes. I'm the squirrel. How the hell did you know?"

"I just . . ." Lily frowns, slightly bewildered by her own astuteness. "I don't know, really. I just kind of *knew.* The comments were so sweet. Plus . . . when we were kids, didn't your neighbors have a squirrel living in their garden that you used to call Lucy? And weren't your neighbors called Jones?"

I frown. "Yes. Blimey, I'd totally forgotten about that."

"Well, it made me feel better anyway. Every time the squirrel said something nice to me, I'd imagine it was you and that you didn't hate me completely, and it would make me so happy and so relieved. So thank you, for that. It meant a lot."

She doesn't need to know I made those comments out of spite, and I suddenly wonder if I *did*. Entirely, anyway.

If I wasn't watching her from afar, just because I missed her.

"You're welcome, Lil."

I'M NEARLY HOME—rushing to meet Henry—when my phone rings.

"You're too early!" I try to shift my handbag so I can find my house keys and accidentally drop it. "I'm not ready yet! But I am *so* bloody ready for all the rampant sex we're going to have and I hope you like expensive silk things because my new knickers are basically disposable, is what I'm saying."

Bending over, I pick up my bag, slightly out of breath.

"I *do* like expensive silk things," Charlie says calmly. "I'm just not entirely sure we've reached that stage of our professional relationship yet, Margot."

I blink at the screen, then silently yell "FUCK" into the sky.

"Hi, Charlie." Worst wannabe children's TV presenter ever. "I thought you were my boyfriend. Please accept my apologies and be assured that I won't be throwing my knickers away, as suggested."

"Good to know." I can hear her smiling. "I won't keep you long, I just have news."

Piece by piece, my future is coming. I am one step closer to the happiness I've seen and felt. So even though I know exactly what Charlie's going to say before she says it, I let her say it anyway.

"The board loved it." She chuckles. "The decision took all of thirty minutes. You got the job. You are now Margot the

Meteorologist, our brand-new children's TV presenter. Oh, and your cat got it too. You're both in."

I look up at the sunny sky and feel the sharp, sweet ache of happiness.

Funny how both grief and joy can make you hurt.

Funny how entangled they are: woven into one big piece of fabric that makes us whoever we become.

"Thank you," I say simply, shutting my eyes.

"You're so welcome, Maggie. I can't wait to see this all come to life."

"Me too," I say, smiling slightly, because it's one thing being shown glimpses of the future and a very different thing to actually live it.

When she's gone, I take my other phone out: my burner phone.

The phone I used to split my life in half.

To split myself in half too.

Then—with a quick flick of my wrist—I flip back the lid on my neighbor's rubbish bin and chuck the phone in. There is no need for me to be two people, two versions of me. One is finally enough.

This is my future now.

And it all starts with Henry.

32

MARGOT!" THE CAR horn beeps again. "Get your lovely bottom out here right now so we can start our Big Sexy Weekend, please!"

Grinning, I swing open the window and lean out.

"Henry! *Please.* I have *neighbors.*"

I don't actually care about the neighbors—I'm quite proud of Henry's shouting—but I'm slightly conscious that I'm now a children's TV presenter and shouldn't be having the word *sex* yelled at me in the middle of a public street.

Or *bottom*, for that matter.

"They can't come!" Henry roars back. "I'm sorry, but there's just no room!"

Giggling, I blow him a kiss and close the window.

Then I run to the mirror again, like a teenager. I'm in a little floral blue dress—it looks a bit like the bedding we eventually get, maybe that's why—and my dark hair has decided to be inexplicably chic and European. My eyes are bright, my cheeks are pink, and *joy* is scribbled across my face. I am lit from within by some kind of internal source, and it's transformed scooped-out, hollow-cheeked Margot into a goddess with cheekbones for days and a fringe that knows exactly what it's doing.

This is going to be the best weekend of my life: I can feel it.

Blowing a quick kiss at myself—better get that out of the way before I start doing it in Cornwall and Henry questions every decision he's ever made about me—I automatically look round the room for Cheddar, then realize Eve picked him up half an hour ago and gave the distinct impression she wouldn't be giving him back.

Quickly, I glance around my flat to see if I've forgotten anything.

It's still pretty empty, but not quite as empty as it used to be. Over the last few weeks, I've gradually collected a few bits and pieces: a rug, a couple of cushions, a plant. Polly's painting is still on the wall, and when I get back on Sunday night I might think about turning my kitchen yellow. It looks so nice in my visions. Like a real *home*. It's all happening, exactly as the universe wants it to. No: as *I* want it to. Because I'm choosing this. It's not fate, or destiny. These are my own decisions, pushing me forward.

With a jubilant bounce, I grab my suitcase—very light, it's basically just lace—and wheel it out of the front door. Then I essentially skip (embarrassing) toward the little blue Mini with its small red seats parked outside.

"How am I supposed to focus on driving when you look like that?" Henry leans over and kisses me. "You're a bloody health-and-safety hazard."

"I *know*," I giggle. "I should come with a warning on the bottle."

"Dangerously attractive: do not take while driving."

"Or using heavy machinery."

"Ugh. I'll have to put the tractor back."

We both laugh and as I turn to put my seatbelt on, I see Pol pause by the window in her living room. She sees me, grins, winks; I wink back.

"Hurry up," Henry grins impishly. "We need to get going, because I am *way* too eager to get you naked."

With a laugh, I look down and realize he's wearing his pink-star jacket: the little embroidered patch is glowing on his arm. He won't be wearing it for long, I can tell you that. I'm going to rip it off him as soon as appropriately possible.

Gently, so it doesn't ruin the stitching.

Let the sexy times commence.

NO ROAD TRIP has ever been this fun.

I dreaded going anywhere with Aaron: his ridiculous road rage, his impatience, his desire to "get there" so we could "start." He'd huff and puff; he'd snap at me if I talked at the wrong moment and we took a late exit; he'd ask me to stop singing because I just didn't have "the vocal cords for that kind of volume." If we bought sweets, he'd intermittently hold out his hand in silence and expect me to obediently place one there, as if summoning a genie.

When we eventually reached wherever we were going, he'd breathe out in relief, collapse on the bed and say, "*Finally.*" As if sitting next to me in a car was some kind of arduous task he'd been asked to complete by an angry God and now it was time for his reward. Which, predominantly, was asking me to move out of the way so he could see the telly properly.

This is completely different territory: a different country, a different *planet*.

Henry is in no rush at all—if anything, he's driving slightly too slowly and keeps insisting on "pit stops" so we can buy more "snacks"—and instead of simply holding his hand out and expecting me to deliver the right thing at the right time, he opens his mouth until I put a sweet or crisp in there. Which, while it may *sound* like the same thing, doesn't feel the same at all. It feels trusting and organic, as if he's a baby bird and knows that whatever I feed him is going to be lovely.

It's only a three-hour drive, but I find myself willing it to be longer.

We chat, we joke and we point out interesting things on the side of the road; we turn the radio up, duetting one of the worst harmonies I've ever witnessed, let alone been part of. We're both completely tone-deaf, but Henry doesn't seem to care: he knows the words of every song in every genre and is bellowing them out at the top of his lungs.

As we finally turn off the motorway and start heading into the countryside, I open the window and lean out to watch the greenery, the narrowing roads, the hedges with their tiny little yellow flowers and—

Oh my God. I'm here. I've reached another vision.

I'm not sure how I know this, unless it's the intense sense of déjà vu I suddenly feel, but—with a tingle—I turn to look at Henry.

His face is in profile.

The hawk-like nose, the bushy eyebrows, tanned hands on the wheel. He glances toward me briefly, dark eyes warm, and I feel a rush of something intense, giddy, almost solid. Then he turns back to focus on the road and I look around the car again, recognizing all of it: this moment, exactly as I was shown. The seats are bright red, ripped and worn, our knees are slightly bunched because the car is so small. Green and yellow on either side of us: the tiny flowers, the hedges, the narrow road.

I'm in the vision I had in the spa and—as if watching myself from a distance—I see my hand instinctively reach out and touch the pink star on his elbow, to hold on to him, to make sure he's really here. Henry looks at me and smiles, happy and kind and relaxed and generous and clever and the sweetest soul I've ever met.

I feel myself glow at him like a nacreous cloud, illuminated from below.

And I realize: I love him.

I love him.

I *love* this man.

And it doesn't matter that we've only known each other properly for five weeks, or that a lot of this love is coming from a future I wasn't supposed to see, or that it's too early, or too fast, or too nonsensical, a complete sidestepping of every bit of the logic I claim to adhere to.

I love him. I can feel it now, and I felt it then; I just didn't know what it was.

I love him.

Then—just as I know he will—Henry reaches forward to twiddle with the car radio: the air crinkles with a sand shaker—no, it's a *cowbell*—and an electric guitar, he hits the wheel with his palms and says:

"TUUUUUUNE."

Beaming at me, he begins to bop up and down in his seat, swaying his head from side to side like a parrot. "Don't fear the reaper," he shouts at the top of his voice. "Don't fear it, Margot. Do *not* fear it. Come on, baby. What are we not going to do?"

"Fear it," I grin at him happily. "Not going to fear the reaper."

"Don't do it!"

"Not going to do it! I promise!"

"It's the *one* thing they're asking from us, Meg." Henry laughs loudly, and takes a slow corner. "That's all they want, and in return we get . . ."

"THE COWBELL," I shriek.

"THE BLOODY COWBELL," Henry yells.

We both start laughing, and this is it, this is as happy as one person gets. It's not the future anymore, I'm here, this happiness is mine and I'm going to hold on to it as hard as I can for as long as—

Everything goes cold.

THE SUNSHINE HAS gone.

I'm in a small street in Bristol, down by the river. It's gray, cold, overcast, getting ready to rain. Blinking, I look down. I'm not in a blue floral dress anymore, I'm wearing a big pink coat to the knees, large buttons, high-collared. Curious, I touch it with my hand. Blimey, is this coat . . . *cashmere*? Wool? Alpaca? It feels *expensive*.

Oooh, Other Margot. You're doing well for yourself. Good job, you.

Then I look a little further down at my boots: leather, black, a small heel. They look expensive too. Quickly, I touch my hair.

It's short. Very short. A crop. Oh my God, I crop my hair? Does it look nice? Does it look French? Is it a mistake? Am I currently growing it out, pulling at it every evening, crying in the bathroom when nobody notices?

To place myself in time, I look down at my hand.

No rings: just my grandfather's emerald.

That puts me roughly in the next three years, before the wedding or engagement, but after whenever I give myself this pretty dramatic and brave makeover. Future Margot is getting ballsier by the minute, and I love this for both of us.

Then I stare at my hand again.

Wait.

My hand looks different.

Not hugely different, but . . . more veiny. Paler. A few splodges on the back of it. Alarmed, I stretch my other hand out just to check. Unsurprisingly, that looks the same. A tiny bit . . . smaller than usual? Drier? More lined? Do I need to start using an expensive hand cream? It looks like I can *afford* to, so why am I not investing in my skincare routine?

Alarmed, I glance up and see myself reflected in a shop window.

The shock rips my breath away.

I'm older.

I'm quite a lot older—in my fifties.

I look good—sophisticated, even—which is a relief, but I am, without any doubt, now a middle-aged woman. The days of being called a "girl" have long ended. The woman staring back in amazement is me, but also not me. Other Margot is somebody I hoped I'd become one day, if I was lucky. I just thought I'd get there gradually: not all at once, while sitting in a car, eating Jelly Babies and shouting to '70s rock.

My stomach twists and I feel abruptly sick.

My rings. *Where the hell are my rings?*

"Margot?"

Slowly, I turn around.

Henry is so much older too: completely silver-haired, his

eyes more crinkly and the lines around his mouth more pronounced. He's wearing a big coat too—green, I don't recognize this either—and is possibly even more gorgeous: like he's been dipped in silver.

"Henry," I say, then my breath stops.

Out of the shop next to us has walked a young woman: beautiful, tall, with long brown hair tied back in a messy bun. For a second, I don't recognize her, can't place her, as if she's my dentist and I've just run into her at a local supermarket. Those hazel eyes, though. That little chin. Those slightly sticking-out ears . . .

Then my chest suddenly hurts: it's Winter.

"Meg!" Winnie bounds toward me and wraps me up in a tight hug: she's taller than I am now. "What are you doing here? Oh my God, did I get the date wrong? I thought we were meeting tomorrow? Have you heard from Gus? The little bugger won't answer my texts. I'm probably not cool enough to talk to anymore. I just saw Posy for coffee. How's Aunty Eve? Jules? Lil? Did you do that thing in the end? Or decide against it? I'm so busy with uni, I've barely had time to catch up with anyone. I've become so boring."

She's at uni, so that makes her—what?—nineteen? Twenty?

That puts me and Henry . . . in our fifties.

Then she starts laughing and pulls back so she can kiss my cheek. "Sorry, too many questions. We can talk about it tomorrow in *full*."

Blinking, I stare at her perfect face.

What's she studying? What *thing*? And of course Gus won't answer her texts: he's two years old. Except he's not, is he? That tiny, curly-haired boy is now a gangly, spotty teenager, playing video games in a basement and driving Eve up the wall.

Winter frowns. "Meg? What's wrong?"

Licking my lips, I turn back to Henry again. It requires every bit of energy I have, because I know what it is I'm looking for and I don't think I can see it; I don't think I'm physically strong enough.

Heart in my mouth, I look down at his hands.

He's not wearing his rings either.

And the pain is so unbearable, I have to stop myself from crouching on the pavement with my arms wrapped around my stomach and screaming.

"Hi," Henry says softly. "How are you?"

It's not a *How are you?* from someone I see regularly, it's a *How are you?* from someone I don't see at all, and my throat clamps shut. This is Other Margot's pain too, I can feel it. Both of us are heartbroken.

Please, I can almost hear future me saying. *Please don't ruin this for me.*

With every bit of control I can find, I manage to nod and smile. I will not be the ex-wife, screeching hysterically in the street. I won't do that to either of us.

"Yeah. I'm OK. You?"

"Yeah. Good. Surgery's a bit manic, but you know how it is."

He's a surgeon now—he did it—but I don't know "how it is," I don't know how it is because we're not together anymore; we were supposed to be together, we were supposed to die in each other's arms, and this is not *right*, this is not *fair*, this isn't the way it was meant to—

"Yeah." I nod. "I know how it is."

Henry's quietly watching me with that careful, clear-eyed expression—the one I love so much—and I can *feel* the love inside me: Other Margot still loves him too. She misses him, horribly. She's in pain. What has happened? Why aren't we together anymore? Does he just stop loving me? Do I do something wrong? *When* do we break up? It has to be quite far into the future because Winter and I are still close, so we must have built a bond over many years.

But I can't ask him what happened.

If we're divorced—which we clearly are—asking him why we're divorced at random outside a shopping center is going to make me look absolutely crazy, and I do not think Other Margot will appreciate it.

"It's nice to see you," I say as my eyes fill with tears and I quickly brush them away. "Sorry. It's . . . just cold."

Henry nods, but his eyes are full of tears too. He still cares about me: that's something, I suppose. It's not acrimonious, and we don't hate each other. But we're not a couple anymore, and I don't know what to do with this pain.

"It's nice to see you too, Margot."

Not *Meg*. Not *Megalodon*. Just Margot.

Winter shifts from side to side—uncomfortable, her eyes desperately sad—and I realize she still has the same tiny movements she had as a child. But I've lost her too. I've lost it all. All of it—my future, my life, my love—has gone.

My chin crumples and I feel Winnie wrap her arms around me.

"It's you, isn't it," she whispers.

I blink as she pulls away and puts a hand on either side of my face.

"It is." She studies me. "It's you. You're Other Margot."

I can't speak—can't find a single word—so she pulls me toward her again.

"*Thank you*," she murmurs so Henry can't hear it. "For literally *everything*. I'm so sorry I'm going to be such a brat as a teenager. Hold on tight, Meg. I love you and I don't mean any of it."

I've told her. Somehow, at some point, I have told Winter about my visions.

She knows that I'm me, that for these few seconds I'm not my future version anymore: I'm Past Margot, the Margot of years ago, scared and confused and unsure where I am or what I'm doing. She *sees* me, and she wants me to know it'll be OK. That when she's screaming at me, or yelling at me, it doesn't mean anything: she just feels comfortable enough to push me away, knowing I'll always come back. She feels secure and loved enough to fight.

With a lump in my throat, I nod: *Yes. I'm Other Margot.*

Then I look back at Henry, because I don't know how long

this vision is going to last—how much more I can find out—and I need to ask, to see what I can do, what kind of changes I can make, how I can avoid whatever forces us apart, but I can feel myself slipping, fading, leaving him behind without knowing why.

"This is it," Henry states quietly. "Isn't it."

The end, is what he means.

And it's not a question, because this is the end, and I can feel it: of us, of everything, the final chapter to our story, and I wasn't supposed to see it, shouldn't be here, it's all in the wrong order and it's ruined everything.

I open my mouth to ask him to stay, to try again, but it's too late.

I've gone and so has he.

"LA LA LA LA," Henry croons. "La la la la."

Then he turns briefly to me with a tiny frown.

"Why aren't you la-la-la-la-ing, Meg? The reaper demands our la's as payment for his cowbell."

With a deep sob, I bend in half and clutch my stomach.

"Meg?" Henry slows the car and turns to me properly. "Oh my God, what is it? Are you in pain? What's happening?"

"Stop the car," I bleat. "Please. Stop the car."

Panicked, Henry pulls into the next dip in a hedge and slams on the brakes.

"You're scaring me. Do I need to call a hospital? Is it your appendix? Have you had your appendix out? Where's the pain? Is it in the lower-right-hand side of your abdomen? Show me. Show me where the pain is."

But I can't show him, because the pain is *everywhere.*

"I need to . . ." I can't breathe, I can't swallow, I can't unfold myself: I am cut in half. "I need to get out."

With immense effort, I push the door open and tumble into the road.

Desperately, I look around me.

It's nothing but countryside. I need quiet, I need space, I need time to *think*, but Henry's getting out too and I don't know what to do and I need him to tell me it's going to be OK, but I can't because he can't, so—with the saddest sound I've ever heard—I curl up in a ball and start crying.

33

I DON'T WANT THIS gift anymore.

It's given me everything and then taken it all away, and it's too cruel, too unkind, too unnatural. I wasn't meant to *know*. I was supposed to meet Henry and fall gradually in love, get married, be happy and then have divorce thrown at me like a surprise hand grenade, the way it is for everyone else.

I wasn't supposed to see the end coming like this.

"Margot." Henry gently nudges me further into the hedge for safety, then sits on the ground next to me. "Margot, are you OK? Whatever it is, you can talk to me."

"Please." I press my forehead into my bare knees. "Henry. I need to think."

Because what do I do now?

I could just go with it, let this future happen—take the happiness and treasure it, hold on to it, enjoy it while it lasts—but it's not that simple. If this was a three-year fling, I'd say: sod it. Let's have a lovely time and say goodbye when it reaches the end, then move on. Consider it a lovely life experience, pocket the memories: thanks for your love and all the great sex. But this isn't going to be that. It'll be a *huge* chunk of my life. It's not another ten years, it's fourteen, possibly *fifteen years*. I'm thirty-six now. By the time it's over, I'll be in my fifties. I won't have my own children, or my own family: Winnie didn't mention any siblings or babies, and there are none with me on that street. If we'd had children together, I would have to see Henry more often, and it wouldn't have been *How are you?* It would have been *I'll take the kids next weekend* and *Have you packed their sports gear for the school football tournament?* I realize that Winnie didn't mention Cheds either and my chest aches more.

It will be too late to have a family, to start again.

If I live as long as my grandfather—which is optimistic but not impossible—that's another *forty years* alone. Four decades, just me. In a very expensive coat and nice boots. With a shitload of memories. A dead cat. An adult stepdaughter I see for coffee sometimes. And an ex-husband who's wandering around the world as a silver fox and a successful surgeon, more gorgeous than he's ever been.

Henry.

This is going to destroy him too. Henry won't have any more children either, and I know he wants them: I've seen it in his face, in future visions. He'll lose *another* wife, and go through that grief all over again. He'll be heartbroken too. And Winter: I'll be forcing myself into her life as a mother figure, making her need me and love me. And then I'll take it all away for a second time. I can't do it to that beautiful, sweet little girl.

How *can* I go through with this relationship, knowing what happens at the end? I'll be watching, constantly. Anxiously studying, waiting, looking for the Red Flags: the signal that it's going to be over. Trying desperately to avoid it. Every beautiful, happy moment will now be tinged with sadness, knowing that it's not permanent.

Logically, I know what the answer is. With the data I've now collected, there is only one possible solution that doesn't ruin both our lives.

But it's more than that: my heart can't do it either.

Not again. Not with Henry.

I love him now—more than I loved Aaron—but I don't love him as much as I'm going to in the years to come, when we've become part of each other: growing round each other like tree roots. I don't know him now like I will eventually. When every single part of him is dear and familiar to me, when I won't be able to live without him.

And, in the meantime, I've thrown away any chance at another future.

Closing my eyes, I stand up.

This has to be done, and it has to be done now.

It's going to hurt him—of course it is—but I'm just a woman he's dated for five weeks who will be forgotten about in a month if I handle this properly. Henry hasn't seen what I've seen: the engagement, the wedding, the birthdays. He hasn't felt the love I've felt—hasn't fast-forwarded into our future together—so this isn't going to be as hard for him as it is for me. He'll move on, he'll meet someone else, and I have to let him do that.

I have to let us *both* do that.

So that we both have a chance at a future that sticks.

"MEG?" HENRY KISSES the top of my head. "What the hell's going on?"

Wiping my eyes so he can't see, I stand up slowly and face him.

"I am so sorry," I say as clearly as I can. "But this isn't what I want."

Henry stares at me in amazement.

"You're very nice." I clear my throat. "And this has been super fun."

He winces slightly and I have to dig my nails into my hand to keep going.

I am so, so sorry, Henry.

"But I don't think it's going anywhere. We're just not right for each other."

In a way, it's the truth: it's *not* going anywhere. It'll just take us a decade and a half to realize that, by which time it'll be too late.

"And I apologize for this sudden realization," I say, somehow managing to keep my voice neutral, my eyes dry. "Truly. The last five weeks have been lovely."

They haven't been lovely: they have been *life-changing.*

It has been the single greatest period of my life. Henry has altered me permanently and I cannot believe I'm not going to be standing at our wedding, screwing up our vows, beamed at by a little girl for whom I will now become a distant memory, her ex one-time babysitter, cat-adopter and not-cleaner.

"But I don't want to waste your time," I finish lamely.

Because it's always, always the *time*: running out, like a bucket with a hole in it. *Drip, drip, drip*, and before you know it you turn around and there's nothing left. Just a stupid giant, looming ever darker while we hold on to our miniature teacups and look up at the sky.

Then I lift my chin and try to make my eyes steely: cold and unflinching.

Let me go.

"OK," Henry says simply.

Now it's my turn to flinch: it wasn't supposed to be *that* easy. "OK?"

"OK." Henry nods. "I don't want to be with someone who doesn't want to be with me, Meg. It's the most basic, fundamental cornerstone of a relationship. So if this isn't what you want, you've made the right choice."

My heart thumps painfully: yet again, he is showing such grace and dignity.

Henry is everything I've ever wanted—everything I've ever wanted to *be*—and I cannot believe I have to let him fly off into the sunset to meet some lovely, normal woman who doesn't have bloody visions of the future at random intervals.

"OK." I nod and swallow. "I'm sorry."

"I'm sorry too."

He smiles, looking so sad, and I smile back at him.

Fuck my fucking life. Again.

"Shall I drive you home, then?" Henry scratches his head.

"I don't really fancy wandering the countryside of Cornwall on my own."

Our weekend: our beautiful, sexy, lace-trimmed weekend. All gone, just like our future.

"Yes, please." I nod. "Thank you, Henry. For everything."

34

THE VISIONS STOP.

I wait, but nothing happens: I've cut the thread, and whatever was glistening and pulling me forward has gone. Without Henry, that future doesn't exist anymore. I've chosen a different path, and it's the right thing to do—I know it, even if I don't feel it—but I'm also sadder and more lost than I have ever been before. I miss Henry, I miss Winter, and I miss my visions. What seemed frightening at first, then an inconvenience, then—frankly—a bit of a burden, suddenly seems like an integral, much-loved part of me.

I also miss Other Margot.

I'm not sure where she is or what she's doing anymore, but I think about her a lot, and I hope she's happy. That I haven't made a mistake she's paying for.

But what to do with the present now I'm not staring into the future?

So I throw myself back into work. I research and make copious meteorological notes, I practice making child-friendly props out of papier mâché and balloons, I visit the TV set as it's developed—it's even bigger, madder—and try to smile at everyone as if I'm not heartbroken, as if I don't feel like there's a bit of me missing, all of the time. While filming the first season, I wake up at 6 a.m. and work straight through until 11 p.m., at which point I go home and pass out on my bed. I have a quick twenty-minute sob at 3 a.m., when I realize Henry's gone for good, automatically check my phone just to see if he's messaged (he hasn't), then it's back to sleep again to finish the night off as best I can.

I worry about Winter all the time, hoping she's OK, that she's happy, that the puppy hasn't peed on her bed again.

But I'm not saying there's no *joy*, because there is.

My new job is truly exciting; Polly is amazing, as usual, and jubilantly getting ready to leave Peter in the next couple of months. Jules buggers off to South America with Sim—"better than sanding, we'll just buy a rug"—and is littering the group chat with photos of her hang-gliding with two middle fingers jauntily held up to the camera, backward.

Lily and I have our promised coffee, which is just as awkward and stilted as we both knew it would be, but we plow on diligently: another coffee, a quick lunch, a few texts, laborious small talk that slowly expands into something that feels like friendship again, albeit a new, slightly altered one. Lil never mentions Aaron after our initial conversation, so I leave the topic alone and pray that she's OK, that she's happy, that he's treating her better than he treated me, that Jules can be there for the intimate details she will never share with me. Although she does—just once—let it slip that Aaron broke his arm by falling off a table, drunk, and I take the news like the gift it is.

Eventually, Lil rejoins the group chat (much to Eve's delight).

And as weeks turn into months, I wait for my heart to heal too.

I wait patiently for time to work its magic, just as it lets my hair grow down to my shoulders, thus, I realize with more sadness, erasing just a few more of my visions—my hair is no longer the right length to fit them.

The punching bag has been removed from the corner of my flat—I have no anger left—and I've still got Cheds, who is growing at an unprecedented speed and fast becoming both the bane of my existence and the love of my life. He is my noisy, neon shadow, and has taken to sleeping in various positions usually reserved for accessories: on top of my head, like an orange hat, around my neck, wrapped around my middle. And when I wake up sobbing most nights, he butts his little head against my face and purrs until I stop.

This cat is all I have left of that other life, the only reminder of what I gave up.

But he's also a reminder of what I *gained*.

Because I'm not the same, and everyone around me has noticed. I'm warmer, kinder, less judgmental. I'm softer, more open. Brighter, somehow. Henry went, but he cracked me apart and pulled out the pearl before going, and even without him I'm a better person, more beautiful and more myself. I'm nicer and more patient with my mother, now that she has moved back to Bristol with Dad and is ruling the roost all over again. I tell her things instead of shutting her out. Once, we even attempt a little cuddle—it doesn't go well—but we've decided we might try it again in the future.

I see my grandfather regularly, and we're closer than ever.

And Christmas, somehow, comes and goes without anyone dying.

Which is a relief—obviously—but I'm not sure exactly how that works: whether by stopping the future with Henry, I accidentally saved a life too. I can't see how, it's kind of illogical, but it's the silver lining I need. Just casually stopping the people around me from dying: that's not such a small thing.

You're welcome, whoever you were.

My only *real* fear is that by stopping the future I've seen, I'll have impacted the people around me in a less positive way.

It's Eve I worry about most.

I go with her to two more IVF appointments, but I've also cut the cord that tied her to Gus, and I'm terrified that somehow I've stopped him from coming into existence at all. Which doesn't make *biological* sense, but just by shifting that future, I suppose I've handed everyone around me a different one too. So when my doorbell finally goes—three months after the break-up, two days after Boxing Day—and I open it to see Eve in floods of tears, I immediately blame myself.

"Eve!" I clutch her fiercely to me, hating myself. "Darling, no! We'll keep trying!"

"She won't stop crying." Jules appears in the doorway. "I've never seen this much salt water, and I've just come back from Bolivia."

I squeak and throw my arms around her. "You're home!"

"Apparently so." She turns slightly. "Hurry up, slowcoach."

Lily ambles up the garden path, pink-cheeked and out of breath. The baby bump on her tiny frame is now so prominent she looks like a cartoon snake who just swallowed a watermelon, and any attempt to hide the pregnancy out of "sensitivity to Eve" is now totally out of the question. Luckily, Eve is such a sweetheart she insisted she didn't mind and that it was "actually very good juju to be around all these pregnancy hormones," despite scientific skepticism and raised eyebrows from both me and Jules.

"Go on without me." Lil smiles briefly and presses her hands against the base of her spine with a wince. "I'll get there in three to five business days."

I smile back at her, then usher a still-sobbing Eve inside.

For a few minutes all I can do is rub her back and cast wildly about for something to say to make it better. We've been here before—eight times now—but I've never seen her cry this hard or for this long.

"Sssshhh." I stroke her head slightly desperately. "Should I get the wine?"

I look up beseechingly at Jules and Lily, now standing like total lemons in the middle of my kitchen, watching me carefully.

"Jesus," I sigh in frustration. "Sensitive as a bag of rocks, you are. I'll get the alcohol, then. Got to do everything round here."

"Neerfami," Eve wails into her hands.

"Sorry?"

"She said," Jules grins, "Not. For. Me."

I stare at Jules, then back at Eve, who continues to sob incoherently. One quick glance at Lily tells me everything I need to know: she's beaming all over, and bopping up and down slightly with her hands on her stomach.

"*No.*" I run back to Eve, fighting the urge to start crying too. "Tell me why you can't drink alcohol. Stop crying and tell me *right fucking now*, you numpty."

"BECAUSE I'M PREGNANT!" Eve yells at the ceiling.

"She's pregnant!" Jules punches the air and then gives a little kick that narrowly misses a curious Cheddar. "She only went and finally bloody did it! Two lines and everything! Did the test—how many times?"

"Seveeennnnnn," Eve sobs, starting to giggle hysterically. "Seven, and they *all said yes*. They said yes, Maggie! THEY SAID YES."

A bizarre celebration dance has commenced in the kitchen: Lil wiggling her bottom while Jules grinds wildly against my recently painted yellow cabinets. Eve giggles and hops up to join them, clapping.

"Don't just bloody sit there," Jules calls. "Get in here."

But I'm busy doing the math.

This is the right time. It's *exactly* the right time.

I didn't knock anything off course, not for Eve. This baby is the little boy I have seen. He's coming, just as I knew he would. A little bit of that future is still left over, still shining, still glimmering like a river. And I'm so incredibly happy that it's saved, even if the rest of it has gone. Like running into a burning building to save one precious thing. But my God, how incredibly precious it is.

"Aaaaarrrghhh!" I bounce into the kitchen. "You *did* it!"

"*We* did it!" Eve lobs her arms around me. "*We* did. It's *our* baby."

"I don't think that's a genetic possibility, mate," Jules says, pretending to slap her bottom repeatedly. "But sure. Thanks for the acknowledgment."

"Do you know what you'll call him?" I clear my throat. *Fuck.* "Or her. Could be a girl. Could totally be a girl. I don't know."

I do know.

"Yes." Eve nods, her cheeks bright pink. "Asparagus."

Lily puts a hand over her mouth with a small, alarmed squeak.

Jules stops faux slapping.

"No." She turns to stare at Eve, crossing her arms. "Evelyn Caitlin Williams, you are *not* calling a human child *Asparagus.* Over my dead body. I'll call social services. I swear, I'll do it, just watch me."

I open my mouth in horror: it fits.

"It's . . . cute," Lily says loyally. "Very . . . organic."

"Yes," Jules snaps. "Like a bloody salad."

"Of course I'm not calling a child Asparagus," Eve giggles. "But oh my God, your *faces.* Ah, that was so worth it. No, it's Augustus, after my great-grandfather. Or August, if it's a girl."

"Gus," I say as my eyes fill: there we go. "It's perfect."

Eve grabs us in a hug, and I feel love wrap around the four of us. Lily makes eye contact with me and smiles tentatively. I smile back. We're not *quite* back where we used to be, but it's looking good. There's too much love here for it not to be.

"Now," Eve says, randomly kissing the top of my ear. "Obviously it's very early days, so I don't want to jinx anything, but—fingers tightly crossed—my dreams have all come true, so what are we going to do with *Margot*?"

I blink and pull away from the hug.

"What do you mean, *what are we going to do with Margot*? You're not going to *do* anything with me. I'm not a bloody bit of leftover lasagna."

Jules, Lily and Eve lift their eyebrows at me.

"I'm not!" I can't believe I'm having to clarify this. "You don't have to *do* anything with me. I am doing *great*."

The eyebrows get a little higher.

"In fact, I am doing *brilliantly.* The show launches next week, which—let me remind you—is going to make me very happy and successful." Maybe. "I have a cat. Look. There he is." I point at Cheddar, who is, indeed, a cat. "I have a flat." I wave my hands around violently, in case they've not noticed. "And I look, like, ten percent French, which is the *most* French I have ever looked."

I point at my new, super-short bob: the TV stylist did it to me for "branding."

"I am exactly as I want to be, as I have *chosen* to be, as I am *determined* to be. It is my *decision*."

"Except you're heartbroken," Jules states flatly. "Still."

"Yup." Eve nods. "You miss Henry. A lot."

"A *lot*," Lily confirms.

I stare at them. How do they know? I've been really careful to hide it. Have they set up film cameras in my bedroom so they can see if I'm crying in the middle of the night? I wouldn't put it past them.

"Pffff." I sniff. "I mean, sometimes. Now and then."

All. Of. The. Time.

"I still don't understand it," Eve says, looking to Jules and Lily for support. "It was going so well, you were so happy, so smitten, and then you go away for a weekend and *poof*. It's over? Because it wasn't—"

"Right." I nod briskly. "Exactly. That's what I said."

"Except it bloody was," Jules says crossly. "It *was* right. We saw it. So you obviously got scared and ran away again. And now you're worse than you were after . . ."

She hesitates and Lily flushes, looks down.

"Because that time you were screaming and punching and burning, but it was all just *noise*. And this time you're . . ."

"Actually heartbroken," Eve fills in. "Like, properly."

Bloody hell. I can't win. No matter how I react to a break-up, apparently it's the wrong way. What do they want me to do? Fall to my knees outside Asda and scream *My life feels empty without Henry in it*? It would be true, but how would it help? It's not an efficient use of my time or energy and I am not wasting any more.

"Could you not . . . try again?" Lily looks up and studies my face. "If you're this sad, maybe it means something?"

"I'm *fine*," I say, yet again. "It was the right decision. Please trust me."

They all nod doubtfully.

"In *fact*," I say with not a small amount of triumph, "I actually have a *date* next week. A first date, with a very nice, very handsome set designer called Fred who I met on the show. So there. Not heartbroken. Totally moving on in a healthy way. Getting Back Out There, with capitals, as I have reassured my mother."

"What number date is this?" Jules asks. "Eighteen? Or are you starting again?"

"There is no number," I say firmly. "No number, no list, no criteria. I shall not be taking notes. I'm going to meet this man, see how it goes. And we're getting a curry, because I'm breaking the cycle. My self-destructive pattern is over."

I gave up Henry so that we could meet the right people, so I have to follow through with it. I have to be open to love. Henry did that for me, I realize. I hope he finds his person too. Someone not *too* hot—that's unnecessary—but kind and funny. What I want most is for him to be happy, even if it's not with me.

Admittedly, I'm not at all sure I'm ready to move on, but Other Margot deserves me to at least *try*. She might be gone now, but I still feel her with me: pushing me to meet her, wherever she is now.

I hope that when I do, I'll be my best possible version.

"Right." Eve looks relieved. "Well, that's lovely. Here's to new starts for all of us! What's our plan for this evening, gang?"

"Don't you have dinner with your mum and dad in, like, forty minutes?" Lily frowns and looks at her watch.

Eve stares at her for a few seconds, then starts laughing loudly. "Baby brain!" She's literally giddy. "It's started already! Oh my goodness, this is amazing. I was *waiting* for this to happen. I'm *such* a tit."

"You've always been a tit," Jules says with a tiny, fond smile. "Don't go blaming your pregnancy for that, Eve."

But I've frozen. Such a tit. Such a tit.

Such a tit.

"Say that again." Something is happening in my brain. "That last bit."

My friends all turn to look at me, concerned.

"Which bit?" Lily asks gently, putting a hand on my arm. "Maggie, are you OK?"

There's a sudden lump in my throat.

I know.

I know what the bit of paper in my pocket was, in my funeral vision.

And I'd have worked it out earlier, except—it didn't fit. Somehow, like Macbeth, I've pieced things together in the wrong order. I've snuggled into fate again, comfortable I've been reading the visions accurately, that I knew what was coming.

But I wasn't. I wasn't reading them at all.

"I have to go," I say, my voice breaking. "Right now."

35

QUIETLY, I LET myself into my grandfather's house again. Without a noise, I slip my shoes off and tiptoe into the kitchen, hoping I don't frighten the life out of him while he's trying to make tea. There's nobody there, so I walk straight to the wall where the calendar is hanging: the robin has gone, replaced by a jay, then a finch and—finally—a small, bright-eyed blackbird.

Although I already know, I lift my hand to feel the paper. It's the same: shiny, stiff, thick, not quite card. Just to confirm, I run my finger to the top and pull a little section of the month away until it's crinkled and serrated at the edge. With my eyes shut, I feel along the edge until I reach the little half-circle, cut out so that the calendar can hang on the wall.

It's the blue tit. That's what is in my pocket after the funeral: I have the month of the blue tit clutched tightly in my hand.

Which means it's my grandfather.

"Meg?" I hear him in the living room. "Is that you? Are you creeping around my house again like a helpful little mouse?"

He was always the obvious choice—being many, many times older than the other candidates—but I didn't think it *could* be him. I saw him at my wedding, didn't I? I saw him watching me, his eyes full of love. That vision convinced me I had years left with him. Wrapped me up in false security, sent me down the wrong path.

But I didn't see him at all, I suddenly realize. I *felt* him.

And it's the twenty-eighth of December: they don't take the Christmas tree in the park down until early January. It's the same calendar, and there won't be any more. My hair is short again, exactly the length it was in that vision.

We don't have years left at all: we have days.

"Just a minute!" I call, finally finding my voice. "What kind of mess have you made in here, Grandad? Let me just tidy up."

Breathing out, I lean against the calendar with my head pressed against the bird.

I don't think this is a part of my future I have changed at all. I don't think I *can*. This is not a giant that is going to be moving just because I've held up a few bits of teeny-tiny cutlery and yelled, "I BROKE UP WITH MY BOYFRIEND, NOW GO AWAY."

Straightening, I square my shoulders and hold my chin up.

We have days.

"Well, *hello*." I walk into the living room. "What are *you* doing here?"

Grandad beams at me. "That's what I was going to say!"

"Beat you to it." I smile as I sit down opposite him and try to drink him up, try to remember everything: every vein, every freckle, every tiny hair, every line in his beautiful face. "*Now* what shall we talk about?"

"I guess there's nothing left." My grandfather shrugs. "That's it, all conversation over, thank you for visiting, it's been a joy and an honor."

We both chuckle and I reach out to hold his hand. He can't see me well enough to know that there's a tear trickling down my face, so I let it drip down my nose until it hits his finger. He frowns and I flinch: *shit*.

"Is it Henry?" Grandad's face softens. "Has it happened?"

I frown. "We broke up, if that's what you mean. I told you that months ago."

Now is *not* the time to get arsey, Margot.

"Yes, I know." He shakes his head slightly, looking a bit

confused. "Sorry. You know what old men are like. Always forgetting."

Something else hits me: another thing I didn't see at the time. The clues are scattered everywhere, like raindrops. Data that's easy to miss if you're looking in the wrong direction. The signs are always there, as long as you're paying attention.

I just . . . wasn't.

"You've said that before," I say blankly, my brain starting to reel. "Months ago. You said, 'Is it Henry? Has it happened?'"

"Did I?" Grandad scratches his nose. "How strange."

I stare at him narrowly and he's now avoiding my gaze. My grandfather is lying.

"You didn't say, 'Has something happened?' You said, 'Has *it* happened?'" I think a bit harder. "And you knew I'd gone on a date with someone called Henry before I'd told you, but even Mum didn't know his name at that point. I hadn't told Eve or Jules his name either. Nobody knew."

My grandfather is now staring at the ceiling light.

"You said, 'Stick at Seventeen,'" I point out. "'A good, powerful number,' you said."

"Well, it is." My ninety-four-year-old grandfather has the slightly defiant expression of a little boy who's just been caught with his hands in a birthday cake. "It represents change and new beginnings, numerologically. As I think I mentioned."

I stare at him as he shifts his gaze to a painting, then to a plant, then to the newspaper in front of him.

"Look at me," I say firmly.

"Um, no, I don't think I will."

"Grandfather, you *look at me right now*."

My grandad bites his lip and raises his gaze until he's staring me right in the face with his bright blue, all-seeing eyes. His magical, other-worldly eyes. Because he's not just sitting here, waiting. I already felt that. I knew it, somehow.

He's sitting here and he's *watching*.

"You get them too," I say simply. "Don't you. The visions."

"Oh!" He nods and grins sheepishly. "Those old things? Yes, I suppose I do."

I THOUGHT IT was just me.

This whole time, it never occurred to me *once* that anyone else I knew might also be able to see the future. I assumed this was a big, totally insane, lifelong secret that would die with me and nobody would ever believe it.

And it sure as *hell* never occurred to me that it could be genetic.

Is it genetic? What even *is* it?

"But . . ." I stand up. "I don't—how do you, why didn't you—"

"Do you need a cup of tea?" My grandfather starts to stand up too. "It feels like now is a good moment for a cup of tea, help calm the nerves. I think there's some lovely lemon shortbread in the fridge."

"*Fuck* the shortbread," I say in exasperation, then flinch as my grandad laughs loudly. "Sorry, Grandad. I didn't mean fuck the shortbread. Please forgive me. I'm just, I, uh—this is a lot to process."

"Of course it is." He chuckles and sits back down with an air of relief. "Honestly, I think you've been handling it all with grace and aplomb, Meg. Far better than I did when it started. I was an absolute nightmare. Your poor grandmother nearly divorced me on the spot. 'What are you raving about now?' she'd say."

I stare at him. "You *know* I've been having them?"

"I worked it out." Grandad shrugs humbly. "Put the pieces together. When you came out of the cupboard, you looked like how I felt the first few times. As if you'd been hit by a bus consisting of buses yet to come. Then you started behaving really quite oddly, in a very familiar way."

"Why didn't you *say*?" I'm even more exasperated now. "I

could have asked you questions, sought support. I thought I was going clinically *insane*."

"Well, if I was wrong, you'd have thought *I* was going insane. I'm older. It's riskier. You could have sent me away to a retirement home. And I figured you'd tell me when you were ready."

"What, just casually lob it in? Over tea and biscuits? 'By the way, I can see the future, Grandad. Ring any bells?'"

"Fair," he acknowledges. "I've found that it's a difficult topic to broach in polite conversation, which is probably why I never told anyone."

I sit down heavily on the armchair again. Bloody hell. Where do I even *start*?

"So what is it? Do you know? You know, right?"

Grandad has to know: he knows *everything*.

"Not really." He looks annoyed with himself. "I've spent a very long time researching, trying to understand it, looking for medical possibilities. There weren't any firm explanations—other than wild hallucinations, obviously, but that didn't quite fit because—"

"Too many accurate details," I say quickly. "And they come true."

Grandad nods his head, then shakes it, nods it again.

"*Do* they come true?" I lean forward eagerly. "Because it *feels* like they do, and that's been my experience so far, but I've also *stopped* them, so I guess there's a chance that they don't? That they're guidelines? Alternative versions?"

"I think . . ." Grandad says slowly ". . . I probably shouldn't answer that question."

"What? Why not?"

"Because that's something you have to work out for yourself, Meg. And my experience is not *your* experience. It may be different for each of us. I don't have the answer and I don't want to influence anything."

I know *that* feeling all too well: do I prod fate in the right direction or leave it alone?

"Except you *did.*" I frown again. "You *did* influence. Those twenty dates—they were *your* idea. You told me to go apologize to Henry. Because you *knew.*"

"What can I say?" Grandad grins sheepishly. "I'm an old man and you're my only grandchild. My willpower is fading."

My brain is racing through my entire life: what other signs were there? What else has my Grandad done, not done, seen, not seen? Aaron. He must have known about Aaron before I even met him. And Lily. But he also knew that by saying something, I might not end up where I was supposed to be. He was trapped, just like I've been.

"My current theory," he continues with genuine interest, gazing back out at the garden, "is not that helpful. It does appear to be genetic, in some way. Your great-great-grandmother, on my side, was frequently called a witch by her neighbors, although she did also have very bushy eyebrows, so it's hard to know if it was just misogyny. And when I dug into our surname, *Wayward* does appear to have been a shift from *Weyward*, a very long time ago. Which means—"

"Yes, I know, it means *weird*. Henry told me."

"Actually," my grandfather corrects amiably, "it goes a bit deeper than that. *Weird* means 'the power to control fate.' The word is of Germanic origin, but with the proto-Indo-European root of *wer*, which means 'to watch.' So Weyward technically means 'those that watch the future.'"

I stare at him. "You didn't think you could have mentioned that at some point?"

"Felt a bit on the nose." Grandad shrugs.

I blink at him.

"And that's it?" I collapse back in the chair. "That's all you've learned? That it *might* in some way be an ancient family trait? What about Dad?"

"Oh, no." Grandad shakes his head. "Your father is blissfully bound to the laws of time and space, and for that I am eternally grateful. It must have skipped a generation, bless him."

All I can think about now are the thousands and thousands

of hours I've spent with my grandfather. How long has he lived like this? A long time, I suddenly realize. He's always known so much. Too much.

"Have you ever tried to stop it?" I try to sound casual. "And does it work?"

There's a sudden lump in my throat.

"Ah." Grandad coughs awkwardly. "I once saw that one of your grandmother's figurines was smashed, and she was absolutely devastated. A little shepherdess, it was. With a crook and a lamb under her arm. Not expensive, but she'd had it since she was a little girl and it meant a lot to her."

He gazes out of the window again.

"So I tried to save it. I took that little figurine and I wrapped it in bubble wrap and I took it up to the attic, put it in a box, covered it in a blanket."

"And what happened?" My breath is held. "Did you save it?"

I don't think I'm asking about a shepherdess figurine, if we're being totally honest.

"No. I didn't. There was a storm and a tree broke through the attic. Smashed that little china girl to pieces. If I hadn't had the vision and put her up there—"

"—she wouldn't have broken."

"For me, there was nothing I could do. But it might be different for you, Meg. I suspect you are full of abilities I don't have. You helped me try to fix that figurine, do you remember?"

A sudden memory: me, aged around six, sitting with my grandfather at the kitchen table as we desperately tried to stick together the pieces with superglue.

Unsuccessfully, as my grandmother spicily pointed out later.

"But . . . what do you *do*?" This is the question I really want to ask: the only one that matters. "When you can see everything? How do you just . . . live? How do you live your life, when you know what's coming?"

"I *don't*." My grandfather looks at me in surprise. "I *don't* know what's coming, Meg. Where on earth did you get that idea?"

"What do you mean? I thought—"

"I see glimpses, that's all. Tiny moments, out of order, scattered in fragments. I don't see all the time in between. I don't see context. I don't know how I get from one to another. I don't know how I'll feel, not fully. I don't know what the whole story is. I've just been given a couple of pages, here and there. The rest is for me to fill in. So that's the bit I focus on. It's the only thing I *can* focus on."

My eyes are suddenly wet. "But what if . . ."

I hesitate and Grandad looks at me: his bright, misty eyes seeing so little but so much.

"What if you make a mistake?" I'm speaking too quickly now. "What if you spend your time in the wrong place, with the wrong person? What if it's all just a waste? How can you start something when you know it will end?"

He gazes at me in silence for a few seconds.

"Ah." A tiny nod. "I see. That's what happened with Henry. I didn't know."

My throat catches. "Yes."

"Sweetheart," he says softly. "Do you love me?"

"Bloody stupid question," I mutter crossly. "But yeah. I guess. You're alright."

"Even though you know that one day very soon I'll be gone?"

I stare at him. How *much* does he know? "Of course."

"Do you regret any of the time we have spent together, just because one day we won't have any more time left?"

I try to say *no* and it comes out as a desperate little squeak.

"There's your answer, then. Life ends, but it's no reason not to live. Not a very tricky riddle, as it happens. Alexa could have answered it for you in ten seconds. Honestly, Margot. I thought you were more logical than this. I'm surprised at you."

I laugh wetly, rubbing my face.

"We *don't know*, darling." He takes my hand and pats it. "Even you and I, we still don't know. We don't know where the rain is going to fall, or when. So we can't carry an umbrella our entire lives. We just have to let ourselves get wet."

That's exactly what Henry said too.

Henry.

Oh, God. What the *hell* was I playing at?

I thought I'd grown so much—developed, matured—but I hadn't. I was just scared, again. Scared of losing him, scared of loving him, scared of one day being without him. I don't care if it ends, I don't care if I "waste" the next fifteen years: I want to waste them all with Henry, every *second* of them. I want the wedding and the birthday party and the beach and the attempts to get pregnant and the failure: I want the hours, the days, the weeks in between, that I still haven't seen.

"Grandad . . ." I say slowly. "I . . ."

"Go get him," he says firmly, reaching into the cabinet next to him. "I'll still be here when you're done. I've not met him yet. And I meet him. Henry, and his little girl. Likes purple. Very straight-talking. Reminds me a lot of you as a little girl. I got her this as a gift, but maybe you've seen it before?"

My grandfather hands me a small, familiar toy panda—still bright white and black, both eyes attached—and I nod with an enormous lump in my throat. It feels as if he's restarting my future for me. That little toy is going to be loved so hard, its colors will change, yet it will be no less precious for it.

"You give it to her," I say, standing up and kissing his cheek. "When I see you again."

My grandfather meets them: there's still time left.

Time with him; time to resurrect my future and put it all back on course. But I still don't know if I can. That depends entirely on Henry. I'm not the only person with a choice here. He has to make a decision too.

"It's a connection, I think," my grandfather says as I reach the doorway.

I turn back. "Huh?"

"You asked me what my theory is, Meg. It's a connection.

Something so powerful that it tethers us to another person, pulls us forward in time for a few minutes at a time. A kind of touchstone, just as long as they're there. Maybe sometimes even when they're gone. Like a magical amulet, except it's made from another person."

My eyes fill, because that vision—the one with the broken shepherdess.

My grandfather saw that.

But I was the only person there with him.

"You're going to be so happy." He smiles as if he knows what I'm thinking, always. "And I know that, because all of mine have been about you."

36

I'M TOO LATE.

As I peg it up the steps to Henry's flat, I can feel it: I'm too late.

The lights are all out, he's at work, he's on a date, he's met someone, someone who doesn't dump him every three minutes, someone *normal*, and I cannot believe I allowed someone else to grab this gorgeous human while I was fannying about, worried about something that doesn't happen for *fifteen years*. You come across a genuine Michelangelo painting at the back of a charity shop, you don't let that out of your grubby mitts until it's *on the wall at home*.

I'm about to smash urgently on his front door and yell "HENRY," then remember that tends to frighten people and I'm not going to ruin this by being bloody crazy again.

Instead, I take a deep breath, calm myself and knock politely.

There's no response, so—desperate now—I lean forward and say through the letter box as clearly as I can: "Vinosauraptor."

Come on, come on, come on . . .

The door opens.

It's Henry. Henry is here. He's here and he's him and it's the same face and the same hair and it's not fully silver yet and we're not fifty and we've still got so many years left to—

Oh God, he looks angry.

"Hey, Margot." Henry smiles stiffly. "This is a bit of a surprise."

"I *told* you!" Little Winter—that's how I think of her now—skips jauntily out of the living room, where I now realize it was dark because they're watching a Disney film. "I *told* you she'd be back! What did I say, Daddy? Oh my gosh, I am *so* clever. And you were all 'No she won't, it's over, she doesn't like me,' and I was all 'She *does* like you, don't be stupid, Daddy,' and you were all 'No, she doesn't,' and I was like 'Yes, she does, I *know* she does, she's just being silly,' and I was right and you were wrong, so *ha*!"

Winnie's been doing a little matching dance, and she lands on the *ha* with a finger pointed in the air, like a '70s disco diva.

Henry has never, ever looked this mortified before.

Not in any of the time I've spent with him in the present, and not in any of the times I've spent with him in the future either.

"That's . . ." He blinks. "Fucking embarrassing, actually."

"*Daddy*," Winter reproves sternly, still in a bizarre pointy stance, "I know this is a *very emotional* time for you because the *lady you love soooo much* has come back and you've been *soooo sad*, but there is *no need* for that kind of language."

"Right." Henry snaps to. "That's enough from you, young lady. And later, before bed, we're going to have a *very* long chat about what defines a *private conversation between a father and daughter*."

Winnie cocks her head. "Am I in trouble?"

"No, because it's my fault, so take some chocolate from the sweets cupboard and you can come out and watch the film when Margot and I are done talking."

"Yessss!" She punches the air. "But not toooo much kissing, OK? I'll be *listening*."

Then she grabs an entire armful of snacks from the drawer and saunters off, making triumphant little kissing sounds as she goes.

Henry turns back to me with his eyes shut.

"So . . . Yeah. That just happened."

"It did indeed."

"Can we just . . ." he opens one eye and squints at me ". . . pretend you heard none of that and let me go back to being cool and a bit disinterested in anything you have to say, as planned?"

"Oh, no." I grin at him. "Sorry, but that's completely out of the question now."

"Bugger." He breathes out in frustration. "Right. Fine. Come in, and I'll attempt not to look quite so happy to see you."

A lot of my anxiety has now evaporated, and it's not just because of what Winter yelled (although that helped quite a lot). It's because as soon as I'm with Henry, everything feels easy. As if anything that happens, anything that's coming, I can face as long as he is here. I can even face the end, as long as it's with him.

"Winter was right," I say as I sit down next to him. "I was being *very* silly."

"You were," he agrees. "Remarkably so."

"I knew I was silly." I shake my head. "But I did not know I had *that* level of silliness within me, just waiting to burst out."

"I suspected." Henry is trying not to smile. "And yet I could never have dreamed of the heights your silliness would take you."

"Truly awe-inspiring silliness," I confirm. "Thank you for appreciating it."

Then we look at each other for a few seconds, and he is smiling but also—I can see it in his face—hurt. Unbelievably hurt. I cannot believe I put that pain there. That I hurt this man I care about so deeply, thinking it was the right thing to do.

"Margot, you pushed me away again," Henry says quietly. "And you didn't even explain why. You just . . . bolted."

"I know." My chest tightens. "I didn't know what to say."

Then I hesitate, because I still don't. I can't tell him the truth. Not if I want to keep him. Not if I don't want him to run screaming to the nearest medical center.

"Just . . . try."

I take a deep breath. What can I say that is true without telling him everything?

"I got scared," I admit carefully. "That I would lose you. And Winter. So it seemed easier to lose you both now rather than . . . later. When it would hurt more."

Henry lifts his eyebrows. "That's kind of how a relationship works, Meg. It's part of the deal. You go into it knowing that it might not work out."

I nod, feeling frustrated. Because *might* not work out is very, very different to *will* not work out. But I can't say that. "I know. I just . . . Something told me that this wasn't going to . . . end well."

Now Henry frowns, thinks about it, hesitates.

"Is it . . ." He scratches his beard. "Was it . . ."

I wait for him to say, *Was it about Aaron, did seeing him again throw you off, did you realize you still had feelings for him?* and I get my best, most vigorous rebuttal ready.

"About the, you know." Henry takes a deep breath. "The, uh, visions? Did you see a vision that told you this would end? Is that what happened?"

My mouth snaps shut in shock.

"Oh God, I sound mad." Henry stands up and starts pacing the room. "I shouldn't have said anything, I'm so sorry. I was putting it all together and I've jumped to the weirdest and most insane—"

"You know?" I stand up too. "You *know*?"

"So you *are* having visions?" Henry stops pacing and his entire face relaxes. "Oh, thank goodness. If I'd been wrong, this would have been a *very* awkward conversation."

I stare at him, totally floored. "I . . . *How?*"

"Well." Henry looks quite proud of himself. "I joined up the dots, Meg. Collected the data. Examined the results. You're not the only one who knows how to do that, for the record. I didn't even need a notepad."

Oh my God: he's perfect for me.

Also, this man is going to be the best doctor *on the planet.*

"OK." I sit down heavily, in shock. "Please present your hypothesis."

"Right." Henry sits next to me with the clear satisfaction of a GP who's stumbled on the right, albeit bonkers, diagnosis. "So, first, you were lying about Eve."

I open my mouth to protest and he holds out a hand.

"No, let me finish. I don't mean *lying*. Because I think this is kind of a special circumstance, so you get a dispensation for that. But *covering up*. She rang when you were poorly, do you remember? So when I picked up, I brought up the topic of Winter. You know, conversationally, as her pupil. Eve had no idea who I was talking about. She doesn't work in that school—she's all the way on the other side of Redland."

I open my mouth, and Henry holds out his hand again.

"Not yet. So I was like—huh. Weird. Is Meg a secret stalker? It did cross my mind, briefly. Sorry. But then I remembered that we'd only stuck that unicorn on my screwdriver the night before. Nobody else knew about it. It was a weekend—Winnie hadn't even left the house. So how the hell did you know?"

I flush and try to speak again.

"Nope. My turn. So I was like, huh. Interesting data. I remembered that you'd asked, 'What would you do? If you were in Macbeth's shoes?' after we watched the play. You seemed invested in the answer. You also kept glazing over, and when you came out of whatever it was, your mood was always totally different. Like you'd seen something. I was a bit scared. I thought brain tumor, maybe."

"Me too," I manage.

"But no other symptoms. That's why I insisted on taking your temperature. You seemed to *know* things about me that you shouldn't know. Things nobody else knows. And then tried to cover it up."

I thought I was being so flaming clever.

"Oh!" Henry lifts his eyebrows. "And then, just in case I hadn't already worked it out, you held an axe in the air and screamed, 'I am angry that I keep seeing shit and am expected to handle it all on my own, puzzle it all out, as if I don't have enough to bloody worry about.' And when I asked, you said,

'I'm not having visions of the future or anything, and then trying to piece them together in the right order. That would be crazy.'"

Henry looks at me pointedly and I flush.

"It did, in fact, sound quite a lot like you might be having visions of the future and then trying to piece them together in the right order. Plus, you apparently know the secret code word I have with my child, which nobody in the world knows but us."

Well. Fuck me.

Subtle as ever, Margot. Like a bullet through the head.

"Oh God." I put my hands over my face. "I'm nowhere near as good at hiding this as I thought I was."

"You're really not." Henry unpeels one of my fingers and grins at me through the gap. "I'm not saying I *believe* you, Margot. To be clear. I am a medical man. A human of science, of evidence and data."

"Well, so am I!" I point at myself. "Meteorologist, remember?"

"But I am not arrogant enough to assume I know everything about how the universe works, and soothsayers have existed in some form or another for thousands of years, across many cultures. So let's just say I *did* humor this wild notion." Henry frowns. "You clearly saw something. You had a vision in the car that made you break up with me, and I think I need to know what it is."

"No." I shake my head. "That's not a good idea, Henry. Please, trust me."

"I don't want to know the rest," he states firmly. "At all. Whatever else you've seen, I don't want to know it. I told you, if I ran across three old witches dancing in the rain, I'd get the hell out of there. Not interested. I just didn't realize this particular witch would be so young and so damn hot. So this one, I need to know."

"Why, thank you," I beam automatically, then scowl. "You're not getting around me with compliments, Henry. It's a no."

"Look, I appreciate that you're a mystical being and whatnot." Henry narrows his eyes. "But this involves me. It involves my child. It's my *life*. So I think you need to make an exception this once, Meg. Then we will never, ever mention the visions again. I need to live my life without knowing as much as I can, if possible."

I stare at him as another wave of shock courses through me.

We don't mention the visions.

Neither of us *ever* mention the visions, while we're in the visions. But I've told him now. Henry knows about them. Which means that for every single vision I've had—apart from the first one—Henry has been there and he has known. He has known I'm a different Margot, I'm Past Margot, and I'm confused and scared and lost. He has comforted me, and gently explained where we are and what we're doing, so subtly I didn't even notice.

This was all part of it: the break-up, the reunion.

I haven't knocked anything off course: I've just brought us back to exactly where that future came from, which is right here.

"I love you," I say as my eyes fill. "I am *in* love with you, Henry. Not because of what I've seen, but because of what I *see*."

Henry's whole face lights up and he leans forward to kiss me gently on the lips.

"I love you too, Margot. Ditto, on all counts. Now please tell me."

This is it. Isn't it.

He didn't mean: *This is it for us.* He meant: *This is the vision you told me about.*

I can tell him, because I already have.

"We break up." I take a deep breath. I'm not saying the word *divorce*, it's too much and he doesn't need to know. "I'm not telling you when, or how, and I don't actually know *why* because I haven't been shown. I'm as blind as you are on that one. I just know it's quite a long time away."

"How long?"

"You're old," I say bluntly. "And so am I. *Relatively* old, anyway."

I don't think Other Margot will appreciate me saying that. I'll get to her eventually, better not cast that stone.

"We meet on a street, in Bristol. It's cold. I'm wearing a pink coat. We haven't seen each other for quite a while, I think. We're pretty much strangers."

My heart hurts again. Just face it, Margot. So you'll hurt. We all hurt. It's part of being alive. Deal with it.

"And . . . ?"

"And Winnie—"

"You saw Winter?" Henry abruptly sits forward, face shining. "Oh my God, you *saw* her? Is she OK? How big is she? Does she look happy? Healthy? No. I don't want to know. Yes, I do. Tell me. Quickly, tell me, before I change my mind."

"See?" I laugh. "It's not that easy, is it? Not when it's about people you love."

"*Fine.*" Henry waves a hand. "You're right, I'm wrong, just tell me my daughter is OK, please, because I cannot handle this, my brain isn't big enough."

"She's *beautiful*, Henry." I feel a lump in my throat. "Winter is all grown-up and she's clever and smart and happy and so, so beautiful."

I'm not going to tell him he finally becomes a surgeon—let that be a surprise.

I'll let the tattoo on her wrist be a surprise too.

"*Oh.*" Henry sits back, winded. "Wow. OK, that was a rush. Blimey."

I smile at him affectionately: his intense, complete love for Winter is one of my favorite things about him. One of the many things I will share with him, in the future.

"She does, however, know about the visions," I add.

"Probably from right now." Henry glances at her bedroom door. "Little bloody big ears." Then he shakes himself. "Right. Back to topic. So we break up, and—"

"And? What do you mean 'and,' Henry? We break up. It's over. We're strangers. I've told you. We're strangers and we're old."

Henry looks at me blankly. "So?"

"OK," I say slowly. "I don't think you're quite hearing me.

We're old. We break up. We're strangers. It's over. Does putting it in a different order help?"

"I mean . . . and *then*?"

"Well, and *then* nothing. That's the furthest forward I've gone. I've not seen anything after that. That's the end. My visions are only linked to you. Without you, I don't have them. So when I stop seeing you, the visions stop too."

"Awwww," Henry says, ruffling my hair. "Little creep."

"Mnnneurgh," I say, pushing him away with a pleased smile. "Focus. Do you understand what I'm saying? This is not going to last forever, Henry. We'll end up alone. Both of us. You might not . . ." *have any more kids* ". . . get everything you want from your life. Is that what you want?"

"But we might last forever," he says flatly. "You don't know."

"But I do know, actually," I sigh. "It's why I call them *visions of the future*."

"But what *if*," Henry says, and I watch him desperately clutching at straws the same way I did when I found out. "What if you stop having visions because that bit *hasn't been decided yet*. Hmm? What then? Haven't thought of that, have you?"

"I don't know if that's how it works."

"But you don't know it's *not* how it works."

"Well—no. I guess not."

Henry beams at me, triumphant and smug, and I want to kiss him so badly I can barely breathe. But I won't, not until we've made a decision. I am not leaving this life-altering choice up to lust, thank you very much.

"Except . . ." Henry sits forward abruptly, watching me carefully. "I need to know for sure that you're not going to just run away every time you get scared of what's coming, Meg. No matter what you see or don't see. It's not fair. Not on me, and not on Winnie. If we do this, we're doing it as a team. You have to trust us."

If we're doing this. My heart hops with hope. "Agreed."

"I'm going to need you to say it."

"We're doing this as a team. No more running. I trust us."

I mean it with my whole body, and Henry can tell: he glances toward Winnie's bedroom door, and I see him evaluate her part in this decision too.

"So how about this." He reaches forward and takes my hands in his. "We stay together. We're happy. At some point, we break up, and that's fine. We have our reasons. You're probably being a right pain in the arse, I'd imagine."

I smack him gently, then nod. "Yeah, probably."

"Then we see each other on some street, whenever that is, and it'll be cold, and you'll be wearing a pink coat, and we make a decision *then*. To get back together or not. We don't have to make it *now*."

I stare at him in amazement. "Seriously?"

"I don't bloody see why not. Fate and destiny, Margot. I've never had much time for either. *We* will decide. Nobody and nothing else will do it for us. That's my take on *Macbeth* too, and I'm sticking to it."

This is it. Isn't it.

He doesn't just mean the vision. *This is it. Isn't it.*

This is our chance to try again.

My chin starts to wobble dramatically and I quickly pull my jumper up over my head so I can cry in private. Because I want it all: everything I have seen. I want the fights, I want the love, I want the boredom, I want the laughter, I want the tears, I want the happiness, I want the pain. I want all the good bits and the bad bits and the bits in between: the bits I don't know, haven't reached, won't see until they're here.

My grandfather was right, as he always is.

I want the *life*.

"Sorry." Henry sticks his head under the bottom of my jumper. "Didn't quite catch that, Megalodon."

"I said *yes*," I sob incoherently. "Please. If it's OK with you."

"It's OK with me." I get pulled unceremoniously out of my jumper so that Henry can hold my face, wipe my tears away, kiss my nose, my ear, my mouth. "So it's a deal."

"I CAN HEAR YOU," Winter screams in the background. "*Just so you know.*"

Henry and I both start laughing.

"See you in the future, Margot," he grins, bopping me on the nose, and I love it, I love him, I love her, *I love it all.* "In the meantime, I'll be right here."

FIFTEEN YEARS LATER

It's cold, gray, gloomy.

I'm in my big pink coat, but I've had it years: wearing it every time it gets chilly. Even when Henry and I were still together. He thought it was funny—as if I was trying to ward off what was coming with my sartorial choices—but I didn't care. I would wear my pink coat as often as I could, even when it was too warm for a coat, and I wear it still.

Just in case.

But my mind is elsewhere now: on other things.

I'm fifty-one, and my parents are getting old. My father's sight is failing too, but we're managing it. He's inherited the Alexa, the Kindle, the funny kettle, chopping board and giant TV remote with the huge buttons. He also has my mother, who has remained sprightly and defiant and a little bit rude in the face of old age, so I guess that's something to hold on to. Winter is the beautiful young woman I knew she'd become—studying to be a vet, as she had determined—and remains my girl, my soul, my whole heart. (She still has her panda, and sleeps with it when nobody is around.)

Eve eventually fell in love with and married one of Henry's best friends—Sebastian, the one who wasn't a doctor, who turned up at the pub all those years ago to watch me screech at Jules—and Gus is now a handsome young man with no spots, no basement, no computer games: just excellent manners and a huge extended family who love him immensely. Polly left Peter a month after we started the show, and her children became part of the gang of smaller family members, Posy immediately bonding with Winnie, and the two older girls followed adoringly everywhere by Gus, Perry, Paige and Abi, Lily's doppelgänger little girl with bright red plaits.

Lil and Aaron divorced years ago—when Abi was three—but she's incredibly happy too and part of the group again as much as she ever was: still posting on Instagram, an inspiration for a different generation, with pure silver hair and a wardrobe strangers fight over. Aaron is still Aaron: he's dating a pretty thirty-two-year-old. He still thinks he's going to be a rock star. No surprises there.

Cheds is an international superstar, ancient, grumpy as all hell and enormous, and I still love him to pieces, even if he has taken to sleeping on top of my head at night again, which is decidedly less comfortable than it was when he was a kitten.

It's Jules I worry about most. She had cancer a couple of years ago, and she seems to have recovered—fought as we all knew Jules would fight, swearing, with two fingers up—but I don't know for sure: I haven't seen.

Everything came true.

Every single vision I had—and continued to have—played out exactly as I had been shown. My grandfather died on New Year's Eve, peacefully, in his sleep, but not before he had met Henry and Winter and he finally got that walk. We took him to Brandon Hill, to our special bench. He saw my happiness, just as he had said, and gave Winnie the final pull-out from his very last calendar: the blackbird. She still has it; it's on her wall at Bristol University. (Henry was thrilled, mostly because she stayed close to home.) I think she knew, somehow, that even though she only met him once, my grandfather—this incredible, magical human—was special. Not just to me, although obviously that too, but to everyone. That the light and joy and warmth he had brought to the world wouldn't leave just because he had.

And when Henry and I married—in those fields, surrounded

by yellow and purple—I could feel my grandfather again: watching me.

I wondered, briefly, if maybe it was real.

If, somehow, one of his visions had connected him to me further than he was supposed to go: as if he had seen my happiness there too. "*Maybe sometimes even when they're gone*," he'd said, and I thought about it a lot.

Because he was right again: Henry and I were *happy*.

So, so happy, for so, so long. What we had at the start—what had felt so strong, so immediate, as if it couldn't get any better—just grew deeper over the years, the roots of ourselves entwining around each other until they grew so thick, so solid, that it felt like nothing could blow us over.

But it did.

As my job took off—as I slowly became one of the most recognizable faces on television, flying around the world, speaking about rainbows at packed events—there was just less time to spend together. It was always, always the time. And as Henry got through medical school again, started his residency at the hospital, graduated as a surgeon (mending lots of hearts, not just mine) and began to make a mark on his profession as I knew he would, our daily schedules became totally opposite. Neither of us wanted to make the other give up what they loved, so instead we held on. We started squabbling when we did see each other—nit-picking, snapping, feeling tired and sad—and neither of us could find a way to stop.

Until Henry sat us down, three years ago now, and said what we both knew was coming: had known for a long time.

"It's time," he said.

"I know." I put my head on his shoulder. "Right now?"

"Not right now. Next week, maybe." He kissed the top of my head. "We have to let go before we start hating each other, Meg. You know that. If we're going to give us any chance later, we have to do it now."

We sat in silence for a few minutes.

Over the years, I had seen so many more visions—they'd

started again as soon as we got back together—but none of them went past that last one, the one I'd told him about. I'd seen Winter leave home and Henry graduate university with a first, top of his class (I didn't tell him—not only had I promised, but he'd have been too smug). I'd seen our fights—the big ones, and the little ones, some of which I brought up again before they'd even happened—and I'd seen Henry worry with me when Jules got sick, and me grieve with him when he lost his mum. I didn't tell him about that either: didn't tell him to spend more time with her. I didn't need to. Henry had always lived his life as if it could all be over at any minute. It was one of the things I loved most about him.

Love.

Because it's still there: the love. Still wrapped around me, like roots.

It just couldn't hold us up anymore.

"No regrets?" Henry had turned to me. "Not even now?"

We'd tried so hard to have a baby—even though I knew it wasn't going to happen, had tried to warn him; he'd refused to listen—but in the end, it didn't seem to matter as much as it once did, for either of us. We were surrounded by children constantly—Winter, Gus, Abi, Posy, Paige, Perry. All the love we had we poured into them, into each other, and it was enough.

With Henry, it was always, always enough.

"None." I smiled at him. "You?"

"Nope." He paused. "Actually—yes. We didn't eat enough Italian food."

We both started giggling.

"Oh," I said. "I think we probably did."

But that was three years ago now, and I'm not thinking about it as much anymore. I still miss him, but I'm thinking about my stupid new haircut—everyone says it looks chic, but I'm sorry, I do not carry it off—and I'm thinking about my big offer of a new position as head of a children's TV network. I'm thinking about Jules—is she going to the scans like she says she is?—and about Eve: she needs to worry less about running the entire school. I'm thinking about my brand-new boots, which—frankly—are hurting like hell.

I'm thinking very, very guiltily about when was the last time I saw my parents: some things never change.

"Margot the Meteorologist!" I hear an excited squeak behind me. "It's Margot the Meteorologist! Oh my gosh, can we have a selfie?"

With gritted teeth, I close my eyes.

I'm fifty-one bloody years old, I do not want a selfie when I'm trying to get home before my ankles burst into blood blisters.

"Hello!" I turn round with a warm, welcoming smile: practiced, over the years. "Of course you can!"

Two fully grown adult women (they must have been children when I first started out—God I feel *old*) take a selfie with me. I glance at it and make another mental note: stupid, stupid hair. Grow it out, immediately, Margot.

"Can you say it?" They stand in front of me, excited. "Just once? For us."

"Together we will take the world by storm," I say with a small smile, and they cheer.

Then they leave, waving, and I suddenly feel a little dizzy. Nauseous. As if the ground is starting to move. I look down at my coat—alpaca, I know that now—and touch it with my hand. I look a little further down at my new boots: they were, in fact, bloody expensive. Too expensive. An absolute travesty of a decision. And that's when it starts: that feeling of déjà vu. I've had it so many times, over the years, I became almost blasé about it. But not recently. Not since the big break-up: the real one. This time, it feels new again. Scary, again.

I look down at my hand: my grandfather's emerald, glinting.

It's a hand I recognize—my hand, smaller, older—but I see it as if it's new and I can feel Margot now: Other Margot. The person I used to be. She's here and I'm not scared anymore.

Curious, I turn toward my reflection in a shop window.

There I am, and I feel Margot's shock: her horror at what we have become. *Alright*, I whisper to her in my head with a tiny smile. *It's not that bad. We're actually considered quite "well preserved," thank you very much.*

And he's here. I can feel it. Henry is here.

"Margot?"

Slowly, I turn around.

He's older, but it's not a shock because I grew old with him: watched every line appear, every crinkle deepen, his hair turn steadily silver. He's still beautiful, but I knew he would be. He always was.

"Henry," I say, and feel my breath stop.

Winnie walks out of the shop next to us, and while I'm not surprised—I saw her last week, she's going through problems with her boyfriend—I can feel Other Margot's heart-wrenching reaction: the love, the surprise, the confusion.

It's OK, I whisper, but I know she can't hear me.

I know, because I didn't.

"Meg!" Winter bounds toward me. "What are you doing here? Oh my God, did I get the date wrong? I thought we were meeting tomorrow? Have you heard from Gus? The little bugger won't answer my texts. I'm probably not cool enough to talk to anymore. I just saw Posy for coffee. How's Aunty Eve? Jules? Lil? Did you do that thing in the end? Or decide against it? I'm so busy with uni, I've barely had time to catch up with anyone. I've become so boring."

It's the same, exactly the same, apart from I'm me now.

Winnie starts laughing and pulls back so she can kiss my cheek. "Sorry, too many questions. We can talk about it tomorrow in *full*."

I know how my friends are, and why Gus isn't replying (he has a weird crush on Winter, which creeps me out, but I suppose they're not related and she *is* gorgeous). I know that I'm veering away from the network job—I want to do more meteorology, go back to my roots, slow it all down—and I know that this is my daughter.

But I feel Other Margot's shock, her fear, her confusion, and I stand there patiently while she takes it all in.

"Meg?" Winnie calls me Meg most of the time—sometimes "Mama" when she's sad or hungover. "What's wrong?"

Licking my lips, I turn to Henry again. I look down at his hands, and he's not wearing his ring—just as I knew he wouldn't be; we divorced years ago—but I feel the pain all over again, and I feel my past pain, all of it at once.

"Hi," Henry says softly. "How are you?"

Please, I tell Margot silently. *Please, don't ruin this for me.*

I feel her pull herself together and smile bravely.

Good girl.

"Yeah. I'm OK. You?"

"Yeah. Good. Surgery's a bit manic, but you know how it is."

I do know: I know *exactly*, because it's one of the reasons we're not together anymore.

"Yeah." I nod. "I know how it is."

Henry is still watching me with that careful, clear-eyed expression—the one I know so well, have seen so many times, carved into the base of me like a heart into a tree—and I feel our love for him together: mine, and hers.

"It's nice to see you," I say as my eyes fill with tears and I quickly brush them away. "Sorry. It's . . . just cold."

Still making excuses not to cry in front of anyone: no change there.

Henry nods. "It's nice to see you too, Margot."

It happens again—*Margot*, not Meg, not Megalodon—and suddenly I'm scared, I'm terrified, because this is it, this is probably our last meeting. I don't have any more visions after this and if it doesn't go right, I may never see him again.

My chin abruptly crumples and Winter wraps her arms around me.

"It's you, isn't it," she whispers, pulling away and putting a hand on either side of my face, just as her dad does: as if I'm too precious to hold in one in case I break. "It is. It's you. You're Other Margot."

I'm not—I haven't been for some time—but I was.

And I needed that, then.

I need it now.

"*Thank you*," she murmurs, even though I know now that Henry can hear it. "For literally *everything*. I'm so sorry I'm going to be such a brat as a teenager. Hold on tight, Meg. I love you and I don't mean any of it."

I nod. *I know, baby girl. I know.*

Then I look back at Henry, because I don't know what's coming. This is the real future now: a part I've not seen, a place I've never been. And all I know as I look at his face is that I love him as much now as I ever did.

"This is it," Henry says quietly. "Isn't it."

I feel Other Margot slip away, back into the past.

It's just me left now. Me and Henry.

"Yes." I nod. "This is it."

"I can tell." He smiles. "The pink coat. I saw you a mile off."

"Well." I look down at myself and shove my hands in my pockets. "That was kind of the plan. Couldn't risk you missing me, could I? Not after all the fuss I made about this one."

We smile at each other and I quietly touch the small blue marble I have kept with me at all times over the years: the marble that would have let me know that there was still hope years ago, if Other Margot had simply reached for it sooner.

"I'm just gonna . . ." Winter clears her throat. "Go and do something less incredibly in the way. Love you, Meg."

She hops closer, kisses my cheek and disappears back into the shop.

"So . . ." I step forward. "I guess we made it."

"I guess we did." Henry grins. "So now what?"

"I don't know." I blink a few times. "For the first time in a long time, I don't bloody know, Henry. I don't know anything at all."

Henry laughs and it's him and it's us and it's always been us.

"Good." He smiles broadly and holds out his hand. "Because I *do* know, Meg. So now it's my turn."

★★★★★

ACKNOWLEDGMENTS

This book started with my grandfather.

If we're lucky, we have people in our lives who shape us into who we become; if we're very lucky, they shape us into who we want to be. Whether my grandad was patiently saving a baby blue tit (which then sat on his shoulder as he built model boats) or meticulously tending to his beloved garden, he was my constant: always warm, always kind, always wise. As a child, I saw him as a magical, all-knowing Gandalf; as an adult, I realized he was so much more than that. What Gordon Smale didn't know, he researched; what he didn't understand, he learned. His curiosity about the world never faded, and I have spent my life trying to retain that childlike sense of fascination too.

My grandfather was my best friend, and—to the best of my knowledge—we only ever lied to each other once. He told me the baby bird had flown away and didn't admit that it died until I was in my late thirties (I was devastated, and mortified I hadn't worked it out for myself). And—as he reached the very end of his beautiful, long life—I told him that the novel I had just finished would be dedicated to him. That was a lie, because I already knew that my next book—this one—would be about our relationship, and how much I would miss him.

This book is for you, My Grandad. I'm not sure how, but I know you're still keeping an eye out for me. Just like Margot, I think you can see further than you should. I think you have powers you aren't supposed to have: you always did. So thank you—for everything. I wouldn't be Your Holly without you.

None of Margot's story would have been possible without the incredible team behind me: supporting every mad idea I have, encouraging me to be brave and then stepping in when the knots get all tangled up. Kate Shaw and Allison Hellegers, my super-agents, I am constantly in awe of your brilliance, understanding and loyalty. April Osborn: it's such a joy to work with such an insightful, warm and wise editor. Rebecca Watson—I am forever grateful for everything you do to make my work shine on-screen. An enormous thank-you to the entire spectacular team at MIRA: Leah Morse, Ashley MacDonald, Pamela Osti, Margaret O'Neill Marbury, Taryn Ortolan, Emily Bierman and Karen Becker. You are absolute powerhouses of creativity and hard work, and I am so very grateful to all of you.

For the rest of my family: I know you miss Grandad as much as I do. I know we all feel the gap he left behind. But he's still here with us—not just in memories, but in the ways he made and changed us. Hopefully, this book is another tiny way of keeping him here, and of sharing his magic with others too. I love you all. xx